Get You
Good

Also by Rhonda Bowen

Man Enough for Me

One Way or Another

Hitting the Right Note

Get You Good

RHONDA BOWEN

Kensington Publishing Corp.
http://www.kensingtonbooks.com

DAFINA BOOKS are published by

Kensington Publishing Corp.
119 West 40th Street
New York, NY 10018

All Kensington Titles, Imprints, and Distributed Lines are available at special quantity discounts for bulk purchases for sales promotions, premiums, fund-raising, and educational or institutional use. Special book excerpts or customized printings can also be created to fit specific needs. For details, write or phone the office of the Kensington special sales manager: Kensington Publishing Corp., 119 West 40th Street, New York, NY 10018, attn: Special Sales Department, Phone: 1-800-221-2647.

Dafina and the Dafina logo Reg. U.S. Pat. & TM Off.

ISBN-13: 978-0-7582-8137-1
ISBN-10: 0-7582-8137-4
First Kensington trade edition: April 2013
First Kensington mass market edition: March 2015

eISBN-13: 978-1-61773-872-2
eISBN-10: 1-61773-872-7
Kensington electronic edition: March 2015

10 9 8 7 6 5 4 3 2 1

Printed in the United States of America

There is no fear in love; perfect love casts out fear.

Acknowledgments

This book is about love, in all its forms and misperceptions. And so it is only natural that I give thanks for the love that has come to me in all its forms and misperceptions.

Thank you to my eternal Father, Redeemer, and Friend, for loving me first and for continuing to love me throughout all the joys and disappointments. It is only through him that I understand what real love truly means.

Thanks to my families, friends, editors, readers, reviewers, writing colleagues, and supporters for walking with me on this road. Thank you for bearing with my mood swings, forgiving my tardiness, allowing my secrecy, showing up at my book signings, reading my other novels, and loving me in your own individual ways. I hope each one of you gets to experience the indescribable amazing love that can come only from him.

Chapter 1

Sydney was never big on sports.

It wasn't that she was athletically challenged. It was just that chasing a ball around a court, or watching other people do it, had never really been high on her list of favorite things.

However, as she stood at the center of the Carlu Round Room, surveying the best of the NBA that Toronto had to offer, she had to admit that professional sports definitely had a few attractive features.

"Thank you, Sydney."

Sydney grinned and folded her arms as she considered her younger sister.

"For what?"

"For Christmas in October." Lissandra bit her lip. "Look at all those presents."

Sydney turned in the direction where Lissandra was staring, just in time to catch the burst of testosterone-laced eye candy that walked through the main doors. Tall, muscular, and irresistible, in every shade of chocolate a girl could dream of sampling. She was starting to have a new appreciation for basketball.

Sydney's eyebrows shot up. "Is that . . . ?"

"Yes, girl. And I would give anything to find him under our Christmas tree," Lissandra said, as her eyes devoured the newest group of NBA stars to steal the spotlight. "I love this game."

Sydney laughed. "I don't think it's the game you love."

"You laugh now," Lissandra said, pulling her compact out of her purse. "But when that hot little dress I had to force you to wear gets you a date for next weekend, you'll thank me."

Sydney folded her arms across the bodice of the dangerously short boat-necked silver dress that fit her five-foot-nine frame almost perfectly. It was a bit more risqué than what Sydney would normally wear but seemed almost prudish compared to what the other women in the room were sporting. At least it wasn't too tight. And the cut of the dress exposed her long, elegant neck, which she had been told was one of her best features.

"I'm here to work, not to pick up men," Sydney reminded her sister.

"No, we're here to deliver a spectacular cake." Lissandra checked her lipstick in the tiny mirror discreetly. "And since that cake is sitting over there, our work is done. It's playtime."

"Focus, Lissa." Sydney tried to get her sister back on task with a hand on her upper arm. "Don't forget this is an amazing opportunity to make the kinds of contacts that will put us on the A-list. Once we do that, more events like this might be in our future."

"OK, fine," Lissandra huffed, dropping her compact back into her purse. "I'll talk to some people and give out a few business cards. But if a player tries to buy me a drink, you best believe I'm gonna take it."

Sydney smirked. "I wouldn't expect otherwise."

"Good." Lissandra's mouth turned up into a naughty grin. " 'Cause I see some potential business over there that has my name etched across his broad chest."

Sydney sighed. Why did she even bother? "Be good," she said, adding a serious big-sister tone to her voice.

"I will," Lissandra threw behind her. But since she didn't even bother to look back, Sydney didn't hope for much. She knew her sister, and she'd just lost her to a six-foot-six brother with dimples across the room.

Sydney eventually lost sight of her sister as the crowd thickened. She turned her attention back to their ticket into the exclusive Toronto Raptors NBA Season Opener event.

The cake.

Sydney stood back and admired her work again, loving the way the chandelier from above and the tiny lights around the edges of the table and underneath it lit up her creation. The marzipan gave the cream-colored square base of the cake a smooth, flawless finish, and the gold trim caught the light beautifully. The golden replica of an NBA championship trophy, which sat atop the base, was, however, the highlight.

She had to admit it was a sculpted work of art, and one of the best jobs she had done in years. It was also one of the most difficult. It had taken two days just to bake and decorate the thing. That didn't include the several concept meetings, the special-ordered baking molds, and multiple samples made to ensure that the cake tasted just as good as it looked. For the past month and a half, this cake job had consumed her life. But it was well worth it. Not only for the weight it put in her pocket, but also the weight it was likely to add to her client list. Once everyone at the event saw her creation, she was sure she would finally make it onto the city's pastry-chef A-list, and Decadent would be the go-to spot for wedding and special-event cakes.

She stood near the cake for a while, sucking up the oohs and aahs of passersby, before heading to the bathroom to check that she hadn't sweated out her curls carrying up the cake from downstairs. She took in her long, dark hair, which had been curled and pinned up for the night; her slightly rounded face; and plump, pinked lips; and was satisfied. She turned to the side to get a better view of her size six frame and smiled. Even though she had protested when Lissandra presented the dress, she knew she looked good. Normally she hated any kind of shimmer, but the slight sparkle from the dress was just enough to put Sydney in the party mood it inspired. OK, so Lissandra may have been right— she was there for business—but that didn't mean she couldn't have some fun, too.

By the time she reapplied her lipstick and headed back, the room was full.

She tried to mingle and did end up chatting with a few guests, but her maternal instincts were in full gear and it wasn't long before she found her way back to the cake. She was about to check for anything amiss when she felt gentle fingers on the back of her bare neck. She swung around on reflex.

"What do you think you're doing?" she said, slapping away the hand that had violated her personal space.

"Figuring out if I'm awake or dreaming."

Sydney's eyes slid all the way up the immaculately toned body of the six-foot-three man standing in front of her, to his strong jaw, full smirking lips, and coffee brown eyes. Her jaw dropped. And not just because of how ridiculously handsome he was.

"Dub?"

"Nini."

She cringed. "Wow. That's a name I never thought I would hear again."

"And that's a half tattoo I never thought I'd see again."

Sydney slapped her hand to the back of her neck self consciously. She had almost forgotten the thing was there. It would take the one person who had witnessed her chicken out on getting it finished to remind her about it.

Hayden Windsor. Now wasn't this a blast from the past, sure to get her into some present trouble.

She tossed a hand onto her hip and pursed her lips. "I thought Toronto was too small for you."

"It is."

"Then what are you doing here?"

"Right now?" His eyes flitted across her frame in answer.

"Stop that," Sydney said, her cheeks heating up as she caught his perusal.

"Stop what?" he asked with a laugh.

"You know what," she said. She shook her head. "You are still the same."

He shrugged in an attempt at innocence that only served to draw Sydney's eyes to the muscles shifting under his slim-fitting jacket.

"I can't help it. I haven't seen you in almost ten years. What, you gonna beat me up like you did when you were seven?"

"Maybe."

"Bully."

"Jerk."

"How about we continue this argument over dinner?" he asked.

"They just served appetizers."

The corners of his lips drew up in a scandalous grin. "Come on, you know you're still hungry."

He was right. That finger food hadn't done anything for her—especially since working on the cake had kept her from eating all day. But she wasn't about to tell him that.

Sydney smirked. "Even if I was, I don't date guys who make over one hundred thousand dollars a year."

He raised a thick eyebrow. "That's a new one."

"Yes, well," she said, "it really is for your own good. This way you won't have to wonder if I was with you for your money."

"So how about we pretend like I don't have all that money," he said, a dangerous glint in his eyes. "We could pretend some other things, too—like we weren't just friends all those years ago."

"I'm not dating you, Hayden," Sydney said, despite the shiver that ran up her spine at his words.

"So you can ask me to marry you, but you won't date me?"

"I was seven years old!"

"And at nine years old, I took that very seriously," Hayden said, his brow furrowing.

Sydney laughed. "That would explain why you went wailing to your daddy right after."

He rested a hand on his rock-solid chest. "I'm an emotional kind of guy."

"Hayden! There you are. I've been looking all over for you!"

Sydney turned to where the voice was coming from and fought her gag reflex. A busty woman with too much blond hair sidled up to Hayden, slipping her arm around his.

"This place is so packed that I can barely find anyone." The woman suddenly seemed to notice Sydney.

"Sydney!"

"Samantha."

Samantha gave Sydney a constipated smile. "So good to see you."

Sydney didn't smile back. "Wish I could say the same."

Hayden snorted. Samantha dropped the smile, but not his arm.

Sydney glared at the woman in the red-feathered dress and wondered how many peacocks had to die to cover her Dolly Parton goods.

"So I guess you two know each other?" Hayden asked, breaking the silence that he seemed to find more amusing than awkward.

"Yes," Samantha volunteered. "Sydney's little bakery, Decadent, beat out Something Sweet for the cake job for this event. She was my main competition."

"I wouldn't call it a competition," Sydney said, thinking it was more like a slaughtering.

"How do *you* know each other?" Samantha probed.

Hayden grinned. "Sydney and I go way back. Right, Syd?"

Samantha raised an eyebrow questioningly and Sydney glared at her, daring her to ask another question. Samantha opted to keep her mouth shut.

"So this is where the party is," Lissandra said, joining the small circle. Sydney caught the flash of recognition in Lissandra's eyes when she saw who exactly made up their impromptu gathering.

"Hayden? Is that you?"

"The very same," Hayden said, pulling Lissandra into a half hug. "Good to see you, Lissandra."

"Back at you," Lissandra said. "Wow, it's been ages. I probably wouldn't recognize you except Sydney used to watch your games all the—oww!"

Lissandra groaned as Sydney's elbow connected with her side.

"Did she?" Hayden turned to Sydney again, a smug look in his eyes.

"Well, it was nice to see you all again," Samantha said, trying to navigate Hayden away from the group.

"Samantha, I can't believe you're here." Lissandra's barely concealed laughter was not lost on Sydney or Samantha. "I thought you would be busy cleaning up that business at Something Sweet."

Sydney bit back a smirk as a blush crept up Samantha's neck to her cheeks. Samantha went silent again.

"What business?" Hayden looked around at the three women, who obviously knew something he didn't.

"Nothing," Samantha said quickly.

"Just that business with the health inspector," Lissandra said, enjoying Samantha's discomfort. "Nothing major. I'm sure the week that you were closed was enough to get that sorted out."

Hayden raised an eyebrow. "The health inspector shut you down?"

"We were closed temporarily," Samantha corrected.

"Just so that we could take care of a little issue. It wasn't that serious."

"Is that what the exterminator said?" Lissandra asked.

Sydney coughed loudly and Samantha's face went from red to purple.

"You know," Samantha said, anger in her eyes. "It's interesting. We have never had a problem at that location before now. It's funny how all of a sudden we needed to call an exterminator around the same time they were deciding who would get the job for tonight's event."

"Yes, life is full of coincidences," Sydney said dryly. "Like that little mix-up we had with the Art Gallery of Ontario event last month. But what can you do? The clients go where they feel confident."

"Guess that worked out for you this time around," Samantha said, glaring at Sydney and Lissandra.

"Guess so," Lissandra said smugly.

Sydney could feel Hayden eyeing her suspiciously, but she didn't dare look at him.

"Well, this was fun," Sydney said in a tone that said the exact opposite. "But I see some people I need to speak with."

Sydney excused herself from the group and made her way to the opposite side of the room toward the mayor's wife. She had only met the woman once, but Sydney had heard they had an anniversary coming up soon. It was time to get reacquainted, and get away from the one man who could make her forget what she really came here for.

By the time the hands on her watch were both sitting at eleven, Sydney was exhausted and completely out of business cards.

"Leaving already?" She was only steps from the door, and he was only steps in front of her.

"This was business, not pleasure."

Hayden's eyes sparkled with mischief. "All work and no play makes Sydney a dull girl."

This time her mouth turned up in a smile. "I think you know me better than that."

His grin widened in a way that assured her that he did. "Remind me."

She shook her head and pointed her tiny purse at him.

"I'm not doing this here with you, Dub."

He stepped closer and she felt the heat from his body surround her. "We can always go somewhere else. Like the Banjara a couple blocks away."

Sydney scowled. Him and his inside knowledge.

"If we leave now we can get there before it closes."

She folded her arms over her midsection. "I haven't changed my mind, Dub."

He grinned. "That's not what your stomach says."

Sydney glanced behind him, and he turned around to see that Samantha was only a few feet away and headed in his direction. Sydney wasn't sure what string of events had put Samantha and Hayden together that night. The woman was definitely not his type. Or at least she didn't think Samantha was.

"I think your date is coming to get you," Sydney said, her voice dripping with amusement. "Maybe *she* wants to go for Indian food."

"How about I walk you to your car?"

Without waiting for a response, he put a hand on the small of her back and eased her out the large doors into the lobby and toward the elevator.

"What's the rush?" she teased.

"Still got that smart mouth, don't you."

"I thought that was what you liked about me," she said innocently, as he led her into the waiting elevator.

"See, that's what you always got wrong, Nini." He leaned toward her ear to whisper and she caught a whiff of his cologne. "It was never just one thing."

Sydney tried to play it off, but she couldn't help the way her breathing went shallow as her heart sped up. And she couldn't keep him from noticing it, either.

His eyes fell to her lips. "So what's it going to be, Syd? You, me, and something spicy?"

He was only inches away from her. So close that if she leaned in, she could . . .

"Hayden!"

A familiar voice in the distance triggered her good sense. Sydney stepped forward and placed her hands on his chest.

"I think you're a bit busy tonight."

She pushed him out of the elevator and hit the DOOR CLOSE button.

He grinned and shook his head as she waved at him through the gap between the closing doors.

"I'll see you soon, Nini."

For reasons she refused to think about, she hoped he kept that promise.

Chapter 2

It was one hour and a quick stop later before Sydney found herself walking through the front door to her home.

"Syd? Is that you?" JJ called from somewhere upstairs.

"Yeah, it's me," Sydney called back to her sister as she kicked off her shoes at the door. She padded through the short hallway into the open-concept living-dining area. Her eyes glanced carelessly around the house that had been her home for the last eleven years, after she'd moved out of her mother's home to live with her dad, Leroy.

Leroy had initially bought the five-bedroom dream house for himself; Sydney's mother, Jackie; and all the children they hoped to have. But somehow it had not worked out the way he had planned, and when Leroy and Jackie split up, Jackie packed up Sydney, Lissandra and JJ and moved them to a dream house of her own. That dream house had seen Jackie through a rebound marriage that produced Sydney's half-sister Zelia; a short-lived reconciliation that produced her brother Dean and another rebound marriage that gave Sydney her other half-sister Josephine. As it was, Jackie had been with that house longer than she had been with all of her husbands combined.

By the time Sydney had hit eighteen, the drama of living with a revolving door of stepfathers had been too much for her, and she decided to move in with her father. Her two closest younger sisters, Lissandra and JJ, followed suit not long after, and the four of them became each other's new family. That was, until Leroy died a year and a half ago. Then things changed again. Now it was just her and her two sisters.

"Oh my goodness, what is that smell?" JJ asked, coming down the stairs and into the kitchen. She went immediately to the take-out bag that Sydney had placed on the counter.

"Is that curry?" Lissandra asked, entering from the living room. "From Banjara?"

"Yup," Sydney said, as she helped JJ remove the food containers from the bag.

"Whose idea was this?" Lissandra asked, pulling up a stool to the counter and grabbing a plate for herself.

"Syd had a craving, apparently," JJ answered

"Really, now," Lissandra said, dishing out a large helping of everything. "Did your craving have anything to do with the tall, dark, and handsome man who was all over you this evening?"

JJ looked up at her sisters. "What man?"

"Hayden Windsor," Lissandra supplied.

JJ's mouth fell open. "You're lying."

"She is," Sydney said as she reached for a napkin. "He was not all over me."

"But he was there," JJ confirmed. She squinted at Sydney. "You two got into it, didn't you?"

"That they definitely did," Lissandra replied.

JJ shook her head. "I never understood the two of you. I remember you guys were together like every day when we were growing up, but you would never date him."

"Because he wasn't serious," Sydney said. "I was just convenient and he was just bored."

"There were a lot more convenient girls, if I remember," Lissandra said. "Like our entire high school cheerleading squad."

"I heard he *did* date all of them," JJ said, going to the fridge for a pitcher of water. "He was a legend."

"She's right," Lissandra said with her mouth full. "He was NBA bound . . . from the start . . . everyone knew it." She swallowed. "Which is why I didn't get his fixation with you."

Sydney raised an eyebrow. "What am I? Dog meat?"

Lissandra waved away the comment with her spoon. "You know what I mean."

"Well, whatever it was, it's all in the past," Sydney said, wiping her fingers on her napkin.

"Not entirely in the past," Lissandra said, reaching for the container with the masala. "My guess is that Indian wasn't the only thing you were really craving tonight."

Sydney grabbed the container before Lissandra could reach it and put the cover on.

"Either way, it worked out for you and your stomach, didn't it," Sydney said dryly.

Lissandra scowled and reached for the mutter paneer, but JJ moved it out of her reach as well.

"It's after eleven thirty, Lissandra," JJ said, ignoring her sister's scowl as she covered the leftovers. "Your size twelve-going-on-twenty behind will thank me to-morrow."

"Don't count on it," Lissandra said, getting up and grabbing a piece of naan before her sisters could get in her way. "You're lucky I love your trifling little selves."

"We love you, too," Sydney called after her grouchy sister as Lissandra headed toward the stairs.

"Guess it would be too much to expect her to help clean up," JJ said as she wiped the counter.

"Please, JJ," Sydney said with a laugh as she rinsed the dishes in the sink. "You know better than that."

JJ tossed the washcloth in the sink and leaned back against the counter to watch her sister finish up.

"So was it weird when you saw him?" JJ's voice dropped to a conspiratorial tone and her eyes sparkled. "Does he look as good as he used to when he was playing for the Celtics?"

"No and yes," Sydney said with a chuckle. "He was exactly the same guy who used to come around to Decadent with his dad when we were kids."

"Oh, this is great," JJ's voice went up an octave as she clapped her hands together. "So is he back in Toronto? Are you going to see him again?"

"I don't know." Sydney rolled her eyes. "I barely spoke to him for five minutes. Like I said, I literally ran into him."

JJ grinned and slipped out of the kitchen. "Well, he must have made some impact. 'Cause I haven't seen you smile this much since you got that do-everything Vita-mix blender your last birthday."

Sydney tossed a dishcloth at her sister, but JJ only laughed and dodged it as she escaped from the kitchen. Sydney shook her head. She should have known better than to discuss Hayden with her sisters. True, she and Hayden had never dated, but there had always been something going on between the two of them and everyone had known it.

It shouldn't have been a surprise, though, since Hayden was just like his father, Dalton Windsor, and Sydney was just like Leroy, and Dalton and Leroy had been lifelong friends. Sydney had been told that it was a friendship that began the day Dalton sold Leroy the tiny bakery that would later become Decadent. Even when Leroy transformed Decadent from the small bakery on College Street to the larger gourmet dessert shop on Queen Street, Dalton was there. And wherever Dalton was, Hayden was, until he got drafted into the NBA after high school. Then he was nothing more than a memory.

The memories of her childhood years around the bakery with Hayden were still fresh in Sydney's mind, but she resisted the temptation to make that trip into the past.

Drying her hands on a kitchen towel, Sydney glanced around the clean kitchen before pouring herself a glass of water to take upstairs with her. She was just about to hit the light switch at the bottom of the stairs when a picture on an end table beside the couch caught her eye. The glass slipped from her fingers, sloshing water all over her feet, when Sydney caught sight of the happy bride and groom. She picked up the photo to confirm that the familiar man in the picture was exactly who she thought it was and her head instantly began to pound.

She thought seeing Hayden again was going to be the biggest surprise of the evening. She thought wrong.

Chapter 3

"Dean's what?"

"Married." JJ opened the refrigerator door and pulled out yogurt. "As in tied the knot."

Sydney dropped the yogurt onto the table with a thud that seemed to reflect the weight of the shocking news that preceded it.

Lissandra's eyes looked like they would fall out of her head. "Shut up!"

"It's true. I saw the ring myself," JJ said from the other side of the dining table. "Looked like about half a carat."

"I can't believe you didn't tell me this last night," Sydney said. Her hand with the knife paused mid-slice through a shiny red apple. She missed one family dinner at her mother's house and she missed everything. Her only brother, Dean—her twenty-one-year-old brother—had gone and gotten himself married, and no one had known about it. Even though she had seen the picture the night before, it hadn't seemed real until JJ said the words.

"Oh, it's real," JJ said, stirring the yogurt absently.

"Dean came home from college with more than just a degree."

"Shut up," Lissandra said again, this time banging the table for emphasis.

"Did any of you even know this girl?" Sydney had abandoned the apple with the knife still stuck in it and was standing beside JJ, hands on her hips. "I didn't even know he had a serious girlfriend."

"I did," Zelia said, bringing a plate with toast to the table. "I met her when he came home for a visit a couple months ago. They've been together for a while—hence the frequent visits home."

Sydney looked at Zelia for a long minute. Her younger sister's blasé attitude to the news of Dean's wedding wasn't lost on Sydney. She suspected that Zelia may have had more time to process the information than she was letting on.

At twenty-two, Zelia was Sydney's second-youngest sister and the closest to Dean. Though she lived with their mother, Zelia spent an inordinate amount of time at Sydney's house. The arrangement worked to Zelia's advantage as she was undoubtedly the most well-informed member of the family.

"Well, he sure did a good job of hiding her from all of us," JJ said. "Not even Mom knew who she was."

Zelia shrugged. "They weren't that serious. At least that's what I thought. They definitely weren't even engaged, let alone married."

Sydney let out a deep sigh as she poured hot water onto a tea bag in her own mug. "Great. Dean goes and does something dumb again and we have to get him out of it. Again."

"What do you mean 'we'?" Lissandra said. "Dean's

not a teenager anymore. We can't exactly order him to unmarry Miss what's her face."

"Her name's actually Sheree," Zelia corrected.

"Whatever." Lissandra shot an annoyed look at her younger sister.

"Well, we can't just do nothing," Sydney said, throwing up her hands before dropping them to her side. "This is not just about Dean anymore. He's twenty-one now."

A wave of silence washed over the table as the four sisters stopped eating and looked at each other.

"Has he said anything yet?" JJ asked after a moment, her eyes on Sydney.

Sydney dug her fingers into her hair. "It doesn't matter. Dad's will was specific. Once he reaches twenty-one, Dean is eligible to exercise his ownership rights over Decadent. Add that to the fact that he's finished school and unemployed. . . ."

"Let's not jump to conclusions," JJ said, finally taking a spoonful of yogurt. "He just graduated a month ago. He hasn't even moved back to Toronto yet. He's probably not even thinking about the shop. And even if he was, he knows you've been running it since Daddy died. I don't think he's going to interfere."

"And wasn't he doing some music program anyway?" Lissandra asked, dishing some fruit onto her own plate.

"It's a dual degree, audio production *and* business management," Sydney said.

Zelia cleared her throat. "Uh, yeah, it's not so dual anymore."

"What?" Sydney and JJ said.

"He kinda dropped the business management part." Zelia kept her eyes on the piece of toast she was meticulously cutting up. "The music program was really intense. It was hard for him to keep up with both. . . ."

"In other words, he was failing his business courses," Sydney said dryly.

Lissandra shook her head as she spooned sugar into her glass of orange juice. "I warned ya'll. I told ya'll he was gonna waste that money. Daddy was wrong to pay for Dean's tuition like that. He shoulda made his behind pay for it with loans and elbow grease like the rest of us. Bet he wouldn't be failing nothin' if it was coming out of his own pocket."

"With all that good English you just used, it sounds like you failed something," Zelia muttered.

"Don't start on me, Miss unfinished degree," Lissandra growled, pointing her spoon at Zelia. "At least Dean's done. You been at school almost six years now and still ain't finished your four-year degree."

"It's only been five years and you know I switched majors. . . ."

"Maybe you need to switch brains. . . ."

"OK, ladies, break it up," Sydney said. "All of us are going to have to switch jobs if we don't figure out this thing with Dean and Decadent."

"I still think you're overreacting. Dean's not going to change anything anytime soon." JJ wiped her mouth with a napkin and stood. "But I'll leave that to you and Lissandra. I've got a dress shop to run."

Sydney absently watched JJ leave the room to gather her things before she headed out to the dress shop she ran with their mother.

"Don't worry about it, Syd," Zelia said, drawing Sydney's attention back to the table. "I'll talk to Dean and see what he's thinking."

"No, that's OK," Sydney said. "I'm gonna arrange

something with him myself. I think I should be the one to bring it up."

"You sure?" Zelia asked. Sydney could see the worried expression in her younger sister's eyes.

"Yeah." Sydney waved away her sister's concern. "It's no big deal. JJ's probably right anyway."

"Zelia! You coming or what?" JJ asked as she walked back through the dining area toward the front door. "You know Mom doesn't like opening up the shop on her own."

"Yeah, I'm coming," Zelia called back. She threw Sydney another sympathetic look before dashing off behind JJ.

Moments later Sydney heard the front door close, followed by the sound of a car engine, which soon faded. She turned to look at Lissandra.

Lissandra took a sip of her juice. "You know this Dean thing is gonna be a mess, right?"

"Oh yeah," Sydney said. "Without a doubt."

The mess was waiting for Sydney by the time she got to work.

Though it was only after ten, the shop was already open for business. While catering special events was the bulk of Decadent's business, they still provided a menu of specialty drinks, desserts, and sandwiches for walk-ins from ten in the morning until ten at night. They were no Starbucks, but they had their share of the lunch crowd around midday, and an even greater share of the couples and first-date crowd in the evening.

"Good morning, Sydney," Wendy said brightly as Sydney entered Decadent through the back door near the kitchen.

Sydney slipped off the sunglasses that shielded her eyes from the bright mid-morning sun. The city famous for its cold winters was holding on to the summer sunshine and warmth as far into fall as possible. Sydney hadn't even had to wear a light jacket to work that morning.

"Morning, Wendy," Sydney said, smiling at the plump, olive-skinned woman who worked the early shift for Decadent. "How's the morning going?"

"Good, but not as good as last night apparently," Wendy said as she used a box cutter to split open the top box on a pile in front of her. "The phone has been ringing off the hook all morning."

Sydney grinned and grabbed a pile of menus. "Oh yeah?"

"Yes." Wendy grabbed a handful herself and followed Sydney to the front of the shop. "At first I was answering and taking messages. But there were so many that after a while I figured I might as well let it go to voice mail if I want to get anything done."

Wendy was about to say something more when the front door to Decadent opened and a sharply dressed woman carrying a purse almost twice her size breezed through the door. She looked around, unsure for a moment, then smiled when her eyes met Sydney's and Wendy's.

"Welcome to Decadent. Can I help you?" Wendy asked with a bright smile.

"Yes." The woman stepped forward. "I'm looking for Sydney Isaacs."

"That's me," Sydney said, handing the menus to Wendy before stepping forward. "What can I do for you?"

"I need to order a cake."

Sydney glanced at Wendy, who shrugged before busying herself with the menus.

"Sure." Sydney motioned to a table nearby. "Why don't you have a seat? Wendy will get you something to drink while I grab a few things. I'll be right back."

"OK." The woman slipped into a chair by a table for two and was on her BlackBerry before Sydney even left the room.

By the time Sydney had grabbed her order binder and iPad and returned to the table, Wendy had served the woman tea and left a cup of peppermint for Sydney.

"So I'm not sure what you know about me, but I probably should introduce myself formally," Sydney said with a small laugh. "I'm Sydney Isaacs and I'm one of the pastry chefs here at Decadent. I have one other chef and a team that works with me and we do everything from dessert orders for events to simple cakes to wedding and other specialty cakes."

"Yes, I was told that you are one of the city's hidden gems," the woman said with a grin. "I'm Charlotte Grisby from Kline and Grisby Events."

"Nice to meet you, Charlotte." Sydney shook the woman's hand.

"I am sorry to just show up without an appointment or anything, but I was hoping if I came early I might be able to meet you in person," Charlotte said.

Sydney smiled. "Well, usually we do consultations by appointment, but luckily for you I have some time available this morning. What are you looking for?"

Sydney listened as Charlotte explained that she needed a specialty cake for a twenty-fifth wedding anniversary event. Sydney took notes and asked Charlotte questions about the theme of the event, the venue, the number of guests attending, and the kind of menu they were serving. She also asked Charlotte to tell her a little about the couple who was celebrating their anniversary.

"I just love how detailed you are," Charlotte said after they had spent twenty minutes talking. "It's been a while since I've had my cake person be as interested in the event as I am."

Sydney smiled. Common first-timer comment. "Well, our goal is not just to give you a cake. Anybody can do that. But this is a special event—an anniversary. A day when two people are remembering one of the most significant days in their lives. Reliving that memory through the anniversary party is a special experience, and the cake should add to that experience. That's why I asked about the theme and the venue and the couple, because the cake should reflect all of those things and help to draw all those special parts together."

When she was done with her speech, Charlotte was grinning from ear to ear.

Charlotte shook her head. "You just reminded me why I got into the event-planning business so many years ago. Sometimes I get so busy and so lost in the routine and forget it's about creating that experience."

"I know what you mean," Sydney said. "That's why we've kept Decadent so small. Even though there's always the opportunity to go bigger, we never wanted to become a cake factory. It sounds corny, but we want to make sure every customer feels like their cake, and their order, is the most important."

Charlotte leaned in with a smile. "Trust me, I already feel that way."

"Good," Sydney said, wiggling her eyebrows. "Now for the fun part. Picking the cake design."

With a touch of the screen, Sydney began to show

Charlotte all the different types of cakes they had done and all the options available to her. Sydney bit back a smile as Charlotte slowly but surely relieved Sydney of the iPad and began scrolling through the diverse inventory of cakes and pastry arrangements.

"OK, so I have a confession to make," Charlotte said suddenly, putting the iPad down.

Sydney raised an eyebrow. "OK."

"You got recommended to me by . . . someone. And I said I would check you out, but I didn't really think you would be this . . . this . . . amazing!" She sighed. "So I already decided on the design I want."

She pulled out a picture clipped from a magazine and laid it in front of Sydney.

"And I already showed this to my partner; she liked it, so she just told me to go with whoever could make this. But now that I've seen what you can do, I don't want this one anymore."

Sydney looked over the picture of a two-tier round cake iced with marzipan and beautifully designed with gold trim. It was a bit too wedding cakey for Sydney, but she could understand why people would go for it.

"So?" Charlotte pressed, a look of concern on her face. "What can you do?"

"Well," Sydney said slowly. "If you want this cake, I can make it for you. But this cake is more of a wedding cake than an anniversary cake. Also, there's nothing that says you have to follow this rule, but gold is usually for fiftieth anniversaries. I would go with a silver trim for you for your twenty-fifth event."

"OK, I'm liking that," Charlotte said. "Tell me more."

Sydney went on to suggest they go with a three-tiered square cake designed to look like silver-and-white gift boxes stacked on top of each other. The design was simple, clean, and elegant, which fit the conservative, traditional nature of the couple Charlotte had described to her.

Sydney got Wendy to bring out a slice of their two-layer vanilla white cake with buttercream filling for Charlotte to sample and also boxed up a slice for her to take away. By the time they were done, Charlotte couldn't stop talking about how glad she was she had come in.

"I'll call and confirm later this evening, but I am almost positive that you'll be making the cake for this event," Charlotte said as the sheets Sydney had handed to her disappeared into the huge purse, along with several of Sydney's business cards.

"Sounds great," Sydney said. "And when is this event?"

Normally she would have gotten that information on the phone before the consultation, but there wasn't much "normal" about her meeting with Charlotte.

"On the fifteenth," Charlotte said, shouldering her bag.

Sydney blinked as she tried to speak through her rapidly contracting throat. "Wow. That's barely a week away. We usually take ten days for this kind of order."

"We're offering fifteen hundred dollars."

"The fifteenth it is."

Both women stood. "So I'll hear from you later, then."

"Definitely," Charlotte said, heading toward the door. "In fact, I think you'll be hearing from me quite frequently from now on."

Sydney smiled as she waved to Charlotte. She liked the sound of that. In fact, the thought of the fifteen hundred dollars coming her way kept her smiling as she headed around to the offices.

"Whose canary did you swallow?"

Sydney paused to stick her head through the half-open metal double doors.

"A very special someone's," Sydney answered. "I think we just got a big job, and probably a new regular client."

Mario Santos, the only other trained pastry chef at Decadent, smiled even as his hands continued sifting flour. "Oh yeah? How much are we talking?" he asked.

"Possibly around fifteen hundred for a single job."

"Cha-ching," Mario said with a little dance. "I hear a bonus coming my way."

"Then you should get your ears checked out." Sydney leaned against the open door. "Where is everybody anyway? Are you so good now you don't need any staff to help?"

"Funny," Mario said. "I sent Jones to the grocery to pick up a couple items and Michelle is out back shortening her life with cigarettes."

"Don't be too hard on her," Sydney said. "There was a time when you used to be out back, too."

"That was a long time ago," said Mario. He suddenly paused and turned to Sydney. "And speaking of a long time, when you gonna hook me up, Syd?"

"With what?"

"With your sister," Mario said, pausing from the sifting to focus on Sydney. "Come on, you know a brother's been trying to get on that train."

Sydney laughed. "Exactly. You've been trying and you know Lissandra's been shooting you down."

"I know, I know." Mario wiped his hands on a dish towel and stepped forward. "That's why I've been thinking that maybe if you put in a good word for me, she might give me a chance."

"She already gave you a chance," Sydney said. "You took her to Burger King."

"I was seventeen!"

"And now you're twenty-six," Sydney pointed out. "Don't you think you should grow out of this crush you have on my sister?"

Mario shook his head. "I thought I did, Syd, but since I've been working here . . ."

He took off his cap and held it to his chest dramatically. "It's like she's hijacked a brother's heart all over again."

Sydney rolled her eyes.

"Besides, it's more than just a crush." His tone grew more serious. "I knew your sister from back in the day. Before she got so crazy. You know, when she was a good girl. I know she can be like that again with some motivation."

"Come on, Mario," Sydney said. "*I* don't even remember when Lissandra was a good girl. And you're crazy if you think you can change her."

"You don't have enough faith in people, Syd," Mario said, pointing his hat at her knowingly. "I know I can't change her. But I can help guide her in the right direction, you know? That's why you gotta hook me up, Syd. Tell her I'm a good man."

"I don't know. . . ."

"Come on, Syd, I give good love. I'll buy her clothes. I'll cook her dinner, too. . . ."

Sydney laughed. "If you start singing, I'm gonna fire you."

"You're not taking me seriously," he said, putting his cap back on and heading back to the counter.

"OK, fine." Sydney let out a sigh. She had known Mario since they were teenagers, when he used to sweep the floor for her father. Even after he had gotten his culinary degree, he had come back to work for her dad. He was loyal to a fault. And she knew he would be a good influence on her wild sister.

"I'll talk to her," Sydney said with a small smile.

"You will?" His eyes lit up like a Christmas tree as he turned back to Sydney. "Thank you, Syd. You're a real down girl."

"Gee, thanks," Sydney said dryly.

"I mean it," Mario said, pulling out some cinnamon and sugar. "In fact, I know a brother who would be perfect for you. I'ma hook you up."

Sydney leaned off the door. "Please don't," she said as she headed back to the hallway.

"He's a ball player and—"

The door swung closed on whatever else Mario had to say, and Sydney was glad. She had met Mario's friends, and even though she had faith in him, she wasn't as sure about the rest of his crew.

She shook her head as she thought about the idea of Lissandra and Mario. That would definitely be an interesting combination. She was about to pursue the thought further when she came to her office door.

Her open office door.

She pushed it all the way open and stepped inside cautiously. When she saw who it was that had invaded her privacy, she let out a sigh of relief.

"Dean," she said. "You scared me half to death!"

"Did I?" Dean turned around and grinned. "Looks like someone's getting jumpy in her old age."

"Boy, you better come over here and give me a hug

before I beat you down for calling me old," Sydney threatened.

Dean laughed, but came over anyway, pulling his older sister into a warm embrace.

"Oh my goodness, look at you." Sydney shook her head as she held Dean back from her. Her eyes drank in his lean six-foot frame, draped in a henley, slim-fitting jeans, and a leather jacket. Add to that his caramel skin and straight teeth and he was definitely a catch. And of course, he had the trademark copper eyes that all Leroy's children had inherited.

"Wow, you're looking more and more like Dad every day," she said finally.

"Thanks." He rubbed the five-o'clock shadow on his chin. "I think."

"Don't worry, it's a good thing," Sydney said with a laugh. She pulled him over to the overstuffed pastel couch at the side of her office. "Come, sit. I want to hear all about U of D."

"You know what, Syd, it's been great," he said as he folded his long, lanky frame into the couch. "I know for sure that music production is what I want to do. I learned so much over the four years, even made a few contacts. Now I'm ready to get out there and do my own thing."

Sydney nodded as she listened to her brother talk about school. He had shocked them all when he had told them his plans to complete a bachelor of music degree at the University of Denver. Jackie had almost had a stroke when she thought of her only son being so far away from her, but she had eventually gotten over it when she heard how passionate he was about what he wanted to do. Even now, several years later, Sydney could still hear the passion in his voice.

"I can't even believe four years have gone so fast. When you left, you were just a kid, and now, here you are, grown, with a degree. And a wife."

Dean rubbed the back of his neck and grinned. "Yeah."

"So." Sydney turned on the couch to face her brother more fully. "Tell me about her. How'd you meet her, what's she like?"

Dean's eyes lit up. "I met her here actually, after the fall semester when I came up for Christmas. A couple guys I knew from high school invited me to a party by the waterfront and she was there. . . ."

"So she went to high school with you?"

"No, she just knew some old friends of mine. She's actually going to school here in the city," Dean said.

"Oh." Sydney paused for a moment. "So she graduated this year with you, too?"

"Uh, no." Dean rubbed the back of his neck again. "She took a semester off. She's trying to get some things together so she can go back next year and finish up. You know, she's actually working downtown pretty near here?"

"Really," Sydney said, trying to keep the judgment out of her voice.

"Yeah." Dean nodded. "Things haven't been easy for her, but she's working hard to make it on her own and be independent. Just like I am."

Sydney raised an eyebrow but stifled her comment.

"We're so much alike," Dean continued. "We like the same food, the same music, the same movies."

"Wow, you guys could be twins."

Dean shot her a look. "Syd."

"Sorry, go on."

Dean stood and began pacing. "Look, I know you

guys never really got a chance to meet her before, but once you get to know her you'll love her as much as I do. She's so kind and caring. When I got sick in January, she came all the way up to Colorado to take care of me. Every time I got a gig to play, she was there. She understands me. She's supportive of my career dreams, she's . . . she's everything I could ever want in a woman."

Sydney watched her brother get starry eyed as he talked about Sheree.

"I've never met someone I wanted to be with all the time like I do with her," he said, sitting back down beside her. "I've never felt like this about a woman before. Never."

"OK, OK." Sydney held up her hands. "I get it. You're in love with her. But Dean, you're twenty-one. You've known her for less than a year. Don't you think it was a bit soon to marry her? What do you even know about her? Her family? Her childhood?"

"I really love her, Syd." He focused puppy-dog eyes on his sister. She wasn't buying it.

"Dean."

"What?" he asked, standing suddenly. "I do!"

"Dean."

He let out a sigh and his hand went to his neck again. "OK, fine. She's pregnant."

"Dean!"

"Damn, Syd, how many ways can you say my name?"

"Uh-uh, don't cuss at me," Sydney said, her brows furrowing.

"Then stop looking at me like that!"

"You just told me you knocked up your girlfriend—"

"Shhhhh!" Dean stepped over to close the office door. "And she's my wife—not my girlfriend."

"Yeah, she only became your wife because you

knocked her up." Sydney rubbed her palms over her face. "I can't even believe this. My twenty-one-year-old brother is having a kid. I didn't even know you were having sex!"

Dean snorted. "Yeah. I am not talking to you about that."

Sydney's hands fell to her lap as she glared at Dean. "Would you rather talk to Jackie?"

His eyes widened. "No! You can't tell Mom. Or anyone else for that matter. Only Zelia knows."

Sydney squinted at Dean. "Really? Zelia?"

"She promised she wouldn't say anything."

"OK, Dean, I get it. You freaked out about her being pregnant, but this is not 1954. You didn't have to marry her."

Dean's eyes narrowed. "Are you serious? Do you know what Mom would say?"

"Our mother?" Sydney leaned forward to look at Dean. "The one with six children, by three different husbands, none of whom she is currently married to. You thought *she* wouldn't understand. Are you kidding me?"

Dean said. "OK, maybe she would, but . . . you know how she is. I couldn't deal with the disappointment from her."

He sat down and took Sydney's hands. "And despite the circumstances, I really do love Sheree. She was my wifey even before she was my wifey."

Sydney groaned and sat back in the chair, running her fingers through her silky locks.

"So what now, baby brother?" she asked. "What are you gonna do?"

He shrugged. "That's what I'm trying to figure out. We're staying at the guesthouse at Mom's for now."

"You think that's a good idea, given the whole pregnancy thing?" Sydney asked.

"No," Dean said. "That's why we're looking for a place. But it's kinda hard when your financial situation isn't stable."

Sydney tensed. This was it. This was the part where he was going to tell her he wanted to take over Decadent.

"A friend hooked me up with a regular gig playing keys at this lounge downtown," Dean continued. "And there are some other small jobs in the works. But I really want to open my own studio. I know a couple guys getting ready to launch their careers who are thinking of putting together some demos. I figure this is how I can get started, you know? And once they go big, my studio will profit. Plus there's always some up-and-comers looking to buy studio time. I really think this could work."

Sydney blinked. "So you just want to do music? You're not interested in Decadent?"

Dean grimaced. "Honestly, Syd, this place has always been your thing. I know it was Dad's dream to keep it in the family, but it's not what I want for my life."

Sydney let out a breath she didn't realize she was holding.

"Wow. I thought you were coming to tell me you were ready to take over running it." The relief in her voice was obvious.

"No way! I could never take this away from you and Lissandra. Especially you," said Dean.

A rush of warmth filled Sydney's chest.

"But it is part of the reason I came down here."

Sydney's smile faded a bit as the tension began to seep back into her chest.

"OK. Go on," she said cautiously.

Dean looked at her uneasily before getting up and walking over to the other side of the room.

"Like I said, Syd, I want to start my own studio," he began. "But that takes money. A lot of money. Money I don't have. But I do have this shop."

He turned to face Sydney, rubbing his palms together nervously.

"I want to sell Decadent."

Chapter 4

Sydney sprang from the couch. "What!"

She couldn't believe what she was hearing. After all her hard work and the years she sank into this shop, Dean wanted to sell Decadent—right out from under her. How could he betray her like that? How could he betray their family like that?

But the look on his face told her he was completely serious.

"You heard right, Syd. I want to sell Decadent," he repeated. "To you."

Sydney's mouth opened and closed. Then opened again.

"You want to sell it to me?" she squeaked.

"I know you love this place." Dean stuck his hands in his pockets. "It's everything you've done since you were a teenager. The same passion Dad had for this place, you have. It really should be yours."

Sydney felt her eyes moisten. She had never spoken to anyone about how much she loved Decadent. How the shop, the staff, the people felt like an extension of herself. But in some small way, it seemed as if Dean had gotten it. And now, here he was proposing to her something that she had hoped one day—when she had enough money—to propose to him.

"Dean, Dad gave Decadent to you," she protested.

"But you love it," Dean countered. "More than I do. Probably more than any of the rest of us do. So what's it gonna be, Syd? Will you buy it from me, so we can both have what we really want?"

Sydney shook her head. "I want to Dean, but I can't. I don't have the money right now."

"But you've been running this place for almost five years," Dean said, an eyebrow raised. "And Zelia told me you haven't gotten anything for yourself—no new car, no house, no vacations—so what have you been doing with your money."

It was Sydney's turn to pace.

"Honestly, Dean? I've been saving in hopes that one day I would be able to own Decadent, or somewhere like it. But I don't have enough yet. This place could be worth close to three hundred fifty K—"

"Three hundred fifty thousand dollars!" Dean's eyes looked like they would pop out of his head.

"Yes, Dean," Sydney said. "Three hundred fifty thousand. This is prime location. People would kill to be downtown this close to the subway, the business district, and the universities. Plus there's all the equipment, and we haven't even started talking about the value of the brand."

She knew all of this because she had been thinking about buying Decadent since the day they read Leroy's will. And since then she had been keeping track of the value of the business on the market.

"The only drawback is that the recession has hit the market in terms of what people are willing to pay. Nobody's really buying businesses like this anymore, but the property would go fast, for sure."

Dean was staring at Sydney, his eyes wide and his mouth open. Sydney could tell he was still stuck on the three hundred fifty thousand.

"Wow. I didn't even know all of that." He swallowed hard. "You really know your stuff."

Sydney wanted to say that he should, too, seeing that he was the owner. But she didn't.

"Yes, well, it comes with the territory," she said. "What did you think it was worth anyway?"

Dean shrugged and came back to sit on the couch. "I don't know. About ninety thousand maybe?"

"No, baby bro," Sydney said with a chuckle. "If it was just ninety K, I could afford that. But I could never let you sell me Decadent for that. It wouldn't be fair."

Dean nodded and sat back.

"So I guess that plan is out." Disappointment dripped from his voice.

"You could always take out a loan against the business," Sydney said in a small, reluctant voice.

He shook his head. "That's not me. I don't want to deal with the hassle of worrying about the financing on two businesses at one time. To be honest, I'm not trying to be tied to Decadent. I just want to focus on my own thing."

Sydney nodded and tried to keep from showing how offended she was by Dean's words. They sat in silence a moment longer.

"Have you checked out the cost of setting up your studio anyway? Where would it be? What would the equipment and licensing cost? What are the startup expenses you would be looking at?"

Dean sat forward again. "I was thinking I could buy

a house and set up the studio in the basement there. Or I could lease space somewhere. I know a couple locations that could work. I even heard about a brother selling his studio because he was expanding."

Sydney bit her lip. "What if I lent you the money for the studio? Or maybe even bought part of Decadent from you so that you could have the money you need to start up?"

Dean's eyes brightened. "You would do that?"

Sydney shrugged. "Sure. Why not? If this is really what you want to do, then you should be able to do it."

Dean nodded, the excitement lighting his eyes. "That might work."

Sydney grinned. "Great! So come up with the costs for your studio and let me know, and I'll see what I can come up with and we'll take it from there."

"Thanks, Syd," Dean said, pulling his sister into a hug after they stood. "This means a lot to me."

"Glad we could come to a solution," Sydney said with a smile as she headed toward her desk.

"Yeah, me too," Dean said, backing toward the door. "I would have hated to have to turn to my other solution."

"What was that?" Sydney asked, shuffling toward the door.

"Selling the shop outright to someone else."

Sydney's fingers stilled as she felt her blood turn to ice.

"Anyway, I'm meeting Sheree for lunch," Dean said, already halfway through the door. "Catch you later, Syd."

Sydney didn't respond as her brother left. She was still in shock at her brother's words. He was willing to sell the family business to someone else.

That meant only one thing.

If she didn't come up with the money Dean needed to start his studio, she could lose Decadent forever.

"OK, Nini, what's going on? You've been hiding in this office all afternoon. Our regulars have been wondering if you're even in today."

Sydney looked up from her desk at Lissandra, who was standing in the doorway to her office with her arms folded.

"You know I hate when you call me that." Sydney turned back to her computer. "I didn't tell you what Hayden said so you could resurrect that name, *Sandi*."

Lissandra scowled at "Sandi," the pet name that she disliked as much as Sydney disliked "Nini."

"OK," Lissandra said, coming into the office and seating herself on the other side of Sydney's desk. "But you still haven't answered my question. Even the busboy can tell you're in a foul mood, and he's not really the sharpest knife in the drawer."

Sydney sighed and slipped off the glasses she used at the computer.

"I had a chat with Dean this morning."

Lissandra raised an eyebrow. "And?"

"And he's thinking of selling Decadent."

Lissandra sat forward. "Shut up."

"I'm serious," Sydney said. "He wants to open his own studio and do this music thing, but he needs money for the startup."

"So let him go get a loan like regular folk," Lissandra said, annoyed.

"He's not interested in a loan." Sydney pursed her

lips. "Why go into debt when you have three hundred and fifty K worth of real estate at your disposal?"

"That little bastard."

Sydney pinned Lissandra with a disapproving look. She didn't even flinch.

"In fairness, though, he offered to sell it to me first." Sydney sighed. "He said he knew how important it was to keep it in the family."

"I know you've been saving, but you ain't got that kind of money." Lissandra narrowed her eyes. "Or do you?"

"I don't," Sydney confirmed. "Not by a long shot. But he thought I might. Can you believe he thought the shop was worth ninety thousand?"

Lissandra kissed her teeth. "You should have let his ignorant behind sell it to you for that, then."

"I couldn't do that, Lissa. That would be beyond wrong."

"What is wrong is Dean not caring enough about the place he owns to even know what it's worth."

Sydney sat up straight and began to shuffle through the papers on her desk. "Yeah, well, that's the least of my problems now. I managed to delay the sales talks with Dean until he could find out how much starting up his studio would cost."

Lissandra pressed the tips of her fingers together as she sat back. "We can't let him sell Decadent. Not until we can afford to buy it."

"Unless you have two hundred and fifty thousand to add to my one hundred, I am not sure how we're going to do that," Sydney said.

"Hmm. I bet that wife of his had something to do with this. I wouldn't be surprised if she put that idea to sell in his head." Lissandra scowled. "Did he mention anything about her?"

Sydney snorted. "Oh yeah. He went on and on about how great she was. You would think that girl put the stars in the sky the way he talks about her."

"She put it on him, that's for sure." Lissandra crossed her legs with a smirk. "There's no other reason she could have that much power over him."

Lissandra leaned forward. "We should check her out, Syd. Maybe she's just into Dean for the money."

Sydney rolled her eyes and began sorting through the mail that had been sitting on her desk all day. "He said they met for the first time over Christmas. How would she even know if he had anything?"

"I don't know. But I don't trust her."

"You haven't even met her."

"Sometimes you have to go with your gut."

Sydney was about to respond when two blue slips of paper fell from a blue envelope she had just opened. When she took them up and saw what they were, her mouth fell open.

"What is it, Syd?"

"Raptors basketball tickets," Sydney said, still gaping.

"Lies." Lissandra reached across the pile of papers between them to snatch the tickets from Sydney's fingers.

"See for yourself," Sydney said, even as she pulled the included card out of the envelope and leaned back in her chair.

> *I told you I would see you soon.*
> *–Dub*

Sydney couldn't stop the smile that spread her lips.

"Sydney, have you seen these tickets! These are right behind the players' bench. We're so close that when Ben Wallace wipes his sweat it might hit us. Syd . . . Syd, are you even hearing me?"

"Huh? Oh yeah." Sydney pulled her eyes from the window and immediately dropped the finger she had pressed to her lips thoughtfully.

Lissandra smirked. "Mr. Windsor sure didn't waste any time."

"I know, right?" Sydney stretched her arms out on the desk restlessly. "How did he even manage to get tickets like this?"

"He's in the NBA boys' club." Lissandra pulled her chair around to Sydney's side of the desk. "I'm sure there's some sort of lifetime membership. Or at least residual benefits for banged-up ex-players."

"Hey! What are you doing?" Sydney asked as Lissandra hijacked her computer keyboard.

"What do you think? I'm Googling him." Lissandra nudged Sydney's chair and sent it rolling out of her way. "Let's see what homeboy is really working with."

Sydney rolled her eyes as she gave her sister space. "This is so juvenile. . . ."

"There he is!" Lissandra exclaimed.

Sydney moved the screen slightly so she could see it. She whistled when the handsome picture of a grinning Hayden came on screen.

"Yup, that's him all right." She bit her bottom lip. "Looks like he's working for the Toronto Raptors now."

Lissandra slapped her palm on the desk and sat back with a grin. "I told you he was still in the NBA."

"Yeah, but he's only a trainer. . . ."

" 'Only a trainer'?" Lissandra twisted around to meet Sydney's eyes. "Girl, for his 'only a trainer' position he's probably raking in at least one hundred K per year plus benefits, along with a contract that won't get terminated if he shatters his other knee."

"Hmm." Sydney picked up a pen and rolled it between her hands. "Well, that explains what he's up to here in Toronto."

"Part of what he's up to," Lissandra said, picking up the tickets and handing them to Sydney. "Looks like you're the other part. What are you wearing?"

"Wearing?" Sydney turned to Lissandra. "Don't be silly. I'm not going."

"Sydney!"

"Lissandra, I'm not playing this game with Dub. I'm not going to just show up where he wants me to 'cause he sent me some tickets. Do I look like some desperate groupie? Forget that. Besides, I have to work Sunday night."

Lissandra sprang out of her chair and planted herself in the tiny space between Sydney and the desk. "Are you hearing yourself? A brother—a tall, fine, well-employed brother—just sent you four hundred dollars' worth of merchandise and your excuse is you have to work? Don't make me slap you, Syd."

"Whatever, Lissandra. I'm not going. And I'm sending back these tickets."

"No!" Lissandra whined. "Now you're ruining my life, too! Sydney, I may never be able to get tickets like this ever again. This may be our only chance. . . ."

Sydney shook her head, slipping the tickets back

into the envelope. "My tickets, my decision. I'm sending them back."

Lissandra pointed a finger. "You're insane."

"And you're over your break time." Sydney glared at her sister for emphasis.

Lissandra scowled and moved around Sydney's heavy cherrywood desk to head back to the main customer area. "Fine, I'm going. But Syd, please don't send back those tickets. He probably got them for free as a member of the management team so it's not like it cost him that much. Just think about it, OK?"

Sydney tapped the pen against the desk. "OK. I'll think about it. Then I'll send them back."

Lissandra shook her head as she turned to leave. "Some girls have all the luck. If a brother got me tickets like that, I would definitely give him the time of day."

When she was sure her sister was gone, Sydney pulled up the Internet window with Hayden's info again. So he wasn't giving up. She had to admit she was a tiny bit impressed. She would be lying if she said she hadn't thought about him a few times since the weekend.

OK, fine, a lot of times.

But she didn't have time for a man—especially one like Hayden. She had enough drama in her life as it was, like figuring a way to not lose the thing that mattered most to her in the world.

She glanced at the picture again and sighed. It sure would have been fun, though.

Taking out a new envelope, she slipped the tickets in and wrote "Mario Santos" on the front. Then she grabbed her purse, keys, and a list of errands before heading for the door. On her way out, she stuck her head in the kitchen.

"Hey, Mario."

"What up, boss?" Mario asked, coming closer.

She stuck the envelope into his hand.

"Here's your second chance," she said, turning to leave. "Don't waste it."

Chapter 5

The Blakes's twenty-fifth-anniversary party was all class and elegance, as was expected from a family that owned more land and property in the city than any other private holder. Truthfully, Sydney had never even heard of the Blakes before Charlotte walked through the doors of Decadent. But once she did her research, she realized they were attached to several hotels, condos, and apartment buildings around Toronto. These people were in a social circle that Sydney hadn't even known existed. She was playing in a whole new tax bracket.

Sydney tried not to gawk as she took in the high ceilings of the banquet hall in the Blakes's ten-thousand-square-foot home. The heels on her neutral pumps sank into the plush carpet, muting the sound of her steps as she wandered easily through the crowd. Lissandra had taken off as soon as the cake had been delivered, choosing to opt out of spending the night with a roomful of old white married men. That meant Sydney was flying solo. And even though the crowd was mixed in age and race, Sydney hadn't seen a familiar face since

Charlotte had disappeared to check on the drinks a half hour earlier. She didn't mind, though. That just meant more potential business to drum up.

"Sydney, there are some people that I want you to meet."

She let Charlotte lead her through the crowd of mingling guests to near the front of the room.

"Charles and Diane, this is Sydney Isaacs, the creator of your anniversary cake," Charlotte said with a big grin. "Sydney, this is Charles and Diane Blake, the anniversary celebrants."

"Nice to meet you, Mr. and Mrs. Blake," Sydney said, smiling as she took the hand of the distinguished-looking man and then his slightly younger-looking wife. "And congratulations on your anniversary."

"Thank you," Diane said, her pale skin crinkling at the corners of her eyes as she smiled warmly at Sydney. "The cake is absolutely breathtaking."

She slipped her arm through her husband's. "I was just telling Charles, it's so beautiful that I'm not sure I even want to cut it."

"Well, you have to cut it," Charlotte said. "Because I can assure you, it tastes just as good as it looks."

"Listen to the event planner, honey," Charles said. "She speaks wisdom."

As they laughed, a much younger couple, closer to Sydney's age, joined them.

"Oh, Sydney, please meet our children, Will and Elise," Diane said, beckoning the two closer. "Children, this is the woman who made our anniversary cake. Elise, you should think about using her for your wedding."

Elise nodded. "It is beautiful. I was just telling my fiancé that we should do something creative like that for our wedding, instead of the normal round cakes stacked on top of each other. I'll definitely have to have my planner give you a call."

Sydney grinned. "I look forward to it."

"I wish we could give Will some similar advice, but unfortunately, he seems unwilling to give us the one anniversary gift we really want," Charles said with a stern look at his son.

Sydney swore she saw Will roll his gray eyes. But the dimple in his handsome face gave away the amusement with which he regarded his father.

"I'll leave the wedding talk to Elise," he said with a small smile. "I think she's putting you and your pocketbook through enough with that."

Elise slapped her brother playfully as their mother laughed.

Another group of well-wishers approached them and Sydney nodded her exit as she made space for the new arrivals. She was about to step away when she realized Will was still in her path.

"So do pastry chefs know how to dance? Or are their skills limited to the kitchen?" he asked with a teasing grin.

"Some of us are known to be multiskilled," Sydney said, going along with him.

"Then let's see if you're one of them," he said, holding out his hand. "Shall we?"

Sydney let Will lead her and her nude-colored dress into the space in the large room reserved for dancing. Most of the guests seemed to have the same idea and slowly the floor began to fill with waltzing couples. Sydney had almost run out of small talk with Will when she heard a throat clear behind her. She saw Will look over her head and grin.

"Can I cut in?"

Sydney turned around and rolled her eyes when she saw who it was.

"Hayden, my man, glad you could make it," Will said, shaking Hayden's hand.

Sydney shook her head. Unbelievable. Did everyone know him?

"You know I had to be here for your folks' anniversary," he said. "Dad wanted to be here also, but unfortunately he was a bit under the weather this evening."

Sydney thought of moving away, but she was stuck in the middle of the dance floor between two men who were both taller and broader than she. Making an exit would be a bit challenging.

"I see you met Sydney," Hayden continued.

Will glanced down at Sydney, surprised. "You know each other?"

Sydney sighed. "Yes."

"Sydney and I actually grew up together," Hayden said.

"Look at that," Will said. "Isn't the world a small place?"

"Indeed," Hayden said. "You mind if I steal her away for a bit?"

"Not at all." Will stepped back. "As long as she promises to save a dance for me."

Sydney smiled as she realized she had no escape. "Of course."

Sydney turned around to face Hayden as Will abandoned her on the dance floor.

"Are you stalking me?" she asked.

He slipped an arm around her waist and threaded his fingers through her other hand, drawing her closer to him.

"Did you get the tickets?" he asked as he began moving them around the floor.

"Yes," she said, resting her hand on his shoulder.

"Are you coming to the game?"

"You still haven't answered my question," she said. "Are you stalking me?"

"Why would I do something like that?" he asked innocently as he led her into a half spin that took Sydney by surprise.

"I don't know," Sydney said after she caught her breath. "Maybe because you're not used to taking no for an answer."

"No, Sydney, I am not stalking you," he said, pulling her even closer to him.

"Then why are you here?" she asked, trying to sound annoyed, even though she had adjusted to his closeness by moving her hand from his shoulder to around his neck.

"Maybe you should answer the question of why you're here," he said easily.

"That's easy. I'm here to work," she said staunchly.

"Thanks to Charlotte, right?"

Sydney paused and tilted her head back to look at him.

"Right."

He leaned forward, placing his lips right by her ear. "Who do you think told Charlotte about you?"

Of course. He did. That's why Charlotte had been so cagey about who recommended Decadent to her.

Sydney sighed and relaxed.

"You don't give up, do you," she said, resting her head on his chest.

"No," he said, placing her other hand around his neck,

as he put both of his around her waist. "But you sure don't make it easy for a brother."

"Now how would that be fun for you?" she asked, a smile lifting her lips. "You always liked a challenge."

"And you certainly were that," he said with a laugh.

"Aw, are you saying I'm the one that got away?" she asked, tilting her head back to meet his eyes.

He snorted. "More like the one I could never catch."

Sydney grinned. "That's the nicest thing you've ever said to me."

"I'll say more nice things if you'll go out with me," he said, taking her into another quick spin. Man, was he good on his feet. She shook her head and tried to focus on his last statement.

"This again, Dub?"

He shook his head. "Nini, you have to be the most stubborn woman I have ever met in my entire life."

"Because I won't go out with you?"

"Because you want to, but you won't," Hayden said, his eyes challenging her to disagree.

Sydney bit her lip and looked away. He got her there.

"How's your dad?" she asked.

He rolled his eyes but let her change the subject. "He's old."

"What?"

"And he won't retire."

Sydney laughed. "Of course he won't. He loves his job."

"But I wish he loved his life as much," Hayden said, his brow furrowing. "He's almost seventy and his doctors say he needs to slow down. His wife says he needs to slow down. Christian says he needs to slow down. He was supposed to be here tonight, but he was so tired he couldn't make it. You would think that would be a sign for him to start taking it easy. But he's trying not to hear any of that."

Sydney gazed at him with empathy, all too familiar with the habits of a workaholic father. "Is that why you came back? So you could get him to slow down?"

"That was part of the reason." Hayden frowned. "Though it doesn't seem to be working."

"Give him time," Sydney said. "You and I both know you can't get a black man to do anything he doesn't want to do."

"True," he said, gazing down at her. "And unless you want this black man to do something you don't want me to do, I suggest you stop stroking my neck like that."

Sydney's hands froze and her eyes widened. "I'm sorry." She hadn't even realized she had been doing it.

His gaze heated her to the core. "I'm not."

Sydney jumped away from him, narrowing her eyes.

"What's wrong, Syd?" He grinned mischievously. "Scared to dance with me now?"

"No," she said with more certainty than she felt. What had she been thinking?

"So why all this distance?"

"No reason." She rubbed a hand against the nape of her neck. "Just a bit winded."

She fanned her hand near her face. "Whew. Haven't danced this much in a while."

Hayden folded his arms. "Really."

Sydney was saved from answering by the end of the music and a hand urging her forward.

"Sydney, the cake, we need you."

Charlotte was pulling on her arm and leading her over to the side of the room where all eyes were focused. By the time she was close enough, she realized they were about to cut the cake and wanted her present to take a few photos. She smiled at the cameras when it was her turn, and cheered with the rest of the crowd as Charles and Diane cut the first slice, but the whole time she couldn't stop thinking about what had happened with her and Hayden.

And since she couldn't come up with a suitable explanation, as soon as the music started up again, she was out the door and in her car. Because even though she didn't know what had gone on between her and Hayden, she wasn't about to take a chance that it would happen again.

Chapter 6

"Sydney, you're needed up front."

Sydney put her hand over the phone receiver. "Coming," she shouted toward the open door. She directed her attention back to the phone.

"Dean, I know one hundred fifty thousand is a lot less than three hundred fifty thousand, but understand that I don't have that money right now. . . ."

"Sydney, this is important," Wendy called from outside Sydney's door.

"Handle it—I'm busy!" she shouted at the door again.

"Look, Syd, I am trying to be as reasonable about this as I can, but I can't put my life on hold for you," Dean said impatiently from the other end. "This guy is willing to sell me this space for one hundred K. The other fifty is just enough to cover my initial expenses. And he's on a clock, so it's not like I can wait forever."

"Dean, I understand, believe me. But isn't there some other way you can get the money. . . ."

"Sydney!" Lissandra was at the door, a look of urgency on her face. "We need you. Like now. No buts."

"Look, it sounds like things are busy over there," Dean said. "We'll talk later."

"Dean, wait—"

Sydney heard the click as her brother hung up the phone.

"Sydney . . ."

"What!" she snapped at her sister.

Lissandra pursed her mouth and Sydney knew her sister was restraining herself from cursing Sydney out.

"You need to see this," Lissandra finally said.

Gritting her teeth, Sydney got up from her desk and followed Lissandra out of the office and down the hallway. Before she even got to the main customer area, she could tell that something was going on. The after-eight period was always busiest because that was when the first-daters and the after-dinner crowds came in for coffee and dessert. But tonight it was louder than usual. Staff had paused serving; even a few guests were on their feet to see whatever was going on. And those who weren't standing all had their eyes turned in the same direction, toward the back of the shop.

Sydney's heart began to beat faster.

"What's going on? What's wrong?" she hissed at Lissandra as she followed her around the L-shaped guest area.

"See for yourself."

Lissandra stepped aside and suddenly Sydney was looking at the back area of the restaurant. Several tables had been pulled together to make one large table seating eight. That and a corner booth were completely occupied with men. Tall, muscular men. All dressed in sporting gear.

Toronto Raptors sporting gear.

"Is it . . ."

"Yes," Lissandra whispered from beside her. "It's our local NBA franchise. Your boy brought the whole team."

As soon as Lissandra said "your boy," Sydney saw him. He had stood up from the corner booth and was walking toward her, his chocolate brown eyes cataloguing her every move like a ball in play. And for all her knowing better, she hoped that he caught her. When he finally came to a stop, just inches in front of her, she gazed up at him. He returned her stare, a small smile on his lips. Sydney finally cracked, a smile breaking her lips.

"You didn't come to the game." His voice was so low she wasn't sure how she heard him over the din of the room.

"I had to work."

"So Lissandra told me," he said, nodding toward her sister, but never taking his eyes off Sydney. "She said you do that a lot."

"The burden of the independent woman." Sydney shrugged and crossed her arms in unison.

"I see." He smiled. "Well, since you wouldn't come to me, I decided to come to you."

Sydney glanced behind him. "Looks like you brought a few friends."

"I like to make an impression."

"I hope your impression doesn't put me out of business," Sydney said. "I don't know if we have enough coffee and cake in the kitchen to feed all your boys."

He laughed. "I think you'll manage. And I think it will make a good impression if you join your special guests for dessert."

"Oh, I can't. I have to check on the kitchen. . . ."

"No, you don't," Lissandra said. Sydney looked

around, surprised that her sister was still there. "I've got it under control."

"But—" Sydney pleaded with her sister, a don't-make-me-do-this look in her eyes.

Lissandra yanked Sydney away and pressed her mouth to her sister's ear.

"If you don't sit your tiny behind down and have dessert with that fine, spectacularly toned man, who can get me courtside tickets, I will nail your butt to a chair and make you do it. Got it?"

Sydney smiled at Hayden while detangling herself from Lissandra's death grip.

"So where am I sitting?"

With a hand on her back, Hayden steered her over to the corner booth, where three other guys were seated.

"Everyone, this is Sydney. Sydney, this is Sean Denary, Brian Packman, and Gary Forbes," he said, introducing her to the three players at the table.

"Hey, I know you," Sydney said, brightening as she looked at Gary Forbes. "I've heard your name on the radio."

Gary laughed. "She's cute, Dub. I like her."

"Yeah, well, don't like her too much," Hayden said. The other guys laughed.

"Nice to meet all of you," Sydney said with a smile.

"Oh no, the pleasure is ours," Brian said. "We couldn't wait to meet the woman that had Dub watching the stands harder than he was watching us the other night."

"Whatever," Hayden said, shaking his head. "I was not."

"Yes, you were," Brian and Gary said at the same time before laughing. Sydney couldn't help but laugh also.

"So why'd you flake on us, Sydney?" Sean asked. "You're not into basketball? Or did Dub's ugly mug scare you off."

Sydney laughed. "No. I had to work—"

A mutual sound of disapproval went up from all the men around the table.

Hayden leaned toward her and she got a whiff of his cologne.

"Tough crowd, eh?"

"A little," she said, looking up into his smiling eyes. "You would think they would cut a working woman some slack."

Just then the dessert plates with larger-than-normal portions started arriving at the table. When all the plates had been put down, including one for Sydney, Sean looked up at Hayden.

"You want to do the thing, Dub?"

Hayden nodded and turned to Sydney. "Do you mind if we pray over our food?"

Sydney blinked several times, surprised.

"Uh, no. Not at all."

Every head lowered and Hayden said grace. When he was done, everyone dug in and the chatter went up again, but Sydney's eyes stayed on Hayden.

"What?" he asked after a moment.

She shook her head and smiled. "I never heard someone pray over dessert before."

"Well, if this red velvet cake is anything like your dad's back in the day, I better pray that I don't get a heart attack," he said, digging in.

She couldn't help but watch as he took the first fork-ful into his mouth. She smiled. The satisfied sound he made in his throat gave her a warm satisfying feeling in her tummy. She had made that cake herself.

"So what did Dub tell you to get you all to come down here anyway?" Sydney asked, slipping a small bite of pumpkin pie into her mouth.

"Well, he didn't really ask us," Brian said, articulating with his fork. "It was supposed to be just him and Sean. But then when we heard where he was going, we decided to crash his party."

Hayden shook his head as Sydney laughed.

"Wow, you guys must be really close," she said.

"Well, you know, Dub is a cool brother," Brian said, glancing at Hayden.

"Sure, he's our trainer, but he's also one of us, you know?" said Gary. "He used to play in the league. In fact, he should *still* be playing in the league. . . ."

"All right, all right, let's not get into that." Hayden threw up his hands with a small smile. "My days on the court are gone, and I'm fine with that. I love what I do. And I love having a front-row seat to watch you guys do what you do."

"See what I mean?" Gary turned to Sydney. "Dub is good people."

"But anyway," Sean said. "What had happened was, practice ended early and we noticed that Dub was trying to give us the slip. So I was like, dog, where you going? And he was trying to play it off and act like it wasn't nothin' serious, but then we find out that he was going to the restaurant of the woman who stood him up Sunday. . . ."

Sydney glanced over at Hayden. He had a look of amusement on his face as he listened to Sean.

"So of course, being the friend I am, I invited myself along," Sean said with a grin.

"And anywhere Sean goes, those two go," Hayden said. "Before I knew it, all the guys were here."

"Well, most of us anyway," Brian said with a grin. "We figured, dessert with some entertainment at Dub's expense."

Hayden shook his head as they laughed. "I am never telling you guys anything again."

"Aw," Sydney said, nudging him with her shoulder. "You should be happy you have a team that cares about you that much."

"Yeah, you heard that, Dub?" Sean said. "Happy."

"I'll tell you one thing, Sydney," Gary said, putting a forkful of mint chocolate cheesecake into his mouth. "This cake right here? This is making me happy."

"Mhmm," Brian agreed. "Compliments to your chef. We will definitely be popping back here. Right, Dub?"

"Not without me you won't," Hayden jokingly threatened.

The guys continued trading barbs and teasing Hayden. Sydney watched as he took it all in stride. Despite the jokes, she could tell that the players really respected Hayden and that made her respect him. When they finally moved to leave after ordering seconds and in some cases thirds, Sydney couldn't believe that almost forty minutes had passed.

"Sydney, pleasure to meet you, hope you'll make it to the next game," Brian said with a grin as he followed the guys toward the exit.

"Yeah, Dub always has tickets," Sean added. "Make sure he gets you a couple."

"Thanks, guys." Sydney waved to them as they left.

Hayden relaxed back in the booth and let out a sigh as he watched the guys leave.

"Too much to handle, Dub?" Sydney teased.

He grinned. "Sometimes. But I love those guys. I

just met them, but they're like family—even when they're giving me hell."

"Well, they sure made my evening," Sydney said, shifting in the booth so she could face him.

"Only them?" Hayden asked with a raised eyebrow.

Sydney smiled coyly. "It was the package."

His eyes sparkled at hers. "Thanks for hanging with me. After the Blakes's party and you not showing up last night, I thought I didn't have a chance."

Sydney raised an eyebrow. "Who said you do?"

"Oh, I'm pretty sure I do." He grinned slyly.

"I don't remember saying anything to suggest that," Sydney said in mock seriousness.

"Please, you were all over me during dessert," Hayden said. "Rubbing your shoulder up against me, caressing my hand . . ."

"I was passing you a napkin!"

". . . rubbing your leg against mine."

"I needed to get out of the booth."

"Always putting your hands on me . . ."

"I was not," Sydney said, slapping him playfully.

"See, you did it again." He shook his head. "You can't keep your hands off me, can you?"

Sydney folded her arms and tried to glare at him, but ended up smiling.

"You are terrible, you know that?" she said.

She shook her head as she let her eyes take in the whole Hayden package. He was beautiful. And not just because of the whole lose-your-breath-gorgeous thing he had going on. It was something else. He was different from the boy she had known years ago. Different in ways that made it harder for her to ignore her growing attraction to him. And she was tired of trying.

What was the worst that could happen anyway?

"OK, fine, maybe you have a chance," she said, leaning back in the booth beside him.

"Good," he said, handing her his phone. " 'Cause I'm not waiting another week to see you again. Next time without the six-foot chaperones."

"How's this weekend?" she asked, as she put her number into his phone and handed it back to him.

He slipped it into his pocket and turned to meet her eyes. "How's tomorrow?"

She grinned. "That works, too."

"Good, I'll text you the details," he said, standing up. He smiled at her as he backed away. "And this time, please show up."

She laughed. That was not something he had to worry about. Not at all.

Chapter 7

"We're taking the subway?"

The sun glinted off his caramel-colored face as he grinned. "Yup."

Sydney stopped in the middle of the downtown sidewalk in front of Decadent. "Why?"

"Why not?" He grabbed her hand and pulled her forward. "It's a beautiful day. The sun is shining, the air is full of smog. What more could a city girl want?"

"Four wheels and central cooling," Sydney said. "Is this why you told me to wear comfortable shoes?".

"I promise you'll have fun," Hayden said as they walked side by side toward the entrance to the underground. "I got us day passes so we can go wherever we want."

"You know, if you don't have a car it's OK. We could have taken mine. I'm not one of those judgmental sisters. I can work with a brother."

Hayden laughed. "I have a car. It's parked in your spot behind Decadent."

"Then why aren't we driving?"

He stopped walking and turned to look her dead in the eye.

"Because I would rather look at you than look at traffic."

Sydney's heart took a pause, then continued beating.

A smile stole onto her lips and she turned her face away slightly so he couldn't tell how much his words had affected her.

"OK," she said after a moment. "That's a pretty good reason, Dub."

He smirked. "I thought so, too, Nini."

The fifteen-minute ride that she remembered from her days of commuting to university seemed like only a few moments with Hayden. The more time she spent with him, the more she felt like the carefree teenager she'd been so many years ago. It was almost as if only a couple of days had passed between then and now, instead of a number of years.

"OK, so I think we're here," Hayden said as they came out of the College subway station exit to the street.

"You think?" Sydney asked teasingly. She watched as Hayden scratched his head and looked around at the pedestrian-heavy street. She had never seen a man look so good, when he was so totally lost. Actually she had never seen a man look so good, period. Well, there was Boris Kodjoe, but she had never met him in person, so he didn't count.

"No," Hayden said, a little more confidently. "I'm sure. This is it."

Sydney looked up and down the street at the tightly packed structures, which ranged in style from nineteenth century to postmodern and which housed an equally eclectic mix of shops and establishments. "What exactly is *it*?"

He grabbed her hand again and led her around the corner to College Street. Sydney's mouth fell open. There were people everywhere. They poured off the sidewalk into the road like a river, circling around the white tents that lined both sides of the street for as far as she could see. She suddenly noticed the sound of music that had been so faint before. It set the tempo for the movement of the crowd as they made their way unhindered by cars through the usually gridlocked downtown street.

"What is this?" Sydney asked, keeping her hold on Hayden's hand as he led her past the barricades where the vehicular traffic stopped and festival traffic began.

"This is Taste of Little Italy," he said, leaning close to her ear. "Every Italian dish you can think of is somewhere in the next seven blocks."

Sydney scrunched up her face and stopped short. "Italian?"

The jubilant expression on Hayden's face fell like a brick into the ocean.

"Don't tell me." Weariness saturated his voice. "You hate Italian food."

He wiped his hand over his face and looked away and she heard him mumble something with the words "stupid" and "idiot." Sydney covered her mouth.

"I'm sorry," he said, dropping his hands to his sides, his face contorted by regret. "I shouldn't have assumed. I should have asked. . . ."

Before he could finish, she burst into laughter.

"Come on, Sydney, it's not that funny." Hayden stuck his hands into his pockets. "I said I was sorry. . . ."

Sydney shook her head and struggled to speak through

her laughter. "Your face . . . you looked like . . . like I told you your dog died. . . . It was priceless."

"What?"

Sydney wiped her eyes and straightened up. "I think we have a bit of a misunderstanding. I love Italian," she said. "I just wanted to get you back for ambushing me last night."

Hayden looked up at the sky and closed his eyes. When he looked back down at Sydney, he was chuckling.

"You are something else," he said, shaking his head. "What am I going to do with you?"

She grinned and slipped her arm into his. "How about feed me?"

They took their time weaving through the crowd on College Street. Sydney was sure they tasted something at almost every stand. Some of them twice.

"Wow, Nini, you still inhale food like a garbage disposal," Hayden said with a chuckle.

Sydney's eyes widened, but her mouth was full of a beef sausage covered in everything and so she opted to punch him in the arm instead. He only laughed at her effort at injuring him.

"At least I chew my food, instead of swallowing it whole," she retorted when she had swallowed.

"Hey, we all appreciate food in our own way." He draped an arm carelessly around her shoulders. "Admit it, being out with me wasn't as terrible as you thought it would be."

Sydney had never thought being out with him would be terrible. In fact, her fear of how completely unterrible it would be was what had kept her hesitating. But she would never admit that to him.

"I don't know about that, Mr. Windsor. Since we've been here, all you've done is insult me and laugh at me. . . ."

". . . and buy you whatever you want, and carry your girly purse so you could hold more food, and tell you you're beautiful even with mustard all over your face."

He wiped a bit of something off the tip of her nose. Sydney smiled up at him and caught the warmth behind the teasing in his eyes.

"So you think I'm beautiful, eh," she said with a grin.

He shook his head and smiled. "You already know that."

She leaned into his side as they continued walking. "OK, maybe you're not too bad for company."

His laugh echoed through the cool night air and got lost somewhere in the dusk that surrounded the thinning crowd. All the streetlights were on now, and a few vendors had turned on the decorative lights attached to their stalls. Sydney noticed that the sound of the music was mostly behind them, and they were almost at the end of the area designated for the festival. As they turned around to make the trek back up to where they started, Sydney was aware of her own reluctance for the evening to be over. Judging by Hayden's own unhurried pace, she suspected the feeling went both ways.

"When was the last time you were down here?" he asked, breaking the lull of comfortable silence that had fallen between them.

Sydney looked up thoughtfully.

"I don't know," she said after a moment. "It's been a while. We've delivered a few catering jobs around here, but I can't remember the last time I've actually walked on this street in this area."

He nodded. "It sure is different from how I remember it."

Sydney looked up at him curiously. "You mean since you left Toronto?"

He looked down at her for a long moment.

"Come here." He grabbed her hand and pulled her toward the sidewalk. She followed him wordlessly for a few steps until he stopped in front of a storefront halfway between the end of the festival and the subway entrance.

He nodded toward the tiny bar in front of them.

"You remember this?"

Sydney stepped forward toward the busy pub. The front had been redone in new colors, and the sign overhead read COLLEGE STREET BAR, but Sydney remembered when it read DECADENT. This was the exact spot where Leroy's bakery had first been more than twenty years ago.

"You remember," she whispered, turning back to look at Hayden. His hands were stuck casually in his pockets as he observed her. He looked more serious than he had all night.

"Of course I remember," he said easily. "This place felt like home to me more than anywhere else in the world."

He leaned back against a nearby light post.

"I always knew what to expect when I was here. There would always be cream soda in the refrigerator. Uncle Leroy would always have a slice of sweet potato pie for me and there would always be a seat under the ash tree out back that was all mine."

Sydney shook her head. "That ash tree. Mom begged Dad to cut it down. She was so sure it was going to fall on one of us, it was so old."

Hayden laughed. "No way was Uncle Leroy going to cut that down."

"I know," Sydney said. "In the summer he used to string a hammock between the trunk of that tree and the back wall of the shop. If he cut it down where would the hammock go?"

They both laughed as they remembered Sydney's dad.

"I was at the funeral, you know," Hayden said after a moment. "I saw you and your sisters. . . . I wanted to go over, but it had been so long. I should have said something. . . . I'm sorry. . . ."

"It's OK." Sydney waved away his remorse with a flick of her wrist.

"No, it's not," Hayden said, stepping closer, peering into her eyes. "Uncle Leroy was like family to me. And I should have been there for you."

He pulled her close into an embrace and Sydney wished he hadn't, because it was like all his love for her father seeped into her and unlocked the part of her heart that had sealed up her affection for Leroy. Memories of her dad suffocated her and she gasped for breath. She pulled away from him and stepped back. His bewildered expression only made her take another step back.

"I . . . I'm s-sorry," she stuttered.

His brow furrowed as his eyes flitted over her face with concern. "Are you OK?"

She blinked and looked away from him, sticking her hands in her pockets. "I'm fine."

"Are you su—"

"Let's just go, OK?" She began walking away without waiting for him to respond.

She soon heard his steps behind her and moments later, he was falling in step beside her. She could feel him glance over at her every few moments, but she hoped he wouldn't ask her about what had just happened, because she couldn't explain. She was still having trouble herself understanding how she felt about her father. Feelings of love, emptiness, betrayal, and guilt had clashed for so long that she found it easier to lock them away than deal with them. That was why she didn't want to go down this memory lane with Hayden.

She took a deep breath and then another, hoping that the cool air that filled her lungs would clear the tension in her chest. But it was Hayden's hand on hers that eventually did the trick. He didn't say anything, he didn't look at her, but the sure strength of his fingers around hers was enough.

"So seeing that I just bought you half the Italian food in Toronto, think I can score a free slice of red velvet cake?" he asked as they headed toward the subway.

Sydney shook her head and smiled. "Always looking for freebies, aren't you, Dub."

"Hey, at least I'm consistent," he said with a grin.

"Hmm," Sydney said, smirking at him. "Too bad your free-throw average for the Celtics wasn't."

"Oooh!" Hayden groaned and grabbed his chest. "Straight to the heart."

"Don't worry," Sydney said, smiling sweetly. "I'm sure a slice of red velvet will heal the pain."

His loud, heavy laugh rumbled through her, and for a while again, Sydney was able to forget how complicated her life really was.

* * *

"Where do you think you're coming from this time of the night?"

"Yes, where have you been?"

Sydney closed the front door behind her and slipped off her shoes.

"Out," Sydney said, as she walked the short distance into the living room, where her sisters were sitting on the couch watching television.

"Out?" JJ raised an eyebrow. "Is that all you have to say? It's 10:15 on a work night, missy."

Sydney smiled contentedly before dropping down on the couch beside JJ. "Yes, that's all."

"Out with Mr. NBA," Lissandra said from the armchair where she was painting her toenails. "Where ya'll been for the past four hours? I don't know any dinner that lasts that long."

"Depends where you're eating," Sydney said with a grin. "We went downtown for Taste of Little Italy."

"The food festival?" Lissandra glanced up. "Well, he certainly found the way to your heart."

"When are we gonna get to see him again anyway?" JJ asked. "It's been forever since he's been in Toronto. I've almost forgotten what he looks like."

"So Google him." Sydney stretched out her legs on the coffee table. "That should jog your memory."

"Come on," JJ whined. "Lissandra got to see him."

"I know," Sydney said. "And look what happened. She bartered my parking spot for game tickets."

"Hey!" Lissandra said, looking up from her toes again. "Everything worked out for everybody in the end, didn't it?"

Sydney rolled her eyes.

"OK, have it your way," JJ said. She yawned as she

stood up. "Just be careful, though. Fame changes people. He may not be the same guy you remember. And who knows what secrets are lurking in the years since we last saw him."

"OK, Mom, I'll be careful," Sydney said mockingly. She watched incredulously as her sister headed toward the stairs. "Are you going to bed?"

"Yup," JJ said, her foot already on the first step. "I'm really tired."

"Tired, eh," Lissandra muttered. Sydney nudged Lissandra's chair and gave her a warning look when she looked up.

"Yes, tired. I do work all day," JJ said.

Lissandra looked like she would say something, but Sydney cut her off.

"Good night, JJ."

"Good night, all," JJ said, already halfway up the stairs.

Sydney flipped the station to the Food Network. "So what you guys been up to all evening anyway?"

"Talking about Decadent," Lissandra said. She pursed her lips. "Dean came over."

Sydney turned to look at her sister. "What did he say?"

"He was looking for you," Lissandra said. She capped the bottle of nail polish and sat up. "He wants the money, Sydney."

Sydney raked her hands through her hair. "I know. . . ."

"No, I don't think you do," Lissandra said. "He wants all the money. You told him what the restaurant was worth and now all he can see are dollar signs. He came over here talking about he and Sheree want to get a place of their own and move out of the guesthouse, and he and Sheree want to start a fund for their child. Why the heck do they need to start a fund for kids they don't have?"

Sydney sighed.

"And then there's the whole money for the studio thing. Did you know he's gonna spend—"

"One hundred fifty thousand? Yeah," Sydney said. "That's what we were talking about yesterday when he called. He wants to sell me part of Decadent for that. Problem is . . ."

". . . you don't have one hundred fifty thousand," Lissandra finished.

"Exactly."

Both sisters sat staring at contestants battling it out on an episode of *Iron Chef*. Sydney couldn't help but see it as a metaphor for her current situation. The whole thing had become a battle between Sydney and Dean over who would win the shop. Already it was causing tension between them. No longer was her conversation with her brother a conversation with her brother. Everything was potentially a discussion about Decadent.

"Zelia thinks I should let him sell it," Sydney said after a moment.

Lissandra snorted. "She would. She always takes Dean's side in everything. I'm sure Jackie would agree, too. It's not like she and Dad split on amicable terms."

"Don't say that. . . ."

"Why not?" Lissandra snapped. "We all know it's true. And yet we never talk about it, like if we don't mention it, it'll be less real. You know the two of them were crazy. You couldn't even mention Dad in Mom's presence after the first divorce. . . ."

"Couldn't have been that bad. She married him twice."

"Probably 'cause she was pregnant. Twice."

"Lissandra . . ."

"Sydney, can we please keep it real." Lissandra's eyes were hard as they stared at her sister. "You know while Mom and Dad were busy being mad at each other we had to look out for ourselves. Nobody in this family ever gave us anything. Even Leroy; when he kicked the bucket he gave everything to Dean. . . ."

"He gave us this house," Sydney said in an effort to defend decisions of her father that she herself didn't understand.

"Stop making excuses for him," Lissandra said, annoyed. "I watched you pour your whole life into that shop, Syd. Dean never worked there one day in his life. And now as soon as he has ownership for it, he wants to sell it right out from under you."

Lissandra got up and moved to the couch where Sydney was sitting. She took Sydney's hand.

"We are not going to let him take Decadent from us, Syd," Lissandra said. "No one is going to take it from us."

"That sounds great in theory, Lissandra, but in reality it's a lot more complicated." Sydney turned off the TV and threw the remote onto the coffee table with enough force to send the battery cover flying. She understood how Lissandra felt because it was how she felt all the time. Those were the things she thought but would never say; the things she buried by avoiding her mother.

"I don't want to lose the shop, but I don't have a hundred fifty thousand dollars," Sydney said.

"But you have a hundred," Lissandra said. "And I have thirty-five."

"That still leaves us fifteen short," Sydney said.

"I'll give it to you."

Sydney and Lissandra turned around to see JJ sitting at the bottom of the stairs. "I'll put in the fifteen thousand. All together that gives us the one hundred fifty Dean is asking for."

Sydney got up and started pacing. "One hundred thousand dollars. That's everything I have."

"And what, our fifty is chump change?" Lissandra asked, an eyebrow raised.

"No, you don't understand," Sydney said. "This is *everything* I have. Everything I have worked and saved and invested for the past ten years."

"We get it," JJ said. "This is a big deal. I can't tell you what to do, but if you want to do this, if you want to buy the shop, I'll help you."

"Same here," Lissandra said.

Sydney sat down and put her head in her hands. How she wished there was someone she could talk to about this. These were the times when she missed her father the most. But any feelings she had for him were mixed at best.

She took a deep breath and sat back in the couch. Yes, she would be giving up everything she had for a chance at owning just a piece of Decadent. It was a risk. But that everything would mean nothing if she lost the shop that was her life. She had no choice.

"OK," Sydney said with a nod. "I'll do it."

Lissandra picked up the cordless phone from the end table and handed it to Sydney.

"Then call him."

Chapter 8

"Ladies, let's go! You know how Mom hates it when we're late."

JJ's strident voice coming from downstairs grated on Sydney's nerves as she tried to smear more concealer over the bags under her eyes. She was usually in church every Saturday, but not at the early and ungodly hour Jackie had insisted they arrive this week.

Normally she wouldn't have been this annoyed about the whole thing, but her week had been a handful and more. She had spent most of it meeting with lawyers and the Decadent's financial accountant to make the changes for the store. In record time, a new agreement for the ownership of the store had been drawn up, so that Sydney and her sisters now owned forty percent of the store and Dean the other 60 percent. He still had majority ownership, but Sydney wasn't worried.

The main reason they had rushed the whole thing was so Dean could have his money, and now that it had been transferred into his account he was happier than a kid on a snow day. Thomas, Decadent's accountant, had been concerned about Sydney giving Dean the money so soon since it would still take a few weeks be-fore the papers were filed, but Sydney knew her brother had people waiting on him to get things going for his own business, and she didn't want to stand in his way. Besides, it was a pretty simple transaction. Everything would be fine.

"Lissandra, hurry up," Sydney growled as she snapped her compact shut and dropped it into her purse. " 'Cause if JJ calls me again, she's going to make it to church with one black eye."

Lissandra responded with several words unfit for airplay before stomping out of her bedroom like an angry bull.

"Why does she think she can run my life like this?" Lissandra spat. "I am twenty-eight years old, not twelve. She can't make me do anything."

Lissandra tended to limit her church attendance to those mandated by their mother.

"In theory," Sydney said as she headed down the stairs with Lissandra behind her. "But would you rather spend a few hours in church or deal with a month-long guilt trip from Jackie. Come on, she only asks you to show up once a month. And you remember how it was the last time you didn't show up a few months back."

Lissandra grumbled something else unrepeatable as she slipped on a light spring jacket.

"Hmm," JJ mumbled, slipping on her sunglasses. "A mouth like yours could use some Jesus."

"You're breathing your last breath, JJ," Lissandra said.

Sydney pushed JJ out the door, and got between her two sisters. It was going to be a long morning.

The ride to church proceeded pretty much in silence until JJ turned the car into an unfamiliar lot.

"So Mom switched churches again," Sydney murmured. She was hardly surprised. Jackie was about as consistent with her church home as she was with her husbands, and so instead of trying to keep up, Sydney had stuck to attending her father's church, which was only ten minutes from the house.

"Yup," JJ said, pulling into a parking space. "This is Mom's new church, Granville Park."

Lissandra huffed and pushed open the back door. "Great. Now we have to smile and be fake with a whole new bunch of people."

JJ looked over her shoulder. "You don't have to be fake, Lissandra. You could just be yourself. God accepts us all, just as we are."

"Don't start, Saint Judith," Lissandra said, gathering her purse and turning to get out. "And don't think I'm staying here a minute past one."

JJ turned to Sydney.

"She's a grown woman, JJ," Sydney said, searching through her purse for lip gloss. "Leave her be."

JJ shook her head. "I don't know what happened to her. We were all grown up the same way. How did we end up so different?"

"Life," Sydney said, opening the car door. "It punches all of us in the gut eventually. And you can either look up for help, or look down and get bitter."

"Which one did you choose?" JJ asked. Her questions stopped Sydney with one foot out the door.

"Well, I'm here, aren't I?"

JJ slipped on her sunglasses and opened her own car door. "Are you?"

Sydney wasn't sure why JJ's words bothered her, but they did. Sydney was nothing like Lissandra. Sure, she might not be the scripture-quoting Christian JJ was, but she made it her duty to be in church every week-end. Everyone's relationship was different. There was no reason to feel guilty about not being like her sister.

Nonetheless, tense silence followed the three of them across the packed parking lot and up the steps of the colonial-style church building.

The service hadn't begun yet, but already the church was half full. Sydney forced her lips into a smile for the greeter who handed her a program, before following her sisters inside the sanctuary and up the main aisle to the middle rows on the right, where her mother and her two other sisters were already seated.

As always, Jackie sat at the end of the row, nearest to the aisle, while all of Sydney's sisters filled the rest of the bench. It had been that way since they were little, and had served as a strategic point to prevent busy-bodied toddlers from crawling out of the aisle and making themselves a nuisance throughout the church. Sydney guessed it still served as a deterrent for busy-body daughters who might attempt to leave church before the service was completely over.

"Good morning, Mother," Sydney whispered, before kissing Jackie on the cheek.

"Good morning, sweetheart," Jackie replied, touching her daughter's cheek with a smile. "I'm so glad to see you."

"You say that every month," Sydney said with a small smile.

"And every month it's true."

Sydney couldn't help but look at her mother. She was almost sixty, but was holding on to that early fifties look with ease. Except for the highlights of gray in her straight, shoulder-length auburn hair, which her hairdresser took care of with some professional grade Dark and Lovely, there were very few signs of her aging. Her cocoa-colored skin was naturally enhanced with warm undertones that gave a sparkle to her clear brown eyes and highlights to her high cheekbones. Furthermore, while the reality of carrying six children to term had added a bit of extra girth to her short five-foot-five frame, it didn't even come close to putting her in the big-momma category. It was little wonder Jackie had been able to attract three different husbands in her lifetime. She was beautiful. And that beauty had matured well over the years.

Jackie motioned to the others to scoot down to make space beside her for Sydney.

"Oh no, that's OK," Sydney said. "I was just gonna sit behind . . ."

"You'll sit here," Jackie said, motioning to the space beside her.

Sydney paused, but then eased into the space between her mother and Zelia.

Jackie smiled ruefully and shook her head. "I remember when you, Lissandra, and JJ were younger. The three of you would fight each other to see who would sit next to me."

"We were kids then, Mother," Sydney said, scanning the program the greeter had given her. "And back then it was only three of us."

"That is true," Jackie said wistfully. "But I remember it like it was yesterday. You were the sweetest thing. JJ would claim her spot as the youngest, but as soon as Lissandra started to cry you would let her have my other side. You were always looking out for your sisters."

Jackie ran the back of her fingers against Sydney's cheek gently. "You still do. I know I can always count on you for that."

The curse of being the oldest. Everyone was always counting on her to do something, to make the right decision for everyone. Who did she get to count on?

Sydney ignored the emotions that tumbled through her, and she flipped to the other page of the program.

"So what's with the new church?" Sydney asked as she scanned the program for any familiar names. "I thought you loved Toronto Central."

She felt her mother take a deep breath beside her, and she glanced over in time to see Jackie purse her lips and turn her head toward the front.

"Sometimes the Lord calls us to make changes."

Sydney closed the program. "What happened?"

"Nothing happened. . . ."

"Mother . . ."

"I said, nothing happened," Jackie repeated, closing the topic with the look in her eyes.

Sydney shook her head and turned to the front. Something had happened. Jackie only changed churches if she was getting married or if there was drama, and since Jackie hadn't introduced Sydney to any special friends, she knew that it had to do with some drama with her sisters.

She remembered the first time they'd had to move because of something like that. She had only been twelve years old. Rebecca Jenkins' mother had planned an eleventh-birthday party for her daughter and invited every girl at the church except Sydney and her sisters. Sydney hadn't been surprised. She saw the way Rebecca's mother would look at her whenever she saw Sydney and Rebecca talking together. She knew the real reason why Rebecca's mother would never let Rebecca come to their house.

But Jackie thought differently. Even though Sydney tried to tell her that they weren't invited, Jackie wouldn't believe it. She insisted that it had been a mistake, and on the day of the party she packed Sydney and her sisters into the car and took them over to the Jenkins' home for the party. They only got as far as the front door. There they were told that the party was almost over, and there was no point in them staying since all the food was gone and everyone was getting picked up soon anyway. Mrs. Jenkins had smiled and apologized, but her smile hadn't reached her eyes, and never once did she look at Sydney or her sisters, who were standing behind Jackie. Sydney watched a look pass over her mother's face that she would over the years become very familiar with. The next weekend, they were headed off to a new church.

Sydney sighed as she looked around the pool of unfamiliar faces. Maybe this was why she preferred going to a huge church where almost no one knew her. She hated being a new person, being the outsider. She despised the way people stared at you and whispered out of the corners of their mouths at you when they thought you weren't looking; the way they judged your clothes and your hair and the car you parked in the parking lot.

She could hear the stories they came up with as they watched Jackie walk in with her six children trailing behind her. "She never heard of birth control?"; "How many men did she go through?" or "I bet those girls are as wild as their mother." They might as well have been speaking their judgmental words aloud. Sometimes they did, and sometimes their children would then repeat them out loud to Sydney and her sisters. And sometimes Sydney and her sisters, usually Lissandra, would have to respond to those words with a fist in the face. And sometimes that would lead to another move. Was it any wonder that Jackie had to resort to ultimatums to get them to go to church together now that they were adults?

Sydney was about to check her watch for the fifth time in as many minutes, when she heard the organ at the front. The congregation stood and the service began. Sydney had been to enough of them that she could go through the motions with her eyes closed. It was only when they called for a Sis Isaacs for special music that she looked down the bench for JJ. Sure, the rest of them could carry a tune if necessary, but JJ was the singer. It was Josephine, however, who stood up.

Sydney's eyes met Lissandra's equally surprised ones.

"What the hell?" Lissandra mouthed. Sydney shrugged. She didn't know what was going on either.

Sydney leaned close to Zelia's ear and whispered. "I didn't know Josephine could sing."

Zelia glanced at Jackie before whispering back. "It's Josephine. Is there anything she can't do?"

Sydney bit her lip to keep from laughing as she turned back to the front to listen to her sister. Josephine's voice was OK, but it was nothing compared to JJ's. But you couldn't tell from the look on Jackie's face. Sydney shook her head. A mother's love.

"So I guess it's a competition now," Sydney whispered to Zelia. "JJ versus Josephine."

Zelia shook her head. "There's no competition. JJ doesn't sing anymore."

Sydney raised an eyebrow. "Seriously?"

"Seriously," Zelia whispered. "And can you blame her. Who wants to compete with that?" she said, nodding toward Jackie.

Sydney looked over and saw the look of utter pride on her mother's face as she hung on Josephine's every note. Sydney and Zelia need not have bothered themselves whispering. They could have been shouting at the top of their lungs and Jackie would have heard no one but Josephine.

Letting out a deep breath, Sydney crossed her legs and prepared to wait for the most awkward two hours of her month to be over. She never got anything from coming to church with her mother. She never heard anything because she was always waiting to hear someone's slick comments about her family. She never saw the Spirit move, because she was watching for every eye that might turn their way. It was like gingerly sitting on a cracked bench, waiting for your behind to hit the floor.

As soon as the last words of the closing prayer fell, she was on her feet and down the aisle toward the back. The only person who beat her outside was Lissandra, whom she found puffing on a cigarette behind the car.

"I thought you quit that," Sydney said frowning, though she had secretly suspected that her sister hadn't. More than once she had smelled cigarette smoke near the back door of the house.

"I tried," Lissandra said, taking one last puff before dropping the cigarette on the ground and grinding it out with her shoe. "But Saturday mornings at church put me over the edge."

"You put yourself over the edge," Sydney said unsympathetically. "You're going to kill yourself, and kill me with all that secondhand smoke."

"Everybody's gotta die sometime," said Lissandra as she fished gum out of her purse. "Where is Saint Judith? Does she know it's one fifteen?"

"The service just ended," Sydney said, leaning back against the car. "You know she's got to talk to everybody."

"Like your boy?" Lissandra asked, squinting toward the church building. "Isn't that him?"

Sydney followed Lissandra's line of sight to the tall, suit-wearing man standing near the steps with JJ and the rest of her sisters. Hayden in church? This was interesting. She watched him hug her mother and chat with the people around him. Then someone pointed over to the car where Sydney was watching, and he turned around and met her eyes. Sydney thought she saw him grin from where she was standing, but as he walked over to the car, she was sure.

"So is this a publicity stunt?" Sydney asked as she craned her neck up to keep her eyes on his face. "Toronto Raptors reaching out to the church folk in the city?"

"Good afternoon to you, too, Nini," he said, pulling her into a hug that immediately improved her mood.

"I didn't see you inside," Sydney said, as he released her from his embrace.

"I came late," he said, playing with her fingers absently. "I like to keep a low profile. What's your excuse?"

"I don't need one," Sydney said. "I was here on time."

"But you weren't here last week," he said knowingly. "I saw your mom and sisters, but not you."

"They didn't mention seeing you," Sydney said.

"Stop avoiding my question."

"Sydney's not really big on church with the family," Lissandra said. "She's more of a solo act." Sydney glared at her sister.

Hayden raised an eyebrow. "Is that true?"

"I go to another church," Sydney said. She pulled her hand out of his and folded her arms. "You have a problem with that?"

"I have a problem with you not going to any of my games," he said, gently unfolding her arms and stringing her fingers through his again. "What are you doing tomorrow night?"

Sydney was set to say "working," but the way he was looking at her, and the feel of his thumb running circles on the back of her hand, made her hesitate.

"I don't know yet," she said with a sigh.

He smiled, and they both knew he had won. "Game tomorrow night. Eight p.m. I'll call you later with details . . ."

". . . and with tickets for her and her sister, right?" Lissandra asked.

Hayden laughed. "Right."

"Hey, what about me?" JJ asked, finally appearing at the car.

"You don't even like basketball," Lissandra said, getting into the backseat as JJ unlocked the doors.

"Yeah, but maybe a girl just wants to have the option of going," JJ said, opening the driver's side.

Hayden shook his head. "OK. JJ, would you like me to send a ticket for you to go to the game?"

"Nah. I don't really like basketball," JJ said with a grin before slipping into the car.

"So I'll call you later?" Hayden said to Sydney.

Sydney smiled. "Fine."

"Excellent." He kissed the back of her hand quickly and opened the passenger door for her.

"See you later, ladies," he said as he helped her in and closed the door.

Sydney rolled her eyes as her sisters singsonged, "Bye, Hayden."

"That man is sprung over you," JJ said with a laugh as they exited the parking lot. "You make sure you keep him around."

"Yeah," Lissandra added. "At least until the play-offs."

The three of them laughed and Sydney realized that maybe the morning hadn't been so bad after all.

Chapter 9

"**D**e-fense! De-fense!"
The floor shook beneath Sydney's feet as hundreds of fans stomped and cheered for the Raptors. Her own throat was hoarse from screaming, and she hadn't sat down in her fourth-row seat for at least twenty minutes as she watched her city's NBA team battle it out against the Boston Celtics. The energy from the crowd electrified the air, and she understood what Hayden meant when he said it was different watching the game live. From where she stood, she could see the back of his head and catch the movements of his shoulders as he paced the sidelines of the court near the coach and the GM. They were all rooting for the players. But tonight it wasn't enough. The Celtics were wiping the floor with them.

"Come on! Block that shot!"

A groan of disappointment ran through their side of the stands as the Celtics sunk another basket, lifting their score to 79 against the Raptors' 71.

"Dang, these brothers got no defense," Lissandra said

with disgust from Sydney's side. In the same breath she shouted at the court. "Come on, Bargnani! Do something!"

"Well, they've got five minutes left," Sydney said. "They could turn it around."

Lissandra glanced at her sister. "Please, even the coach knows that's not going to happen." And when the final whistle blew for the end of the match five minutes later, Sydney admitted that her sister had been right. The Celtics had beat the Raptors 80–75 on the Raptors' own home court. The stands emptied quickly and quietly.

"Well, that's that," said Lissandra, gathering her things and preparing to follow the crowd toward the exit. "You ready?"

"Actually I'm gonna hang back and wait for him," Sydney said. "See if he's OK."

"Want me to stick around?" Lissandra asked.

Sydney shook her head. "No. I'll be fine."

"All right," Lissandra said shouldering her purse. "But if he's not too depressed, can you ask him if he can hook a sister up with Chris Bosh?"

Sydney rolled her eyes. "Even I know that Chris Bosh doesn't play for the Raptors anymore. And you're already seeing someone! Remember Mario?"

"Yeah yeah," Lissandra said. "Just because Chris doesn't play for Toronto anymore doesn't mean your boy doesn't know him. A sister has to be on the lookout for an upgrade, you know?"

"Lissa, you need Jesus," Sydney said, shaking her head.

"So is that a yes?"

"Bye, Lissandra!"

Lissandra grinned and waved as she walked away,

and Sydney couldn't help but smile. She loved her sister, but Lissandra was a mess.

It didn't take long before the stands were empty. The court had cleared almost immediately after the game, but Sydney knew that Hayden would have some last-minute things to do before he went home. The team didn't play again until next week, so she knew he would have the night off to rest. He was probably tired, but she wanted to check in with him before she left. His old team had just beaten his new team, and she knew that he would be taking it hard.

She took her time exiting the stands and making her way to the parking lot where she knew he was parked. The night air was cool in the almost-empty lot. Most people had already left, but in the distance she could see the lights from the traffic on the expressway nearby. Getting out of the downtown area, especially after a sporting event, was always a pain. She knew it would probably take her sister about an hour to get home.

Sydney felt like she spent about an hour sitting on the bonnet of Hayden's car before she saw him exit the building in sweats and Nikes. She watched him as, with his sports bag flung over his shoulder, he nodded to a couple of guys who had come out with him, before splitting off and heading toward her.

Sliding off the car, she came around to the driver's side. She saw a small smile break the gloom on his face when he saw her.

"Hey," he said, slipping his hands into his pockets as he came closer. "Glad you made it. Sorry it couldn't have been for a better game."

She smiled. "They played hard. It was a good game," she said. "How are you doing?"

He shrugged casually, but Sydney saw the disappointment cloud his features once more. She stepped forward and slipped her arms around his tall frame, holding him close.

"Sorry it didn't turn out the way you wanted," she said against his chest.

She felt his arms go around her and his head rest against the top of hers.

"Thanks," he said quietly against her hair.

"Want to talk about it?" she asked, pulling back to look up at him.

"Not really," he said, letting his hands slide down her arms to catch her fingers. "But I am hungry. Eat with me?"

It took them twenty minutes to get to a Gabby's, where there wouldn't be too many basketball fans talking about the game. To Sydney it was worth it if it would mean Hayden relaxed even a little.

"OK, so I generally am a healthy eater," Hayden said, leading Sydney to a booth in the back. "But bar food is my craving when I'm trying to fight off a bad mood."

Sydney grinned. "Hey, you don't have to justify it to me. I haven't had bar food in so long that I'm actually excited."

He handed her the menu. "Then pick your poison, Nini."

Between the two of them they ordered a bit of almost everything off the late-night menu, from chicken and fries, to nachos and cheese, to salad. When the waitress finally brought the last serving plate, she read back their order to make sure they had everything, then glanced at the both of them before shaking her head and leaving.

Sydney let out a laugh. "Oh my goodness, did you see the look she gave us?"

"Yeah, I caught it," Hayden said with a grin. "But she was a good sport. She'll get her twenty percent."

As Hayden blessed their food, Sydney closed her eyes. When he was done, she opened them and glanced around at the several plates on the table.

She shook her head. "Why does it always look like this when we go out to eat?"

" 'Cause you have a big appetite." He grabbed a nacho chip covered in cheese and salsa.

"Me? You're the one trying to make me fat." She popped a sweet potato fry into her mouth.

"This from the woman with a dessert shop called 'Decadent,' " he said with a laugh. "But don't worry, Nini; I'll watch your figure for you."

She tossed a fry at him. "I'm sure you will."

"So tell me something to take my mind off the horrible game I just had," he said, focusing his eyes on her.

She bit her lip as she served some salad into a small plate for herself. "What do you want to know?"

"How many siblings do you have exactly?" he asked, reminding Sydney that even though they had known each other for a while, some important details had slipped through the cracks.

"Five."

The chicken wing Hayden was reaching for fell from his fingers onto the table. "You're kidding, right?"

Sydney grinned. "Nope. Four sisters, one brother."

Hayden retrieved his chicken wing. "Uncle Leroy sure was busy."

"Not that busy. Only four of us were Dad's. The rest had different fathers, but same mother." She looked away and stuck her fork in some lettuce. "It's a long story."

"I can imagine," he said, finally going back to his

food. "You know me and Christian have the same dad. But I have a sister on my mother's side, so I know what that's like."

"Two bedrooms, two birthday parties . . ."

"Awkward graduations, split summers . . ."

Sydney shook her head. "It definitely was a unique experience."

"Do you wish Uncle Leroy and your mom had stayed together?" Hayden asked after a moment.

Sydney chewed thoughtfully.

"No," she said finally. "They weren't happy together. They never fought that much, but it was just . . ."

Sydney paused, not quite sure how to say Leroy was a better father than husband, without ruining Hayden's image of him.

"I know what you mean," Hayden said, nodding. "My parents were never married, but the way they fought, I know it was a relief that they didn't end up together. It sounds terrible, but I think they were better off apart than together. Plus, I see my dad with my stepmom, and they are . . ." He shook his head and smiled. "They're supposed to be together. I can just tell."

Sydney nodded. "If I remember, you grew up mostly with your stepmother, right?"

"Yes," Hayden said. "She's an amazing woman. She and Dad pretty much raised me on their own. I wish I had gotten to know my mother better . . . but she wasn't always stable. . . ."

Sydney saw pain flicker through Hayden's eyes at the mention of his mother. He was already dealing with enough disappointment for one night. She changed the subject.

"So," Sydney said, grabbing a chicken wing. "Leroy's

daughters would all like to know where exactly you've been over the last twelve years and what skeletons you have in your closet."

Hayden laughed. "Everything I've been doing has been well documented. Did the basketball thing with the Celtics for almost ten years until I tore my ACL. They said I could come back, but . . ."

Sydney raised an eyebrow. "But what?"

"But it was time." He smiled.

She squinted at him. "There's more to that story, isn't there."

"Isn't there always?" he asked. "But we don't have enough chicken wings for that tonight. Let's just say, it was God's answer to my questions."

She shook her head. "You're really different. I never heard you talk about God like this before—not unless you were whining about your dad making you miss practice to go to church."

Hayden laughed. "You're right. But I find that God has a way of getting your attention when he wants to. My dad is a great dad, but no one can love like the Father. And I've learned that we can't really understand that love, or love like he loves, until we know him."

Sydney shifted in her seat. "So you're saying you know him now?"

Hayden sat back, a content look on his face. "I'm getting there."

"I told you he would be here. . . ."

"Shhh, baby, keep your voice down."

A stylishly dressed black woman, with hair that Kim Kardashian would envy, slid into the booth beside Sydney, while a tall man in gray sweats, with the hood pulled over a baseball cap, slid in beside Hayden.

Before Sydney could open her mouth to protest, however, Hayden burst into laughter.

"Dog, it's not that bad," Hayden said between laughs.

"It *is* Dub," the woman said, helping herself to nachos and chips. "We had to leave his car at the arena."

Sydney leaned forward and peered into the face of the man sitting beside Hayden.

"Sean?

"Shhh . . . no names," he said, looking around.

"Baby, no one recognizes you." The woman signalled for the waitress and a handful of gold bangles jingled as they slid down her arm. "No one recognizes anyone here. Why do you think Dub comes here all the time?"

Sydney raised an eyebrow. "I thought you said you usually eat healthy."

The woman let out a laugh.

"I usually get salad," Hayden said, rubbing the back of his neck.

"Yeah, right," Sydney said, pursing her lips.

Hayden cleared his throat. "Uh, Sydney, this is Maritza, Sean's wife. Maritza, this is my . . . uh . . . Sydney."

"Hello, Dub's Sydney," Maritza said with a mischievous grin as she reached over to shake Sydney's hand. "Nice to meet you."

Sydney smiled. "Nice to meet you, too."

"What can I get you, ma'am?" the waitress said, arriving with a notepad and with another waitress, who immediately began clearing the table.

"We'll have everything they just had," Sean said, motioning to the plates that were fast disappearing.

"And two ginger ales," Maritza added. "And the quicker you can bring it all out, the bigger the tip."

Sydney tilted her head to get a better look at Maritza, and Hayden chuckled.

The waitress gave a shrug that said "good enough for me" before turning and heading back to the kitchen.

"So it's like that?" Sydney asked, taking a sip from her drink.

"Listen," Maritza said, with a wave of her long, neon pink fingernail. "I've been here, and if you don't let them know what's up they will have you here for hours. These girls ain't getting nothing but minimum wage. All it takes is a little green to light a fire on their size-two behinds."

Sean sighed. "Sydney, meet my wife."

Sydney laughed. "I guess I know who gets things done in your house."

"Yes," Sean said. "And I feel no shame about it. That's why I married a financial adviser. I play ball. She handles the money. Sounded like a good plan to me."

"You guys seem too young to be married," Sydney said.

"Don't let the gym clothes fool you," Hayden said, leaning back in the booth comfortably. "Sean's almost as ancient as I am."

Sydney rolled her eyes. "Thirty-one is not ancient."

"Thank you," Maritza said. "I'm thirty, and I, for one, never felt better."

"That's 'cause you don't play ball, baby," Sean said. "I can barely keep up with those little eighteen-year-olds. Yo, Dub, did you catch the center for the Celtics first half. You know they drafted him right out of high school, right?"

"Yeah," Hayden said. "We were considering him for our draft pick."

Sydney zoned out as the boys went into game talk.

"Get used to it," Maritza said with a laugh as she caught the blank look on Sydney's face. "These men eat, sleep, and breathe basketball. It's like the default conversation when they get together."

"I figured as much," Sydney said with a smile. "It's OK, though. At least they're passionate about something. I wish I could get my brother to focus and dedicate himself to working on one thing that made some sort of sense."

"I hear you," Maritza said. "I have three younger brothers, and Lord knows they keep me and my mother on our knees praying they get it right."

Sydney smiled as she found immediate kinship with another member of the big-sisters' club.

"Ma'am, your order?"

Sydney looked up and saw the waitress standing over them. Her mouth fell open.

"Already?"

Maritza grinned. "See? I told you."

Sydney laughed as the waitress put the food on the table. And as she listened to the banter between Maritza, Sean, and Hayden, and joined in a bit of it herself, she found herself laughing more than she had in a long time. So much so that when she finally checked the time, she couldn't believe how late it was.

"Oops, that's my time," Sydney said, sitting up suddenly and nudging Maritza out of the booth. "Scoot over, Miss Wall Street."

"Where are you going?" Maritza asked as Sydney slipped out of the booth.

"Home."

A chorus of disapproval went up from the other three at the table.

"What for?" Sean asked, even as he made space for Hayden to get out. "It's barely after eleven."

"Yeah, but I have a cake tasting for a wedding on Tuesday morning," Sydney said, shouldering her purse.

"Girl, you've been working way too hard," Maritza said with a shake of her head. "You're way into the week and it's only Sunday."

"It's not that, Mari," Hayden said with a chuckle. "A Tuesday-morning tasting for Sydney means she has to make the cakes tomorrow morning so she has time to ice them."

Sydney raised an eyebrow at him in surprise.

"Right?" he confirmed.

"Right." She narrowed her eyes at him. "How do you know that?"

"I do know some things about what you do, Syd," he said with a grin.

"OK, fine, but this means you'll have to come over next weekend," Maritza said. "You're the first girlfriend that Dub has actually claimed voluntarily. You've got to let me in on how you got him to do that."

Sydney and Hayden began speaking at the same time.

"Actually, I'm not his . . ."

"We're not really . . ."

They glanced at each other awkwardly before looking away.

"It's not really like that," Sydney said, fiddling with the edge of her jacket.

Sean snorted and reached for a chicken wing. "OK. Whatever you say."

"No, really . . ." Sydney began.

"We're not . . ." Hayden continued.

". . . together," Sydney finished.

"Mhmm," Maritza said with a mischievous grin. "All right, then. Well, in that case, can you two bring your not-together selves over to the house next weekend?"

Hayden grinned. "We'll see."

"It was nice to meet you, Maritza," Sydney said with a wave.

"Talk to you soon, guys," Hayden said as he led Sydney away.

Sydney grinned as she glanced back at the couple who had moved to one side of the booth together.

"I like her," Sydney said, glancing up at Hayden.

"Yeah, I'm sure you do," Hayden said with a snort. "Sometimes when I hear her and Sean, I get flashbacks of arguing with you."

"Aww," Sydney teased as she stepped out the front door he held open. "Are you saying you missed me, Dub?"

"I'm saying you better move your behind," he said, taking off in a sprint. "Unless you want to walk it all the way home."

Sydney laughed as she took off behind him. It was going to take a lot for her to keep up with this man—in more ways than one.

Chapter 10

Sydney hated early mornings. Especially at this time of the year when six a.m. looked like midnight. But it was the price she had to pay to have the kind of job that never felt like work. In any case, getting up was really the worst part. She knew as soon as she was elbow deep in flour and sugar she would be wide awake. The best part was that she would have the kitchen all to herself. That was when she did her best work.

The silence welcomed her as she stepped through the back door of Decadent, in from the nippy, late-fall breeze. She shed her coat, closed the door securely behind her, and went straight to the kitchen, where she went through her routine of putting up her hair, setting the radio in the kitchen to the jazz station, and getting out the items for the first cake. She planned to work on three cakes for her client. The first two were obvious choices: devil's food cake and a vanilla layer cake, two of the most popular cakes for weddings. However, to stir things up a bit, she was also making a coconut cake with lime-curd filling. It was not as traditional as the other wedding cake options, but whenever she'd offered it to brides in the past, five out of ten times they went with it.

Special-occasion cakes were Sydney's favorite orders. That's when she could get as creative as she wanted, and pull out the cake decorating skills that she had no opportunity to use with her walk-in patrons. It was a bonus that they brought in the most revenue.

She pulled out a couple of mixing bowls, wooden spoons, whisks, and other items, leaving the heavy equipment in its place. For the final product, she would use the electric mixers and other appliances. But the sample cakes she would do by hand—the traditional way. The way that her dad used to do them. When she thought about it now, she couldn't believe he used to make huge wedding cakes and orders for hundreds of people without the aid of modern equipment. Sydney couldn't possibly do that.

With the sound of Coltrane's *Lush Life* in the background, she sifted together flour, baking soda, and salt in one bowl before moving to another to combine sugar and butter. She was just finishing up combining the dry ingredients with the buttermilk mixture to complete the batter when a knock at the door made her start. When the knock came again only moments later, she set down the whisk and made her way to the back door.

"Delivery for Ms. Sydney Isaacs?"

Sydney smirked and opened the door wider for a track suit- and sunglasses-wearing Hayden to come inside.

"What are you doing here?" she asked, trying to mask the delight in her voice as she closed the door behind him. "It's not even seven yet."

"I came to bring you tea," he said, holding out a tall cup from Tim Hortons, Canada's answer to Starbucks.

"Don't you have to work today?" she asked, taking the steaming hot gift gratefully and leading him back to the kitchen.

"How about, thank you, Dub, you know I haven't had anything all morning," he said groggily as he slumped onto a stool near the counter.

She turned around and walked back over to where he was sitting, then leaned over and kissed him on the cheek.

"Thank you, Dub." She smiled and lowered her voice. "You know I haven't had anything all morning."

His lips stretched into a grin from behind the sunglasses. "Well, if that's what I get for some tea, I might have to go back out and get you a whole continental spread."

"Too late," Sydney said with a smirk. "That will teach you not to skimp on breakfast."

"Tease."

"Cheapo."

"You're so lucky you're beautiful."

Sydney stuck out her tongue at him before going back to mixing.

"So how many are you doing today?" he asked.

"Three," she said, pouring most of the thick brown batter into two baking tins. "This one is the devil's food cake."

"Ooh, can I taste . . ."

Hayden stretched his hand toward the bowl, but Sydney slapped it away.

"You can't eat sugar first thing in the morning, Dub," she scolded lightly as she poured the rest of the batter into a smaller tin. "After you eat breakfast, you can eat cake."

"But Nini . . ."

"Breakfast first, cake later," said Sydney, firmly moving the bowl out of his reach, before placing the two baking tins in the oven.

"See, this is why I didn't marry you," Hayden grumbled, heading toward the fridge. "What do you even have in here anyway? It's not like you guys make real food here."

"I'm sure you can find something," Sydney said as she pulled out the ingredients for the second cake.

He did, and within moments he was whipping up breakfast burritos, complete with sautéed bell peppers and onions.

"Ooh, that smells good," Sydney said as she put the batter for the second cake into the oven.

"Tastes good, too," he said, handing her a plate.

Sydney took a bite of the warm burrito and groaned. "Oh, this *is* actually good."

Hayden grinned. "Told you."

"No, seriously," Sydney said, taking another bite. "I haven't had a decent burrito in ages. Did you put garlic in this?"

"My burrito, my secret," he said from his place on the stool.

"I'll remind you of that when you're reaching for my cake," Sydney said, wiping her mouth on a napkin.

The sound of jazz floated between them in the kitchen as Sydney set the tester cake to cool and moved around preparing the filling and icing. She could feel Hayden's eyes on her without even looking. But every now and then when she did look, and she caught his eye, a smile would pass between them and Sydney would feel a flutter in her stomach. She wasn't sure what kind of feelings she was having for him, but whatever they were, they were growing fast.

"You know, I always thought of this place as Uncle Leroy's," he said after a moment. "But watching you here . . ."

She glanced at him as she sliced one of the devil's food cakes in half horizontally to make the two layers. "What?"

"This is your place now, Syd," he said with a small smile. "I'm really proud of you."

She smiled. "Thanks," she said without looking up at him. "But this isn't my place. Not really."

He frowned. "What do you mean?"

"Decadent belongs to my younger brother, Dean," Sydney said with as much lightness as she could muster given the lump in her throat. "Dean was Dad's only son, and when he died, he left Decadent to him."

Sydney busied herself shifting the cakes around on the cooling rack so she wouldn't have to see the pity she knew was in Hayden's eyes. She already knew how pathetic she was, pouring her life and soul into something that wasn't even hers. But she didn't need to see that in someone else's eyes. Especially someone else who knew just how much of her life was in this place.

"I'm sorry, Syd," she heard him say from behind her. "I thought . . . I'm sorry."

She shrugged. "It's OK. That's just the way life is."

He sighed. "I don't know why Uncle Leroy did what he did, but he must have had a reason. He knew how much you loved this place. Maybe he was hoping you could get Dean to love it as much as you do. Or maybe he thought you would one day go out on your own. I don't know."

"Neither do I," Sydney said. "Sometimes the people you love do things you don't understand. But you can't stop loving them because of it, right?"

Sydney hoped her words didn't sound as hollow as they felt. The truth was she still couldn't come to terms with how everything had worked out and she wasn't sure from one day to the next how she felt about it.

"Well, at least it's still in the family," Hayden said.

"For now," Sydney said, still not looking at him. "Dean wants to sell. And since me and my sisters can't afford to buy the place, he may already be looking for other options."

"You're kidding, right?"

Sydney laughed dryly. "I wish I was."

"Do you know how soon?"

"We've talked about it almost every day since he came home from college a couple weeks ago," she said. She moved quickly to pour the batter for the coconut cake into tins, partially to try and finish up quickly and partially so she didn't have to focus on the topic floating around the kitchen.

"We can't come to a resolution." She moved one cake from the counter into the oven, shifting another tin to another shelf.

"My sisters are fighting with my brother." She closed the oven and took off her mitts. "My sisters are fighting with each other."

She grabbed the last tin off the counter and pulled open the oven again.

"It's splitting our family apart." She shoved the last tin in, moving another to the side to make more space.

"Ouch!" She jumped back from the oven as her bare finger burned on contact with a hot tin. She squeezed back tears, mad at herself for letting the topic of Dean make her so careless.

"Hey, hey, easy." Hayden was beside her in moments, closing the oven door, taking her burned hand and holding it under the faucet.

Sydney tried to turn her face away from him so he couldn't see the moistness in her eyes, but it was almost impossible with him standing so close to her.

"It's OK to be upset, Syd." He spoke the words softly and close to her ear. "You put everything into this place and you might lose it. It's OK to be upset about that."

Turning off the water, he pulled Sydney against him. She buried her face in his chest and let a few teardrops escape. She had always felt guilty about her feelings about losing the store. She had no right to expect anything from her dad or Dean. They were free to do whatever they chose. But that hadn't helped lessen the hollow ache in her chest whenever she thought about what her life would be like without Decadent.

After a moment, she pulled away from him and wiped her face.

"You didn't answer my question earlier," she said, grabbing a cloth to wipe the counter as she changed the subject. "Don't you have training or work today?"

"Nothing with the team," he said, gathering the empty breakfast dishes and taking them to the sink. "I have a few appointments. But not until later."

"What kind of appointments?" Sydney asked. She took out the tester and began adding filling to the first layer.

"Physical therapy appointments," he said as he started on the dishes. "At my private practice across town."

Sydney raised an eyebrow. "Private practice, eh? Look at you. Hayden Windsor, the businessman."

He laughed. "Nothing in the NBA is guaranteed. I could be here today and out of a job at the end of the year."

"I highly doubt that," Sydney said as she set the second layer of the tester and continued icing.

"Yeah, well, better safe than sorry," Hayden said distractedly. Sydney looked up and noticed he had finished cleaning up and was watching her as she carefully spread the buttercream icing.

"Dub, it's not done yet," she said, knowing exactly what he was thinking. "The icing has to set."

"Just a taste, Syd," he said, stepping closer. "Come on, I had breakfast."

She tried to put on a stern face, but it was no match for his puppy-dog eyes.

"Pleeeeese," he said in an intentionally childish voice.

She rolled her eyes. "OK, fine."

She laughed as she watched his eyes light up.

"Come here." She cut a small piece of the iced cake. "Taste this."

Instead of waiting for her to set it on something, he grabbed her wrist and brought her fingers to his mouth, pulling her closer to him in the process.

Sydney felt heat cascade through her as he ate the delicate confection right from her hand. Then he took her fingers into his mouth to secure the last bits of icing, and Sydney couldn't breathe. His warm, moist lips on her fingers, his eyes on her . . . she couldn't turn away. And before she knew what was happening, he was placing her hand around his neck and cupping her cheek.

And then he kissed her.

His buttercream-tainted lips caressed hers with all the finesse of a man who knew exactly what he was doing, and exactly how to do it to leave a woman completely senseless. Sydney knew then that she was in trouble, because this kiss—the one that she had admittedly waited almost thirteen years for—was the best she had ever had.

The knife clattered noisily to the counter as it slipped from Sydney's fingers, freeing her hand to join the other around Hayden's neck.

"How was it?" She breathed against his lips.

He chuckled, his breath tickling her face. "Good." He pressed his lips to hers briefly. "Very good."

He kissed her again. And then a second time. And a third. And then she lost count, and lost awareness of anything other than Hayden. It was only the slam of a door that shattered the moment and brought them back to the present. They jumped apart only moments before the kitchen door banged open.

"Sydney, do you know how long I've been outside knocking? And I called your cell phone like a million times," Lissandra said, annoyance all over her face. "What the heck were you doing?"

"Uh . . ."

"Eating," Hayden said, cutting another slice off the tester cake and stuffing it into his mouth. "We were eating cake."

Sydney looked at her sister and then at Hayden, before bursting into laughter. She could almost see the steam pouring out of Lissandra's ears, but she couldn't stop herself. The look on her sister's face and the buttercream on Hayden's were too much for her. And at that moment it occurred to her that she had laughed more with Hayden in the past few weeks than she had all year.

Chapter 11

"So we'll see you next week to review the design for the cake?"

"Wednesday, ten a.m. sharp," Sydney said, smiling wide at her newest clients.

"Can't wait!"

Sydney waved at the couple as they exited the store holding hands. They had loved all the cakes, and had tasted them more than once before finally deciding on the coconut cake with the lime-curd filling. The early hours preparing for the tasting had been so worth it.

Still floating on cloud nine from her great morning, she drifted through the shop and into her office to file the contracts for the job. When she opened the door, however, her face fell.

"Geez, don't look so happy to see me," Dean said from where he sat lounging in Sydney's chair.

"Good morning, Dean," Sydney said, trying to force some enthusiasm into her voice.

She was not a fan of the way Dean kept showing up in her office unannounced. She knew that it technically was his office and his space, but it still irked her. That and the fact that she had heard through the family grapevine that Dean and his wife had made a down payment on a house. He sure was spending money fast.

"Don't worry, this time I have good news," he said, jumping up. "I actually wanted to show you something."

Sydney set her notes from the morning meeting on her desk cautiously.

"OK. I'm listening."

With his iPad in hand, Dean moved over to the couch, beckoning Sydney closer.

"Check this out," he said, pulling up some pictures. "I went to see some spaces this week. Tell me what you think."

Sydney didn't have time for this. She had a business to run, more clients than she had seen in years, and desserts to replenish for her walk-in customers. She didn't have time to consult with Dean on properties for his studio. But he had gone out of his way to work out a deal for Sydney to stay at Decadent. The least she could do was support him in his own dreams.

"OK, show me what you've got," she said.

"All right, this one is on the east end." He flipped through some pictures of a small storefront. The front area was small and a little dingy. The second room off the first was larger, but gray and poorly lit.

Sydney wrinkled her nose.

"You don't like it," he said.

"Well . . ."

"OK, forget that," he said quickly. "Here's another. This one is more north of the city. Near Sheppard Avenue and Yonge Street. It's a bit newer, and comes with kitchen equipment and display cases."

Dean flipped through the pictures of the admittedly

better-looking space, not noticing the confusion on his sister's face.

"Now, it is a bit smaller, but it's the price of staying in the city. . . ."

"OK, Dean, these places look more like storefronts. Shouldn't you be looking for somewhere more enclosed for your studio?" Sydney asked.

"Studio?"

"Yes," Sydney said. "Isn't this what you're showing me?"

She watched Dean pause, then swallow hard.

"These aren't for me, Sydney," he said. "They're for you."

It was Sydney's turn to pause.

"Excuse me?"

Dean put the iPad down on the couch in the space between them and rubbed his sweaty palms on his pants.

"These are potential new locations for Decadent."

"Oh my God . . ." Sydney's head was spinning, but Dean kept talking, his words speeding up as if he was trying to get everything out while she was still in shock.

"They're great locations, Syd. Me and Sheree checked them out ourselves. They get lots of traffic, both come with kitchen equipment so you wouldn't have to buy a lot of new stuff, and the rent is pretty reasonable. . . ."

"What's going on, Dean?"

"What do you mean?" he squeaked.

"Don't play games with me."

"I found a buyer."

Dean might as well have pulled the pin out of a grenade and tossed it into the middle of the room. The level of shock that Sydney was experiencing would have been about the same.

"I know this wasn't what we planned," he said, getting up and pacing. "But me and Sheree have been talking about this, and we agreed this was an opportunity that we couldn't pass up."

"You and Sheree?"

"Yes," Dean continued. "Sheree and I met with the buyers. They are willing to pay above what we thought this place was valued, and they are willing to pay everything upfront. No long-term payments, no installments. One solid money transfer. It would be a smooth exchange, and I know it's not what we planned, but I feel like this is the best for every—"

"Dean, we had an agreement!"

"I know you're disappointed, Syd, but . . ."

"Disappointed?" Sydney repeated. "I was disappointed when you walked in here and told me you were thinking of selling Decadent. I was disappointed when you made it clear you couldn't even wait long enough for me to get the money to buy it outright. But this, Dean? This is not disappointment."

Dean tried to explain again, but Sydney could barely hear him over the steam pouring out her ears.

This was not happening.

This was definitely not happening. Not after the perfect weekend she had just had. Not when things were finally starting to look like they were going her way. She was on her way to owning the shop she loved and she had someone in her life she really cared about. Heck, she was even getting along with all her sisters and her mom. And then this happened. Her brother had walked into the office and told her he had a buyer for the store.

"Dean, this is crazy," Sydney said. "We had an agreement. I signed it. You signed it. You received our payment on our portion of the store. It's already done."

Sydney laughed a little. What was she getting so worked up for? She was safe. She had a legal agreement binding her to the store. Dean couldn't sell without her.

"Actually, it's not that simple," Dean said slowly. "I talked to my lawyer, and he said the agreement states that within one week of signing either party can opt to dissolve the arrangement. In any case, the filing of the paperwork is not yet complete, so . . ."

"So you're saying that the law compensates for your irresponsibility."

"Sydney . . ."

"You took our money, Dean," she said, jumping to her feet. "The money that we pinched and scraped to pull together as soon as possible because you needed to have it."

"I know and you'll get it back. All of it. Plus, I'll help you with whatever you need to get set up at a new location—"

"I don't care about the money, Dean! I care about this shop. This is all that I have. Don't you get that?"

"Yeah, Syd," Dean said, his face hardening. "You had this shop. You had Dad all the time before he died, you had your dream. And what do I have? Nothing."

"I worked hard for this," Sydney snapped. "I sacrificed everything to make sure this place stayed afloat, even after Dad was gone. . . ."

"Yeah, 'cause you thought it would be yours, too, right?" Dean sneered. "Admit it, Syd. You hate that Dad gave this to me. You probably even hate me."

Sydney shook her head. "I don't hate you, Dean.

But I hate that you went about getting what you want like this. When did you even go looking for a buyer anyway? Were you going behind my back to do this all along?"

"Of course not!" Dean said, his brows furrowing deeply. "You really think that I could do that?"

"I don't know, Dean," Sydney said, folding her arms. "I didn't think a week after you sold me a percentage of the business that you would try to sell the whole thing out from under me to someone else."

"I didn't plan this," Dean said, throwing up his hands. "But I got an offer I couldn't refuse. I guess people heard we were thinking about selling. A couple days ago I got a call with an offer from a holding corporation that owns a similar line of pastry stores. I don't remember the name, something nice or something delicious . . ."

Sydney felt her heart fall into her stomach. "Something Sweet?"

"Yeah, I think that's it," Dean said absently.

"You sold to our competition?"

"What?"

"That's why they're willing to pay above value. So they can put us out of business." Sydney squeezed her eyes shut. "You sold our father's life's work to his competition."

Silence hung in the room as the magnitude of what Dean had done dawned on both of them in equal measure.

Sydney turned away. She couldn't look at her brother. Because at that moment, all she wanted to do was put her hands around his ignorant neck.

"Maybe it's not that bad," Dean tried after a long moment. "We didn't sell the brand. You can still use the name Decadent and run the business somewhere else. The space is not the business."

"This space *is* the business," Sydney countered, whirling around to face him. "We've been here for twenty years. Twenty years, Dean. This is where people know us. You think we can just change locations and continue business as usual?"

"What the hell is going on in here?" The door burst open and Lissandra flew inside Sydney's office where Sydney and Dean were squared off on opposite sides of the room.

Neither of them answered or even looked at their sister.

"Well?" Lissandra asked, her tone riddled with annoyance. "I mean, it's not like we have a floor of customers who can actually hear you!"

"Tell her," Sydney ordered, nodding toward Lissandra but keeping her eyes on Dean. "Tell her how you want to go back on our agreement and sell the store to someone else."

The door slammed shut under the pressure of Lissandra's anger. "What?"

Dean looked back and forth between his two sisters nervously and at the door, which was out of his direct line of access.

"Lissandra, just listen—"

"No, I don't need to listen to you," Lissandra said, her finger pointed at Dean. "I'm about tired of listening to you. You just need to answer one question: Are you trying to sell this store."

"It's not about Decadent, it's about—"

"You're not answering me, Dean," Lissandra hissed, stepping closer to her brother. "Are you trying to sell this store to someone else?"

Sydney watched her brother swallow and take a step back.

"Yes. But . . ."

"You stupid, selfish little bastard. . . ."

Lissandra lunged toward Dean, but Sydney grabbed her before she could rake her nails across her brother's face. Dean took the opportunity to scramble behind Sydney's desk, out of Lissandra's reach.

"I am so sick of catering to your spoiled little behind. . . ."

"Lissandra!"

"You better have my money, you little prick, or I swear I'll . . ."

"Lissandra, stop," Sydney said more forcefully, physically moving her sister much farther away. She was managing to hold her off so far, but Lissandra had more than a couple of pounds on Sydney and she knew she wouldn't be able to contain her sister for much longer.

"Dean, leave."

He didn't need to be told twice. Before Sydney could turn around, she heard the door open and close behind her.

"Lissandra, you need to calm down."

"Let me go."

"Lissandra . . ."

"Let me go!"

Sydney let her sister go, and Lissandra immediately charged out the door. A few moments later she came back, her face still stony in anger.

"How could you let him leave, Syd?" Lissandra snapped, glaring at Sydney. "How could you let him do this?"

"Let him?" Sydney snapped back. Her anger with

her brother was still burning inside her. If Lissandra didn't watch herself, she was going to get scorched.

"Yes, let him."

"And what exactly do you think I should have done?" Sydney spat. "Thanks to our father, Dean is the owner of this store. Dean's name is on the deed for the property. Dean is the one who gets to decide what happens."

"But we own it, too," Lissandra insisted. "We gave him that money. He can't go back on us."

"Actually, the law says he can," Sydney said. She sank into her chair, drained. "The filing of the papers hadn't been completed yet, so he still could dissolve it—money or no money."

Lissandra shook her head and began pacing. "This can't be it. He has our money. There must be something we can do. There must be a way we can sue him. . . ."

"No," Sydney said firmly. "I am not taking my brother to court."

"But Sydney—"

"No, Lissandra," Sydney said, the disappointment and shock at her sister's suggestion evident in her voice. "It doesn't matter how bad we feel about this, this is our brother. Our family. We don't do that."

Lissandra folded her arms and pouted, making it clear she disagreed.

"This place means as much to me as it does to you," Sydney said. "But I will not split our family up any further than it already is. I'm already dodging calls from Jackie because of this whole thing. How do you think she would react if she heard we were planning to sue Dean over the store? Daddy would roll over in his grave."

She sighed. "This is not the legacy he wanted for Decadent."

Lissandra sat down across from Sydney, still pouting. "So what are we supposed to do, Sydney? Just give up?"

Sydney ran her hand over her eyes tiredly.

"I don't know, Lissandra," she said finally. "I don't know anything anymore."

They sat in silence as the weight of the situation fell on both of them.

"So he already found a buyer."

"You'll never guess who."

"Don't tell me . . ."

"Samantha and her people."

Lissandra swore. "And they're willing to pay?"

"Above the asking," Sydney said.

Lissandra swore again.

"He's giving our money back." She shook her head. "Can you believe he came in here, showing me some tired storefronts that we could move to? Said he was trying to help."

"I'll tell him what to do with his help."

Sydney looked around at the office that she had shared with her father for several years and used on her own since Leroy died. The eggshell blue made the windowless room look brighter than it actually was. Books on food, pastry making, and decorating lined the bookshelves on one side while a large board covered with pictures of specialty cakes and creations, catered events, and favorite customers hung on the other. This place was her life. The one thing she could depend on to be there and to be the same. She couldn't imagine not coming here every day. What would she do?

The air in the room suddenly felt thinner and Sydney's chest hurt as she struggled to breathe. She bolted up from her seat and grabbed her purse.

"I have to go."

"You can't go now, Syd," Lissandra began. "We have to deal with this. . . ."

Sydney grabbed her iPhone in response. "I'll be back later."

As she went through the door, she heard her sister call after her, but she didn't stop. She barely smiled as people called out to her on her way through the doors to the parking lot. Her cell phone rang as she started the car. It was Thomas, Decadent's accountant. He had probably heard from Dean and wanted to know what was going on. But Sydney didn't want to talk to anyone right now. So she shut off the phone and pulled out of the parking lot. She didn't know where she was going, but anywhere but here would be good enough.

Chapter 12

"Anywhere" turned out to be the backyard behind the house. After driving around for what felt like hours, it became her final stop. Still dressed in her clothes from work, Sydney slipped through the back door into the gated yard behind the house. She looked around the ground at the thin layer of grass that was bucking the winter and holding strong. The time for barbeques and evenings out back was long gone with the fall, but Sydney didn't care. She couldn't think of anywhere else to be, so here she was.

The empty wrought-iron benches beckoned to her, but she chose the tire swing instead. It had survived their childhood and was still useful as a source of entertainment for kids on the rare occasions that there were any at the house. She dusted off a thin layer of leftover leaves before fitting her legs through the hole and making herself comfortable. At the right angle her feet didn't even touch the ground.

She took a deep breath of the crisp, dry air and noted that yesterday's clear blue skies, which had today become gray and murky, were an uncanny reflection of the way her life had suddenly changed in only a few hours.

As the tire moved gently in small circles, Sydney wondered for the hundredth time what she was going to do. The one thing she had feared the minute Dean had come home was the very thing that was happening. She was losing the shop. But it was much worse than she had anticipated. In her worst-case scenario, Dean had just assumed ownership of the store and run it into the ground. Sydney could have dealt with that. She would have let him crash and burn first, but then she would have helped him figure out how to run Decadent. Then they would have done it together and everything would have been fine. But never had she imagined that she might literally lose the store—that it would no longer be in the family but belong to someone else. She didn't have a plan for that.

"Want some company?"

Sydney twisted the swing around and found Hayden standing by the door, his hands in his pockets and concern in his eyes.

"What are you doing here?" She let the tire turn her around as the swing righted itself.

"I called you several times on your cell, but it kept going straight to voice mail," he said, walking over to where she was. "I got worried, so I called the shop. Lissandra told me what happened."

He stooped down in front of her. "I'm sorry, Syd."

She realized tears had begun to run down her face. Hayden reached over and gently wiped them away with his thumbs.

"I don't know what I'm going to do," Sydney said, her voice cloudy. "If I had known this was coming like a year ago, then I could have planned for it. I would still be upset, but I wouldn't feel so . . . so . . ."

"Blindsided?"

"Yeah," she said, nodding. "How am I going to fix this in a couple weeks? There's no time to find a new space, to let all our customers know we're moving, to change all our stationery and business cards, and reschedule all our orders, to move all the equipment— that's if Dean didn't sell all of it with the store. Plus, I know Samantha, and she's just going to swoop in and steal all our clients with our location. . . ."

"Easy, Syd," Hayden said, taking her hand and squeezing her fingers. "One thing at a time. . . ."

"Yeah, but which one thing first?" Sydney asked. "I feel like someone took my life, put all the contents in an electric mixer, and pressed START. Now everything's tossed around and all the things I care about are not how they should be. How do I deal with that?"

Hayden sighed. "I wish I could give you an answer, sweetheart, but I don't know either. What I do know is that everything that happens in our lives happens for a reason, and if God is letting this be taken from you, it's because he has something better for you."

Sydney shook her head. "I don't know, Dub. In this past year, so many things have been taken from me. If something better was coming, it should have been here by now. Instead, it's just one thing after another. And I know you mean well, but if you start preaching to me, I'm gonna kick you out."

"I'm not going anywhere," Hayden said, unfazed by her words. "You already know that. I'm here for you for whatever, so you can quit the tough act. I'm not try-ing to preach to you, I'm just telling you I've been where you are. I lost hundreds of thousands of dollars, a multiyear contract, and my entire career when I tore my ACL. In one night, one game, with five minutes left in the quarter, it was all over. The other dude walks away with a flagrant foul and a one-game suspension. I walk away with a bad knee and a lifetime suspension from the only thing that I knew how to do."

"What did you do?" Sydney asked, watching as the emotions from the memories played over his face.

"I sulked and wallowed and hid from the world for a couple months," he said with a small smile. "Then on May seven 2008 I prayed that if God gave me a sign, I'd pull my life together. Within seconds, my phone rang. It was my dad telling me it was time to get up."

Sydney raised an eyebrow. "You remember the exact day?"

"How could I forget?" He smiled. "It was the first day of the rest of my life. My dad said exactly what I needed to hear, what I already knew—that God had a new direction for my life. I knew my dad's words were a message straight from God to me. That was the day I started moving, started living again. And since then I've never stopped."

"But at least you had something to keep going with. . . ."

"Not much," Hayden said. "What's worse, I had no plan for the future. And without a plan, you might as well have nothing. I thought I would play ball forever. I didn't even finish my degree. So I had to go back and do all that. It took me two years to get back on track, Syd. But you know what?"

"What?"

"I'm in the best place now that I've been in a long time."

Sydney sighed and looked down at the grass.

"I know, baby, it doesn't look that way now. I couldn't see it then, either. But the God who loved me would never let me go through all that for nothing. And he's not letting you go through all this for nothing, either."

He tilted her chin up so she had to look at him.

"It's OK to be upset," he said gently. "It's OK to be angry and hurt. But don't give up. Give God a chance to show you what he's got for you."

Sydney pursed her lips to try and hide a smile. "I thought you weren't going to preach to me."

He smiled.

"Sorry." He leaned over and brushed his lips against hers gently. "Sometimes it just happens."

She reached out to touch his cheek as her eyes roamed his face. Who was this man, and what had he done with the arrogant boy she had grown up with? His eyes smiled at her, as if he heard her question, and he placed a hand over her fingers, holding them to his cheek a moment longer.

"Syd! Thank God you're here. I need you to help me in the kitchen."

Sydney and Hayden turned to where JJ was standing by the doorway.

"Help you with what?" Sydney asked, not feeling in a particularly charitable mood.

"With dinner! Dean's going to be here in a few minutes. Remember, we told them six o'clock."

Sydney rubbed her hand across her eyes. She had forgotten. With everything that had happened that morning, she had completely forgotten that Dean and Sheree were supposed to be coming by for dinner.

"I'm not having dinner with him." Sydney shook her

head. "Not after what happened today. And I'd be surprised if Dean was still planning to come."

JJ sighed. "Yeah, he called about that. But I told him it was OK. Come on, Syd. It's been weeks since he's been back and you haven't even met his wife yet. . . ."

"You mean the woman who's been whispering in his ear and convincing him to sell the family business?" Sydney snapped. "Yeah, I'd like to meet her. My fist would like to meet her face, too."

"I know you don't mean that," JJ said, her tone slightly scolding. "Can't we put everything about the shop aside for just one night and try to remember we're family?"

"No," Sydney said. "Not tonight."

"Sydney . . ."

"Sorry, JJ, I can't be in a room with Dean tonight." Sydney got out of the swing. "And if you're smart, you better hope Lissandra doesn't come either."

"She's not," JJ said dryly. "She said Mario's taking her somewhere where she's far enough away from Dean so she can't kill him."

"Lucky for him." Sydney walked toward the door. "I'll be back around midnight."

"Where are you going to go?" JJ asked.

"We'll find somewhere," Sydney said, pulling Hayden with her.

JJ groaned. "This is not how this evening was supposed to happen."

The three of them walked through the house toward the front door. Sydney had her hand on the doorknob when the doorbell rang.

JJ bit her lip. "It's Dean."

Sydney felt Hayden's hand on her arm. "Easy," he whispered in her hair. "Just say good night, then we'll leave."

Sydney pulled the door open. She suspected that the scowl on Dean's face was identical to the one on hers. They glared at each other in silence until a small woman, with caramel-colored skin and Beyoncé-blond hair stepped in front of Dean and stretched out her hand.

"I'm so sorry we had to meet like this," she said apologetically. "Hi, I'm . . ."

Sydney was about to give her a piece of her mind when she heard Hayden's voice.

"Sheree?" There was no missing the surprise in his tone.

Sydney watched the smile on the woman's face change to shock. "Hayden?"

Sydney whirled around to look at her boyfriend, then back at Dean's wife. They both wore a strikingly similar look of surprise on their faces.

"You two know each other?" JJ asked, voicing the question that Sydney was sure she and her siblings were all thinking.

Sydney watched several expressions she couldn't read pass over Hayden's face.

"Yes," he said finally, as he folded his arms. "Sheree is my sister."

Chapter 13

Jackie's house was in the community of Thornhill, situated near the northern border of Toronto. Yonge Street, which served as the east-west dividing line of Toronto, ran straight through Thornhill, dividing the community into Thornhill-Markham on the east and Thornhill-Vaughan on the west. Sydney's mother had bought her home, in what was now Thornhill-Markham, more than twenty years ago. She had gotten in right before the large housing developments began to move in. Since then, the size of the community and the value of Jackie's house had more than tripled.

Despite its closeness to Toronto, however, Thornhill, particularly the part where Jackie lived, still had a suburban feel. For one, it was still far enough from train lines and highways that one could sleep peacefully. In addition, Jackie's backyard had enough space that it could have fit Leroy's house and still have room for more trees than most downtown parks.

Sydney wasn't even sure why she was on her way to Jackie's. She loved her mother, but they didn't have the kind of run-to-you relationship that Jackie had with Sydney's younger sisters. Sydney didn't remember exactly when it had gotten that way, but she suspected it was some time after her parents' second divorce.

However, on this particular day, she was running out of places to go. Her own home was off limits, as was the shop. And after finding out the news about Sheree and Hayden's relationship, Sydney had needed a breather from her boyfriend also. At this point she was fresh out of options.

Her mother's car was the only one in the driveway when Sydney finally arrived. Parking behind it, she walked up the steps and rang the doorbell. When there was no answer, she tried the door. Open.

Sydney closed her eyes and sighed.

"Mother, how many times do I have to tell you, you can't keep leaving the front door open," Sydney called out as she locked the door behind her and headed through the large entryway, past the sitting room to the kitchen. The house was quieter than she had heard it in ages, and she realized absently that it was the first in a long time she had been there without at least some of her siblings.

"Mom?" Sydney's voice echoed through the empty kitchen.

She stuck her head through the back door into the yard that was already growing dark as the night approached. No one.

"Mom, where are you?" she called out as she headed through the back hall past the laundry room.

"Jackie?"

"Child, who you calling Jackie? You think the two of us were born the same day?"

Sydney grinned and stuck her head into the large downstairs bedroom that Jackie had decades earlier converted into a sewing room.

"Hey, Mom."

"Hey, yourself," her mom said as she strung the needle on her Singer. "Why are you walking through this house, shouting at the top of your lungs like deaf people live here?"

"Why are you still leaving the front door open?" Sydney responded with an equal measure of chastisement. "This is not the eighties anymore, Mom. You can't just leave your door unlocked. It's not safe."

"Don't you worry about me being safe," she said, turning the reel of thread that she had just run through the needle. "God will take care of me. He and Alarm Force."

Sydney rolled her eyes.

"Come over here and give your old mother a kiss. I can't tell the last time you came here."

Sydney gave her mother a hug and a kiss before sinking down into the couch nearby. She remembered, as a child, spending hours reading in that same couch while her mother worked away at the machine. It was in the peaceful years after her parents had gotten back together. It seemed like so long ago.

"What are you working on today?" Sydney asked.

"Costumes for the Christmas play at church," Jackie said. "You know, Josephine is directing it this year."

Sydney fought her gag reflex. "I'm sure she is."

"Now, why do you have to say it like that?" Jackie paused to look up at Sydney. "I can't talk about my own daughter now?"

"Of course you can talk about your daughter," Sydney said. "I just wish she wasn't the only daughter you talked about."

"Oh, please." Jackie huffed. "I talk about the rest of you."

"Zelia is not the rest of us, Mom," Sydney said.

"So you think I only talk about Josephine and Zelia?"

"Yes," Sydney said with a laugh, nodding at her mother. "You do."

Jackie sighed. "OK. Maybe I do talk about them a little more. But it's only because they're the youngest. And they're the only ones who let me know what's going on in their lives. Like I said, before today I barely saw you. You never even told me you were dating that basketball player."

"He's not a basketball player, Mom, he's a trainer," Sydney said, resting her head against her propped-up hand. "And who told you about that?"

"Doesn't matter who told me. You didn't."

"It was Zelia, wasn't it." Sydney pursed her lips. "That girl can't hold water."

"Don't blame your sister," Jackie said. "I never said it was her."

"You never said it wasn't, either."

"I just wish I had heard it from you," Jackie said. "You know, that man is at church every week. Which is more than I can say for you."

Sydney's head fell back against the couch. "Here it comes . . ."

"I don't know what we did to you that you would rather worship in that big old church where nobody knows you, than worship with your family."

"I come with you once a month."

"Under duress," Jackie said. "You can't grow your relationship by just going to church for two hours every week. You need other things—including fellowship with other believers who know you and can help you in your struggle."

She shook her head. "Sometimes I wonder what happened to you."

Sydney lifted her head and pulled her bare feet up under her on the couch.

"Nothing happened to me," she said quietly.

"Uh-uh," Jackie side-eyed her daughter. "Something happened to you. The Sydney I know had real relationships with other people. The Sydney I know wouldn't ruin her relationship with her brother over concrete and stone."

"I did not ruin my relationship with Dean," Sydney retorted with a frown. "He did that all by himself. . . ."

"And the Sydney I know wouldn't walk out on her brother and her new sister-in-law because she was in a bad mood. . . ."

"Unbelievable." Sydney sat forward and her eyes widened. "Does Zelia have you on a live feed?"

Her mother stopped sewing and turned to her.

"Look, Sydney, I know this whole business with the store has been hard for you, but remember at the end of the day all these things pass away. But what you do, the relationships you have with the people around you, your family, that's all that you will have."

Sydney stared down at the arm of the couch for a long while.

"Did you know he was going to give it to Dean?" Sydney asked suddenly.

Her mother sighed. "No. I didn't know that Leroy

would give the shop to Dean. He must have changed his will since the last time I saw it."

"What was it like before?" Sydney asked.

"It doesn't matter," Jackie said.

"It does to me," Sydney said.

"Come on, Sydney. Your father was a good man, but you know he was old school. He loved you girls, but when Dean was born, his first son, it was a whole new set of rules. He wanted Dean to carry on his legacy and he was dead set on making that happen. No matter what anyone said."

It was brief, but Sydney caught the look that crossed her mother's face. It was a look that told her that Dean had been a source of strong disagreement between her parents more often than she cared to know.

"Your father was who he was," Jackie continued. "He did things his way and he was not the kind of man to explain himself to a woman. But he's gone, Sydney. And we may never understand why he did what he did. But your brother is still here."

"He sold the shop, Mom." Sydney blinked back tears. "After he agreed to sell us part of it, he went ahead and sold it to one of Dad's competitors. And then he told me after the fact. Do you know what I got on my phone on my way over here, Mom?"

Jackie sighed.

"An e-mail from the company that he sold to, with proposed dates for a meeting to work out the transfer details." Sydney sniffled and wiped her nose with the back of her hand. "Dean already closed on the sale. I have to pack up everything and be out in six weeks. Did you tell Dean that I am still here? Did you give Dean this speech about how his relationship with me should still matter? Or was that just for me?"

134   *Rhonda Bowen*

Jackie got up from the machine and moved to sit beside Sydney on the couch.

"Honey, I know you're hurting. And I know it's unfair to ask you to make amends with your brother. But I'm asking because I know that you can. You're the older one. You're the more mature one. Dean doesn't know what he's doing. That boy just went and married a girl he barely knows because she's pregnant."

Sydney looked up at her mother. "You knew about that?"

"You know your sister can't hold water."

Zelia.

"The point is, he needs us more than he knows." Jackie squeezed Sydney's hand. "We have to love him, Sydney. And loving him means giving him the freedom to make those selfish choices, but letting him know that we still love him at the end of it. It's like God and us. He knows what's best for us. And he could force us to it, but that wouldn't be love. Love is the freedom he gives us to choose to do things his way, or to choose our own way."

"I'm not God, Mom."

"I know." Jackie pulled Sydney into a hug. "But you still have to love your brother."

"And what about my career while I am doing that?" Sydney asked. "Should I run Decadent from a food cart on King Street?"

Jackie raised her hand to the ceiling and closed her eyes. "Honey, if that's where the Lord is leading you, who am I to stand in your way?"

Sydney smiled in spite of herself.

"On a serious note, though, I have a feeling things will work out the way they should," Jackie said. "If we do things God's way, he will take care of us. Of course, it works better when we have a relationship with him and lean on him."

Sydney groaned. "Not you, too."

"Not me too what?"

"With the preaching," Sydney said. "I already got a dose from Hayden."

"You did, eh," said Jackie, getting up and going back to the machine. "You keep that one. He's a good man."

"Yeah." Sydney got up and headed to the kitchen to see what she could scrounge up to eat. "That's what everyone keeps telling me."

She was rummaging through the fridge for leftover chicken when her cell phone rang.

"Hello?"

"Hey, it's me. Can we talk?"

Speak of the devil.

Sydney closed the fridge and sat down on one of the stools by the counter.

"OK."

Hayden let out a deep breath. "I didn't know about my sister and your brother."

"I know."

"I didn't even know my sister was married," he continued. "We don't exactly have a close relationship. In fact, I barely see her a couple times a year. We have the same mother, but that's about the depth of our connection."

Sydney heard him take another deep breath.

"Does that bother you?" she asked.

He paused. "Yeah," he said finally. "Sometimes I feel guilty about not having a better relationship with her. She didn't do too well growing up. I lived with my dad, and he was able to give me everything I needed and more. But she lived with Mom, and, well . . . that wasn't always easy."

"Oh yeah?"

"Yeah," Hayden said with another sigh. "If you met my birth mother you would understand. She was never married, and I don't think Sheree knew a lot about her father. I know she moved out of Mom's house not long after she graduated high school, and she's been bouncing around since. I try to help her where I can, but she's pretty stubborn and independent."

He chuckled. "A little like you, actually."

Sydney felt her spine stiffen. "I doubt it."

"Anyway, she always took care of herself, but like I said, we didn't have a close relationship. I would go years without hearing from her. And after I left Toronto and moved to Boston it got even harder. Today is the first time I've seen her in over a year. I knew she was dating someone, but I . . . I couldn't even imagine this."

"OK," Sydney said, letting out a deep breath. "I believe you. I didn't really think you knew, but it was just too much. I just needed some space."

"I know, baby, I understand. It was a shock for me, too." He let out a deep breath. "So are we good?"

"Yeah, we're good."

Sydney paused. "I just need to ask. Sheree . . . she wouldn't . . ."

"She's a good person, Sydney," Hayden said. "She's had some difficulties, but all she ever needed was someone to love her. To give her a chance. And it looks like your brother really loves her."

"I just don't want him to get hurt," Sydney said. "I

may be mad at him. But if anyone hurts him they'll have to deal with me."

"Well, you don't have to worry about that from her," Hayden said. "She seems a lot more settled now than the last time I saw her. And happy."

"Glad to hear it," Sydney said.

"So where did you end up anyway?"

"At my mother's," Sydney said, returning to the fridge. "We've been lacking quality time."

"Well, I better let you get off the phone, then," he said. "I'll talk to you soon."

Sydney put the makings of a chicken sandwich on the counter and sat down on the stool. But as she thought about the situation ahead of her she lost her appetite.

She closed her eyes and rested her head in her hands.

If there was ever a time she needed to hear from God in an up close and personal way, it was now. Because at that moment, she had no idea what she was going to do next.

Chapter 14

It was barely six fifteen when Sydney dragged herself out of bed and into the shower. Almost four weeks had passed since her life had fallen to pieces, and even the distraction of Christmas and New Year's hadn't tamed the urge she had every morning to stay buried under the comforter. But as much as she wanted to, she couldn't. Life wasn't stopping so she could have her pity party. And even though she still didn't know what she was going to do at the end of the month when her time at Decadent ran out, she still had to keep going.

This morning she had the joy of meeting with the development team Something Sweet had hired to take care of the transition and prepare the store to become just like the others in the franchise. Watching the place her father had bought and turned into his own being stripped of its individuality made Sydney want to hurl. Instead, she stood under the hot spray a little longer and let it beat more reality into her.

"Syd. Hurry up and get out of the shower. I gotta get to work," JJ hollered from the bathroom doorway. "Besides, there's a gorgeous man cooking breakfast in our kitchen."

Sydney stuck her head around the side of the shower doors. "Huh?"

"You heard me," JJ said, her hip leaned against the doorway and a plate piled high in her hands. "Your man is pulling an Iron Chef downstairs."

Of all of Jackie's children, JJ was the least prone to lying. But this, Sydney had to see for herself. Jumping out of the shower, she quickly dried off and pulled on some jeans and a T-shirt before padding downstairs to the kitchen. Her mouth fell open when she saw Hayden standing in her kitchen. As if sensing her presence, he turned around and grinned. His smile was almost as bright as the sunflowers on JJ's apron that he wore over his starkly contrasting navy blue dress shirt and pants.

"Good morning," he said, his eyes sparkling.

Yes, it definitely was.

"Good morning yourself." Sydney was unable to stop her lips from spreading into a huge smile. "How did you get in here?"

"I let him in," Lissandra said from the small breakfast table off the side of the kitchen, where she was stuffing food into her face. "And I'll get him his own key if he'll come cook breakfast like this every morning."

"Let me get back to you on that," Hayden said, winking at Sydney.

Sydney shook her head and smirked as she slid onto one of the breakfast stools by the counter. "Never gonna happen, babe," she said.

"A brother's gotta try." He leaned over the counter

and gave Sydney a deliciously slow kiss before turning back to the stove.

She rested her chin on her hand, a dreamy expression on her face. "Mmm. Now that I could get used to."

"You know what I could get used to," Lissandra said through a mouthful of food. "These boiled dumplings. Can a sister get another one of these?"

"Absolutely." Taking another one of the small, firm spheres from a pot on the stove, Hayden placed it on a plate and hand delivered it to Lissandra. While he was on his way, Sydney slipped into the kitchen and began opening the other pots. An amazing aroma of codfish and ackee hit her as soon as she opened one of the smaller ones. She was about to stick a fork in to sample, when a wooden spoon lightly tapped her knuckles.

"Hey hey," Hayden said teasingly, slipping an arm around her waist as he pulled her out of the way. "No peeking into my pots. You just sit and wait."

"But I just—"

"Sit."

Sydney put her hands on her hips. "But this is my—"

"Sit."

Hayden's raised eyebrow was enough to move her back to her stool.

"Why do you have to be so stubborn?" He took a plate from the drainer and dished food from all the pots onto it. "Can't you just let me do something for you?"

"But I just wanted to see how you made it," she said, biting her lip.

Hayden laughed. "Do you go into the kitchen at Banjara and tell them you just want to see how they make it?"

"Actually, she has," Lissandra called out from the table. Hayden turned to look at Lissandra, surprised.

Lissandra laughed. "Oh yeah. You don't know who you're dealing with."

Hayden turned to look at Sydney for confirmation.

She shrugged. "We have a good relationship with the guys over there."

He shook his head at her as he placed the plate in front of her. "I have two words for you, baby. Control. Freak."

But as Sydney looked down at her plate filled with boiled green bananas, boiled dumplings, ackee with codfish, and tomatoes, she decided that she could definitely give up her controlling tendencies for this.

She looked up at him for a long moment, wondering what she had done to deserve such a wonderful man.

"Thank you," she said quietly, for his ears only. It didn't cover the gratitude she was feeling, but it was the best she could come up with at the moment.

"You're welcome." He leaned forward, his elbows resting on the counter. "I'll admit I'm motivated by mostly selfish reasons. I wanted to see you before I went out of town tonight, but I have a packed afternoon, and I know you have that big meeting this morning. I figured this might be the only way it could happen."

Sydney nodded, remembering that he had mentioned he would be away for a while.

"How long will you be gone?" she asked, cutting a dumpling with her fork and spearing a piece.

"Week and a half," he said.

Sydney pouted.

He smiled. "I know. But I'll call you."

"You better." She pointed her fork at him threateningly.

"I promise," he said. "We have a bunch of away games, so we'll be on a bus most of the time. It will be nothing but cramped seats, hotel food, and living out of a suitcase."

"Along with court lights, fast-paced games, and screaming fans." Sydney smiled. "Admit it. You love the life."

Hayden tilted his head to the side. "Yeah, I do. Basketball runs through my veins. And I love to see these players develop from rookies to stars. Coach says it's probably because I love building players more than I love being a player."

"It's true." Sydney paused from her eating to look up at him. "I can see it when I see you with them. That's one of the things I like about you. Among other things."

Hayden raised his eyebrow, mischief tilting his lips. "What other things?"

Hayden's watch beeped and Sydney laughed. "I guess that part's gonna have to wait until after you come back."

Hayden let out a deep breath as he glanced at the time. "Guess so. Gotta go." He looked around at the kitchen. "As soon as I clean up this mess."

"Don't worry," Sydney said. "Lissandra will do it."

"I will?"

Sydney glared at her sister, who was scanning the morning's paper. "You will."

"Thanks, Lissandra," Hayden said with a grin as he grabbed Sydney's hand and pulled her with him toward the front door.

"All the best with your meeting this morning." He pulled her into his arms for a brief moment.

Sydney turned away a second, but he touched her cheek and turned her downcast eyes back to his.

"Don't worry. God knows what he's doing. As the

heavens are higher than the earth, so are his ways higher than ours," he said, referencing Isaiah 55:9.

Sydney nodded but said nothing.

Seeing her doubt, he pulled her into another embrace.

"It will be fine," he said, kissing her forehead. "I promise."

He pulled away and began to dash through the door when Sydney grabbed his arm.

"Wait!"

"Huh?"

Sydney drew him close, wrapped both arms around his neck, and kissed him so hard she felt his arms shake. When she finally let him go, it took him a moment to find his voice.

"Baby." He gazed at her through eyes glazed with desire. "I *am* coming back."

"I know," she said with a grin, as she pulled JJ's apron that he was still wearing over his head.

He laughed when he realized the real reason she had stopped him.

"But with all those groupies, I just don't want you to forget what you're coming back to."

Backing her up against the doorframe, he dipped his head toward hers and caught her lips in a smoldering kiss of his own. And as he easily lifted her slim body slightly off the floor so he could have easier access to her mouth, Sydney felt every inch of her heat up like a furnace. When he finally set her feet back on the floor, he pressed warm lips against her ear.

"No chance of that."

Sydney slumped back against the doorframe, breathless, and fanned herself with her hand, as he laughed and backed away toward his car. It was a good thing he was leaving. Because after a kiss like that, she wasn't sure she could remember their boundaries. She watched his car disappear down the road before she drifted back into the kitchen, where she found Lissandra washing up the pots and dishes from Hayden's meal.

"You guys finally wrap up that PDA session?" Lissandra asked.

"Hey," Sydney said, barely looking up from her plate where she had resumed eating. "It was all PG."

"Please. More like rated R."

"No," Sydney said, motioning with her spoon. "Rated R was you and Jeremy Wilkins on the front steps the night of your senior prom."

Lissandra paused and looked up as if trying to recapture the memory. "Yeah, you're right. That was R," she said after a moment.

Sydney shook her head. "I thought Jackie was going to die. She was so mad. . . ."

"Oh man, Jeremy was so scared," Lissandra said, glancing back at Sydney. "Especially when Mom came back with that gun."

Sydney laughed. "Where did she get that again?"

They turned to look at each other as they remembered at the same time.

"Bill!" They burst into laughter, as they remembered Zelia's dad's gun collection, a part of which he seemed to have forgotten at the house after the divorce.

"Poor Momma didn't know what she was doing," Lissandra said, turning off the faucet. "The thing wasn't even loaded."

"Jeremy didn't know that, though," Sydney said with a gasp. "I never saw a boy move so fast my whole life."

Both of them were so doubled over with laughter

they never saw JJ come into the kitchen. But when they finally looked up and saw her stone-set face, all the laughter disappeared.

"What's wrong?" Lissandra asked.

"Zelia just called. We need to go over to Dean's." Her voice was tense. "Now."

No further explanation was needed. Lissandra turned the faucet off on the half-washed dishes and hurried upstairs to get dressed.

"Go on ahead," she threw after them. "I'll meet you all over there."

Sydney and JJ were out the door in five minutes.

Questions burned Sydney's lips on the drive over, but JJ was too wrapped up in a phone conversation with their mother to answer any of them. Sydney knew how uncomfortable her sister was giving their mother a vague explanation about why she would be late opening up the shop. But there was no use alarming Jackie until they knew exactly what was going on.

Zelia's and Dean's cars were already parked in the driveway when they arrived.

"OK, JJ, I'm sufficiently freaked out," Sydney said as they headed toward the front door. "Just tell me what's going on."

"I'm not sure. Zelia just told me to get over here." JJ fished the spare key from the ledge above the door where it was taped flat and unlocked the door. She glanced back at Sydney before stepping inside. "We're about to find out."

The first thing Sydney noticed was the way her shoes echoed loudly off the hardwood floors as she stepped inside. When she turned from the front hallway into the living room, she understood why.

"What in the world . . ."

This place looked nothing like the one she had been to over Christmas. Dean's living room, which before had been tastefully decorated with an expensive three-piece living room suite, Persian area rugs, glass end tables, and a collection of lamps and other furniture that Sydney knew Sheree paid too much for, was now stripped to nothing. There was not one piece of furniture in the living area. Even the paintings on the wall were gone. Only the drapes remained, to give an appearance from the outside that the house was still the same as it was the last time they saw it.

The two women walked around the room examining the emptiness from every angle as if there was furniture hiding in a corner in the ceiling or some other clearly uninhabitable spot.

"It's the same in every room," Zelia said, appearing at the bottom of the stairs, panic and alarm written all over her face. "She took everything. That little demon took everything."

"What do you mean 'she took everything'?" JJ asked, shock and confusion in her voice as she walked across the hall and into the equally empty kitchen. "Who took everything?"

"Sheree," Sydney said, standing at the door of the kitchen. Even before Zelia said it, she somehow knew exactly what had happened.

Sheree had cleaned Dean out.

Chapter 15

"I don't believe this." JJ shook her head as she pushed past Zelia and went up the stairs of Dean's three-bedroom home. "That's impossible. Are you sure she did this?"

"We're sure," Zelia said, her jaw set. "Dean came home this morning and everything was gone. She is the only person who could have done all this so fast. It doesn't help that she's completely disappeared."

Sydney and Zelia followed her upstairs, and sure enough, except for Dean's clothes, every bedroom, every bathroom, the library, and every closet was empty, from the bed to the bedding. Nothing was left. Not a lamp in a corner, not a rug on the floor, not a towel in the closet. Save Dean's clothes, the whole house was empty as the day the builder had handed the keys of the new house to Dean and Sheree. Scratch that. It was emptier, because the Queen of the Damned had even taken the new appliances that came standard with all the new homes.

"I can't believe this," seemed to be the only words

that JJ could manage as Sydney followed her sister from one empty room to another.

When they got to the master bedroom, they found Dean sitting on the floor in a corner, his head in his hands. Sydney's heart broke at the sight of her little brother.

"Oh God, Dean," Sydney said, squatting down beside her brother and putting her arms around him. "I'm so sorry. I'm so sorry."

JJ slipped down on the other side and followed suit, rubbing the back of his neck gently. "What happened, Dean? Did you guys have a fight or something?"

Dean shook his head. "No," he said, his voice cracking with his effort to speak. "We never fought about anything. I thought we were good—we were happy. But this morning I came home, and she was gone."

"He was out of town scouting some new artists for about a week," Zelia supplied from the door. "He just got back a couple hours ago."

"I love her, she loves me." Dean grabbed his head in his hands. "She would never do this. . . . Someone must have made her. She would never just leave like this."

"Have you tried calling her?" Sydney asked.

"It just rings, then goes straight to voice mail," Zelia answered.

"When was the last time you talked to her?" JJ asked.

Dean sniffled and rubbed his eyes. "Last night. We talked for about an hour. She wanted to know what time I was coming in today so we could have lunch together when she got off work."

Sydney looked over at Zelia. "Call her job and—"

Dean shook his head. "She never came in."

Zelia rolled her eyes. "They said she quit last week. She hasn't been there since last Friday."

So she had planned this. In fact, since Dean had been away since last week, technically Sheree could have been gone for days.

"When you spoke to her last night, did you talk to her on the landline or her cell phone?" Sydney asked.

Dean sniffled again. "Cell phone. There've been some problems with the landline. Sheree says sometimes it rings and she doesn't hear it."

"What a coincidence," Sydney said dryly.

"She mentioned it on Tuesday evening when I spoke to her," Dean said. "But she told me she was taking care of it with the phone company."

He wiped a hand across his nose. "She always took care of everything. Made sure I didn't have to worry about buying the furniture or paying the bills. Once we put everything in our joint account, I knew I didn't have to worry about anything."

The lightness in Sydney's head increased and she began to have trouble breathing. Sydney looked over at JJ, and they exchanged the same panicked look.

"What do you mean you put everything in your joint account?" JJ asked.

"What do you think I mean?" Dean asked, seemingly irritated by the multiple questions. "I mean everything! She's my wife. I'm her husband. We don't keep anything from each other. She's my partner on everything."

"Dean," Sydney began trying to keep her voice calm. "Please tell me you didn't put the money from the sale in your joint account."

"The sale?" Dean pulled away from Sydney and glared at her. "My life is falling apart. My wife is missing and you're asking about the shop?"

"Dean, sweetheart, just relax." JJ squeezed his shoulder lightly. "She didn't mean anything. She just wanted to make sure that you would be OK. We are all just concerned about you."

Dean looked at JJ, then back at Sydney, before looking down at his feet and sighing.

"No," he said. "The money from the sale is in the business account."

Sydney and JJ exchanged another relieved look and Sydney let out a breath she was holding.

"I'm sorry, Dean," Sydney said. "I'm so sorry this happened to you. I know how much you love—"

"Oh hell no!"

Zelia pursed her lips. "Guess Lissandra is here."

"Zelia, can you stay . . ." Sydney began.

Zelia nodded, and Sydney got up from the floor and headed downstairs with JJ, leaving Zelia upstairs to comfort Dean.

As they descended the stairs, they saw Lissandra stomp past them angrily into the kitchen.

"Oh hell no!"

Sydney and JJ finally caught up with her in the dining room.

"She did this, didn't she? That trick even took out the chandeliers!" Lissandra screeched. She squeezed her eyes shut. "Oh hell no."

"She took everything," JJ said, her anger mounting as the reality set in. "Down to the freakin' toilet-seat covers."

"Where she at?" Lissandra cracked her knuckles as she paced the floor. "Where that chick at? I'm about to rip her track-wearing head off. . . ."

"We don't know where she is. . . ."

"I'll find her," Lissandra said angrily. "And when I do, I'ma bust her a—"

"Shhh," Sydney hissed at Lissandra. "Can you lower your voice? Dean is upstairs, and he still thinks that maybe something happened to Sheree and she's the victim."

"That Negro better open his eyes," Lissandra said. She shook her head. "I knew this was going to happen. I knew it, I knew it. I told him and Jackie that girl was trouble. . . ."

"We need to call Jackie," Sydney dug through her purse. "And we should call the police before Sheree gets too far."

But before she could reach her phone, it started ringing. It was Thomas.

Sydney winced as she realized she had forgotten all about her meeting.

"Hey, Thomas," Sydney said, pre-empting the man. "I'm so sorry—I forgot about the meeting. I'm sort of in the middle of a family emergency."

"Sorry to hear," Thomas said. "I hope it's not too serious. Is something wrong with Jackie? One of your sisters?"

"No, no, nothing like that," Sydney said, not wanting to go into details until she was 100 percent sure of what had happened.

"Oh," Thomas paused. "Does that mean you and Dean had a chance to talk about what will happen with the closing costs for the sale now that he moved all the money?"

Alarm bells began going off in Sydney's head like crazy.

"Moved what money?"

"The money from the sale of Decadent," Thomas said, like it was the most obvious thing in the world. "He wrote a check for all of it to SV Records. I assumed that he told you. The check came to the bank yesterday."

The room began to spin before Sydney's eyes.

"Thomas, please tell me that you did not just say the money from Decadent has left the account," Sydney said weakly.

"All the money has left the account, Sydney. And I must say I am rather offended that none of you advised me beforehand that you were planning to make such a large monetary transaction before all the final details of the sale were complete. We still have some remaining expenses that we need to cover."

Sydney thought Thomas said more, but she never heard it as the phone slipped from her hand and she stared at her sisters.

"She took the money."

"What money?" JJ asked.

"From the sale."

JJ leaned against the wall as the color began to drain from her face. "How much."

Sydney choked on the words. "All of it."

Lissandra dropped her purse and screamed. "Oh hell no!"

Chapter 16

Five hundred thousand dollars.

Every time Sydney thought about it she couldn't breathe, and she had done nothing but think about it all day, hence the reason she was sitting on the couch in her living room with a paper bag in her hand.

Once they had explained to Thomas what had happened with Sheree, he had called the bank and some other connections of his to find out if there was a way they could get the money back. But it was too late. Sheree had already moved the money out of the SV Records account she had created, divided it up into smaller amounts, and distributed it into other accounts. And that's where the trail of bread crumbs pretty much ended. Beyond that point her transactions were so secure and totally unconnected to Dean that even Thomas, with all his Rolodex of contacts, couldn't find out any more.

If that wasn't bad enough, Thomas noted that it would be nearly impossible to charge Sheree with anything beyond check fraud since she was Dean's wife. In order for things to get even that far, Dean would have to be willing to bring charges against his wife. And since last time Sydney checked Dean hadn't progressed past believing in Sheree's innocence, she didn't see him pressing charges against his missing wife anytime soon.

Sydney sighed and looked around at the living room of her house—a house that once belonged to her father, Leroy, but which now belonged to her and her sisters. Sydney realized that this was all she would probably have left after the dust cleared—one-third of an old house just north of downtown Toronto. She reached for the paper bag again as she felt herself begin to hyperventilate.

She had just managed to calm herself down when the front door opened. She shifted her eyes to see which of her sisters it was.

"Hey." JJ kicked off her shoes at the door and stepped down into the sunken living room.

Sydney didn't answer, only sighed. JJ echoed her sigh as she sank into the couch beside her sister, placing her head on Sydney's shoulder.

"What are we going to do?"

"I don't know," Sydney said tiredly. She had spent all morning just trying to come to grips with the reality of their situation. She hadn't gotten to the point of problem solving yet.

"How's Dean doing?" Sydney asked.

"Not good," JJ said, a worried edge creeping into her voice. "He wouldn't leave the empty house, and when he finally did, we had to take him back to Mom's and give him a sedative. When I left, he was asleep."

"Has anyone talked to Jackie yet?"

"No. She's still at the shop and Zelia's busy taking care of Dean. So it's going to be you."

Sydney closed her eyes. There it was again. That burden of being the oldest.

"Where is Lissandra?" Sydney asked, even as the front door opened again.

"I'm here," Lissandra said with about as much enthusiasm as the rest of them felt. She dropped her keys on the table and added her shoes to the pile at the door before joining Sydney and JJ on the couch.

"So my police friend called back." She put her feet up on the coffee table.

"And?"

"And she basically said the same thing as Thomas. Since Sheree is Dean's wife, it will be nearly impossible to charge her unless Dean grows some common sense. And even then, they might look at the whole thing as a domestic issue. Like all she did was move some of her money without telling her husband."

Sydney had been hoping for a ray of hope from the law enforcement corner. So far it hadn't happened.

JJ shook her head. "This is crazy. How can that woman clean out our brother, steal our family money from underneath us, and get away with it?"

"Because they were married, there wasn't a prenup, and everything we have technically belongs to Dean," Sydney answered matter of factly.

Sydney partly blamed herself for this. She should have gotten the money back from her share of Decadent sooner. She should have been more diligent about finding out who Sheree was. She should have made Dean put the money from the sale in a completely separate instrument, secured through the bank rather than in a regular account. But who was she kidding? If she had been in Dean's place, she would have done things Sheree's way, too.

There was no point dwelling on what ifs. They couldn't change the past. But Sydney wasn't about to let the future run her over.

"We've got to get Dean to press charges."

JJ sprung up like a jack-in-the-box at Sydney's statement.

"No way." She shook her head so vigorously Sydney thought it might fall off. "He won't do it and we shouldn't force him. He can't handle it. Not now."

"Who cares if he can handle it now," Lissandra snapped. "The longer we wait, the lower the chance that we're gonna get back our money. This is not just about the three fifty K from the store. That trick went on the run with our one fifty K also."

"She's right," Sydney said. "Plus what if this isn't Sheree's first time pulling a stunt like this? You can't create multiple accounts, forge signatures, and disappear completely in less than a week unless you know how. And if that's the case, then our chances of finding her drop even lower."

"Then let's hire a private investigator or something," JJ suggested.

"Haven't you been listening?" Lissandra countered. "We can't afford jack."

"We could all pool together . . ."

"We would still need Dean's cooperation. He's the one who knows the most about her and would have the info that could help us find her," Sydney said.

JJ looked at her two sisters a moment longer before slumping back into the chair, defeated.

"I'm just worried about Dean," she said quietly. "He's not taking this well at all. I'm afraid . . ."

She bit her lip.

"I'm afraid he might not pull through this."

Sydney and Lissandra exchanged a look.

"You don't think he might . . . he wouldn't try to hurt himself, would he?" Sydney asked.

"I don't know what to think," JJ answered. "I've never seen him like this. Not even after Dad died."

Sydney got up off the couch. "We need to go see Mom," she said.

"Good luck," Lissandra said, easing down farther in the chair.

"Uh-uh," Sydney said, grabbing her sister's hand and pulling her up. "You're coming with me. Both of you."

JJ headed for the coat closet as Lissandra whined.

"Do I have to?"

"Yes," Sydney said, slipping on her winter jacket. " 'Cause when Jackie hits the roof, there is no way I am dealing with that on my own."

Chapter 17

Sydney read over the weekend schedule a third time without ever really seeing any of it. She finally put it down on her desk and sat back, rubbing her palms over her face.

It was Thursday night. Almost a week had passed since the news of Sheree's disappearance. But they were no closer to answers than they had been the morning the shocking news came to them. When they had told Jackie what happened, she had nearly had a heart attack. She had started feeling chest pains, and they had given her an aspirin and almost taken her to the hospital. After she had recovered, she'd called Thomas to find out exactly how much money had gone missing and then made a beeline to Dean's side, where she had been ever since.

Sydney wished she could have dropped everything as easily to deal with this latest catastrophe. However, when you weren't your own boss, you didn't have that freedom. Instead of being by her brother's side, she had to be at the shop.

The details of the transition had been finalized. Sydney and her staff had two weeks until Decadent as they knew it would close forever. There would be one week to get all their stuff out, and then that would be it. There would be job opportunities for the existing staff, but they would have to apply to the new management and they would be on the same level as anyone on the street looking for a job. As far as Sydney was concerned, it was like firing them.

She personally would rather eat dirt than work for Something Sweet. But that was about as much as she knew when it came to what she would do next. With no savings, no job prospects, and nothing but misery wherever she turned, she had not been very motivated to think about what would happen when Decadent expired. She figured she still had time to work out the details. Until then, however, Sydney had to make her way in every morning and put on a smiling face as if her world wasn't crashing down around her.

Her cell phone rang and she picked it up. She sighed when she saw the name on the screen. Hayden had been calling her for days, but every time she let it go to voice mail. She didn't want to talk to him. Not now. Not after his sister had ruined her brother's life. She knew that once he got back from out of town she would have to face him. But she would worry about that then.

A knock on the door distracted Sydney, pulling her from her thoughts.

"Boss?" Mario stuck his head around the slightly ajar door.

"Hey, Mario," Sydney said, sitting forward. "Come in."

Mario came in briskly and stopped in front of Sydney's desk, a serious expression on his face.

"You wanted to know those of us who were interested in working here after the change, so you could put in a good word for us with Something Sweet."

Sydney nodded. "Are you interested?"

"That's the thing," Mario said, tilting his head to the side. "I came to tell you that I'm with you, Syd. No way am I working for those cats. My loyalty is to your old man."

Sydney smiled slightly. "That's kind of you to say, Mario, but it's a tough economy. We all need every opportunity we can get. If there's a chance for you here after all this, you should take it. It won't make you any less loyal to Decadent."

"I feel you, Syd, but I can't do that. Your pops was like a dad to me. If he had never given me that job here when I was a kid, I woulda never made it to college. That degree, all my experience, I owe it to him. And I can't turn my back on him now."

He shook his head. "I'll work somewhere, but it won't be here. I just wanted to let you know."

Sydney didn't know why, but she felt her eyes moisten. She blinked the wetness away before it could embarrass her.

"Thank you, Mario," she said, her voice taking on an unusual softness. "It means a lot to hear you say that."

He nodded. "No problem."

He grinned. "Besides, your sister would probably kill me if I even considered working for them. And seeing that she's finally feelin' a brother, I'm tryin' not to mess that up, you know what I'm saying?"

Sydney smiled knowingly. "Yes, I know what you mean. She would definitely kill you."

Mario grinned and headed for the door. "Keep your

head up, Syd. Everything's gonna work according to God's plan."

Sydney raised an eyebrow. "You're a Christian?"

Mario popped his collar. "No doubt."

She shook her head. "All these years and I didn't even know that about you."

"Yeah," he said. "That was your dad, too. And you know what, I've never regretted that decision. Not one day in my life."

Sydney nodded and considered him thoughtfully, seeing him in a whole new light.

She suddenly sat up. "Wait, if you're a Christian, how come you're dating my sister?"

He gave a little smile. "I have faith in her. Like I told you, Syd, she just needs a little direction. She's gotten a little sidetracked during life. But she'll find her way back."

Sydney didn't know whether to admire or pity Mario. He had more faith in her sister than most.

"Anyway, I gotta go clean up before the end of the shift," he said, heading through the door. "Remember what I said, Syd. It's gonna work out. And if you ever decide to open another Decadent, know that you got me."

Sydney watched him leave but felt his words still hang after him. Everything's gonna work according to God's plan. She had heard that text before. But it took a few clicks in Google to give her the exact reference in Romans 8:28.

And we know that all things work together for good to them that love God, to them who are called according to his purpose.

She read it over and over until she was pretty sure she had it memorized. It sounded like the kind of thing to keep someone hopeful. All things work together for good. How? How could losing Decadent and her savings work for good? She couldn't see it. But maybe that was only the case for people like JJ and Jackie. People who had that perfect relationship with God. People who were so good that they were liable to ascend at any moment.

She was far from that point. Sure, she showed up at church, but her time with God outside of that was relegated to two-line prayers over her food if she remembered. She didn't talk about him every day or weave the topic of him into regular conversation like her mother or Hayden. She did love God. Or used to anyway. But her ideas on loving God were tangled up with memories of going to one church with Leroy on some weekends and a different one with Jackie on others; it was confused with childhood memories of family worship at Jackie's, where Josephine took center stage; it was lost in the whispers of church people who told their children not to talk to *those* kids, not to date those girls—the ones whose mother had all those husbands. She had had a hard time conceptualizing God's love through all of that. And she suddenly realized that at some point she had stopped trying.

She glanced at the clock: 10:45. It was time to get ready for closing. Forcing her mind to stay focused, she went over the schedule one more time before approving it and e-mailing it to all the staff. It would be one of the last schedules she ever sent them.

Powering down her computer, she packed up her things and prepared to make the final round through the shop floor before closing. She was almost through the door when the phone rang. She glanced back at it but kept going. Whatever it was, it could wait.

When she was almost at the end of the hallway, she felt her cell phone vibrate at her hip. Without pausing, she pulled it out and answered it.

"Hello—"

"Sydney, it's Dean!" The panic in JJ's voice sliced through Sydney like a knife.

"What? What's wrong?"

"There was an accident." JJ began sobbing and Sydney's heart beat faster. Her mind had suddenly flashed back to the last time her sister had called her crying. It had been a year and a half ago when Leroy died.

"When? Where? What happened?" Sydney was already on her way back to her office to grab her car keys.

"Dean . . . he was drinking . . . there was an SUV . . . oh God . . . Syd, he's not conscious."

After that it was pretty much impossible to get anything out of JJ. But somehow she managed to get the name of the hospital. With quick instructions to Wendy to lock up, Sydney dashed through the door and was in the car before she even got JJ off the phone.

By the time she pulled out onto the main road, she'd called Lissandra and relayed the news. The traffic seemed heavier than ever as she made her way over to Toronto Western Hospital on the west end of the city. She tried to temper the millions of thoughts in her head, but they were completely out of control. She didn't want to think about what her brother's fate might be. Whatever it was, he was too young. This shouldn't be happening to him.

She squeezed her car into the first available space,

ignoring the parking information sign a few feet away. When she finally got into the lobby, Zelia's boyfriend, Luke, was pacing the waiting area.

"Where are they?" she asked, skipping the formalities.

"Fell Pavilion, first floor," he said. "I'll take you. . . ."

"No, you stay here," Sydney said, already running toward the hallway. "Lissandra's coming and she'll tear this place up if she doesn't know where to go."

Sydney felt like she ran through the confusing hallways of the hospital forever, but she finally found the waiting room where her sisters were. Zelia immediately fell on Sydney in tears.

"Where is he?" Sydney asked, her eyes moving from Zelia's sobbing form to JJ, who was walking back and forth nearby, barely holding it together.

"He's in surgery," JJ said, her eyes already swollen. "Several of his ribs were crushed and one punctured his lung. Plus they say he has head injuries."

JJ's face crumpled as tears began to pour out of her eyes, and she rocked back and forth to calm herself down. Sydney turned away from her sisters as much as she could, with the weight of Zelia pulling her down. She couldn't afford to break down now. One of them had to keep it together. She suspected that no one had managed to call their mother.

"What happened?" Sydney asked after a moment, when JJ seemed to recover a little.

"We don't know for sure," JJ said. "Zelia said he took off a little after eight this evening. We don't know where he was, who he was with; all we know is that Zelia got a call about half an hour ago. They found his driver's license on him, and she was listed on his file at the hospital as one of his contacts."

"They didn't call Mom, did they," Sydney asked, even as feelings of panic began to stir in her.

"No," JJ said, shaking her head.

"Thank God," Sydney breathed. "I don't know how she would have taken it on top of everything else that's already happened."

"I know." JJ said. She sniffled. "Syd, they say he was wasted. His blood alcohol was almost three times the legal limit."

"He was drinking?"

JJ nodded. "It's been happening almost every night since Sheree took off."

Sydney shook her head. She hated that woman for what she had done to her brother.

She sank into the chair and pulled out her cell phone and dialed. After several rings, her sister Josephine answered.

"Hey, Sydney. How's it going?"

Sydney winced. Only Josephine could be this perky at 11:15 at night.

"Not so good."

Josephine's tone changed. "What's going on?"

Sydney took a deep breath. "I'm going to tell you something and I need you to stay calm because I need you to get Mom."

There was a pause on the other end. "OK. Go ahead." Josephine said finally.

"Dean was in a car accident. He's here at Toronto Western, and he's having emergency surgery," Sydney said.

Josephine gasped. "Oh God. Is it serious?"

"Yeah," Sydney said. "But I don't have the details."

"So you want me to tell Mom."

"Yes," Sydney said. "But don't tell her everything.

Just tell her there was an accident and bring her here. We'll explain everything when she gets here. All she needs to know for now is that Dean is alive. Can you do that?"

There was a pause and for a moment Sydney wondered if this was too much for her nineteen-year-old sister.

"You know what, I'm sorry," Sydney began. "I shouldn't have asked you to do this. Forget it. I'll be over to get her. . . ."

"No, it's OK," Josephine said. "I'll bring her."

Her voice sounded surer than Sydney felt and Sydney remembered why she had asked her: because on most days Josephine was more mature than most of Sydney's other siblings. Sydney hoped today would be one of those days.

Sydney let out a deep breath. "Call me when you get here and I'll tell you where we are."

"See you in a few."

Sydney leaned back in the chair and rested her head against the wall, closing her eyes. The gentle sobs of Zelia in her lap and the sniffles of JJ blended with the beep of machinery, intercom messages, and other hospital sounds. Sydney remembered the last time she was here. It was when her dad had his stroke. It had been his second one, and somehow she had known that it would be his last. Before her thoughts could descend into any further gloom, JJ's voice broke the silence.

"Sydney?"

"Yeah?" Sydney answered without moving.

She heard JJ take a ragged breath. "What if—"

"Don't," Sydney said, cutting her sister off before she could release the negative thought into the open. "Just don't."

She heard JJ sigh again. She didn't know how long they sat there. Every moment waiting to hear something, anything, felt like eternity. When the phone rang again, Sydney didn't even check the caller ID before answering.

"We're in the emerge waiting room on the first floor, Fell Pavilion," she said. "If you get lost, ask for nursing station 4."

"Syd?"

Sydney's eyes flew open and she sat up.

"Hayden?"

Hot and cold feelings ran through her at the sound of his voice. More than anything, she wished he was there right then. But there was something else there. A sudden resentment that she couldn't explain. The emotions were too much for her to handle and she felt herself break. She tried to cover her mouth to hold it in, but her sobs betrayed her.

"Syd, Syd? Baby, why are you crying—what's going on?"

Instead of soothing her, the tenderness in his voice sliced Sydney through with grief and anger.

"My brother's in the hospital. He's lying unconscious on an operating table fighting for his life because of what your sister did to him—that's what's going on."

"Whoa, Sydney, wait a minute. I don't even know what you're talking about. What did Sheree do? I don't understand—"

"Yeah, me either," Sydney said hoarsely. "Look, I can't talk to you right now."

"Hold up. Sydney, wait—"

But Sydney didn't hear the rest. She ended the call and tossed her phone on the empty seat next to her. She looked up and caught JJ staring at her. But when she met her gaze with a scowl, JJ looked away.

Time seemed to move in slow motion as they waited. Lissandra showed up next. JJ and Sydney took turns retelling whatever they knew and they all took turns crying as they came to grips with the reality of what had happened already and the possibility of what could happen in the next few hours. The real crying began, however, when Jackie showed up.

The other residents of the waiting area, whom Sydney had caught watching them curiously as their party grew in number, watched intently as Jackie came in leaning heavily on Josephine. She already looked weak, as if she had been in an accident of her own, and they immediately made space at the center of their huddle for her to sit. But when she looked up, Sydney knew that her mother still had a lot of fight left in her.

"What happened?" Jackie asked. Her voice was steady and sure, and had taken on the deep quality it did whenever there was a situation to be dealt with.

Sydney stared into her mother's expectant eyes and tried to construct the least painful version of the events as she understood them.

"Don't try and sugarcoat it, Sydney," Jackie said. "I've outlived two husbands. I'm not going to fall apart. Just tell me what happened."

Sydney nodded and took a deep breath. Then she related the details to her mother exactly how she knew them. She watched her mother's jaw tighten and her eyes close as she listened. When Sydney was done, Jackie let out a deep, shaky breath. With her eyes still closed, she opened her hands, and Sydney saw that they were shaking. She gripped one firmly as JJ grabbed the other, and she felt her mother's fingers close tightly around hers. The shaking intensified, and Sydney held Jackie's hand between both of hers as her mother began to rock back and forth. Jackie had lost husbands. But she had never lost a child. Sydney knew that the thought of losing her only son was too much for her mother.

Josephine, Zelia, and Lissandra wrapped their arms around Jackie while Sydney and JJ continued to hold her hands as she moaned quietly and shook.

Then, with her eyes still closed, Jackie did the last thing Sydney expected.

"Father, I know that all life is in your hands. I know that you see my son on the table and I know that by faith, you can heal and restore him. And so I claim your promise, trusting that you will heal him, believing that my son . . ."

Jackie's voice broke as she choked back a sob.

"The only one that you gave me. That he will not die."

When Jackie was done, JJ went next. Then Josephine, then Zelia. The air in the waiting room grew thick with her sisters' prayers, and as Sydney listened to them, something stirred inside her. Something that had been dead a long time, but was now starting to wake up. When the chain of prayer was over, JJ began to sing softly. The sound of her voice was so haunting that it triggered the tears that Sydney had been trying to hold back.

She had forgotten JJ's voice. She had forgotten how JJ used to sing almost every week in church when they were teenagers. Even then she'd had that deep, husky, soulful voice. The kind that should be coming out of a robust life-weary black woman and not a skinny cocoa-colored young girl. It was the kind of voice that made you feel everything you didn't want to feel and think about everything you wanted to ignore. But as she sang Jackie's favorite hymn, "I Must Tell Jesus," it made Sydney want to dig inside herself for some faith—even if she knew she didn't have any.

They huddled together in a cluster of clinging arms and hands until a nurse appeared to inform them that the surgery was over and that a doctor would be with them shortly to give an update. Moments later he was.

"Hello." The young man in scrubs and sneakers had freckles on his nose and couldn't have been much older than Dean. "I'm Dr. White, and I was one of the surgeons working on your son."

He clasped his hands together. "The good news is that we have managed to stop the bleeding in his brain and repaired the damage caused to his lung by the fractured ribs."

"And the bad news?" Lissandra asked.

His brow furrowed. "As you know, your brother came into the hospital unconscious due to head trauma sustained during his accident. Though we have managed to repair some of the damage, he is currently not responding to external stimuli and is showing no motor movement. . . ."

"Translation?" Zelia asked.

"He's comatose," Josephine said weakly from where she was sitting.

They all glanced from Josephine to the doctor.

"She's right. Your brother is in a coma."

Sydney felt her chest tighten as the doctor dropped the bomb on them.

Coma?

She could barely breathe.

Sydney drew a long, shaky breath before she could speak. "Will he come out of it?"

"We hope so," the doctor said. "He could wake up tomorrow, or next week, or it might be longer. It's just too early to tell right now. We've put him in a room on this floor and are having him closely monitored."

Sydney felt like the room was spinning. This couldn't be happening. Her brother was in a coma? How? This was for other people. People who were careless and who drove one hundred miles per hour over the speed limit on the highway. People who were alcoholics, who didn't care about anyone but themselves. This was not for people who followed the rules. This was not supposed to be happening to her family.

Jackie, who had been silent throughout the exchange, suddenly stood. "I would like to see him."

The doctor nodded. "That's fine. But keep the visit brief. And only two people at a time."

Josephine jumped up. "I'll go with you."

Sydney and her sisters watched as Josephine and their mother followed the nurse to Dean's room. Almost as soon as they left, Lissandra was on her feet.

"I need coffee." Without waiting for anyone's response, she headed down the hallway.

No one seemed to be able to speak. It was as if the doctor's words had robbed them of their voice. So instead, they held on to each other, joining hands like they had when they were little girls, Sydney holding JJ's hand on one side and Zelia's on the other. If only life was as simple and painless now as it was then.

Sydney hadn't even realized her eyes were closed, until she felt the pressure on her fingers from JJ. She opened her eyes and there he was. Sydney's heart fell into her stomach. The conflicting emotions that had run through her before took on greater force as his compassion-filled eyes met hers. Seeing him was worse than hearing his voice.

"You found me."

"There aren't that many hospitals with a Fell Pavilion," Hayden said, his hands in his pockets.

Sydney stood up and began to walk away. "I didn't ask you to come here."

"You didn't have to ask me," he said, less than half a step behind her. "You know I wouldn't let you go through this alone."

"I'm not alone," she said, doing double time down the corridor. "I have my sisters."

"And you have me," he said.

"I don't need you," she snapped, lashing out at him with pain and anger that she couldn't account for. "I don't want you. Since you and your family came into our lives it's been nothing but chaos. You let your sister take everything from me. Everything. And now my brother might die. So as far as I'm concerned, you can all go straight to hell."

He grabbed her arm to stop her, but she pulled back, beating her fists against his strong frame. She knew her blows hurt. She saw him flinch a couple times, but he never let her go. Instead he put his arms around her.

"It's OK, Syd. . . ."

"No! Let me go," she screamed, not caring who was looking at her as she struggled against him.

"It's OK. Do what you need to do. Hit me if you need to. But I'm not going anywhere," he said gently near her ear.

She hated that he wouldn't get angry with her. She wanted someone to shout at, to scream her frustrations at, to wear herself out fighting with so she wouldn't have the energy to hurt for Dean.

"This is your fault," she sobbed, her blows growing weaker and more far apart. "You did this, this is your fault."

She finally gave up and let him crush her against his chest. Then she cried the deep, angry sobs she would never let her sisters see. Her eyes hurt and she knew they were swelling up like tennis balls, along with her nose, but she didn't care. It didn't even matter that he was about to see her at her worst, because after tonight, he wouldn't see her at all.

But for the time being, she was content to drench his shirt and let him massage her head gently as he tried to convince her it would be OK. Then he started to pray over her, and it occurred to Sydney that this was the most prayer she had heard in one night in a long time.

As her sobs faded away, she felt his hold loosen, and she pulled away and moved toward a bench against the wall a few feet away. She sat down and rested her elbows on her knees as she covered her face with her hands. A few moments later, she felt him sink down beside her.

"So you're telling me you don't know anything about what happened," Sydney said hoarsely after a long moment.

"No," Hayden said, shaking his head.

Sydney sighed and sat back.

"Sheree took off about a week ago with everything Dean had," Sydney said. "Dean came back from his trip and the house was stripped bare. So were his bank accounts. She took everything, Hayden, even the money from the sale of the shop."

Sydney watched Hayden tense up right before her

eyes. His jaw tightened and he closed his eyes as his head fell back against the wall.

"That's why you haven't been taking my calls." Hayden rubbed a hand over his face. "Let me guess, you can't get in touch with her."

Sydney nodded. "No one has seen her since she walked out of the bank. She might as well be a ghost."

Hayden let out a frustrated sigh. "That's why your brother's here."

"He took it hard. At first he thought something might have happened to her. But when he realized the money was gone"—Sydney shook her head—"that's when things got really bad. He was drinking tonight. . . . That's how he ended up in an accident."

"Syd . . . I . . . I don't know what to say." He leaned forward and turned to look at her. "I'm so sorry. I had no idea Sheree would pull something like this. I wish I could have stopped her."

He reached for Sydney's hand, but she pulled away. "Syd . . ."

"You told me she wouldn't hurt him," Sydney said, staring straight ahead. "I asked you, and you told me we could trust her."

Hayden's eyes widened and he leaned forward to try and meet Sydney's gaze.

"Syd, I never thought she would do something like this. . . ."

"When Dad died, Dean took it hard. Really hard. But he was finally starting to deal with it. He had his whole life ahead of him," Sydney continued, her voice calm and even. "We had the shop. And I had a plan. And then you all came along."

"Sydney . . ."

"And now we have nothing."

Hayden clasped his hands in his lap and looked down.

"I know you feel like you've lost everything—"

"You don't know how I feel," Sydney said, cutting him off. No one knew how she felt. How she'd felt for the past two years as the life she planned slowly crumbled like a hill of bread crumbs. First she had lost her dad. Then the shop. Then her savings. And now her brother. There was nothing left for anyone to take from her. It was all gone.

"You told me it would be OK," Sydney said, willing the tears that burned at the back of her eyes to stay at the back of her eyes. "You said it would work out; that it would all be fine."

She stood up. "This is not what fine feels like."

"Don't do this, Sydney," he said as she began to walk away. "We can find her. We can fix this."

"No, we can't," Sydney threw over her shoulder. "There is no more 'we.'"

Sydney kept her gaze straight ahead as she walked back to where her family was. She could feel his eyes on her with every step she took, but she didn't look back. Sheree and everything connected to her was toxic to Sydney's family.

Cutting him out of her life was the best thing to do and she knew it. Even if it felt otherwise.

Chapter 18

By the time Sydney returned to the waiting area the Isaacs family had hijacked, her sisters had already returned.

"Where you been?" Lissandra asked before Sydney could sit down. Sydney ignored her. Her emotions were still close to surface level and she didn't have the patience for Lissandra at that moment.

"Is he gone?" Zelia asked.

"I hope so," Sydney said.

"Did you ask him about Sheree?"

This time Sydney did look at her sister.

"He doesn't know where she is," Sydney snapped.

"Hmm," Lissandra said, her lip curling. "Pretty convenient, don't you think?"

JJ and Zelia looked back and forth between Lissandra and Sydney. They knew better than to insert themselves into a potential squabble involving Lissandra.

"No," Sydney said, her annoyance showing. "I think he just doesn't know where she is. Why would he lie about it?"

"Why?" Lissandra asked, raising an eyebrow. "I could think of five hundred thousand reasons why."

"The man's employed by an NBA team and runs his own private practice with pro-level athletes," Zelia said, rolling her eyes. "You really think he's gonna screw that up for half of Sheree's five hundred thousand? He probably makes that much in six months."

"So I guess you believe him, too," Lissandra said, scowling.

"I believe that he's not an idiot. And getting involved in Sheree's brand of moneymaking would be an idiot move. Anyone with half a brain can see that," Zelia said.

"What you trying to say?" Lissandra said, easing off the wall she had been leaning against and stepping forward. "You trying to say I'm stupid?"

"Ladies, quit it," Sydney said, cutting things off before they went where they usually did with Zelia and Lissandra.

"Lissandra, I asked him. He said he doesn't know where she is. If he said he doesn't know anything, he doesn't know anything," Sydney said, closing the topic.

"Well, I'm glad you're sure," Lissandra said, swinging her hips as she walked slowly over to a chair across from Sydney. " 'Cause I'm not."

Lissandra glared at Sydney, but Sydney was familiar with Lissandra's mind games and this time she wasn't getting drawn in. There were more important things to worry about.

Just as she was about to lean back, Jackie and Josephine returned to the room.

"How is he?" JJ asked, as they all stood up and moved toward their mother.

"Just as the doctors said," Jackie answered. Their mother had seemed to age several years since she had gone to Dean's hospital room. She barely looked strong enough to hold herself up, and JJ and Sydney carefully lowered her into a nearby chair.

"The nurse says he's fairly stable, but he's still not responsive," Josephine continued. "They're going to keep him in ICU until his blood pressure stabilizes and his other vital signs are at normal levels."

Sydney turned to their mother. "Mom, there's nothing else we can do tonight. You need to go home and get some rest. . . ."

"I can't leave my son here alone. . . ."

"He won't be alone," Sydney said gently, rubbing her mother's hand. "I'll stick around for the rest of the night."

"Me, too," JJ added.

"You all listen to me," Jackie said. "None of you helped me carry my son the eight-and-a-half months he sat in my belly before he came into this world. You all want to go home, go ahead. But I am not leaving my son tonight."

Jackie had spoken.

"Fine, I'm staying, too," Sydney said.

"Same here," said JJ.

Lissandra rolled her eyes. "Does that mean I have to stay?"

"No, your selfish behind can take itself back home," Sydney snapped.

Lissandra scowled again and sat back down in her chair.

"I'll stay, too—" Josephine began.

"No," Jackie said, cutting her off. "It's already late. You need to get home. You and Zelia."

"No, it's OK," Zelia said. "I can stay. . . ."

"No, you can't," Jackie said firmly. "I don't want you girls here all night. Get some sleep and you can come back in the morning."

Zelia nodded, and she and Josephine kissed Jackie and said their good-byes before leaving.

A throat cleared and they all looked up to realize that the nurse from before was standing near them.

"You are welcome to stay through the night, but visiting hours end shortly. If you want to see your relative, you only have a few minutes left."

Sydney and JJ stood at the same time.

"Mom, we'll be back in a bit," JJ said, squeezing their mother's hand before she and Sydney followed the nurse down the hallway to Dean's room.

There were wires and tubes everywhere. They'd connected Dean's arm to the IV drip that hung above his head. They'd connected his chest to the machines that beeped continuously, and they connected his nose and mouth to the machine that pumped oxygen into his lungs. There were so many Sydney could barely see her brother through it all. But what she did see was enough to double up the tight knots already in her stomach. JJ started crying softly again and Sydney tried to hold her upright as her younger sister's weight collapsed against her.

"Is it as bad as it looks?" JJ asked.

Sydney nodded as she remembered what the nurse had told her right before they entered the room. "Right now he can't even breathe on his own."

Sydney felt the pull of JJ's weight as she began to sink, and she lowered her sister into a chair near Dean's bedside.

She grasped her brother's swollen hand and tried to

find the boy she had watched grow up in the bruised and bandaged face that was in front of her. This could not be it for her brother. He was only twenty-one years old. He had his whole life ahead of him. He may have been hardheaded and impulsive, but he didn't deserve to have his heart broken because of it. He certainly didn't deserve to die because of it.

Sydney suddenly couldn't breathe, as she considered the possibility of Dean dying. Of her brother not being there. The tears that had been welling up poured down her cheeks as she leaned close to Dean, lifting his still hand to her cheek.

"Dean." Tears clouded her voice. "I know you can hear me. You need to come out of this. You are too young to be lying here like this. And I am too young to watch my baby brother waste away. I need you to wake up, Dean. Just . . . wake up."

Her body shook with sobs as she held her brother's hand close to her heart. He was her heart, just like all her sisters and mother were. Just like her father had been.

There was a knock on the door and then she heard the nurse. "A few more minutes, ladies."

They sat at Dean's bed until they couldn't any longer. Then they said their good-byes and exited the room.

As soon as the door closed behind them, JJ put her arms around Sydney and started crying again and Sydney had feelings of déjà vu as she remembered her sister doing the exact same thing a little over a year earlier. They were at this same hospital, and they had just left a hospital room. Leroy's hospital room. The day they left that room there had been no machines beeping, no oxygen masks, and no IV drip. There had been no need.

As Sydney walked with her sister back to the waiting area, she prayed that the outcome this time would be different. She was tired of losing the men in her life.

Sydney's joints ached from exhaustion and from being folded into the uncomfortable waiting-room chairs for too many hours. Sleep beckoned her like a child to a loose ball, but she couldn't reach for it. Not until she knew someone would be there with Jackie. Even though her eyes had been closed most of the time, the woman hadn't slept a wink all night. Instead, she had alternated between talking to Sydney and JJ about the things she remembered from Dean's past, and talking to God about Dean's future. Lissandra, in true Lissandra style, had gone to the bathroom at about two a.m. and not come back. A text message half an hour later confirmed that she had gone home. Sydney was just impressed that her sister had managed to hang around for that long.

"What time is it?" Jackie asked. She had been more quiet the last couple of hours.

"It's almost seven," Sydney answered. "Mom, you should go home and get some rest."

"So should you," she replied. She turned to JJ. "You, too."

"We'll go when you go," JJ said.

Their mother sighed. "Fine. I'll go home for a little while. As soon as one of your sisters gets here. I don't want Dean to be alone."

Sydney exchanged a look with JJ. There would be no talking Jackie out of this one.

"OK, fine," Sydney said. "Zelia said she should be here a little after nine. Luke's going to pick her up and they'll stay for a while. Can you promise me that as soon as they get here, you'll go home?"

Jackie pursed her lips. "When they get here, then I'll consider going home."

JJ shook her head. "And you wonder where Lissandra gets her stubbornness from."

"Child, hush your mouth," Jackie said. But Sydney and JJ saw the slight tilt of her mouth toward a smile.

Zelia and Luke got to the hospital sooner than they thought.

"I got Luke to come a little earlier," she explained as she entered the waiting area, with her boyfriend just steps behind her. She leaned down and hugged Jackie. "How are you, Mom?"

"I'm fine, dear," Jackie said with a small smile. "Just glad that someone is here for Dean."

"I'm so sorry, Ms. Isaacs," Luke said, his pale skin flushed with concern as he leaned down and kissed Jackie's cheek. "If there's anything I can do, please let me know."

"You and Zelia just let me know if you hear anything about Dean," Jackie said.

He nodded his agreement.

"Now can we take you home?" JJ asked, standing and shouldering her purse.

Jackie sighed and stood tiredly. "All right. But only for a couple hours. I'll be back later."

"I'm gonna drop Mom off and then I'll meet you back at the house," JJ said.

Sydney nodded and watched as her sister and mother walked away.

"Any change?" Zelia asked, once they were out of earshot.

Sydney shook her head. "No. Same as when you left

last night. They think he's going to be like that for a while, at least until his internal injuries heal."

Zelia nodded, then looked at Sydney with concern. "You OK? I know you, and somehow you've probably figured out a way to blame yourself for this."

Sydney sighed. "I just keep wondering if somehow we could have stopped this from happening. I should have asked Hayden more about her. How could he not see that she could do something like this?"

"It happens," Zelia said with a shrug. "People can hide who they really are, even from the people closest to them. I admit it doesn't look good for him, but maybe he really didn't know anything."

Sydney nodded while stifling a yawn. "Yeah. Maybe."

"OK, you need to go home," Zelia said. "You're almost as bad as Mom, thinking you can stay up twenty-four hours. You're not nineteen anymore, girl."

"Don't I know it," Sydney said dryly as she stood up. "I'm going to head home. But I'll check in with you later."

"All right, sissy."

Sydney gave a weak wave to her sister as she headed down the same corridor her mother and sister had taken toward the parking lot. She was so exhausted. She really should take a cab home. But with her finances in the land of uncertainty, and Dean's hospital expenses on the horizon, she wasn't about to spend any money she didn't have to—even on something as small as cab fare. Instead she took the highway home, and managed to get there without incident in twenty minutes.

"Any change?" Lissandra asked as Sydney stepped through the front door.

Sydney barely glanced at her younger sister, who

was sitting on a stool near the kitchen counter with an oversized mug in her hands.

"No." Sydney slipped off her shoes and slipped onto the couch.

"So, what, you're gonna be mad at me for leaving? You and JJ were already there!" Lissandra protested.

"That's not me you're hearing in your head, Lissandra." Sydney's eyes were already closed. "It's your conscience."

Sydney heard her sister kiss her teeth but still didn't bother to open her eyes. All she needed was an hour's rest and she should be fine. However, when she felt the couch sink near her hip she had a feeling that might not be happening right away.

"Here, drink this." Lissandra nudged Sydney with her elbow.

"What?" Sydney protested, cracking her eye open. She groaned when she saw the mug. "Go away. I don't want to drink anything, Lissandra. I just want to go to sleep."

"Not yet," Lissandra said. "I need to talk to you about something."

"Now?" Sydney whined.

"Yes, now."

Sydney groaned into the cushion by her head. Lissandra had slept the whole night in her own bed. Couldn't she give Sydney a minute to just get some sleep herself?

Sydney sat up with a frown. "OK, what is it? You have sixty seconds. Literally."

"So I've been thinking . . ."

"That's never good. . . ."

". . . and the only way we're going to get back that money is if we find Sheree ourselves."

Sydney's mouth fell. "Seriously? That is what couldn't wait until I got an hour of sleep?"

"This is serious, Syd."

"No, Lissandra," Sydney said, her voice going up a decibel. "Serious is our brother, lying on a hospital bed, teetering between death and life. I couldn't care less about Sheree right now."

"But this *is* about Dean," Lissandra insisted. "If we don't find that woman and that money, how are we going to afford Dean's care?"

Sydney sighed. "There are five of us. Six if you include Mom. Among the lot of us, we can come up with the money."

"Can we?" Lissandra challenged. "Last time I checked, you and I are pretty much broke, and Zelia and Josephine are still in school."

"That still leaves Mom and JJ and the shop . . ."

"Please. Mom and JJ and their dress shop that takes as much money as it generates?"

Sydney sighed as the reality of Lissandra's words came home to her.

"We aren't the Joneses, Syd. We don't have anything to fall back on. If Dean ends up being in that coma longer than expected, we're going to be in trouble. Even if he doesn't, once he's awake, you know he's probably going to need a lot of care before he's back to normal. That kind of care costs money."

Sydney took the mug from Lissandra. "What are you thinking?"

"We need to talk to Essie," Lissandra said.

Sydney almost choked on the hot liquid.

"What?" Sydney and Lissandra both looked up at JJ, who had just come through the door. "You want us to call Essie?"

Lissandra hissed her teeth. "This is why I wanted to have this conversation *before* she got here."

"I can't believe you are letting her even suggest this, Syd." JJ closed the front door before coming into the living room.

"OK, Lissandra," Sydney said, trying to hide the amusement in her voice. "I know we need to do something, but Essie?"

"Yes, Essie, the former police officer and current private investigator. If anyone can track Sheree, she can."

"If anyone can get Momma's blood pressure up, she can," JJ countered.

"Hey, just because Mom doesn't talk to her own sister doesn't mean we can't," Lissandra said.

"OK, OK, let's just calm down." Sydney raised the mug, to silence her sisters.

"JJ, Lissandra's right. You know Aunt Essie can find a priest at a gay pride parade. If we really want to find Sheree, she's the one."

"Thank you!" Lissandra said.

"But," Sydney continued, "if Mom finds out that we went to see Aunt Essie, she's gonna hit the roof. . . ."

"Exactly," JJ said.

"So." Sydney paused. "We can't tell her."

"That's what I'm talking about," Lissandra said, getting up triumphantly.

"Sydney, I can't believe you."

"I know, JJ, and if you come up with a better suggestion in the next two hours, then we'll consider it." Sydney got up and headed toward the stairs. "Otherwise, I'm going to bed. And if anyone wakes me up again, I can't be responsible for what I do to you."

Sydney ascended the stairs to the sound of her sisters arguing. Going to see Aunt Essie was always a last resort. But desperate times called for desperate measures. And right now, things looked more desperate than ever.

Chapter 19

Essie's office was located near Old Toronto, just a stone's throw from the infamous Regent Park community that most people wouldn't visit in broad daylight, much less at night. It was in the middle of a street of tightly packed shops and businesses whose edifices had seen better days. The entrance to Essie's second-floor office was strategically located between a shady-looking law office and a Cash Money payday loan center, with which she often shared customers.

"This is a bad idea." JJ pushed her shades farther up her nose as she, Lissandra, and Sydney climbed the stairs to Essie's office.

Lissandra glanced back at her younger sister, who was almost unrecognizable in the head wrap and oversized sunglasses. "No one asked you to come, Erykah Badu."

"Well, someone needs to be the voice of reason in this, since Sydney has clearly lost that ability."

"JJ, the wisest man said there's a season for everything under the sun," Sydney said as she crowned the top of the stairs.

"I didn't see anything in there about a season for going behind your mother's back," JJ grumbled.

Sydney pressed the doorbell. "Well, you can't expect the man to list everything."

The door opened to reveal a gorgeous, slim-but-toned man whose racial ambiguity made him an advertiser's dream and eye candy for women of all backgrounds.

"Model," Lissandra whispered.

Sydney shook her head. "Too short. Actor."

JJ tipped her sunglasses down. "Uh-uh. Singer/dancer."

"Actually, it's actor." He opened the door wider, letting them into the main area.

"Told you," Sydney said as she stepped inside.

"That's actor slash receptionist, so can I help you?" he asked, when he had taken a seat behind his desk.

"We're here to see Essie," Sydney said.

"Do you have an appointment?"

"We don't need one." Lissandra stepped past him toward her aunt's office.

He jumped to his feet. "Now, just wait a minute. . . ."

"Essie, we're here," Lissandra said, knocking twice on the door before opening it and letting herself in, with Sydney only steps behind her.

"Sorry." JJ threw him an apologetic look before following her sisters inside.

He was at the door of the office in less than a second.

"Ms. Isaacs, I am so sorry. . . ."

"Don't worry about it, Mars." She stood up, revealing toned, leather-clad legs. "These are my twin sister's kids."

His mouth fell open. "You have a twin sister?"

"Close the door on your way out, would you?"

The actor/receptionist looked back and forth between the four of them before shaking his head and exiting the office, closing the door behind him.

"What happened to the last guy?" Lissandra asked, making herself comfortable in one of the chairs across from Essie's desk.

"Too much drama." Essie's long, blood red nails clicked together as she waved her hand. "That's what I get for hiring all these wannabe actors."

She grinned. "They sure are easy on the eyes, though."

JJ groaned and Sydney couldn't help but chuckle as she took in her aunt.

One would never believe that Essie Isaacs had shared a womb with Jackie and was in fact seven minutes older than her. Sydney herself would have doubted the fact that they were identical twins, except she had seen the pictures. But as far as she could tell, Essie and Jackie were night and day. While Jackie was curvy from carrying six children in her body, Essie was lean and toned, as if she spent every day of her life in a gym. Jackie's features were soft and motherly. Essie's identical ones had a sharper edge. And while Jackie had never strayed far from her natural auburn hair color, Sydney had never known her aunt's to be anything but a golden blond. In fact, Essie had been dying her hair blond for so long that Sydney suspected it had probably started growing out of her head that color.

But the physical differences were just the tip of the iceberg. Even though both Jackie and Essie had grown up in a Christian home, and even though both had wandered away, Essie had yet to find her way back. It wasn't that she didn't believe there was a God. She just didn't believe that he had anything to do with her.

There were a few things they did have in common, however: specifically, their inability to remain married to one man and their refusal to take any of those men's last names.

"So, what kind of trouble have you girls gotten yourselves into now?" Essie asked, leaning her hip against her desk.

"Can't we just come see our aunt?" Lissandra asked, sticking a cigarette in the corner of her mouth and pulling out a lighter. "Why do we have to be in trouble?"

" 'Cause that's the only time you're willing to risk my sister's wrath to see me." Essie pulled the cigarette out of Lissandra's mouth and tossed it into the garbage. "No smoking in my office."

"You're right, Auntie . . ." Sydney began.

"Hey, none of that 'Auntie' stuff," Essie said, cutting her off. "Makes me feel old. Just Essie."

Sydney rolled her eyes. "OK, Essie. We do have a bit of a situation. Your nephew went and got himself married."

"What?"

"Yes," Lissandra continued. "And the gold-digging spawn of Satan got him to sell Decadent and then cleaned him out."

"She took everything," Sydney said.

"Everything?"

"Everything," the three sisters echoed.

"Dean took it so hard he got drunk and ran his car into a tree," JJ put in. "He's in the hospital in intensive care."

"And Mrs. Dean Isaacs is still MIA," Sydney added.

"Along with five hundred thousand dollars of our family's money," Lissandra finished.

Essie looked back and forth between the three of

them, then reached into her purse and pulled out a cigarette.

"I'm gonna need a smoke for this."

"I thought you said no smoking in your office?" Lissandra protested.

Essie slid open a door to a tiny balcony and stepped
out onto it. "This ain't the office."

"So let me guess: you need to find her," Essie said
after she had taken a few puffs.

"Yes," Sydney said.

"What about the police?"

"We already went through that," JJ said. "They
couldn't find anything on Sheree in the system."

Essie nodded. She took a few more puffs, then put
out the cigarette and dropped the butt in a planter on
the balcony.

"OK," she said, unbuttoning her jacket as she sat
down in front of her computer. "Tell me what you know
about this heifer."

Sydney gave her everything she knew about Sheree,
including her last known address in Toronto, her last
place of employment, and her social insurance number,
which Sydney had been able to find on some documents included in the paperwork for the sale of the
shop.

"OK, I got something," Essie said, squinting at the
screen.

The three women leaned forward.

"What is it?" Lissandra asked eagerly.

"You said this girl was twenty-two, right?"

"Yeah," JJ said. "Her birthday is May fifteen."

"Now, that's your first problem. 'Cause according to
the government of Canada, Sheree Vern's birthday is

September twenty-two, and as of that last birthday, she was twenty-six."

"What?"

"Twenty-six?"

"She doesn't look like twenty-six."

"Come on now, you know black don't crack," Essie said. "But that's not even your biggest problem."

Sydney pursed her lips. "Keep going."

"Well, based on the records here, Sheree Vern graduated high school in Ontario in 2004."

"OK," Lissandra said. "So?"

"So, up to 2004, there is activity for her. Bank accounts, medical records, tax information, basically proof of life," Essie began. "But after that, there's nothing."

"Nothing?" JJ echoed. "What do you mean 'nothing'?"

"There's no registration at a college, no credit card or bank account activity, no doctor visits or dental checks, no nothing. She didn't even file taxes. It was as if she dropped off the map from 2004 until about two years ago," Essie said. "As far as this country is concerned, for seven years she didn't exist."

Sydney shook her head, confused. "How could she just not exist? She must have been somewhere doing something."

"Exactly," Essie said. "And I have a feeling if you figure that out, you'll be a lot closer to figuring out where she is."

"This is ridiculous." JJ shook her head. "This is not some TV show. There must be an explanation for where she was. Maybe she was out of the country or something. Living overseas. For the year I was away, my record probably looks like that, too."

"No, sugar," Essie said. "Even if she was away, there would be some clue. Flight records, immigration records, visa requests, border check-ins. Plus you still have to file your taxes even if you're out of the country. There is nothing for this woman. Her passport was not used in 2005 or during the time that she was off the grid."

Sydney got up and began to pace as thoughts began to stir in her mind. It was ridiculous. So ridiculous that she didn't want to say it out loud. But she had to.

"What if . . ." Sydney paused as her sisters and aunt turned to look at her. "What if she was someone else?"

"Huh?"

"In the seven years that she was missing, what if she was using a different identity?" Sydney asked. "It would explain why she was able to be off the grid for so long."

Essie shrugged. "Could be. But you said this girl has family, right?"

"Yeah," Sydney said.

"So why didn't they report her missing or dead that whole time?" Essie asked. "They must have been in touch with her. They must know something. They're the ones you need to talk to."

Lissandra cleared her throat, JJ's eyes fell to her lap, and Sydney avoided looking at both of them.

Essie's eyes passed over the three of them one by one.

"OK, spit it out," she said finally.

"What?" JJ asked.

"You girls are hiding something," Essie said, narrowing her eyes. "You stink of it. So you might as well tell me what it is."

Sydney waved away her aunt's suspicion. "It's noth—"

"Sydney's dating Sheree's brother."

"Lissandra!"

Essie turned to Sydney, an eyebrow raised.

"It's not what you think," Sydney began. "We actually started dating before we even knew our siblings were married. We grew up together. His dad was friends with our dad. And Sheree is only his half sister."

"Half is better than none, sugar," Essie said. "And if you want to find this Sheree girl, you're going to need to work that half."

"We already broke up," Sydney said.

"Only in your mind," Lissandra supplied. "He called twice while you were still at the hospital."

Sydney sank into a chair and rubbed her eyes.

"This isn't right, Syd," JJ said. "You can't use his feelings for you to pump information from him about Sheree."

"JJ, if you don't have anything useful to say, why don't you shut up," Lissandra snapped.

"I am not going to sit here and act like this is OK," JJ shot back. "We want to find Sheree, but we can't walk on people to do it. That's not the way."

"And what other way—"

"No," Sydney cut Lissandra off. "JJ is right. We're not going to use Hayden to find Sheree. I'll ask him what he knows, and if he doesn't know anything, we'll find another way."

"You sure that's going to be good enough?" Essie asked, leaning back in her chair.

Sydney stood up as they prepared to leave. "It will have to be."

Lissandra kissed her teeth as she stood up. "I swear I am the only one with any backbone in this family."

"If that's what backbone looks like, then thank God for that," JJ muttered.

"Girls, I'm sorry about Dean," Essie said. "Let me know what ward he's on and I'll send over a basket."

Sydney looked at the sadness on her aunt's face. "Or you could come visit."

Essie snorted and busied herself with some papers on her desk. "Please, you know your momma and me can't be within twenty feet of each other. And I know she won't leave that boy's side till he opens his eyes."

Sydney nodded.

"But if I can help you find this hussy, I will," Essie said with renewed vigor. "You find out what you can from that boyfriend of yours and let me know. In the meanwhile, I'll keep digging. If it's there, Essie will find it. You can believe that."

Sydney and her sisters said their good-byes to Essie before exiting the office. Lissandra blew a kiss at the actor/receptionist, who scowled in return.

"See, it was a good thing we came," Sydney said as they headed down the stairs to the sidewalk. "Now we know something that we didn't know before."

"What's that?" JJ asked.

Sydney slipped on her sunglasses as she stepped out into the bright sunlight, even as the harsh reality of their situation hit her.

"When it comes to Sheree, we're not dealing with an amateur."

Chapter 20

Sydney paced the entryway inside the front door as she waited. It had taken her a week, but she had finally gotten the nerve to call Hayden. Their discussion had been brief and had consisted mainly of him agreeing to come over after he got done with his two-o'clock client. He had suggested they meet for lunch instead, but Sydney had made up some excuse about having to work. The conflict, however, had little to do with her working and more to do with her ability to be in the same room with Hayden for an extended period of time. She had not seen or spoken to him since the day at the hospital, and she wasn't sure how she would feel when she finally saw him, especially given the conversation they were about to have.

The sound of tires crunching gravel alerted Sydney to his arrival.

"He's here," Lissandra said, coming out of the kitchen.

"Thanks." Sydney didn't try to hide the sarcasm. "I know. Why are *you* here again?"

"Moral support." Lissandra threw the door open before Hayden could even get his hand on it.

"Hey, Hayden," Lissandra said, beckoning him inside. "Long time no see."

"Back at you." Even though his response was for Lissandra, his eyes locked on Sydney and stayed there.

"Hey." Sydney's eyes drank in his tall, handsome form. She could tell he hadn't shaved that morning, from the shadow on his jaw. She longed to reach out and touch it, rub her thumb across his full lips. It had just been one week, but it felt like forever since she had been in his arms. When had she gotten so attached to him?

"Hey, yourself," he said with half a smile. "Thanks for calling."

"Thanks for coming."

Sydney heard a throat clear and realized that Lissandra was still there.

"Uh, why don't you have a seat." Sydney motioned to the living room. "I'll be right with you."

Hayden seemed to weigh the option of declining, but then nodded and made his way to the couch.

"I'll be in the back," Lissandra said, lowering her voice for Sydney's ears only. "Don't punk out."

Sydney watched her sister disappear down the hallway, then made her way into the living room where Hayden sat waiting on the couch.

She chose the chair opposite him, on the other side of the coffee table.

"So," she began. She spun her watch on her wrist as she tried to think of what to say next.

Hayden watched her before shaking his head and sitting back.

"Wow. This is awkward."

She sighed. "I know. And that's my fault. I shouldn't have gone off on you at the hospital like that."

He shrugged. "It's OK. How is Dean?"

"Still in the coma," Sydney said, her eyes dropping to the floor. "The doctors say his lower-body injuries seem to be healing well. But until he wakes up, they won't know about his brain functioning."

"I've been praying for you all. My dad and the family have been, too," he said. "I'm sorry you all had to go through this."

"Yeah," Sydney said. "It's only been a few months since Dean's been back home, and already so much has happened."

Hayden let out a deep breath. "I'm sorry about Sheree, too. I just can't believe she would do something like this." He shook his head. "I don't know what happened to her."

Sydney began spinning her watch again.

"Have you spoken to her?" Sydney asked.

Hayden looked down and shook his head.

"I tried calling our mother, to see if she had seen or heard from her. But she hasn't spoken to Sheree in over a year. She didn't even know she was married."

Hayden put his head in his hands.

"How could she do something like this?" Sydney asked, an edge stealing into her voice. "What kind of person does that?"

"She wasn't always this way," he said, shaking his head. "Things have just been hard for her, that's all. And I'm not saying that makes what she did right, but that's the only way I can try and explain it."

"That's not good enough." Tears sprung to Sydney's eyes. "Because if my brother . . ."

She covered her mouth as unexpected sobs stole her voice.

"If my brother dies," she sobbed, "it would be her fault."

She closed her eyes as the hot tears slid down her cheeks. She hadn't allowed herself to think that way until that very moment. But it was a very real possibility that Dean would not recover. The doctors were hesitant to say it, but Sydney could see it in their eyes. And the longer he stayed unconscious, the more unlikely a full and complete recovery seemed.

She felt arms around her and she realized that Hayden was kneeling in front of her, pulling her close. She let him cocoon her in his arms as she pressed her face against his chest and cried the tears for her brother that she thought she had been done crying.

"He's not going to die," he whispered to her as his hand traced soothing circles on her back. "God is going to heal Dean. I believe that, and you have to believe that, too."

Sydney wanted to believe, but it was hard. She had prayed for God to heal her dad and he hadn't. In her mind she knew that her father had already been living in pain because of his first stroke, and that God had his reasons for doing what he did, but in her heart that hadn't made it hurt any less.

When she finally pulled away, she found Hayden's coffee-colored eyes staring at her with concern. Could eyes like that lie to her? If he knew where Sheree was, would he tell her?

"Look, I know I can't make up for what my sister's done," he began. "But if there's any way I can help . . . If you need help with Dean's medical bills, anything . . ."

"No," Sydney shook her head. "We're fine. But thanks."

"OK," he said. "But if that changes . . ."

"I'll let you know," she said.

He gently wiped the tears from her face with his fingers.

"How about you?" he asked. "How are you dealing with this?"

She knew what he was asking. They both knew her last few interactions with Dean hadn't been the most positive.

She took a deep breath. "I'm fine. I don't care about the shop or anything. I just want Dean to be better."

He nodded, then pulled her closer, kissing both her eyelids.

"You know I'm here for you," he said softly, his forehead resting against hers. "If you need anything, or you just want to talk, or you need to get away, I'm here."

Sydney closed her eyes. He was making it hard for her to not trust him.

"OK," she said with a sigh. "Just promise me something."

"Anything."

"If you hear from Sheree, you'll tell me."

"Sydney, forget about her for now. Right now, you need to focus on Dean. . . ."

"Hayden, promise me."

He sighed and kissed her forehead. "If I hear anything major, I'll let you know."

"Thank you."

She slipped her arms around his shoulders and he stood, lifting her off the floor as his strong, steady arms returned her embrace. Yes, she had definitely missed being close to him.

"I have to get back to the shop," she said, when they finally let go of each other.

"Yeah," he said with a nod. "I have to get back to the clinic, too."

She nodded and followed him to the door.

"So we're good?" he asked.

She nodded. "We're good."

"Great," he stepped closer. " 'Cause, baby, I've really missed you."

His lips found hers briefly, but it was enough to make Sydney wish she could blow off the rest of her afternoon. Minus the blip at the hospital, it had been more than two weeks since she'd last seen him.

"Later?" she breathed against his lips.

"Definitely."

"Leaving already?" Lissandra asked, appearing at the doorway with them.

"Duty calls." Hayden glanced at Sydney affectionately. "But I'll be back."

"Well, thanks so much for coming by," Lissandra said, throwing her arms around Hayden in a hug. "I know it meant a lot to Sydney."

"Uh, no problem." Hayden patted her back awkwardly as he shot Sydney a questioning look.

"OK." Lissandra stepped back. "Take care."

Sydney eyed her sister suspiciously as Lissandra watched Hayden make his way to his car.

Sydney folded her arms. "What was that about?"

"What?" Lissandra's eyes were still outside, where Hayden was starting his car.

"You don't even hug your own brother." She narrowed her eyes at her sister. "What's with the sudden affection toward my boyfriend?"

"Because"—Lissandra waited until Hayden had driven off before closing the door—"I needed this."

She held open her hand with Hayden's cell phone in it.

"You lifted his cell phone!"

"Hell yes," Lissandra said. "Once you went all weepy, I knew your little lovesick behind wouldn't get anything from him."

"I'm lovesick because I get emotional over my brother in a coma in the hospital?"

"Save the dramatics." Lissandra headed to the living room. "I just need to see if there's anything on this phone about Sheree."

"Well, you won't get anything. It's password protected." Sydney followed her sister into the living room. She sank into the couch. "I can't believe you stole his cell phone. Where did you learn to do that?"

"What's the password?"

Sydney let out a laugh. "You must be smoking more than just cigarettes if you think I'm going to help you break into his phone."

"Come on, Sydney," Lissandra said in frustration. "All we need to see is if there's a number for Sheree, or a record of a last call, or a text message from her."

"He said he hasn't heard from her."

"And you believe him?" Lissandra asked in disbelief. "If the tables were turned, would you rat out Dean?"

Sydney bit her lip. "Maybe."

Lissandra threw her a knowing look.

"OK, I don't know," Sydney admitted.

"Exactly." Lissandra's eyes went back to the screen as she tried different combinations. "Look, the worst that could happen is we find nothing, you can say I told you so, and you have an excuse to have him come back over here."

Sydney bit her lip. Lissandra did have a point. Plus she liked the thought of having Hayden come back. Somehow being with him made everything else bearable.

"OK, fine," Sydney said. "But we don't look at anything unless I say it's OK."

"Whatever," Lissandra said, moving over to where Sydney was sitting and squeezing in beside her. "Let's just get this done before he figures out it's missing."

"OK, so what have you tried?"

"Your birthday, your first name, and your middle name, the date of the NBA party where he first ran into you again . . ."

"Try his graduation date, 062000."

"Nope."

"Try 200607, that's when he won MVP."

"Keep going."

"Sheree's birthday?"

"Which one?"

"Try both."

"Nope," Lissandra said. "How about his birthday."

"Too easy."

They kept tossing out options, but each one turned out wrong. Suddenly Sydney sat forward.

"What?" Lissandra asked, curious.

"Try 050708."

Lissandra sat forward. "That's it!" She turned to look at Sydney. "What's that?"

Sydney closed her eyes. "The first day of the rest of his life."

"Huh?"

"Never mind." Sydney shook off the sense of guilt that settled around her. "Let's just get this done."

Sydney felt awkward going through Hayden's phone. She had never been an insecure girlfriend. Even though she knew that Hayden got a lot of attention from women, it never bothered her. But going through something as private as his cell phone was different. All it took was one text message out of context to change things.

It wasn't long before they found Sheree's number in the address book. It was the same as the one they found in Dean's phone, so it didn't help much. The call history showed that Hayden had been in touch with his sister quite a bit, but nothing past the week she went missing. Same with text messages.

"See? I told you," Sydney said. "He's not a liar."

"Whoa, not so fast," Lissandra said. "There's a missed call, from her."

"What? Where?" Sydney asked, pulling Lissandra's hand with the phone closer.

Lissandra scrolled through the list until Sheree's name and number showed up again.

"It's from a week ago," said Lissandra.

"Look at this, though," Sydney said. "One minute before, there's another missed call from another number. Maybe she called from that number first, he didn't pick up, then she called back from her number, thinking he would recognize it and answer."

"Only one way to find out." Lissandra pressed the green call button for the unknown number and put the phone on speaker. It rang twice before a cheery female voice came over the line.

"Welcome to Best Western Mississauga, how can I help you?"

Lissandra and Sydney looked at each other.

"Hello?"

Lissandra ended the call.

"Call Essie," Sydney said, taking Hayden's phone from Lissandra and getting up. "Tell her we'll be there in ten minutes."

"Why?" Lissandra asked, even as she followed Sydney to the coat closet.

Sydney slipped on her jacket and gloves before opening the front door.

"We need to get into his voice mail."

"So in less than a week you've figured out where this girl was staying, figured out she called her brother, and managed to jack his cell phone. Man, I should have you all working for me."

Sydney handed the phone to her aunt, then took the chair next to Lissandra's.

"Lissandra stole the phone, not me," Sydney said. "If anyone ever asks, I'm throwing her under the bus first."

"Thanks for the warning," Lissandra said dryly.

"So I have a few ideas, but what do you want me to do with this?" Essie asked, her eyes on Sydney.

"First, we want to get into his voice mail," Sydney said. "I think she's too smart for it, but there is a possibility that Sheree may have left him a message there."

"You can do that. Right?" Lissandra asked.

Essie laughed. "Sugar, you can't imagine some of the things I can do."

"Well, let's just limit it to that for now," Sydney said, as she watched her aunt connect Hayden's phone to her computer.

It wasn't long before she had accessed the voice mail and was going through the most recent messages. She asked Sydney if she wanted to hear, but Sydney declined. The less she knew, the better. The only thing she was concerned about was information about Sheree.

"OK, I got something," Essie said after a few minutes. "Listen to this."

Essie disconnected the headset so all three of them could listen to the audio.

"Message received at seven thirty p.m.: I can't believe you called Mom. Now she's blowing up my cell every ten minutes. I can't deal with her and your girlfriend's people on my back. Look, don't worry about me. I'm fine. But I'm ditching this phone. I'll call you when I can."

"When was that message?" Sydney asked.

"Last week," Essie said. "After the missed call you guys caught."

"So you can bet she already got rid of the phone," Lissandra said.

"And she's probably not at the Best Western anymore either," Sydney said. "Do you think they would have a record of her, though?"

"Probably not under her name," Essie said. "And she probably paid cash. We don't know how long she was staying there, if she was actually staying there, or if she was just using the phone."

"Great," Lissandra said with a huff. "So we're back to square one."

Lissandra got up and went onto the little balcony to light a cigarette.

"I don't get it." Sydney got up and began pacing. "Sheree stole that money a week before she made that call to Hayden. Why was she in Mississauga, just an hour away from here? Five hundred thousand dollars can get you far, far away. Why stick around?"

"Maybe she wants to be close to her brother or mother," Essie volunteered. "Maybe she has other ties to the city that we don't know about."

"I couldn't care less why she stuck around," Lissandra chipped in from the balcony. "I just want to know where she is with my money. Essie, you said you had ideas."

"I do," Essie began. "This girl said she would call your man back. She may have already done that. But in the event that she hasn't we may be able to track her through your boyfriend's phone."

Sydney stepped closer to her aunt's desk. "How."

"There's software we can download onto his phone that will allow us to connect into his calls and messages. He won't even know it's there, but if she calls again, we may be able to listen in."

"That's great," Lissandra said. "Let's do it."

"That's your sister's call." Essie turned her eyes from Lissandra to her other niece. "What do you want to do, Syd?"

Sydney paced the floor behind the chairs again. First they were just looking at text messages and call records. Now they were tapping into Hayden's phone. What was she doing? Hayden had promised her he would tell her if he heard from Sheree. He knew how much what had happened had affected her family. He told her he was there for her. He cared about her.

However, he had also told her he hadn't heard from Sheree, when the voice mail message they had just listened to said the opposite. She knew he wouldn't intentionally hurt her, but she had seen the look in his eyes when he talked about Sheree. He wanted to save his sister. Just like she wanted to save Dean. In the end, blood was always thicker than water.

"OK, put the tap in," Sydney said. "But no one listens to those calls but you, Essie."

"You got it."

"And I only want to hear about the stuff that has to do with Sheree. Nothing else."

"You have my word."

A sudden feeling of anxiety swept over Sydney. But as she waited for Essie to finish loading the software onto Hayden's phone, she ignored it. What she couldn't ignore was the smirk on Lissandra's face.

"Well, well, look who grew a backbone." She gave Sydney a once-over. "Good job, big sister. I knew you had it in you."

Sydney turned away. Now she knew she had crossed over. Because if Lissandra thought it was a good idea, it was definitely all bad.

Chapter 21

After leaving Essie, Sydney swung by the shop to check in. Things had been pretty slow in the past two weeks, since Sydney had stopped taking jobs past the date when Decadent would close. Dean had sold all the equipment with the store, so there was no way she would be able to fulfill the specialty orders she used to. Her oven at home could only handle smaller jobs. She could still swing a couple wedding cakes or simple specialty cakes if she had enough lead time. But cakes like the one she had made for the Raptors party were absolutely out of the question.

It had been even harder to be in the shop over the last week since the sign had gone up about the closing. Sydney couldn't deal with the stream of "why" and "what will you do next" questions that seemed to flow from people who had patronized the shop for years. She knew it was unfair to leave it all to Wendy and the other staff. But they had been trained in what to say, and at least there was no risk of them breaking down when people started to tell stories about the good old days when Leroy Halton used to be there.

After a brief meeting with a client for a birthday cake and cupcakes, she went into the kitchen to prep for the job, which she would complete early the next morning.

"Hey, boss lady, how's it going?" Mario asked from the sink where he was washing down some tins.

"I'm hanging in there," Sydney said with a small smile. "How have things been going here?"

"Same old same old," Mario said. "Sad staff, sad customers. It's a regular pity party."

"I know," Sydney said. "I was thinking maybe we should have a farewell event for our staff on the last day. What do you think?"

"I think it's too early to be talking about farewells," Mario said. "Where's your faith, Syd?"

"It disappeared with the last of my bank balance, after I paid our last Hydro bill yesterday," Sydney joked.

"Seriously, Syd." Mario turned off the pipe. "Don't you believe God will find a way to save this store?"

"I believe that faith is for people who have a strong relationship with God." She measured out sugar into a glass container. "And honestly speaking, I can't say I have that."

Sydney had come to this sad realization recently when she had started praying for Dean. She had realized that she couldn't remember the last time she'd gotten on her knees to talk to God personally about anything. She had even begun to ask herself what she bothered going to church for. Maybe it was just a routine. Something she did because she was supposed to do it. But as for a relationship with God? She wasn't even sure what that looked like.

"Then what's stopping you now?"

"It's not that simple."

"Why not?" Mario leaned against the sink to watch Sydney. "You go to church. . . ."

"Just because I go to church doesn't mean I have a relationship," Sydney said. "Look at Lissandra. She used to go to church all the time, too. You think she has a relationship with God?"

"Don't judge your sister," Mario said. "She's on a path of her own, and when God's ready he'll get to her. You need to worry about yourself, because all this happening around you right now may be God's way of trying to get to you."

Sydney covered the sugar and moved to the spices.

"Well, he sure has a funny way of doing it."

"Hey," Mario said, wiping the counter. "Some of us he calls in the silence, others of us he calls in the storm."

Sydney was still thinking about Mario's words hours later as she got off the elevator at the hospital on Dean's floor. Visiting hours would end in a few minutes, but the staff at the hospital had overlooked the policy for Sydney and her family, as long as they didn't make too much noise coming to and going from Dean's room.

Jackie was dozing in a chair by Dean's bedside when Sydney slipped inside the quiet room. Jackie had all but shut down the dress shop she ran with JJ since Dean had been hospitalized. Not once in Sydney's hospital visits had she found her mother absent.

Instead of waking her, Sydney sat down in the chair on the other side of Dean's bed. He looked a lot better than that first night. The swelling around his face had gone down, and the bruises looked less gruesome than before. A little hair had begun to grow back where they had shaved his head for the initial surgery and he was finally starting to look like the Dean she knew.

She took his hand in hers and squeezed it.

"Dean, it's me," she said quietly, hoping not to wake her mom. "I know you can hear me, so you can quit it with the silent treatment."

She smiled, knowing that if her brother was awake, he would have given some smart-aleck response followed by the handsome grin that he had inherited from their father. Dean had always been carefree like that. He did whatever he wanted whenever he wanted. Though it often drove Sydney crazy, sometimes she envied him for it. Maybe it had to do with being the younger of several siblings. He always knew that there would be someone to take care of him in case anything happened.

"I'm sorry for the way things ended between us," Sydney said, still holding her brother's hand. "You know you drive me crazy, but it's only because I love you. I guess I just took it for granted that you would always be there."

Sydney sighed. "You have so much life ahead of you. I didn't always get your music thing, but I know how talented and passionate you are about it. The world needs to see that. So, whenever you're ready to come out of this, we're here."

"Glad to hear it," Jackie said with her eyes still closed.

"Mom!" Sydney scolded. "I was having a private conversation with my brother. Were you awake the whole time?"

"Of course I was," Jackie said. "Just because my eyes were closed doesn't mean I was sleeping."

"Yeah, OK. Guess that snore was just you clearing your throat."

"Hush now," her mother said, straightening up in her chair. "Don't spoil this good day. You know they took him off the ventilator today? He breathed on his own for a few hours."

Sydney's eyes widened. "Really?"

"Yes." Jackie smiled. "They want to watch his vitals some more and then tomorrow they might take him off it for good."

"That's great." Excitement filled her voice. "That means he's recovering."

"That it does." Jackie squeezed her son's other hand lovingly. "They keep telling me to not get too excited, that he has a long way to go. But they don't know my God. I've been talking to him and he told me my boy is going to be all right."

Sydney watched her mother, a bit envious of her certainty.

"Don't look at me like that," Jackie said. "If you knew God like I know him, you would be sure, too."

Sydney was starting to wonder if the people in her life had had a meeting about her.

"If you say it's so, Mom, then that's good enough for me," Sydney said.

"You can't survive on someone else's relationship, Sydney," Jackie said, getting up and walking toward the door. "You have to have your own."

"Where are you going?" Sydney asked, watching her mother.

"Cafeteria," Jackie said, wrinkling her nose. "I'm not a fan of their food, but I haven't eaten all day."

Sydney frowned. "I can run out and get you something. . . ."

"Don't trouble yourself," Jackie said, waving a hand at Sydney. "I just need a little snack to hold me over until Zelia brings me something later. You spend some time with your brother."

Sydney had only spent a few minutes with Dean when she felt her phone vibrate. When she dug through her purse, however, she realized that it wasn't her phone but Hayden's. She had called him at work and then on his house phone and left messages earlier that afternoon, but he still hadn't gotten in touch with her about his missing cell phone. She was beginning to get concerned that he might be missing important calls, and so she left the room briefly to try calling again.

She listened to his line at the clinic ring as she walked to a quiet spot near the end of the hallway where she could still keep an eye on Dean's room. After what seemed like forever, the line finally picked up.

"East York Athletic Clinic."

"Dub! Finally," Sydney said, relieved.

"Nini." The warmth in his voice made Sydney melt. "I got your messages, but I've been backed up all evening. I had a last-minute client and then I had to run over to the ACC for an evening meeting with the boys."

"No, it's fine," Sydney said. "It's just that your phone rang a couple times and I was worried that it might be important."

Hayden laughed. "Baby, that phone rings off the hook. I probably got more done not having it than having it."

"Mhmm," Sydney murmured distractedly, as she noticed the door to Dean's room swinging closed. She hadn't seen who had gone in, but it must have been a nurse. Her mother couldn't have made it back that fast.

"So I know this might put you out of your way, but can you bring it to me?" he asked.

"Uh, sure," Sydney said, taking a few steps closer to Dean's room. "Where will you be?"

"I'll probably be at the ACC until ten tonight. I'll let Robby know that you're coming by and he'll send you up when you get here."

"Yeah, OK, I'll try to make it by that time," Sydney said. "Have you eaten? Do you need me to bring you anything?"

"No, they're ordering us dinner," Hayden said. "Just bring yourself. That will be good enough for me."

Sydney smiled. "OK, baby, I'll see you later."

"See you," Hayden echoed before ending the call.

Sydney was about to slip the phone into her pocket when she saw Dean's door open and a woman with dark hair step out. Sydney frowned. That wasn't a nurse. She knew all the nurses on the floor, and none of them wore their hair out like that. Besides, the woman wasn't wearing a uniform.

Sydney walked faster to see if she could catch up with the person.

"Excuse me, ma'am?"

The woman turned around, caught sight of Sydney, and started running. Without thinking, Sydney took off after her down the hall, barely dodging a food cart and skirting around a group of nurses headed in the opposite direction.

"Wait!" Sydney called out. But the woman kept running down the halls, into the stairway. By the time Sydney got to the stairs, the woman was already two floors down. All Sydney could see was the top of what she now recognized to be a wig.

She went as fast as she could, but even taking the steps two at a time she couldn't catch up with her. The woman finally reached the bottom and burst through the doors to the exit. By the time Sydney made it out the doors, she was gone, swallowed up in the night.

Sydney leaned against the rail of the outside landing and fought to catch her breath as she searched the dark night for any trace of Dean's mystery visitor. There was nothing. Sydney leaned back against the door, more confused than ever, until her eyes caught a figure in the distance standing under a street light. The wig was gone and Sydney was too far to distinguish any features, but she knew it was her. There was no mistaking that short blond hair under the streetlight. Sydney stared at the woman who stood staring back at her and immediately understood why Sheree hadn't left town.

She was staying for Dean.

Chapter 22

Sydney pulled the knee-length fitted sweater dress carefully over her head, then adjusted the huge loose turtleneck until it sat elegantly on her shoulders. The rust color picked up the golden highlights in her dark-colored hair, which she had curled and pinned up for the night for Hayden's benefit. She knew how much he loved any hairstyle that gave him a full view of her neck. She was in the process of applying mascara to her lashes when Lissandra came into the room.

"Look at you, all dressed up to meet the parents." She slipped onto Sydney's bed to watch her get ready. "Guess I'll be the only one at home tonight."

"Really?" Sydney capped the mascara and reached for lip gloss. "I'm almost sure I heard JJ moving around downstairs."

"Yeah, she was," Lissandra said, curling her lip. "And then she went to 'bed.' "

Sydney laughed as Lissandra put air quotes around the word *bed*.

"You think we should ask her where she goes when she sneaks out?" Sydney asked.

"And force Saint Judith to add lying to whatever sin she's committing when she leaves the house at ten o'clock at night? No, thanks," Lissandra said dryly. "If she can't even tell us, it must be really bad."

Sydney rubbed her lips together. "I don't know. This is JJ we're talking about. It's probably some guy."

"Yeah." Lissandra lay back on the bed. "Some married guy."

"Speaking of men, where's Mario?" Sydney asked, glancing back at her sister.

"Men's ministry meeting at his church."

Sydney didn't miss the disdain in her sister's voice. "Has he invited you to church yet?"

"Tries every week." Lissandra sounded like she had indigestion. "I swear, being with this man is doing something to me. Last week he asked me something, and I was about to lie, when I get this weird sensation in my chest. What is that?"

Sydney laughed out loud. "It's called 'guilt.' "

Lissandra shuddered. "How do you deal with that all the time?"

"By not doing things that make you feel that way." Sydney shook her head. "I still can't believe you've lasted this long with a church boy."

"Look who's talking!" Lissandra said. "You might have everyone else fooled with your going to church every week, but I know you are nowhere near that man's level of commitment."

Normally Sydney would have been offended by Lissandra's comment. But her sister had spoken truth.

"I know," Sydney conceded with a sigh. "I've been thinking about that lately."

"What do you mean?"

Sydney sat down on the bed beside Lissandra as she tried to explain how she had been feeling.

"Do you believe everything happens for a reason?"

Lissandra squinted. "You mean like Karma?"

"No." Sydney bit her lip. "Like everything that has happened to us in the past few weeks, to me. Losing the shop, losing the money I had saved, Dean in the hospital, even meeting Hayden and finding out that he's gotten all religious. What if all these things I didn't plan, and can't control, happened for a reason?"

"What reason could that be?"

Sydney shrugged. "What if God wants to get my attention?"

Lissandra wrinkled her nose. "Why would he want to do that?"

"I don't know." Sydney sighed as she caught her own reflection in the mirror. "I don't know much of anything anymore. Especially this thing with Sheree."

Lissandra sat up. "What do you mean?"

"I mean, I don't feel right tapping my man's phone." Sydney got up. "It's been a week, and Essie says there's been no contact between him and Sheree."

"So? He still lied to you when he didn't tell you about her voice message," Lissandra said.

"Look, all I'm saying is it's getting harder and harder for me to look him in the eye, knowing that I have an ear in on his conversations."

"I'm sorry. Is this the same woman who got us the cake job for the Raptors' opening season party by helping me release a colony of ants into Samantha's cake shop?" Lissandra asked in disbelief.

"Yes! And look how that worked out," Sydney said, throwing up her hands. "The health department shuts her down for a week. She buys our shop and shuts us down for eternity."

"So you're saying that we brought all this on ourselves?" Lissandra asked.

Sydney sighed and tossed the lip gloss into her purse. "I'm saying that I'm not sure that we've been going about this the right way."

"Oh, God." Lissandra sounded as if she was about to hurl. "You are becoming like the Bible thumpers."

"I never said all of that," Sydney protested. "I just said it doesn't feel right. That's all."

Lissandra rolled her eyes. "You're gonna tell Essie to stop listening in, aren't you."

"I'm gonna see how tonight goes first." Sydney headed toward the bedroom door. "But yes, that's what I'm leaning toward."

By the time Sydney rang Hayden's doorbell, she had pretty much made up her mind. No more spying on Hayden. If they were going to find Sheree, they were going to do it without him.

The door swung open and the tension in her body melted away as her eyes met Hayden's.

"Hey." His eyes lit up as his gaze swept over her.

"Hey, yourself," she said with a smile equal to his own. She already felt lighter now that she had made her decision, and that left her free to enjoy every moment as he whisked her into his arms and parted her lips with his for a kiss that made her toes curl.

"Well," Sydney said, slightly breathless. "I hope that's not the welcome you give all your visitors."

"You'll have to ask them yourself."

Sydney slapped his arm playfully, before letting him

take her coat and hang it in the closet. Her eyes eagerly drank in everything in Hayden's townhouse. Though he had been to her home on several occasions, this was the first time she had opportunity to be in his. Before she had even gotten through the door, she had been impressed with the contemporary architecture of brick, stone, and stucco façades. But the inside was just as modern, with its dark-stained hardwood floors and high ceilings. He had kept the decor fairly neutral with tan walls, a brown shag rug in the living room, and a dark-stained wood entertainment center. But pops of deep red throughout gave life to the rooms.

"Mom, Dad, look who's here."

Sydney followed Hayden into the kitchen, where she found Dalton Windsor and his wife, Staffine, at the island counter.

"Sydney, girl, come here." Sydney got lost in his arms as the six-foot, two-hundred-fifty-pound man pulled her into a huge bear hug. He may have been much older than the last time she saw him, but there was no absence of strength in his arms as he embraced her.

"Look at you." He held her back from him, his crinkled brown eyes looking her over. "It's been more than a decade since I've seen you."

"I know," Sydney said. "Whose fault is that, though? You never stop by anymore."

"I know," he said apologetically. "I'm an old man now, but they keep me busy over at Lakeshore Holdings."

"Mhmm." Sydney pursed her lips in mock disapproval. "I think you keep yourself busy, Uncle Dalton."

Dalton rolled his eyes as Hayden and Staffine began clearing their throats.

"You don't listen to them," he said with a shake of

his head as he sat down on one of the chairs by the island. "If it was up to them, I wouldn't do anything."

"Please, as if you ever listen to anything we have to say," Hayden muttered as he went back to the stove.

"Sydney, it's nice to finally meet you." Staffine pulled Sydney into a more delicate embrace than her husband's. "I've heard so much about you from your father when he was alive, and from Hayden over the past few weeks, that I feel like I know you already."

"We also heard about your brother," Dalton said, his tone taking on a serious quality. "He's been in our prayers every day. How is he doing?"

"A little better," Sydney said, appreciating their concern. "They were able to take him off the ventilator a couple days ago and he's breathing on his own. It's a good sign."

"God be praised," Staffine said. "I just know God is going to bring him to a full recovery."

"Thank you for all your prayers and concern," Sydney said. "It means a lot. Now I know why Dub speaks so glowingly about you. It's great to finally put a face to the name."

"So tell me, Sydney, did you cook all this and then sneak out to make it look like Dub did it?" Dalton asked. "You don't have to lie to me. I know my son."

Sydney chuckled. "Then you should know that he's an excellent cook. He doesn't need me."

"Thank you, sweetheart," Hayden said. They both smiled as their eyes met. "But I do need you. Would you grab the potatoes out of the oven for me?"

Just as Sydney was pulling the oven open, the doorbell rang.

"That must be Christian and Jennifer," Hayden said as he set the salad on the countertop.

"Don't worry, I'll get it," Dalton said, heading toward the door.

"Is that the gravy?" Sydney asked, resting a hand on Hayden's back as she peered around him to see what he was stirring on the stove top.

"Yeah," he said. "Want to taste?"

He dipped a spoon into the pot, then held it close to Sydney's lips.

"Mhmm, babe, that's good."

"I know, right?"

Staffine chuckled and they both turned to look at her.

"What?" Hayden asked curiously.

"Nothing," she said with a smile. "Just young love."

Sydney's eyes met Hayden's and she couldn't help but smile. Is that what this feeling was?

"Sydney, I don't think you've met my other son before, have you."

"I've heard lots about him, but I don't think I have met him," Sydney said, wiping her hands on a towel.

"This is Dub's younger brother, Christian, and his fiancée, Jennifer," Dalton said. "Christian and Jennifer, this is Sydney."

"Hey, are you the girl who wanted to marry my brother?" Christian teased.

Why did everyone remember that? Oh yeah, because her dad and Dalton had kept telling the story.

"I was seven!"

That started a round of laughter, but it didn't make Sydney feel out of place. In fact, it made her feel like she was part of them—like they had already accepted her into their family. That feeling stayed with her the rest of the night as she talked and laughed with Hayden and his family. And when Hayden grabbed her hand under the table and intertwined his fingers with hers, she knew that he felt like she was part of them, too.

They had just cleared the table and were about to bring out the apple and rhubarb crumble that Sydney had brought for dessert, when Hayden's phone rang. He excused himself to take the call as Sydney and Jennifer finished carrying the last of the dishes to the kitchen.

"I've got to tell you, I've heard nothing but amazing things about the desserts from your shop," Jennifer said. "Last time Dub came over, he brought your red velvet cake. Girl, it was gone in two days."

Sydney laughed. "I bet he ate most of it. That man does love some red velvet cake."

By the time Hayden returned to the room, the crumble as well as the dessert plates were already on the table.

"Don't let me keep you waiting," he said, taking his seat beside Sydney. "Dig in."

The conversation started up again as the dessert moved around the table, but something was different.

"Everything OK?" she whispered to Hayden when no one else was looking.

"Fine." He kissed her briefly on the forehead, but didn't meet her eyes. "Everything's fine."

Everything was not fine. But she would get to that later.

She was about to take the first bite out of her dessert when her own phone started ringing.

"So sorry," she apologized, as she scrambled to get to it. "I thought it was on vibrate."

"You young people and your twenty-four-hour access," Dalton said. "In my day, if they didn't catch us from nine to five, they didn't catch us at all."

Sydney was about to end the call and turn off the ringer when she saw who it was from. With a glance behind her at the table, she took the phone to the bathroom and closed the door behind her. "What's going on?" she whispered.

"She just called him." Essie's voice came with an urgency that caused Sydney's muscles to immediately tense. Even though her breaking heart already knew the answer, she still had to ask.

"Who called him?"

"Sheree."

Chapter 23

The temperature in Hayden's guest bathroom felt like it went up a notch as Essie began to give Sydney the details of Sheree's call to Hayden.

"It was less than five minutes ago," Essie said. "And it doesn't sound good. It sounds like she's getting ready to move, but she left something important at her brother's house that she needs to get first. Why are you whispering? Where are you?"

"At his house. I'm having dinner with his family. Did she say what she left?"

"No, but it was important enough that she wasn't willing to leave it behind."

Sydney sat down on the closed toilet lid and tried to think. Through the door she could hear the sound of Hayden's family laughing and talking. It wouldn't be long before they started wondering where she was.

"Look, she didn't say when she was coming," Essie continued. "But she said it would be sometime this week. It sounded like she was mad about your boy Hayden changing his locks so the key she had wouldn't work. She's planning to come by one day when he's there, but she wouldn't say when. Sounded like she didn't trust him to not turn her in."

"Did you get the number she called from?"

"Phone booth."

Sydney scraped her fingernail against the ribbed fabric of her dress. "That doesn't give me much to work with. What should I do?"

"Find out what she's coming back for before she comes back for it. If it's that important, maybe you can use it to bargain with her."

Sydney squeezed her eyes shut. How was she supposed to do that?

The sound of footsteps in the hallway raised the urgency.

"Gotta go, call you later."

Sydney ended the call, then flushed the toilet and washed her hands in the sink.

When she opened the bathroom door, Jennifer was standing on the other side.

"You OK?" she asked, looking at Sydney curiously. "I thought I heard you whispering in there."

"Yeah," Sydney said. "Just on the phone with one of my sisters. Everything's an emergency with them."

Conversation swirled around Sydney once she reclaimed her seat at the dining table, but she barely heard any of it above the noise of the questions in her mind. What had Sheree left behind? Money? Travel documents? Information about where she might be headed? Where would she have put it? Did Hayden know what it was? Was he hiding it for Sheree?

Out of the corner of her eye, Sydney watched him as he chatted with his family. Other than the kiss on the forehead, he hadn't touched her since he had come back to the table. She wondered if he remembered the promise he had made to her, and whether he planned to tell her about the call.

At Dalton's suggestion, the group moved to the living room, but Sydney stayed behind to help clean up the table with Hayden.

"Hey, you go ahead and sit with your family," she said. "I'll put these in the dishwasher for you."

"I can't let you do that," he said. "You're a guest."

"And you spent all day preparing this." She took the dish from his hand. "Let me do this for you."

He looked at her a long moment, then removed the dish from her hands and replaced it with his hands. They were so warm and strong and welcoming. She wanted to trust them. She wanted to trust him.

"Syd, there's something I have to tell you." His brow had furrowed and he stared at her with such intensity that she felt a chill run through her.

Her heart beat faster. She prayed that he was going to tell her about Sheree. She didn't want to believe that he was lying to her. And if he told her now, then they could do this together. Sydney wouldn't have to go to the plan that her mind was already formulating.

"What is it, babe?" She squeezed his hands in encouragement. "You can tell me."

He let out a deep breath. "It's about . . ."

"Dub, come talk some sense into your brother," Dalton's voice came from the living room. "You believe this boy really thinks that Boston will make it to the play-offs this year?"

Hayden glanced up at the hallway to the living room, then back at Sydney as he debated what to do next.

"Come on, Dub, tell him that Boston is the best defensive team in the league," Christian shot back.

"I'm coming," Hayden threw over his shoulder.

"Dub . . ."

"We'll talk later," he said, squeezing her hands.

"Dub, wait," she pressed. "What do you need to tell me?"

He gave a forced smile. "You know what? It's not even important."

Then, before she could protest, he kissed her forehead and made his way to the living room. As she watched him walk away, the truth sank into her. He wasn't ever going to tell her.

Her phone buzzed again. This time it was Lissandra.

"Essie told me about the call," Lissandra said. "Did he tell you about it?"

"No," Sydney said with a sigh.

"Can you talk?"

Sydney glanced at the hallway. "Not really."

"Then I'll make this quick," Lissandra said. "You need to take a photograph of his key."

"What?"

"Use your phone and make sure you get in close. It needs to be clear, so use the Macro focus function. You have to take the picture beside something with a scale. Check the kitchen or bathroom; there must be something in one of those rooms with a ruler on it."

"How are we gonna get a copy from a photograph?" Sydney whispered, not believing that she was even having this conversation with her sister.

"Don't worry, I know a guy."

"I can't believe I am even considering this," Sydney said as she began loading dishes into the washer.

"You better consider it. If Sheree gets what she needs from that house, we may never be able to find her again. This is our only window," Lissandra said. "Look, just get the picture. You can decide later if you want to actually use it."

Sydney hung up the phone and finished loading the washer, then began her search for the keys. She found them hanging on a hook near the kitchen cupboards. There were three bunches: one for his car and the other two she guessed were for the house and the clinic. She was about to panic when she noticed that one set of keys had an East York Athletic Clinic key ring attached, and the three keys were labelled "office," "Exam Rm," and "Main." That only left the last bunch of two keys. It was almost too easy. With her heart pounding, she rummaged quickly through the kitchen drawers until she found millimeter markings on the back of a box of nails. Grabbing the box of nails and the keys, she slipped into the bathroom once more and took pictures of both keys and forwarded them to Lissandra.

She had just put the keys back on the hook and placed the nails in the drawer when Hayden walked back into the kitchen.

"Hey, what's taking you so long?"

Sydney gripped the edge of the counter to steady herself. Her heart was beating so fast that she thought it would explode out of her chest.

"What were you looking for in there?" He pointed to the open drawer.

"Oh, just some Saran wrap to cover the rest of the crumble," Sydney lied.

"Oh. It's in the bottom drawer." He paused. "You could have just asked."

Sydney closed the drawer and opened the bottom one. "I didn't want to bother you."

She pulled out the box of plastic wrap, but when she

straightened to set it on the counter she found Hayden watching her. The temperature in the room seemed to drop a degree as they stared at each other, and an odd sensation began to creep through Sydney. A sadness she couldn't describe began to fill her, so much so that she was almost sure she saw it reflected in his eyes.

He stayed with her as she covered the crumble and put it into the refrigerator. Then they joined the others in the living room. She was sure no one else noticed it, but something had changed between her and Hayden. Though he was sitting with his arm around her, she had never felt more far away from him. And as she thought about the moment in the kitchen, the moment when they seemed to see right into each other, she couldn't shake a single disturbing thought:

She was losing him.

Chapter 24

Sydney waited a whole day for him to come clean. Despite the fact that the copies of the keys were sitting on her dresser; despite the fact that every passing day increased their chances of not finding Sheree; despite the fact that Lissandra was wearing out her last nerve, she waited a whole day before doing anything. Though she knew in her heart that he had chosen to protect Sheree, she hoped that he would change his mind and tell her what he knew.

In that day, she went to see Dean. When she arrived at the hospital, she found Jackie and JJ talking with a group of doctors. Whatever they were talking about wasn't good, because Jackie was crying and leaning on JJ.

"What's going on?" Sydney asked, coming up to her mother and sister moments after the doctors had left.

"Mom, why don't you go back and sit with Dean. We'll be right in," JJ said, opening the door to the room so her mother could shuffle inside. Sydney watched her mother move slower than she had in a long time. The last few weeks had changed her mother. The youthful look that she usually carried effortlessly was slipping away.

"Dean's regressing," JJ said once Jackie was out of earshot. "A couple days ago, they noticed blood clots forming, so they put him on blood thinners temporarily. Unfortunately, the thinners caused him to start hemorrhaging in the brain."

"Oh my God." Sydney gripped her sister's hand tightly.

"They're doing all they can, but that's not the only issue." JJ rubbed her eyes. "Dean's bills are piling up. You know he had no insurance, and he's too old to be considered Mom's dependent, so everything has to be paid out of pocket. Every day he's in here, it's more and more debt. Mom's thinking of taking out a second mortgage on the house. . . ."

"No." Sydney shook her head. "She can't afford to do that. If she loses the house . . . no."

"Well, do you have a better idea?"

"We have to take out a loan against Leroy's house," Sydney said, letting out a deep, despairing breath.

JJ bit her lip. "You know, all three of us have to agree."

"Don't worry, I'll deal with it," Sydney said.

JJ looked at Sydney in concern. "Are you sure about this, Syd? I mean, you and Lissandra are pretty much in the hole, and things aren't that great with me either, with business slowing down at the dress shop since Mom and I are here so often. How are we going to manage the payments?"

"Don't worry about it," Sydney said. "I'll take care of it."

"All right." JJ sighed. "But do it quick, 'cause I think

the hospital is dragging its feet on treatment until part of the balance on Dean's medical fees is taken care of."

"As soon as I get Lissandra's agreement, I'll call the bank to get the paperwork done up."

"You have my OK," JJ said. "Anything to get Dean through this."

"Anything" was right. And as she stepped away from her sister to call Lissandra, she knew exactly what "anything" had to be.

"Speak to me."

"All right, I've decided," Sydney said. "No more waiting. It's time for Plan B."

Chapter 25

Sydney's stomach was in knots and her nails were suffering. A spot on her pants was beginning to wear away, and a fingernail beginning to chip because of how long she had been scraping it against her jeans-clad leg. The sweat trickling down her spine despite the frigid air outside was enough to let her know that she was not OK. This was not OK. In fact, it was plain wrong. And she was woman enough to admit to herself that she was having second thoughts. Stealing Hayden's cell phone and breaking into his voice mail was one thing. But breaking into his home? Now she was entering felony territory. This was the kind of business that could get a sister sent to prison. And it wasn't like Hayden lived in some seedy apartment downtown. This was a two-story townhouse in Leslieville, where a desperate housewife, soccer mom, or recession-unemployment victim could be behind every sheer curtain.

"You ready, Syd?"

Sydney took a deep breath and scanned the street from the front seat of Lissandra's heavily tinted rental sedan.

"Syd, did you hear me? I asked if you were—"

"Yeah, I heard you," Sydney snapped. "Can you just give me a minute?"

Lissandra squinted at her sister from the driver's seat. "Look, if you were thinking of backing out, I'm not going to argue with you. This is a whole new ball game. And we don't know what the deal is with his alarm system. . . ."

"It's OK," Sydney said. "I got the code."

All it had taken was a forgotten watch at Hayden's place. She'd had to time it right. If she had gotten to his home five minutes after he had arrived, then she would have missed spying over his shoulder as he punched in the deactivate code. But everything had worked out well. As long as he hadn't changed it in the past twenty-four hours, they would be fine.

"Even so, this is really toeing the line."

Lissandra was wrong. This wasn't toeing the line. This was across the line and 20 meters away. If she got caught, there was no way she would be able to explain it away. But the numbers on Dean's hospital bill had pushed Sydney over the edge. She had no choice. Since Hayden wouldn't volunteer the information she needed, she would have to find it herself.

"I'll make it quick."

Lissandra pursed her lips. "All right, fine. Then you need to get your behind out of the car. We've already been sitting here too long. You know how white folk love to talk. Hmm, I don't know why your man couldn't kick it in a black neighborhood like everyone else."

"Make sure you keep the line open," Sydney said, slipping the ear bud for her cell phone headset into her ear before exiting the car. Pulling her wool cap down around her hair, she thanked God for the cold, snowless day. It gave her a reason for the scarf, cap, and long coat, but kept her from leaving footprints as she walked down the sidewalk.

Lissandra's car drove past and headed around the block just as Sydney turned up the walk to Hayden's front door.

She rang the doorbell with her gloved hands.

"Hello! Anyone home?"

There was no answer, just as she had expected. The night before, Hayden had told her he would be in a meeting all morning. And when she had called his office only five minutes earlier, his secretary had confirmed the fact.

With a quick glance around, she slipped the dangerously acquired copy of Hayden's key out of her pocket and into the lock for the front door. She held her breath until she heard the lock click and felt the door slide open with her pressure. She stepped inside and quickly punched in the alarm deactivate code before closing the door.

She looked around the house she had only been in two times before. It felt a little colder without Hayden, but there was still a sense of his presence there, and a nervous sensation ran through her stomach.

This was a bad idea.

A really bad idea.

But she had already committed the crime of entering. There was no point turning back now. Though her shoes were fairly clean, she knew better than to take chances. She slipped out of them and left them on the mat at the door as she padded in stocking feet toward the stairs. She was on the first step when she paused and looked back at the shoes.

A girl could never be too careful. She turned back

and ran to grab them, choosing to stick them deep in the back of the coat closet instead.

This time she decided to walk through the living room and kitchen first. Everything was immaculate. And save for an old family picture on the ledge above the fireplace, there was no hint of Sheree anywhere. Sydney flipped through a stack of mail on the kitchen counter. Bills, coupons, fliers, an invitation to some upcoming event. Nothing Sheree.

Upstairs she found two bedrooms, a bathroom, and a linen closet. The first bedroom was without embellishment and clearly served for guests. The second was obviously Hayden's. Everything about the room breathed Hayden—from the Raptors-red-and-gray drapes and bedding, to the oversized four-poster bed, probably custom made for his large frame, to the 32-inch plasma screen television on the wall. Even the large, worn black Bible sitting on his bedside table was exactly what she expected from her man. And then there was his scent. The mix of Gucci and Hayden that she had come to associate with him wrapped tighter around her the deeper she stepped into the room. The house was for everyone else, but this room was for Hayden, and in that moment she knew that by being in that room—by entering without being invited—she had violated him in a way that he would probably never forgive.

Her eyes fell on a picture stuck in the corner of the dresser mirror. It was from the weekend they'd had dinner at Sean and Maritza's place. All four of them were smiling at the camera; she was leaning against Hayden and he had his arms around her. She couldn't forget that moment, that feeling of being in his arms. She had never felt safer.

Sydney backed up. She couldn't do this.

She had reached the top of the stairs when her hip
vibrated. Lissandra.

"How's it going?"

"Lissandra, I can't do this. This is too much—even
for us."

"What?" Lissandra hissed. "Girl, have you lost your
mind?"

"Yes," Sydney said. "And I'm in the process of getting it back. This can't be the only way to find Sheree,
Lissa. This . . . this . . . it's just wrong."

"Is it?"

"Yes," Sydney continued. "It's a downright viola-
tion."

"You mean like the way Sheree violated Dean? Violated our whole family? Took from us one of the most
precious things we have? Our daddy's legacy."

"Sheree did that, not Hayden."

"Yes," Lissandra said. "But if he knows what she
did, and he knows where she is and isn't telling us—
he's just as guilty. A man who claimed to love you
wouldn't keep letting your family suffer if he could
stop it. A good man wouldn't do that."

Sydney bit her lip. On some level she agreed. But
she still wasn't absolutely sure.

"Look, Sydney. We're not robbing him, we're just
looking for some information," Lissandra said. "See
what you can find in the next ten minutes. If you don't
see anything, we'll go."

"Fine."

Sydney ended the call and took a deep breath before
heading back into the room. This time she didn't waste
time looking around. She went straight for the small
desk in the corner and skimmed through the papers
there. Most of them were documents for the Argonauts,

for billing, for X-ray clinics—nothing useful to Sydney. She opened the first drawer and found some old receipts. The second drawer produced some blank paper and stationery. Sydney almost felt relieved that there was nothing there to lead them to Sheree.

Third and final drawer. More bills and bank statements. Nothing interesting, restaurant charges, supermarket purchases. Movers.

Movers?

Sydney paused and looked at that one more carefully. It was the third charge on a VISA card issued in Hayden's name. Sydney checked the date. January fourteen. Two days before Dean found out Sheree was missing!

Sydney's chest began to tighten as she scanned the rest of the statement. A hotel stay at a Best Western. A rental vehicle charge for a week and a few other out-of-town charges. Sydney's heart hammered in her chest. She didn't want to believe what she was seeing, but the evidence was right before her. The cardholder's name was Hayden Windsor, and since he had the bill, that meant it came to him. Did Hayden help Sheree in her scheme?

No, he wouldn't do that. Even Sydney knew that.

So why then would he pay for it? Maybe she had used the credit card without him knowing. But if he had the bill he must have figured out what she had done. He could have traced her through the movers. Why didn't he tell Sydney? Why had he acted like he didn't know anything about where Sheree was?

Sydney felt a pain within her chest. She knew what it was, but she didn't have time to deal with it. She had gotten what she came for. Pulling out her phone, she snapped a few photographs of the statement before turning to the other documents in the pile. She was almost at the end when she heard a sound.

She froze.

She had begun to think it was her imagination, when she heard a door close loudly followed by footsteps on the stairs. Then a voice.

Hayden's voice.

Chapter 26

"Yeah, I should be back in ten minutes, by the time the break is over," Hayden said. "I just need to grab a few things."

Panic seized Sydney. If Hayden caught her here, in his house, in his bedroom, there would be no explanation that would be good enough. With only seconds to spare, she slipped the papers back into the drawer before falling to the floor and crawling under the low bed.

Sydney prayed her thumping heart would not give away her position. As it was, she was barely breathing for fear that he might hear her.

Dear God, if you get me out of this, I'll go to church every weekend.

"OK, Paul, I'll see you in a few."

She watched his stocking feet move around the room. Then the surface above her shifted as he sat down on the bed. Sydney ceased breathing as she watched his feet to her right. There was nothing under the bed, and so no reason for him to look under it. But she couldn't find any comfort in even that logic.

The moments seemed to stretch into eternity for

Sydney as she listened to Hayden shuffle through papers. A few moments later, he got up and Sydney let herself breathe again. The stress from the situation was making her so tense she felt she would pass out.

She heard more movement and then a beep.

"You have three messages. . . ."

The answering machine. Well, at least she no longer would have to worry about who the messages were from.

"Message one: Hey, it's Samantha. Heard you're finally back in Toronto from all those away games. Would love to catch up over dinner. Call me."

Sydney's eyebrows shot up. Call her? What was that heifer doing tracking her man?

"Message deleted."

Sydney pursed her lips. Smart move.

"Message two: This message is for Hayden Windsor. This is James Bright calling from TD Bank. Please give us a call as soon as possible. It's in regard to your VISA card."

"Message saved."

"Message three: Hayden . . . it's me."

Sheree.

Sydney froze. And apparently so did Hayden, as the movement she had been hearing previously ceased.

"Look, I'm only going to be here for a few days more. I hope you're not having any visitors tonight."

So she was planning to stop by that night. Well, maybe Sydney needed to make a surprise visit.

"No more new messages."

She felt the bed sink again as Hayden sat down, but there was no movement after that. Sydney could almost feel the waves of his concern. He was thinking about Sheree. Then all of a sudden she felt her hip vibrate. Sydney bit her lip hard as she tried to discreetly reach for the phone. The buzzing of the phone had never sounded louder than it had in that moment. When she finally managed to access it, she realized the call was from Hayden. Guilt washed over her. With a touch of the screen she sent the call straight to voice mail.

"Hey, Syd, it's me. Look, remember the other night I said I needed to talk to you about something? Well, I still do. Call me when you get this."

She closed her eyes and rested her forehead against the floor. So he was finally going to tell her. If she had just waited one more day . . .

Sydney was so lost in her guilt that she barely noticed when the bed shifted again. It was only when she heard the muted sound of his footsteps that she realized he was leaving. She listened until she heard what sounded like a door shut downstairs. Then she waited. . . . Until fifteen minutes had passed since she'd heard movement in the room. Until Lissandra had called her three times in a row. And until her intuition told her it was safe to get from under the bed. As she did, her foot hit something sharp and metal. She scooted around to see it was just a vent under the bed.

But when she looked closer, she realized that the vent was only loosely secured to the wall. Scooting closer, she used her fingers to untwist the screws until the whole thing came loose and the vent fell from the wall. Sydney pulled a tiny wooden box out of the space. When she opened it, she found it crammed full of items, from a well-worn piece of paper folded multiple times, a creased black-and-white photograph, and a locket with a cross pendant. But it was what was at the bottom that told Sydney she had found what she was looking for. She replaced the vent, crawled out from under the bed, and made her way downstairs.

"Girl, I thought you were done for when I passed back and saw his car at the gate," Lissandra said with a shake of her head as she opened the car door for Sydney. "Did you find anything?"

"Yes," she said, opening the box so Lissandra could see it. When she did, Lissandra's mouth fell open.

"You've got to be kidding me, that isn't . . ."

"Yes, it is," Sydney said, strapping on her seat belt. "It's a key to a safe-deposit box. We got her."

"So I guess the two of you really went through with it."

Sydney stepped out of the downstairs bathroom and froze when she rounded the corner and found JJ standing by the kitchen counter, the box with the key and the rest of Sheree's junk open in front of her.

"What are you doing here?" It was the middle of the day. Lissandra had already left to return the rental car and Sydney was about to leave to pick up a box of items she had left at what used to be Decadent. She hadn't expected anyone to be home.

"Don't change the subject, Syd," JJ said, folding her arms. "I can't believe you would break into Hayden's house. Lissandra, yes. But you?"

Sydney pursed her lips. This was exactly the guilt trip she had wanted to avoid.

"How did you know about that?"

"I overheard the two of you last night." JJ shook her head with disappointment. "How could you do that, Sydney? Apart from the obvious legal issues, how could you do that to a man who loves you like that?"

Sydney brushed past her sister as she made her way to the fridge. "He left me no choice."

"You always have a choice."

Sydney put the orange juice decanter down on the counter, hard. "Not always." She met her sister's eyes. "He was lying to me about Sheree."

"You can't know that. . . ."

"I do," Sydney said matter of factly. "I know she called him. I heard the conversation."

JJ's mouth fell open. "Wha . . . When? How?"

"Trust me, you'd rather not know."

JJ narrowed her eyes. "This has something to do with Essie, doesn't it?"

Sydney poured herself a glass of juice but didn't answer.

"Have mercy, Sydney," JJ said, staring at her sister. "What have you been doing?"

"Don't look at me like that, JJ. Everything I did, I did because I had to. I tried it your way. I asked Hayden to tell me the truth about Sheree. He promised me he would let me know if he was in contact with her. Since then he's spoken to her twice."

"And?"

"And what?"

"And did you give him a chance to tell you?"

Sydney took a swig from her juice as the voice mail on her phone came to the forefront of her mind.

"He should have told me as soon as he knew," she said stubbornly. "He knows how important this is."

"Sydney, Sheree is his sister!"

"And I am his girlfriend and Dean is my brother, and Dub made a promise to me," Sydney said. "Doesn't that count for something?"

"Sydney, think about it," JJ said, placing her hands

on the counter. "What if Dean had done this and Sheree was the victim. What would you have done?"

"I wouldn't have told Dub jack," Sydney snapped.

"Exactly!"

"But I wouldn't have made the kind of promise he made to me, either," Sydney said. "And while I would probably hate whatever he would do to find out what he wanted, I would understand it."

"Sydney, you're not being reasonable. . . ."

"No, I'm being real," Sydney said, moving to the sink to rinse her glass. "We're about to send ourselves into debt to pay for Dean's care, when that woman is out there running around with our money. You bet your behind I'm going to do everything I can to find her and to take care of our family."

"Well, guess what," JJ said. "Sheree is married to Dean, so she is our family, too."

"Maybe *your* family," Sydney said, drying her hands on a kitchen towel before leaving the kitchen. "Not mine."

"Sydney, I know you're not that cold," JJ's words trailed after her. "I know somewhere inside, you know this is wrong. This is not what you do to someone who loves you."

"He doesn't love me!" Sydney's voice came out louder and harsher than she'd intended as she turned to face her sister. "If he loved me, he couldn't look in my face and lie to me. He couldn't watch my family fall to pieces, knowing how to help and not doing something. He couldn't betray me like this."

"Don't do that, Syd," JJ said, shaking her head. "We want to blame someone, but the truth is no one is innocent here. Not Sheree, not Hayden, but not us, either."

"You don't understand, JJ."

"Understand what?" she asked softly. "That you love him? Yeah, I understand. He couldn't have upset you that much, and you wouldn't be standing over there crying if you didn't have strong feelings for him."

Crying?

Sydney looked over at her sister at the same time that her hand reached up to touch her own face. Wet. JJ nodded just as Sydney realized she had indeed been crying.

Sydney sighed and headed into the living room. "It will pass."

"Are you sure?" JJ asked as she followed.

No, she wasn't. But she hoped she was right, because the alternative was unbearable.

Sydney picked up the phone. "I need to call Essie. Now that we know the moving company she used, maybe we can find out where she went."

"Why don't you just talk to him?" JJ asked, putting her hand on the phone to pause Sydney's dialing.

"I'm done talking to him," Sydney said, gently removing JJ's hand. "Whatever he has to say, it's too late."

Chapter 27

The two-car driveway was empty at 1069 Park Place. Sydney glanced at the address on her GPS to confirm that she was at the right place, then parked her Nissan at the end of the driveway. She and JJ got out just before Lissandra pulled in behind them, effectively blocking the rest of the entrance. Lissandra had insisted on the three of them driving two different vehicles. Sydney thought it was just so her sister could take off on her own in the event she got bored.

Sydney walked slowly up the driveway toward the house, taking in all two stories spread out across what had to be at least half an acre of land. She stopped halfway and took off her sunglasses.

"So this is what she did with all that money," JJ said, giving voice to the exact thought in Sydney's head.

Lissandra sucked on her teeth. "I don't understand this trick. What does she alone need so much house for anyway?"

Sydney replaced her sunglasses. "Who said she's alone?"

Without waiting for her sisters' response, Sydney headed up to the front door, ringing the doorbell. She wasn't surprised when she didn't get a response. After trying the door and finding it locked, she turned to Lissandra.

"It's locked."

"What you telling me that for?" Lissandra asked with a touch of annoyance.

"You know I don't agree with all of this," JJ said, folding her arms. "But we're here, so we might as well go in. And since we don't have a key . . ."

JJ and Sydney looked at Lissandra expectantly. Lissandra cursed under her breath.

"Fine. But can you at least back up and give me some space?" she asked, stepping toward the door. "And make sure we don't have an audience."

Sydney turned her back to Lissandra, glancing out across the front yard and the driveway. As the sounds of metal against metal clinked behind her, she felt grateful for the tall shrubs that created a bit of a barrier around the front door. A few moments later, the door clicked open and Lissandra stood up, slipping a couple pieces of metal back into her purse even as she used the edge of her coat to wipe off the doorknob.

They all paused at the slightly ajar door. Lissandra and Sydney glanced at each other. This would be the second house they had broken into in less than a week. This was becoming a disturbing habit.

Sydney began to step forward, but for a brief moment it felt like something held her back. Quick images of Hayden, Jackie, even her father flashed across her mind. It was almost enough to make her change her mind. But then she thought of Dean lying in the hospital bed at Toronto Western Hospital and everything else seemed minor in comparison. She had to do this. For her brother.

She slipped on her winter gloves and stepped forward. "So what are we waiting for?"

Dark-stained hardwood floors covered the wide foyer and the even wider living room that it opened up into. Sydney walked through the space carefully, touching the brand-new, cream-colored, three-piece living-room suite, the glass end tables, the matching Tiffany lamps, and the 72-inch LED TV. The cash register in her mind kept ringing as she calculated the cost of the items, many of which were the same as the ones in the house she had shared with Dean.

"Syd, get in here. You will not believe this!"

After what she had seen so far, nothing could surprise her. But what could anger her were the three chandeliers hanging over the ten-seater dining table in the dining room.

"Do you believe this?" Lissandra asked, adding a few more colorful words for emphasis.

Before Sydney could respond, JJ came flying down the stairs.

"She has four bedrooms, Syd. Four." JJ's eyes were wide in shock. "All completely outfitted from Pottery Barn! I know 'cause I was just in there looking at everything I couldn't afford! Those are five-thousand-dollar rooms."

"You're talking about rooms? Look at these chandeliers, JJ? We could feed our family for a whole year on one of these—"

Her sisters' voices faded out for Sydney as she looked around and continued calculating the cost of everything. Between the house and the furniture, Sheree had already spent a chunk of their money. It wasn't half, but if she had done all this damage in the two weeks since she had been MIA, who knows what else she could do? If she was buying up assets this fast, how long would it last? Would they ever get any of it back?

The air left her lungs at that thought, and visions of the future began to materialize in her mind's eye. Visions of them going into debt over the cost of Dean's care; having to sell Leroy's house to cover the bills; having to move back in with Jackie. In an instant, she would go from being a young woman with a business, a home, and a budding career, to a thirty-year-old spinster living with her mother. She sank down into one of the plush dining chairs to catch her breath.

"Sydney, this ain't no time to be chillin', girl. What we gonna do?"

"Yeah, Syd, this woman is burning through our money. By the time we finally get to her, there may be nothing to get back." JJ added the wringing of her hands to her pacing. "We have to do something."

Sydney didn't know why they were both looking at her. She was tired of people looking to her for answers. This whole thing had begun with Lissandra's investigation into Sheree. But without Sydney and her connection to Hayden, it would have never come this far. And somewhere along the way, Sydney had taken the lead in this dangerous operation.

The feeling of apprehension she had felt at the door came back to her again. She should end this here. They had found Sheree. If they had been unsure about it before, they were even more certain when they walked into the kitchen and saw a picture of her and an older woman with similar features tacked up on the fridge door. They could go back outside, get in their cars, and call the police. Let the officials handle it. But Sydney didn't trust the officials. They had told them before that because Dean was legally married to Sheree, whatever was his was hers—especially now that he was in the hospital and she would have power of attorney over his assets. Never mind that Sheree was the reason her brother was in the hospital; the law was on her side.

But even though the law was on Sheree's side, the Isaacs girls were on Dean's side. And sometimes, that was all you needed.

Sydney stood up.

"OK, ladies, it's time to get down to business."

JJ and Lissandra looked at each other, then back at Sydney.

"And what business do you have in mind exactly?" Lissandra asked.

"The business of finding out everything we can about Sheree Vern." Sydney pulled her hair up into a ponytail. "Search every room, every closet, every drawer, and every loose floorboard. There's got to be something here that will tell us exactly who she is and what she did with our money. And you can bet your life we're going to find it."

Chapter 28

"Sydney, are you sure this is a good idea?"

It had been a little over an hour since Sydney and her sisters had begun to turn Sheree's house upside down. Since then, they had discovered that Sheree liked to collect expensive things. And not everything they found had been from Dean's house, which meant that at some time in the past Sheree had been involved in some other profitable scam. Just as Sydney had suspected, this wasn't Sheree's first time around the block.

She was about to go through the slide-away cupboards under the bookshelf when JJ posed her worry-ridden question.

"Good idea or not, it's what's happening." Sydney barely paused to address her sister. "We don't have many other options left."

"What if we just call the police? Or even Essie? Maybe she could give us another way to find out what we need to without the risk of a breaking-and-entering charge." JJ's copper eyes were wide, and her butterscotch skin flushed as she pleaded with Sydney. Sydney paused to consider her sister and couldn't help but feel sympathy. She knew the whole situation must be excruciating for JJ, who wouldn't even burn a CD for anyone because she thought it was wrong.

Sydney turned to face her sister fully.

"JJ, I appreciate all you've done for me up to this point," Sydney said. "But you don't have to do this. If you need to leave, then go. You don't need to get caught up in all of this."

And Sydney didn't need to have JJ's conscience dulled, either. Sydney needed to know that in the future, she could count on JJ to pull her back from the edge when she was about to dive over a precipice. If JJ became like Sydney and Lissandra, then there would be no one to do that.

"You don't need to get caught up in this either, Sydney," JJ said, grabbing her older sister's hand. "We can stop this right now. Let's just go."

Sydney shook her head. "I can't. I have to see this through."

Turning back now would make everything she had done before all for nothing.

JJ's eyes pleaded with Sydney before the words even came.

"Syd, please. Stop this. . . ."

"Ladies, we talking or we working?" Lissandra called out from the doorway. She had ditched her shirt and was wearing an Angry Birds tank top that matched the scowl on her face.

"I'm working," Sydney said, standing up. "JJ was just leaving."

"Sydney . . ."

"JJ, go." Sydney pulled out her car keys and handed them to JJ. "Take my car. I'll get a ride with Lissandra."

Lissandra snorted. "I knew you would chicken out eventually."

"It's not about chickening out, Lissandra," JJ said. "This . . . all of this . . . is a really bad idea. What if Sheree comes back?"

"Then I can flatten her face with my new Louis Vuitton boots."

"What Louis Vuitton boots?" JJ asked.

"The ones I found in her closet that happen to be my size."

Sydney grabbed JJ's hands and put the keys in them, folding her sister's reluctant fingers around them.

"Go," Sydney urged. "You shouldn't be here."

"Neither should you," JJ tried one last time.

Sydney shrugged. "That's debatable."

JJ gave her sisters one last look before heading toward the front door.

"You call me if anything happens," JJ said as she held on to the open door. "Anything."

Sydney nodded.

"You OK?" Lissandra asked after the door closed behind JJ.

Sydney turned and went back to the cupboards. "I'm fine. Let's just get this done."

And get it done was exactly what they did. The minutes flew by as they pored over every room, coming up with more expensive but virtually useless things. Sydney was about to hit what looked like an office upstairs when her cell phone rang. She assumed it would be JJ, trying to talk her into leaving again. She assumed wrong.

Hayden.

She stared at the name on the display and considered not answering. But it had been days since they had spoken to each other directly. His next move might be to visit her house and then, finding it empty, her mother's house. That would be bad. The last thing she needed was Jackie figuring out that her three oldest daughters were MIA. She would sniff out trouble faster than a drug dealer could sniff out a cop.

She sighed before pressing the green phone symbol.

"Hey!" She hoped he bought her enthusiasm.

"Hey, yourself. I've been trying to reach you all week," he said. The concern in his deep husky voice tightened her stomach into knots.

"Yeah, it's been really busy," Sydney said, pacing the hallway upstairs. She hated lying to Hayden. And she hated that it was starting to become a regular occurrence.

"Yeah? What's been going on?"

"You know, the usual drama with my sisters," she said, adding more layers to the deceit.

"Sydney, come help me move this couch. There's something underneath it. . . ."

Sydney scrambled to cover the mouthpiece of the phone.

"Is that Lissandra?" Hayden asked. "You guys are moving? How come you didn't tell me?"

"Umm, yeah—no . . ." Sydney bit her lip. "I mean, yes, it's Lissandra, but no, we're not moving. One of my other sisters is."

"So that's why you've been so busy," Hayden said, understanding flowing through his voice. "You've been helping your sister move. Baby, you could have told me. You want me to come over and give you a hand? The guys are off today, so I have time."

"No!" Sydney squeezed her eyes shut. "No, babe,

you don't need to do that. We already have a lot of people over here. You know all the sisters have to show up for everything."

"Oh." He tried to hide it, but Sydney heard the disappointment in his voice. She knew he thought she had left him out of a family thing, and she couldn't explain otherwise without lying to him or hurting him. She held back a sigh. This was why she hadn't wanted to answer the phone in the first place. No matter what she said, it would be the wrong thing.

"Babe, I wanted to ask you, but I knew you were out of town for most of the week for games. I figured you'd be tired like you usually are when you do a string of away games," Sydney said. "I didn't want to bother you. . . ."

"Spending time with you is not a bother, Syd," he said. "As it is, I feel like we've been playing phone tag since the day you picked up the watch from my place. Are you mad that I didn't get to see you before I went on the road?"

"No, of course not," Sydney said, her heart constricting from the tight layers of guilt around it. Her initial anger at Hayden for hiding his knowledge of Sheree's whereabouts had kept her from worrying about what Hayden might think about her avoiding his calls. But JJ's well-placed words had helped to wear away some of that anger, leaving just enough space for her guilt to creep in.

"Sydney!"

Sydney turned her back to the stairs, where Lissandra's voice was coming from, and ducked into one of the bedrooms, closing the door quietly.

"But you're right," Sydney said with a sigh. "We haven't seen much of each other lately."

"How about I come over tonight?" he offered. "You can relax, I can cook you and your sisters some dinner, and we can just chill for a while."

He had no idea how good that sounded and how much it would kill her to say no. But apart from the obvious fact that she didn't even know when she would be home, there was no way she wanted Hayden anywhere around the likes of Lissandra and JJ. Especially Lissandra.

"Sorry, babe. Tonight's no good," Sydney said. "I don't even know when we'll be done here. But how about we meet up tomorrow night?"

There was a pause on the line and for a moment Sydney wondered if Hayden suspected she was lying to him. But if he did, he didn't let on.

"OK, baby, I'll see you tomorrow, then."

Sydney swallowed another sigh. "OK. Have a good night."

"You, too," he said tiredly. "Love you. Bye."

Sydney's mouth fell open.

"What!" she squeaked.

"Huh?" Hayden asked, suddenly alert.

"What did you just say?"

"Uh, nothing, I just said good night. Bye."

"No, no. You said something else."

"I did?"

"You did."

"I did, didn't I," he said.

Sydney smiled. She could envision the sheepish look on his face. "Yes, babe, you did."

She heard him let out a deep breath on the other end. "So."

"So?"

Another deep breath. "So how do you feel about that?"

At any other time, from any other man with whom Sydney felt the same way she did with Hayden, it would have been great. But Hayden wasn't any other man. He was Sheree's brother.

It was her turn to let out a deep sigh.

"Hayden . . ."

"You know what, you don't need to answer," he said quickly. "Just . . . just think about it. And know . . . that I meant it. OK?"

"OK."

"Good night, Syd."

"Good night, Dub."

She ended the call and slid down the wall until she was sitting on the floor. Hayden had said he loved her. What was she going to do?

The door burst open.

"Sydney . . ."

"Just give me a minute and I'll help you with the sofa," Sydney said, closing her eyes.

"This isn't about the sofa."

Sydney opened her eyes to look up at Lissandra.

"You need to see this."

Without another word, Sydney followed her sister downstairs, through the living room, and into the kitchen. The cupboard of the island was open and pots and pans were strewn all over the floor. Lissandra kicked a few of them to the side in order to get to the flashlight, which was on the counter. She flicked it on and handed it to Sydney.

She nodded toward the open cupboard. "Go ahead. Take a look."

Sydney crouched down and shone the flashlight into the now-empty cupboard. She soon discovered that it wasn't as empty as she thought.

There was a square-shaped hole in the floor of the cupboard. She noticed a flat piece of wood that had concealed it from view before Lissandra uncovered it. What was more interesting, however, was what was in the hole.

Money.

And lots of it. Bundled in stacks and wrapped in bags of clear plastic for purposes of preservation.

"Oh my God," Sydney breathed. "How much do you think is in here?"

Lissandra dropped down beside Sydney. "Only one way to find out."

They began pulling out the bags with the bundles. Most of them were stacks of fifties and hundreds, with a couple stacks of twenties thrown in for good measure. Sydney assumed those allowed Sheree easy access when she needed to use some of the money in a hurry. By the time they had pulled all of it out, Sydney estimated it to be about fifty thousand dollars.

Three-hundred-thousand-dollar house. Thousands of dollars in clothes and furniture, and now fifty thousand dollars in cash. Her father's twenty years of hard work; of denying himself and his children; of long hours and low pay; her ten years of struggling to prove herself to him, to everyone. Here it all sat, in houses and cars and furniture. In fur coats and designer clothes that Sydney had found in closets upstairs. In bundles of fifties under the kitchen floorboards. All in the possession of a woman who probably didn't know the value of an honest day's work.

Sheree had taken everything from Sydney. Her livelihood, her family's money, her security, and her brother. And because of Sheree, she would probably lose the first man who had loved her without making her prove herself.

She was done playing games with Sheree. It was time they had a face to face.

"Let's get back to work. If there's anything else like this, we need to find it. I don't want us to miss anything."

An hour later, as the sun sank down behind the trees, Sydney stood in the living room looking at the loot they had found. There had been another stash of about ten thousand dollars in the bedroom upstairs to add to what they had found under the sink. It was nowhere near what Sheree had taken, but it was more than Sydney had expected to get her hands on at that moment. She should be satisfied, but she wasn't. They had been there all day, but there had been no sign of Sheree. That heifer had barely worked a day since her wedding to Dean, but even if she had grown some work ethic and gotten a job, she should have been back by now.

"I'm gonna get the car so we can pack this up before we go," Lissandra said, heading out the front door.

"OK." Sydney said, stopping outside the doorway. "But I'm not leaving."

"What?"

"You heard me," Sydney said, sitting on the step. "I am tired of this woman getting the upper hand over us. We've been eating her dust since she came to Toronto, and even after she left. She's always been one step ahead of us. But it ends here. I'm not leaving here until I see her."

"Syd, we don't even know if she's coming back." The tiredness in Lissandra's voice was thinly veiled.

"For all we know, she peeped us while we were here and took off. I hate her as much as you do, but you got to admit she is one crafty chick. And like you said, she's always been ahead of us."

"Yeah, and I'm sick of it," Sydney said. "That's why I'm not moving till I look into her conniving face myself. I can't look my brother in the eye knowing she got away with all this."

Lissandra's gold bangles jingled as she wiped a hand wearily over her face.

"OK." She sat down on the step beside Sydney. "We'll wait."

Sydney looked over at her sister for a moment before looking away.

"Go home, Lissandra," Sydney said. "You don't need to be here."

"Neither do you," Lissandra said. "But this whole crazy mess was my idea. And Dean is my brother, too. We started this together, we'll finish it together."

Sydney looked at her for a long time. She leaned over and nudged her sister with her shoulder.

"Thanks."

"Back at you," Lissandra said. "Just make sure we end up in the same cell when we go to prison for this."

Sydney laughed. But deep inside she wondered if that just might be a possibility.

"By the way, when I was going through the bedrooms, I found this." Lissandra pulled out an envelope and handed it to Sydney. The first thing that fell out was a small circular pill pack with space for twenty-eight pills. Almost half were missing.

"She's been on birth control?" Sydney asked, looking over at her sister.

"At least for the past two weeks," Lissandra said

dryly. "And last time I checked, pregnant women don't take birth control."

Sydney shook her head. Sheree had not only stolen from her brother, but she had lied and manipulated him into marrying her. It seemed like there was nothing this woman wasn't capable of.

"Party ain't over," Lissandra said. "Keep looking. Now we know why we couldn't find anything on her after 2004."

Sydney slowly perused the envelope of personal documents that included a passport, credit cards, and miscellaneous IDs for a woman named Shayla Vaughn. When she opened the passport and checked the photo, however, she saw that Shayla was none other than Sheree.

Sydney jumped up. "Why didn't you show me this before?"

Lissandra shrugged. "We already found her home. I didn't think it was that important. We were too busy searching."

Sydney began pacing. "But don't you get it? Now we can find her. We thought we couldn't track her because she was only using cash, but she was just using different cards. We were looking for the wrong person."

Sydney pulled out her cell phone. "We have to call Essie—"

"Already on it," Lissandra said, her phone to her ear. "Hey, Essie, can you run a search for me on Shayla Vaughn? We have her passport number and social insurance number."

Sydney held up the documents for Lissandra as she read off the details to Essie. Their aunt ended the call, promising to call back when she found something. As soon as Lissandra hung up the phone, Sydney heard her stomach growl.

"Dang, girl, you need to get some food into you before you eat me," Lissandra said.

Thoughts of Hayden's offer to cook for her came drifting back into her head. She glanced at her watch. If they left now, they could be back in Toronto by eight thirty. Maybe not too late for Hayden to make good on his offer.

"I passed a fish-and-chips place on our way in. Let's see if it's still open," Lissandra said, getting up.

Sydney paused. "I can wait. I don't want to chance her coming while we're gone."

"We have her real info now," Lissandra said. "We can find her easy. Plus, if you're that hungry, she'll probably beat down your scrawny behind, no problem."

"All right, but let's be quick," Sydney said, getting up.

Lissandra paused and glanced back at the front door. "What about the money?"

Sydney cracked a smile. "Yeah, we should probably do something about that."

Within fifteen minutes, they had hidden the money in a different part of the house and found the small diner that Lissandra had seen before. The crowd in the diner was pretty thin. Sydney guessed that most people probably stayed in on a Sunday night. All the better for getting them quickly in and out.

The waitress had just brought their order when Sydney's phone rang.

"Hey, it's me," Essie came across the line.

"You have anything for me?" Sydney asked, her hunger passing almost immediately.

"Yeah," Essie said. "Looks like our girl has been busy. A friend of mine managed to access her credit card records. She made some purchases in Montreal late last week and yesterday. But yesterday evening, we have her making purchases in Ogdensburg and Alexandria Bay."

"So she's on her way back."

"That's right," Essie said. "In fact, she could be there already."

"OK, thanks," Sydney said, even as she signalled the waitress for a check. "Anything else?"

"Yes," Essie said. "My contact says she uses her card a lot at some place named The Toucan. You might want to check there."

"Thanks, Essie," Sydney said honestly. "I owe you."

"Don't worry about it. You just be careful."

Sydney hung up the phone just as the waitress was placing the bill in front of them. Given her most recent conversation with her aunt, she decided to pay in cash.

"Quick question." Sydney handed the woman the tray with the bill and the money. "How do I get to The Toucan from here?"

Chapter 29

From the outside, The Toucan didn't look like a bar. Darkly tinted, tall arched windows contrasting elegantly with gray brick walls made the place look more like an architectural piece than a pub. Sydney suspected that it probably was, until the city discovered that it could be used as revenue and decided to lease it out. Inside, however, was a totally different story.

It was definitely classier than your corner pub. With TSN and ESPN live on strategically placed flat screens and framed athletic jerseys on the wall, there was definitely more of a sports bar vibe. But the ever-present haze of smoke and the smell of alcohol quickly reminded Sydney that it was still a bar like any other.

She heard Lissandra cough from behind her.

"You sure she's here?"

"No," Sydney said, looking around as her eyes adjusted to the dimness. "But there's a high possibility."

"Hey, ladies, welcome to The Toucan," a skinny girl with a high forehead and dirty blond hair called out from behind the bar. "Can I get you anything?"

Lissandra flashed a big smile and stepped forward.

"Thanks! We're actually new in town."

"Oh, really!" the bartender said, her eyes brightening. "Well, welcome to Kingston, and welcome to the best spot this side of Ontario. I'm Mindy and I'll be your bartender tonight. What would you like to drink? We have a great brew on tap tonight. . . ."

"Actually, we were here to meet our friend Shayla?" Sydney said, adding her smile to Lissandra's. "She never stops talking about this place. We heard so much about it, we decided to stop by on our way through town and grab a drink with her here."

"You know her, right?" Lissandra asked.

"Shayla?" Mindy said, her mouth forming into a smile of her own. "Who doesn't know Shayla in here? She's one of our best customers." Mindy laughed. "She comes here so often we might have to offer her a job."

Sydney forced herself to laugh like Lissandra was already doing, and tried not to roll her eyes.

"That's our Shay Shay," Lissandra said, with all the affection of a cobra.

"You wouldn't know if she's come by yet, would you?" Sydney asked casually.

Mindy smirked. "Oh yeah, she's here. She's with Junior in the back at their regular booth, of course."

Sydney and Lissandra exchanged the same look. Who was Junior?

"Let me go call her for you. The lights are pretty low back there, and she's such a tiny thing, she can be hard to spot."

Lissandra snorted. "You don't have to tell me."

"But don't trouble yourself with that," Sydney said quickly. "You've already been a big help. We'll just pop back and say hi."

"But thanks," Lissandra threw after her as Sydney dragged her away.

They walked carefully through the narrow bar toward the back, trying to not trip over anyone as the light grew dimmer. Suddenly Sydney felt her hand jerked back as Lissandra stopped and tightened her grip.

"There she is," Lissandra hissed.

"Where?"

"There!" She jerked her head in the direction of a booth on the back left. "The woman with the dark brown hair and the tight dress."

Sydney's mouth fell open a little. "That's her?"

"Yeah," Lissandra said. "I could spot those fake lopsided silicones anywhere."

Sydney was not about to get into a conversation about the authenticity of Sheree's breasts or anything else. There would be time for that later. After she beat the conniving out of her.

This was the moment they had waited for. And now it was time to get the show on the road. With a hand over her mouth, Sydney screamed.

"Oh my goodness, Shayla! Is that you?" Sydney squealed and ran over to the table, throwing her arms around a redfaced Sheree. Sydney almost lost it when she saw the shocked look on Sheree's face. She would never forget that look. It was priceless.

"Oh my word, look at you, girl!" Sydney continued, releasing Sheree and looking her up and down. "You look good. Sandi, get over here and look at Shayla."

"Mm, mm, mm," Lissandra said, sauntering over to the table and looking at Sheree, her eyes sparkling. "Shayla, girl, you done gone and done the thing. Look at you!"

"Doesn't she look great, Sandi?"

"Fabulous, Nini," Lissandra said with a shake of her head. "Must be the inheritance from her dead husband."

Sydney glared at Lissandra. "Sandi, stop, you know her husband ain't dead."

She turned back to Sheree, whose caramel skin had gone through three shades of red. "Ain't that right, girl?"

Sheree opened and closed her mouth several times, but no words came.

"Shayla, darlin', what they talking about?" Junior asked.

Sydney looked over at the man on the other side of the table. So this is who Sheree ditched her brother for? This ashy-skinned man, with sunken cheeks and two-day-old stubble who looked like he weighed less than a hundred pounds soaking wet? Sydney scowled and wondered if she could toss him through the glass windows of The Toucan so she could focus on Sheree.

"N-n-nothing, Junior," Sheree stuttered. "I don't even know these women. Come on, let's just go."

Sheree stood shakily and Lissandra and Sydney exchanged an amused look. This chick was crazy if she thought she was going anywhere.

"Sit down, Sheree."

Junior paused halfway from getting up, his eyes widening. "Who's Sheree?" He looked at Sheree with a mix of confusion and suspicion. "Why they calling you Sheree, Shayla?"

"Why you listening to them for," Sheree said, raising her voice at him. "I said let's go."

"And I said sit your behind down," Lissandra ground through her teeth. She held up her right hand. "These rings? They ain't just jewelry."

Sydney put a hand on Sheree's limp shoulder, pushed her back down into the booth, and sat down beside her, blocking her in.

Lissandra looked over at Junior, who was standing and looking at Sheree as if he had never seen her before.

"Shayla . . ."

"Her name's not Shayla," Sydney said, sitting back and looking up at Junior. "It's Sheree. She's not from Kingston or wherever else she told you. And she's married, to my brother, who she put in the hospital after she ran off with all his money."

Junior's mouth fell open. He turned his eyes slowly to Sheree as if trying to confirm their story. She looked away at the wall.

"You lied to me? How could you . . ."

"Yeah, yeah, look, buddy, we kind of have some business to do with your girl here, so can you take up the whole broken-hearted routine with her later?" Lissandra asked impatiently.

"But . . ."

"Beat it."

Junior looked up and down at Lissandra as if considering his options, then slipped on his baseball cap and slumped out toward the exit. Lissandra took the seat he exited, effectively blocking Sheree in on both sides. Finally they had her—and there was nowhere for her to run.

Sheree pulled a cigarette from her purse and lit it, taking a deep draw. She had either recovered from the shock of seeing them and was planning her next move, or was resigned to whatever was coming next. From everything Sydney knew about Sheree so far, she suspected that it was the former.

"So you found me," she said finally. She clapped her hands mockingly as she blew out a puff of smoke. "Congratulations. Now what?"

"What do you think, heifer? We want our money back!" Lissandra snapped.

"That's my money. Me and my husband's money," Sheree spat nastily. "And who you calling heifer, you fat cow."

Danger flashed in Lissandra's eyes as she began to stand up, but Sydney caught her arm and gave a slight shake of her head.

"Nice try, Sheree," Sydney said. "You're not going to get us kicked out on a bar fight so you can get away. So how about we quit playing games. Give us the money, and we can just walk away from all this right now."

OK, so all of them knew that Sheree walking away was not going to happen. But it made them sound more civil to put it out there as an option.

"It's gone," Sheree said, taking another drag from her cigarette as she flipped a lock of her dark brown bob out of her eye. "I already spent it."

"Yeah, we know," Lissandra said dryly. "We saw the house and the clothes. And the fifty thousand in the kitchen cupboard."

The smug look slid off Sheree's face. Sydney suspected that she was starting to realize how tight the noose was around her neck.

"You're a liar, Sheree. You said you were pregnant, but you weren't. Now you're saying the money's gone, but my guess is it isn't," Sydney said. "I know you must have a chunk of it left. Even *you* can't spend that much money that fast."

Sydney was bluffing. A professional scammer like Sheree *could* spend that much money that fast. She would know to put her money in luxury items and assets. But Sydney was hoping that somehow she was wrong.

"Just give us the money, Sheree," Lissandra said impatiently, her hands pressed on the table. "It wasn't yours. It was Dean's—you stole it from him."

"Oh, please," Sheree snapped. "OK, so I lied about being pregnant and I took the money. At least I'm doing something worthwhile with it. Your brother would have burned through that money in a year spending it on that silly studio and those third-rate artists of his who were going nowhere fast."

That was probably the only thing Sydney and Sheree would ever agree on. She was probably right about Dean burning through the money. But he never would have gotten his hands on that money if it wasn't for her.

"He wouldn't have had the money if you hadn't convinced him to sell Decadent. Don't think for a second that I don't know you were behind that, too. Don't you even care that you destroyed our family's history by forcing him to do that?"

Sheree laughed. "I didn't force your brother to do anything. The idea was all his. I just passed the information that he was planning to sell to the right people and encouraged him along."

She leaned forward. "See, that was always your problem, Sydney. You always thought that Dean cared. Dean didn't give two hoots about the shop. You did, though. He told me how you poured your sweat and blood into that little family shop. How you did everything for Daddy Leroy. Gave all your time after school and during college, sacrificed your social life for Daddy's little business. He told me how sure you were that that little hole in the wall was going to be yours. How you stayed in that little fifteen-dollar-an-hour manager position even after you got your degree, so that when the time came, it would be yours. But that didn't happen, did it?"

She took another draw from her cigarette and sat back watching Sydney with amusement. "When old boy Leroy finally kicked the bucket, he gave everything to Dean. The one who didn't even care about Decadent. The one who had never even worked a day in the shop, much less knew how it operated. And that killed you, didn't it."

She laughed. "That's why you're here, Sydney. You think you're so much better than me. But you're not. You and me, we're the same. I wanted that money for me, and you're here now because you want it for you, too. Well, guess what, sugar. Game's over. I've got the money.

"And just like the day they read Leroy's will"—Sheree paused to take another draw—"you get nothing."

She blew the smoke straight into Sydney's face and laughed.

But before the smoke could even clear, Sheree's laugh was cut off by long, slim fingers around her neck. The cigarette slipped from her fingers onto the table and her eyes widened in fear as she struggled in vain to pull Sydney's ever-tightening hands from around her neck. Her ears rung as she gasped for breath.

"Syd, what are you doing?" Lissandra hissed, looking around nervously. "This is not the place. Syd!"

But Sydney only had ears for Sheree. Her eyes watched the younger woman gasp for breath.

"Look at me." Sydney's voice was so low and so unnervingly calm that it sounded foreign to her own ears.

Sheree focused her terrified eyes on Sydney's cold, calm face.

"Listen very carefully. I'm going to say this only one time." Sydney spoke quietly but she knew that Sheree heard every word—especially since her next breath literally depended on it. "You will give us back that money. One way or another. Do you understand?"

Sheree nodded her head quickly, even though Sydney's grip made it difficult.

Sydney leaned closer. "I'm sorry. I didn't hear you."

"Ye-yes," Sheree squeaked.

Sydney glared a moment longer at Sheree's face, which had gone from red to pale to tinted blue. She let her go and the younger woman slumped back in the booth, gasping for air.

"You ladies doing all right?" Mindy asked, coming to the back with a pitcher of beer and glasses for all of them.

"Oh yeah, we're doing great," Lissandra said cheerfully. "Right, Sher-Shayla?"

Sheree nodded and rubbed her neck, offering a weak smile.

"OK, then," Mindy said cheerily. "I know it's pretty loud in here, but just holler if you need anything."

"Gotcha," Lissandra said.

Sydney was glad Lissandra was doing all the talking, because suddenly she wasn't feeling so good. What had just happened? Had she just put her hands around a woman's neck? She could have killed her. She knew, because for a brief moment she had thought about it. It had crossed her mind. What if she had just kept squeezing . . . just until she couldn't speak . . . just until her words stopped hurting . . . until they stopped being so painfully true?

But that wasn't who Sydney was. She wasn't a killer. Right?

A wave of nausea washed over her and she stood up.

"I'm going to the restroom," she said to Lissandra. "Watch her."

"OK," Lissandra said. Sydney could see the concern in her sister's eyes, but she didn't have time to reassure her, when she didn't even know what was happening inside herself.

She slipped into an empty stall in the restroom and leaned her back against the closed door, closing her eyes. When she did, she could see Sheree's face laughing at her. Hear her words mocking her. Then she saw Dean, and Leroy. Even Jackie. And she imagined that at some point they had laughed at her also. Or worse, pitied her.

Sheree was right. Sydney had thought Decadent would be hers. Why? Because Leroy had told her. A long time ago when she was just a little girl, when she should have been too young to remember. But she did.

It had been the summer before Leroy and Jackie had gotten back together. She had been only nine years old. It had been late. She had been sitting on a table near the exit, waiting for him to lock up so he could take her home. Lissandra and JJ had gone home early and were already at the house. But Sydney had stuck around with her dad until closing time.

She remembered that day like it had just happened. Everyone else had left, all the offices had been locked up, and all that was left to do was turn off the lights and shut the front door. Leroy reached for the switch, but paused just before, looking back at the empty shop.

"What is it, Daddy?" Sydney had asked.

He hadn't answered right away. Just smiled.

"Sometimes I can't believe how good God has been to me," he said with a shake of his head. "I never thought God would ever give me all of this." He turned to Sydney. "And one day, pumpkin, this will all be yours."

Sydney's eyes had widened. "Me?"

He laughed. "Yes, you." He pinched her nose. "I can see the little baker in you already."

"But it's so big!"

He laughed again, this time turning off the lights and opening the front door for Sydney to go outside.

"Don't worry, pumpkin. When you're older, it won't seem that way at all."

Sydney's eyes burned at the memory. She blinked rapidly and was surprised to feel wetness on her cheeks. Was she crying? No, she wouldn't cry about this. Not anymore. That was years ago. Before Dean was ever even born. Before he had a son who could carry on his legacy. She should have known things would not be the same. Not after the years of chaos that had followed.

What she did know, though, was that no one was going to give her anything. And if she wanted to start to get things back in order with her family, she would need to finish what she started with Sheree.

Sydney stepped out of the stall and stared at herself in the mirror for a moment as she tried to figure out who the woman was staring back at her. She gave up trying and instead splashed some water on her face, washing away any traces of tears. She was about to pat it dry with a napkin when she heard a scream.

When she dashed from the restroom, she found Lissandra crouched down at their table, her hands covering her face.

"Where is Sheree?"

Lissandra was still crouched down, but Sydney still managed to catch her muffled words.

"She's gone. Sheree is gone!"

Chapter 30

"Aargh! She threw beer in my face," Lissandra screamed.

"You let her go!" Sydney hissed.

"She threw beer in my face! I can't even see!"

"I'm going after her."

Without waiting for a reply, Sydney dashed through the bar and out the front door. The cold night wind stung her face. She looked around, but there was no sign of Sheree. She suddenly heard a car engine start and tires squeal as a silver BMW reversed quickly out of a parking space.

Sprinting to her car, Sydney jumped in and gunned the engine, keeping her eyes on the direction of the BMW. She was almost sure that it was Sheree. The car peeled through the parking lot, almost hitting a group of pedestrians before turning right and taking off. But the delay with the pedestrians kept Sydney from losing her completely. As she turned right out of the parking lot, she caught a glimpse of Sheree's car far ahead up the road.

Ignoring the speed limit, Sydney hit the accelerator

and began to close the distance between her and Sheree. Her Nissan was no BMW, but it could hold its own. Soon she was close enough to see the custom plates marked SHAY. There was no doubt whom the car belonged to.

She was almost close enough to pull alongside Sheree, but the woman must have looked back and seen her in the rearview mirror and pulled away again. Sydney slammed her hand against the steering wheel before accelerating again. The cars around her seemed to be standing still as she flew past in pursuit of Sheree. The woman weaved in and out of the two lanes of traffic, easily avoiding the scattering of cars that seemed to be on the road. Sydney tried to follow, but the constant lane changing made it hard for her to catch up with Sheree. Car chasing was not her forte.

As Sheree took the road higher and higher, the traffic began to thin out more. Sydney wasn't that familiar with Kingston, but she was sure they were heading east toward the harbor. Sydney didn't know what Sheree was planning, but whatever it was, she wasn't going to let it get that far. The break in the traffic gave her the opportunity she needed, and she floored her gas pedal and caught up with Sheree.

Pulling up beside her, she rammed Sheree's car with the side of hers, nearly losing control of her Nissan in the process. For a moment, fear sliced through Sydney as she felt her car sway onto the other side of the road. It did not look this dangerous on TV.

"Are you crazy?" Sheree screamed. Even though the window was up, Sydney could read the words on Sheree's lips, as well as see the mix of fear and anger in her eyes.

Sydney rolled down her window.

"Pull over!" Sydney screamed back.

"Go to hell!"

Sheree pulled off again, and Sydney was forced to fall behind her as a huge truck came bearing down on the opposite side of the road. Instead of giving up, however, she sped up and rammed Sheree hard in the back. The force of the impact caused Sydney's car to swerve a little, but she grabbed ahold of the steering wheel and kept it steady.

"You better pull over that car!" Sydney screamed.

She rammed the back of Sheree's car again. Sheree's car tilted a little, swinging into oncoming traffic. Sheree suddenly moved to the side and hit the brakes, allowing Sydney to shoot past her. Then she pulled up beside her and rammed Sydney's car on the left side, causing Sydney to skid onto the shoulder of the road and giving Sheree time to take off again.

Sydney screamed obscenities at Sheree before taking off behind her again. By the time she caught up with her, they were speeding along Ontario Street, where gaps between buildings offered glimpses of the harbor that was closer than it seemed. Sydney was right on her tail when Sheree made a quick right onto the La Salle Causeway. It was empty as far as Sydney could see. There was nothing but her and Sheree and the Kingston Harbour on both sides of the road.

Speeding forward, she clipped Sheree in the back again, but this time the car didn't bounce forward. Sydney tried to fall back a little, but she couldn't. She hit the brakes even harder, but all she got was resistance and the smell of burning rubber.

Her heart began to pound in her chest as she realized what had happened. She was stuck to Sheree's car. She floored the brakes but still nothing. She pressed on the horn, somehow trying to alert Sheree to what was happening. But either the woman didn't know or didn't care. She accelerated, pulling Sydney along with her. Sydney twisted her steering wheel, trying to pull herself away as she continued to lean on the horn. Both cars began to swing from one side of the road to the other.

Sydney felt sweat break out on her forehead and nose. What had she gotten herself into?

She tried again in vain to detach herself from Sheree. Sheree, seeming finally to realize what had happened, began to turn her steering wheel and accelerate at the same time. Sydney wasn't sure what happened, but suddenly she found herself pressed against the side of her car as both cars went spinning at high speed across the causeway. They finally became separated, but only in time for both vehicles to go flying off the road.

Time slowed to a crawl for Sydney. In the same moment, her mind seemed to leave her body as the scene unfolded in front of her, as if she were watching it in IMAX on mute. She saw herself suspended in the air over the Kingston Harbour, the shock and fear on her face clearly visible through the car windshield, her dark hair pressed against her face. She suddenly realized, however, that it was not herself she was looking at. It was Sheree, trapped in her BMW. Sydney was seeing her through her own windshield as both their vehicles headed for the water.

Sydney had heard people who'd been through near-death experiences say their life flashed before their eyes. But as her car sliced into the water, she didn't see scenes from her life. Only people. The staff from the shop. Her Aunt Essie. Her sisters. Dean. Hayden. Jackie. Leroy. His disappointed expression cut through the fear and tore her heart in two with regret. His was the last face she saw as water poured in through the windows of her Nissan and soaked her feet as it came up from the floor.

And then Sheree's car fell on hers.

After that everything went black.

Chapter 31

It was hazy around her. Like the sky outside the plane when you're flying through a cloud. The air felt thick, like a light, white blanket. It was so quiet she could hear her heartbeat. A slow steady rhythm that served to keep her anchored.

"Sydney."

The silence was broken by the low whisper of her name. It was so faint she was almost sure she imagined it. Until she heard it again, a little louder than before. She tried to answer, but she couldn't. There was no sound.

"Sydney."

The voice became more distinct even as the sound of her heartbeat became louder, sharper, and somehow mechanical.

"Sydney. Syd, can you hear me?"

She could hear her but couldn't answer. And now the haze began to grow dark. She felt pressure on her hand and she tried to squeeze back but couldn't. Her body wasn't cooperating. She tried to speak again, and this time her voice stirred from wherever it had been hidden.

"Lissa . . ."

"Yes! Sydney, it's me. Open your eyes, sweetie. Open your eyes."

Sydney was sure it was Lissandra. She heard sniffles and hiccups that sounded like crying. Lissandra never cried.

She finally managed to crack her eyes open, though she almost wished she hadn't as the harsh light assaulted her senses. She groaned and closed them for a moment, before trying again.

"Oh, thank God!" Lissandra cried. Sydney could feel her sister's arms around her neck and her long, curly hair against her cheek.

"Lissandra? What's going on?" Sydney asked slowly, squinting at her sister as Lissandra pulled away.

Lissandra's face was wet and her eyes swollen as she gazed at Sydney with a mix of distress and relief.

"You've been unconscious," she said between sobs. "For two days."

Sydney blinked rapidly as she tried to process what her sister had just told her.

"Two days?"

Lissandra nodded. "They haven't been able to revive you since they pulled you out of the water. Even though they managed to pump the water out of your lungs, they didn't know how long you'd been without oxygen in the car, so they weren't sure if you had brain damage. . . ."

Lissandra was still talking, but Sydney could barely focus on her voice as the memories of what had happened began to come back to her in bits and pieces.

The bridge. Speeding along the causeway. The cars going into the lake. Sheree.

"Sheree," Sydney said, suddenly cutting off her sister. "Where is Sheree . . . ?"

"She's . . ."

"Syd! You're awake!" JJ almost tossed the two cups of hot liquid on the table in her hurry to get to Sydney's side.

"Oh, thank God." She threw her arms around Sydney and began to cry. "I was worried that you might end up like Dean."

"Dean?" Sydney felt a streak of panic run through her, though she couldn't remember why. "What's wrong with Dean?"

"The coma," JJ said. "You know, from the accident?"

Sydney looked to Lissandra for help.

"Dean was in an accident a couple weeks ago," Lissandra said slowly. "Remember?"

Sydney searched her brain and slowly bits and pieces began to come back to her.

"What's wrong with her?" JJ asked, glancing at Lissandra.

"She just woke up," Lissandra said. "I think it's taking her a while to remember things."

"We should call the doctor." JJ got up from Sydney's bedside and headed to the door.

Sydney took the opportunity to ask her previously unanswered question again.

"Where's Sheree?"

Lissandra glanced at the door before leaning forward.

"She's here in the hospital," Lissandra said quietly. "She was unconscious like you, but I heard one of the nurses say she woke up yesterday."

So she was still alive. Sydney felt relief rush through her. Even in her impaired state, she knew she had no positive feelings toward the woman, but if she was dead that would make Sydney a murderer. There was no coming back from that.

"But get this," Lissandra said. "I think she may have amnesia. The nurses are saying she doesn't remember anything about who she is."

Sydney knew this was important for some reason, but her brain was still foggy, and even though her sister said she had been asleep for a few days, she still felt tired. Thinking about Sheree would have to be postponed.

"Ms. Isaacs."

Sydney looked up to see the doctor, an older gentleman that reminded her of Elmer Fudd, enter the room with a nurse and JJ just steps behind him.

"Glad to see you're awake." He gave a tight-lipped smile as he checked the readings on the machines beeping away beside her. "How are you feeling?"

"Tired." It took so much effort to speak. Her mouth felt like it was full of cotton. "And a bit disoriented."

He nodded. "That's quite normal. You've been through a great deal of trauma and your body is still working on healing. Are you in pain?"

Sydney shook her head. "Should I be?"

"Well, you've fractured your right leg and we've set it in a cast, but we have you on pain medication, so you may not feel anything right away," he said. "But once we start to lower your dosage, you will start to experience some discomfort."

Sydney nodded.

"When can she go home?" Lissandra asked.

"We want to observe her for a few more days, just to make sure there isn't any serious brain damage, but if all goes well she should be able to go home in about three days," he said, scribbling something on Sydney's chart.

"You're a very lucky woman, Ms. Isaacs," the doctor said as he prepared to leave.

"Not lucky, blessed," JJ corrected.

The doctor smiled. "Take it easy and get some rest. Nurse Weir will be back to check on you later this afternoon."

"Thanks," Sydney said as she watched them leave.

"I just called Mom," JJ said, taking a seat on the side of Sydney's bed not occupied by Lissandra. "She's on her way back from the hotel. She should be here any minute."

Sydney let out a sigh and pressed the switch to adjust her bed into a sitting position.

"What does she know?" Sydney asked.

"Just that you've been in an accident," Lissandra said. "She doesn't know who the other woman was."

"Which is pretty amazing, seeing that the whole thing was all over the news the night it happened," JJ said.

"In Toronto?" Sydney asked.

"Yup," JJ confirmed with a nod. "Essie managed to talk the police into keeping it hush hush, so they didn't reveal the names."

Sydney rested an IV'd hand across her forehead. "Thank God."

"Don't thank him yet," Lissandra said. "We gotta figure out what we're gonna do about Sheree. We still have time since no one knows she's here. Not even Hayden."

JJ glared in disbelief. "Are you serious? I can't believe you're still scheming after what just happened."

"You better believe it," Lissandra snapped. " 'Cause

if homegirl suddenly starts having flashbacks about how Sydney chased her down the causeway, we're gonna be looking at a lot more than just hospital time."

JJ scowled. "If the both of you had listened to me in the first place, this wouldn't even be happening."

Sydney closed her eyes and put a hand to her aching temple. "Ladies, please—"

"Not all of us can sit back and get rolled over without fighting back," Lissandra shot back.

"Maybe you need to—"

"Sydney."

The three women looked at the unexpected visitor standing at the hospital door.

"Hayden."

In two steps he was on the edge of her bed, pulling her into his arms. Sydney forgot all the complicated issues between them and laid her head against his chest, letting his familiar scent comfort her and jog all her memories of him.

Just when she was beginning to feel like she had found the one place she could stay forever, he loosened his grip so he could look at her.

"How did you know I was here?" she asked as his eyes roamed all over her face.

"I called him," JJ said. Her response earned her a scowl from Lissandra, but Sydney barely noticed either of them.

"I came as soon as I heard," he said, rubbing a thumb across her cheek. "How are you feeling?"

"Like someone just pulled me off the bottom of a lake," Sydney said with a crooked smile.

He smiled back and kissed her forehead.

"Thank God you're alive," he said, his lips so close

to her ear that the words reached only her. "I don't know what I would do if I lost you."

"You can't get rid of me, Dub." Sydney rested her head against his chest once more, feeling the rumble of his chuckle. A contented sigh slipped from her lips as he wrapped his solid arms around her. Her man. Why had she been mad at him again? Whatever it was, it sure didn't matter now. He was definitely forgiven.

He turned her face to his and kissed her eyelids gently, then her nose, then both her cheeks before finally getting to her lips. Sydney sighed. He was definitely the best medicine.

A throat cleared somewhere beyond them, and they turned to see Jackie standing at the door with Zelia and Josephine.

"Mom."

Within moments, Jackie and Hayden had exchanged places and Sydney was being crushed against her mother's bosom.

"Child, you nearly gave me a heart attack worrying about you. The Lord told me that something was wrong with one of my children that night. But I stayed on my knees and he heard my prayer."

Jackie held Sydney's face between her cheeks and looked at her as if memorizing every feature.

"I knew God would take care of you. I knew he would bring you back to me."

Jackie crushed her in her arms again for a moment, but soon had to make space for Zelia and Josephine. The hospital room was starting to turn into a zoo, until the doctors came and shooed everyone out so Sydney could get her rest.

The longer she had been awake, the more clear her

mind had become. And by the time everyone had left and Sydney was alone in her hospital room, the fog had completely lifted. Now she had nothing to do but think. Think about how she had almost died. Think about how she had almost killed another human being. Think about how she had lied to and deceived the people she loved most in the world. And all for what? Money? Revenge?

And then there was Sheree. She had destroyed their lives, but that didn't give Sydney the right to destroy hers. She was tired of this. Tired of letting someone else's actions control her own life. She was done with the secrets and lies.

Reaching for the cell phone at her bedside, she sent a message to Hayden. Within moments, he was at the door.

"Hey." A soft smile played on his lips. "You trying to get me in trouble with the doc?"

"Sit," she said, pointing to a chair beside her bed. "I need to talk to you."

He sat, taking Sydney's hand in his at the same time. But she noticed that the smile had been replaced with a look of concern.

"What's going on?"

Sydney looked at him long and hard, memorizing the lines on his beautiful face. Recalling the touch of his hands on her skin, the feel of his lips against hers, the warmth in his eyes whenever he looked at her, the sense of safety in his arms. She remembered the day months ago when he had walked back into her life. She could almost picture him standing in front of her in his perfectly fit suit, his coffee-colored eyes glowing as they watched her. He had been everything she wanted and needed, and she hadn't even known it. And now that she did, she was about to say words that might make her lose him forever.

But she had to. She wouldn't have him under a cover of lies. There would be no more secrets between them. No more half-truths. No more omissions. If they were going to be together, it would have to be on the terms of complete honesty—starting with her.

Sydney sighed. "You know there were two cars involved in my accident, right?"

He nodded.

"The driver of the other car was Sheree," she said.

Sydney watched as a range of emotions passed over his face. He looked away from her as if trying to process the information.

"We found her here in Kingston, at a bar. Things got a little messy. She took off and I took off after her. At the bridge, things got out of control and both our cars went into the harbor."

He slowly sat back, pulling his hand away from Sydney's. She felt the coldness slide between them like a wall as he took in her words. His face was expressionless, but she could see his Adam's apple bob up and down as he swallowed hard.

"So she's here," Hayden croaked. He still wouldn't look at Sydney.

"Yes." Sydney said, not sure how much more she should say. "She's here under an alias, Shayla Vaughn. She . . ."

Sydney stumbled and Hayden turned hard eyes on her. She couldn't speak when he looked at her like that, so she looked away.

"She was unconscious. But she woke up yesterday. She doesn't remember who she is."

She heard the chair scrape against the floor as Hayden got up.

"Hayden . . ."

"I have to go see her." He was halfway to the door.

Sydney felt bands of panic wrap around her heart as she watched him walk away. It felt like he was leaving more than just her hospital room.

"I never meant for any of this to happen." She could barely speak past the lump in her throat.

He stopped but didn't look back at her.

"You found her. How could you not have told me?"

There were so many things she could say to defend herself. But that wouldn't be complete honesty.

"I'm sorry," was all she could come up with.

His voice was quiet when he finally spoke. "Yeah. Me, too."

He opened the door and left without looking back. Sydney curled onto her side and pulled the sheets closer around her as the coldness of his departure wrapped around her. She was almost sure, that this time he wasn't coming back.

Chapter 32

Sydney had always thought she would be much older before mobility would be a problem for her. It had been more than three weeks since she'd been released from the hospital, but timely movements were still difficult. With the better part of her right leg in a cast and a number of bruises on other parts of her body, she had been ordered to take it easy. But taking it easy meant a lot of downtime thinking about all the taking it easy she could do now that she didn't have a job. So she had called up Jackie and offered to make snacks for her next women's ministries meeting at church. Her mother had declined but contracted her to make hors d'oeuvres for the seniors' banquet that weekend. Sydney had nearly fallen off her crutches when Jackie told her the event would host two hundred people. She should have known better than to ask her mother for work. Jackie could always find some.

It was probably a blessing in disguise, however. The busier she was, the less time she would have to think about Hayden. At least, that was the way she supposed it should work. Instead, however, everything reminded her of him. The kitchen reminded her of when he had cooked breakfast for her and her sisters. The living room reminded her of when he had held her as she cried about Dean. The backyard reminded her of the day he had dropped everything to be with her after Dean announced he was selling the store. Her home was infested with memories of him. No matter where she turned, there was no escaping him. But at least the work would help her try.

Sydney was wrist deep in pastry dough when the doorbell rang. In a moment of impatience, she abandoned her crutches and hopped the short distance to the door on her good foot. Slightly out of breath, she pulled the door open.

"Sorry, I didn't hear the . . ."

Sydney lost the rest of her sentence when she saw him. It was the first time she'd laid eyes on him since the hospital. She had thought that time would be the last time. But here he was, standing outside her door looking incredible. The rich chocolate brown of his leather jacket and navy shirt contrasted sharply with his bronzed skin. The midday sun behind him framed his sturdy form in golden light that made him look like he had stepped out of a dream, but the scent of his sandalwood cologne confirmed that he was fully and completely real. She thanked God for the doorframe. Her good leg was completely weak.

"Hey," was all she could manage when she finally found her voice.

She watched his eyes trip all over her face before he answered.

"Hey."

She wasn't sure how long they stood at the door

staring at each other. Sydney had always been able to read Hayden. He had been an open book from the start. Every emotion, every thought, every inclination was always right there at the surface. She had always been the one to hold back. But now the roles had been switched. Sydney felt like everything she felt for him that wouldn't go away was written all over her face. But he was unreadable.

She balanced against the wall and moved to the side. "Come in."

He stepped in slowly and she closed the door behind him, still leaning on it for support. Now they were both standing in the entryway. Sydney knew she would look ridiculous hopping toward the couch or the kitchen, but her crutches were nowhere nearby. She saw Hayden glance at her non-functioning leg, and he seemed to pause as if contemplating his options.

"Where are your crutches?" he asked finally.

"In the kitchen, between the refrigerator and the counter."

Without another word, he strode through the living room and disappeared into the kitchen.

"Thank you," Sydney said nervously, when he returned a few moments later with her supports in his hand.

"Can I get you anything?" she asked, settling the crutches under her arms and turning toward the kitchen. "Water? Soda? Juice?"

"No, I'm fine." He followed her into the kitchen. He sat on one of the breakfast stools by the counter and watched Sydney move the huge roll of dough into a bowl and cover it with a towel.

Something that almost looked like a smile lifted the corner of his lips.

"Stressed out?" he asked.

She glanced at him and remembered how much he knew her. He knew that work was her escape.

Sydney let out a shaky breath. "A little."

When there was finally nothing left to do with her hands, she settled onto the kitchen stool across the counter from him.

She could feel his eyes on her, but she couldn't bring herself to meet them. Every time she looked at him, she felt like she was hurting him all over again. And sorry didn't seem like enough to cover all of that.

"How's Sheree?" she asked.

"She was OK," he said, "while she was with me."

Sydney looked up at him.

"She was at my place for a couple days, then I came home one day and she was gone."

Sydney looked down again. "I'm sorry."

He shrugged. "Some birds can't be caged."

"I'm sorry about everything," Sydney said, looking up at him again.

He looked at her for a long moment.

"See, that's the problem," he said finally. "I keep getting the feeling that there are parts of that everything that I don't know about."

Sydney felt her heart beat faster and she prayed to God that he wouldn't ask her.

"I want to know, Sydney . . ."

"No, you don't," she said, shaking her head.

"I need to know," he said, leaning forward. "Tell me what happened with you and Sheree. Please."

Sydney didn't want to. She really didn't want to. But she had promised herself on that bed in the hospital that she was done lying. Done keeping secrets. If she really accepted that what she had done was wrong and she was really sorry for it, then she had to be ready to be honest about it. Honest with herself and honest with everyone else.

She raised her eyes to his. "OK."

Then she took a deep breath and told him everything: from the cell phone tap, to copying his keys; from the day in his bedroom at his house, to the day they searched Sheree's house. She told him every detail, and she watched every emotion roll over his face as she did it. When she was done, he was somewhere between disbelief and anger.

"You copied my keys?" He had gotten up off the stool and was pacing the floor. "You broke into my house? I can't believe . . . I was there, you were right there . . ."

Sydney watched him rub his hands over his head as he continued pacing. Every couple of moments, he would glance up at her. She knew what he was thinking. What kind of person could do that? How could he have loved someone as vile and deceitful as she was? She knew, because she had asked herself those same questions.

"I can't believe you did that to me." His whole body seemed to shake with anger. "I trusted you, I loved you. How could you do that to me?"

His anger couldn't disguise the hurt that poured out of him as he questioned Sydney. It sliced her heart in two. And even though she thought she was done crying over Hayden and what she had done, she felt tears sting the back of her eyelids.

"I'm sorry," she said. "I know I was wrong. But I had to find her. And you wouldn't tell me anything. You knew and you wouldn't tell me!"

"Oh, so this is my fault?"

"No, I never said that." Sydney couldn't stop herself from choking up. "But we both lied to each other, Hayden. I am sorry for what I did, but I didn't mess us up on my own."

"I was trying to help you," he protested. "I wanted her to give it all back. But I knew once you and your sisters got ahold of her, you would rake her over the coals."

"And what, she didn't deserve it? For what she did to Dean?" Sydney protested. "My brother's been in a coma for weeks. He may never wake up—never come home!"

"My sister *has* no home," Hayden said. "She never did. And I just wanted to be that one person that she could feel safe with. Can't you understand that, Sydney? She never had anyone be on her side. I wanted to be that for her. I needed to be that."

She rubbed a hand across her face to swat away the tears that had disobeyed her. "I know we both have reasons for what we did. If I could do this all over, I would do it different. But I can't. All I can say is I'm sorry. And I know it's not enough, but . . ."

Sydney had run out of words, and the sobs choking her weren't making it any easier. She had never cried this much in her entire life. She wasn't even sure who she was anymore.

"Don't," he said, shaking his head. "Don't do that. You don't get to cry and make me forget. You hurt me, Sydney—in ways that you can't even understand. You disrespected me, violated me, and trampled all over our relationship."

He stepped forward, the heat in his eyes incinerating her.

"And you know what the worst part of it is?" he asked angrily. "Despite all of that, despite everything you did . . . For some reason that I don't even understand, I still love you."

Sydney felt her heart fall to her feet. His words should have made her feel better—consoled some part of her deep inside. But instead, she felt like she wanted to die.

He reached into his inside jacket pocket for something, then dropped it on the counter in front of her without looking at it. She breathed in and got the slightest whiff of his cologne. She looked into his clear brown eyes and saw the sheen of his unshed hurt. He was so close, her fingers ached to touch him— but so far away she felt she could never reach him again.

With one last look at her, he turned and headed toward the living room. His final words cut the last cord of composure Sydney had, and echoed through the empty house even after the door slammed behind him.

"Happy birthday, Sydney."

"Surprise!"

The front door to the house burst open and in flooded Sydney's mother and sisters.

"Happy Birthday to you! Happy birthday to you. Happy birthday, dear Sydney . . . happy birthday to you!"

Sydney burst into tears and buried her face in the cushions of the couch that she had been lying on for the past four hours.

"Sydney, what's wrong with you?" JJ sank into the couch beside Sydney.

"Yeah, girl," Lissandra asked. "How long you been lying on that couch? It looks like it's starting to take shape around you."

"Lissandra, please make yourself useful and bring me a damp cloth for your sister," Jackie said, easing Sydney's head up and sitting before resting her daughter's head in her lap.

"Geez, is turning thirty that depressing?" Zelia asked.

"OK, the rest of you with nothing useful to say can go find something else to do somewhere else." Jackie laced the group with her no-nonsense look.

When the crowd had finally cleared, only Jackie and JJ were left.

"What happened, sweetheart?" Jackie stroked her grown daughter's head, which was wrapped in a scarf.

But Sydney wasn't up for talking and only started sobbing again.

"Maybe it has something to do with that gift she's holding on to like a lifeline," Lissandra said upon her return. She handed the damp cloth to her mother before taking a seat in the empty armchair.

"Can I?" JJ reached for the partially unwrapped gift.

When Sydney relinquished it, Lissandra immediately moved to JJ's side to get a closer look.

"What is it?" Lissandra asked impatiently.

"It's a card," JJ said. "And a whole stack of papers."

"Happy Birthday, baby," Lissandra read out over JJ's shoulder. "Here's to your dream coming true. Dub."

"Oh." A mutual sound of understanding went up from the three women.

"Oh hell no," Lissandra said as she took the papers from JJ and began flipping through the stack. "No, he didn't."

"He didn't what?" JJ asked. "What is it?"

"It's a deed," Lissandra said. "To a property on College Street. And it's in Sydney's name. Both their names, actually."

JJ let out an appreciative whistle. "He bought you real estate for your birthday? What a man."

"What number?" Jackie asked suddenly.

"Huh?"

"What number College Street?"

JJ and Lissandra peered back at the paper.

"It's 572," JJ said finally.

"Dang," Lissandra said with a laugh. "That Negro knew what to do."

Jackie shook her head and smiled. "Five seventy-two College Street."

"I don't get it," JJ said, looking from her sister to her mother.

"That was where Decadent used to be," Lissandra said.

"What?" JJ exclaimed.

"We weren't always over on Queen," Jackie said with a smile. "When Leroy first opened his bakery, it was just that. A little bakery and pastry shop. And it was at 572 College Street. That was the first Decadent. You're probably too young to remember, JJ."

"I remember," Lissandra said wistfully. "It was small and narrow, with only space for a few tables and chairs down the side. But Daddy loved it."

"We had good memories there," Jackie said, nodding.

Sydney began to sob again and Jackie looked down at her.

"Oh, sweetheart." Jackie stroked her daughter's head. "He knew this would mean a lot to you, didn't he."

Sydney nodded against her mother's lap.

"Dang." Lissandra glanced over at the pile of gifts on the floor. "None of us can top that."

"It's OK, sweetheart," Jackie said. But Sydney sat up, pulling herself away from her mother's touch.

"No," Sydney said, her voice nasal from her stuffy nose. "It's not OK and it won't be. Hayden and I are over."

"Don't be so quick to throw in the towel," Jackie said. "God is in control. Even of this."

"Not after what I did," Sydney said. "There is no chance after that."

"You got that right," Lissandra said, earning her a warning look from Jackie.

"Why don't the two of you go help your sisters in the kitchen," she suggested in a way that told them it was not a suggestion.

When they left, she pulled Sydney into her arms.

"Sydney, sweetheart, I don't know exactly what went on with you and Hayden and his sister. And to be perfectly honest, I am not sure I want to know," she said. "But I do know this. Since your father died, I have watched you let your emotions of hurt, resentment, guilt, and confusion turn you into a shadow of the woman I know."

Sydney sat up and looked at her mother.

"You have to let those feelings go, Sydney," Jackie said. "Forgive your father for breaking your heart. Accept the truth that it's OK to feel hurt and disappointed. And for heaven's sake, stop thinking that you have to solve all our problems on your own. Dean's hospital bills will get paid somehow. My mortgage will get taken care of. The staff from your father's store will find work somewhere. And you won't lose this house, either. Even if you do, you and your sisters will be fine and Dean will get over this thing with Sheree. You don't have to solve all these problems to prove that you love all of us. We know you love us and we love you. And you don't have to earn that love."

Sydney looked down at her hands. She had never realized that that was what she was doing. When had she started thinking she had to earn the love of the people around her? Maybe when she realized she hadn't earned her father's love, not completely anyway.

"I know that it will be a long time before you get over what your father did with that store," Jackie said, as if reading Sydney's thoughts. "But darling, unless you get over it and get past it, you're gonna keep finding yourself right here. Your father loved you the best way he knew how. You can keep struggling to understand him and what happened, or you can accept it and get on with your life."

"Today is your thirtieth birthday, sweetheart," Jackie said, stroking her daughter's hair. "Don't you think it's time you made a new beginning for yourself?"

Sydney did think it was time. She knew her mother was right: she had to let go of her disappointment over Decadent. She had been carrying it too long and it had been keeping her stuck in a place that she knew she didn't want to be anymore. It was time to get up and start moving, start living again. It was time for a new direction.

Chapter 33

"OK, Sydney, where are you taking me?" Maritza asked from the driver's seat of her BMW X3.

"You'll see soon," Sydney said from the passenger seat. "Turn right at the light."

"Girl, this better be good." Maritza's neon pink lips curled up in skepticism. " 'Cause I do not drive through midday traffic for just anyone."

"We're here," Sydney said, sitting forward. "See if you can grab that parking space behind the red mini-van."

Maritza glanced suspiciously at the minivan. "That soccer mom better not scratch my truck."

Sydney got out of the SUV slowly and stood in front of the storefront. It looked exactly like it had the day she had come there with Hayden, except now the sign for the bar was gone and it was completely empty. Her grip tightened around the keys in her hand. It had taken her over a week to work up the courage to just come down here. Now that she was here, she wasn't sure she could go in.

This was part of the reason she had asked Maritza to

come with her. Though they hadn't been friends for that long, they had clicked. And there were certain things Maritza understood that her sisters couldn't— like what it meant to date a man of Hayden's status. When you weren't used to being around someone with that much money, it was easy to get caught up and miss the big picture. Plus Maritza probably understood the new Hayden much better than any of her sisters did.

"OK, so what's this about?" Maritza asked between smacks of gum as she came up beside Sydney. "Did you haul me down here to look at storefront property? 'Cause if you're in the market, I can think of a couple better locations."

"You asked me what Hayden got me for my birthday," Sydney said, her eyes still on the store.

"Uh-huh," Maritza said, her bracelets jingling as she put her hand on her hip.

"This is it."

"This what?" Maritza asked.

Sydney glanced over at her friend, then back at the store.

"This," she repeated, adding a tilt of her head for clarification.

Maritza stopped chewing. "He bought you a store? Dub bought you a freaking store! Girl, what did you do to that man? And can you teach me how to do it to Sean?"

Sydney shook her head. "I didn't do anything. Nothing to deserve him, anyway."

"Well, he certainly doesn't think so," Maritza replied, marching toward the door in her eight-inch wedges. "We going in or what?"

Sydney stood rooted in front of the store, staring at the glass.

"Syd!"

Sydney shook her head. "I can't."

"Well, I can." Maritza took a few steps back toward Sydney and stretched out her hand. "Keys."

Sydney reluctantly released the keys into Maritza's hand, then watched as the robust woman sashayed her way over to the door and began trying keys in the lock. It took her less than a minute to get to the right one. Sweat beaded Sydney's anxious forehead as she watched the door swing open easily.

With a glance back at Sydney, Maritza disappeared inside. Sydney wrung her hands as she waited to hear something. She resisted the urge to retreat to the passenger seat of the car even though her right leg, wrapped in a walking cast, begged for reprieve. But even the soreness in her leg couldn't compete with her anxiety as she contemplated whether or not she could go into the store. She didn't know why she was being so weird about the whole thing. Going in didn't mean that she was accepting the store as a gift from Hayden. She couldn't. She had no right to. But she wasn't sure she would feel as strongly if she went inside.

"Well? What does it look like?" Sydney yelled toward the slightly ajar door.

Maritza's voice came from somewhere deep inside the store. "Come and see for yourself."

Sydney wrung her hands some more. This was silly. She would go inside, look around, and then leave. Plain and simple.

"It's just a store," she murmured to herself, before closing the distance between herself and the door.

She managed to hold on to her conviction the first few moments inside. The blinds on the windows were down, and it was still too dark inside to see anything clearly. But then Maritza flipped a switch somewhere and light flooded the space.

Sydney heard her breath catch in her throat. The whole space had been redone. Gone was the ugly dark green paint they had seen the first time, and in its place a fresh coat of a soft eggshell color. The hardwood floor was shiny as if recently refinished, and she could see that the lighting fixtures above the counter and around the store had been recently replaced. All the bar equipment was gone, leaving lots of space behind the counter for anything and everything Sydney could have wanted.

Hayden had redone the entire space.

"Sydney, girl, you're gonna want to see this." Maritza stuck her head through the double doors behind the counter that led to the kitchen. "You're gonna flip."

Sydney could only imagine what Hayden had done in the kitchen. However, when she finally stepped through the double doors, she realized that her imagination had fallen way short.

The entire kitchen had also been done over, with what looked like new tiles on the floor and stainless-steel cupboards and countertops. But the brand-new industrial oven was what Sydney couldn't take her eyes off of. The thing was straight out of a Bakers Pride catalog. Stainless-steel double oven, gas. It was convection, but Sydney knew that with this model, there was the option to turn off the fan, which she hadn't had in the old convection oven at Decadent. She ran her hand over the sleek, shiny body of the oven before opening both doors to look inside. This was a brand-new oven. She knew how much it cost because she had been salivating over one online the last time she'd had to bake a batch of tarts for her mother, and had had to get through the whole order in three rounds because her oven was too small to accommodate them all at the same time.

"I can't believe he did this," Sydney said, shaking her head.

"You and me both," Maritza said. "I don't know much about kitchen equipment, but I know that all of this ain't cheap."

She had no idea. Sydney's brain was still running the numbers. "He talked about not making the best choices with his money."

"Girl, Dub may have been young, but he wasn't stupid enough not to hold back anything. He was into his second multimillion dollar contract when he got hurt. So . . ."

"It's too much." Sydney backed out of the kitchen and into the main storefront. She pulled out her cell phone and dialed Hayden's. But it went straight to voice mail. Just like it had the last twenty-three times she had called him since he had dropped the deed on her counter. But this time she wasn't giving up. She called the clinic.

"East York Athletic Clinic—"

"Yes, I need to speak with Hayden Windsor, please," Sydney said before the receptionist could finish her introduction.

"I'm sorry, ma'am. Mr. Windsor is currently out of the office. Would you like to leave a message or set an appointment?"

There was no point leaving a message. Sydney knew he wouldn't call her back.

"I'd like to set an appointment," she said.

"OK." She could hear the woman's fingers tap away at a keyboard in the background.

"Are you a regular client or were you recently referred?"

"Uh . . . a regular," Sydney said, walking in small circles.

"And your name?"

Sydney cleared her throat. "Maritza Denary."

Maritza emerged from the kitchen. "You hollered?"

"Oh, Maritza! How are you? I almost didn't recognize your voice," the receptionist said, breaking her formality. "How are you doing? Is it that knee injury acting up again?"

Sydney cleared her throat and glanced back at Maritza, who was watching her suspiciously. "Uh, yeah, it's the knee again. You know how it gets this time of year."

"No problem, girl," the receptionist said. "Look, Hayden has a free spot tomorrow afternoon where one of his clients cancelled. I can slip you in if you want, or if it's too soon . . ."

"Nah, girl, tomorrow's fine," Sydney said. "What time?"

"Three thirty," the receptionist said. "I'll book you in right now."

"OK, thanks," Sydney said. "I'll be in for my appointment tomorrow."

"OK, girl," the receptionist said. "And remember those Chanel fragrance samples you promised me!"

"No problem," Sydney said. "See you tomorrow."

She hung up the phone before the conversation could go any further.

"So let me guess," Maritza said, folding her arms and smirking at Sydney. "I have an appointment tomorrow with Dub."

Sydney bit her lip sheepishly. "Yup. And you're

bringing the Chanel samples you promised the girl at reception."

Maritza rolled her eyes. "Great. Now I'm gonna have to go buy something at Chanel on the way home. Sean is going to be mad again."

"Why?" Sydney asked. "You work. It's your money, isn't it?"

Maritza clucked her tongue at Sydney. "That's why you're not married, sugar. You have so much to learn."

Sydney wrinkled her nose. "Apparently."

"So why couldn't you set your own appointment?" Maritza asked.

"Because he would never see me," Sydney said with a sigh as she rested her elbows on the counter. "He won't even answer my calls."

"That bad, huh?"

"Yeah," Sydney said. "And trust me, I totally deserve it."

"So how do you know he won't throw you out when he sees you tomorrow?"

Sydney shrugged. "I don't know. I just hope I can get through to him before he does. We need to find a way to handle this shop thing so that he can get his money back and get on with his life. There is no way I can accept this."

Maritza's eyes widened. "Now hold on just a minute, Miss Bleeding Heart. I know that you're feeling really terrible about what went on with you and Dub, but let's not get carried away, here. This was your dream, remember?"

"I know, but—"

"No buts," Maritza said. "Don't you think you should think about this some more? This is what you worked your whole life for, and now it's right in front of you."

"You're right," Sydney said. "But I don't want it. Not like this. Dub bought this place for us. This was supposed to be something we would do together. But without him in it, I would just be miserable. Every day in this place would just be a reminder of what I did to him, and what I gave up because of my own selfishness."

Maritza narrowed her eyes at Sydney. "You love him, don't you?"

Sydney shrugged. "Is that what this is?"

"Putting someone before yourself? Giving up what you want for someone else, even though you know you probably won't get anything out of it?" Maritza asked. "Kind of sounds like that to me."

Sydney shook her head. "You know, I used to think I knew what love was. I thought it was about me. What I wanted, what would make me feel good. But it's not. Real love is not about yourself. It's about the other person."

Maritza came over to lean on the other side of the counter. "You know, Syd, you remind me so much of myself when I first met Sean," she said. "I thought I knew everything, but that boy taught me so much. He always said you can't really love anyone until you know God's love."

Sydney chuckled humorlessly. "Sounds like something my mom would say. And Dub, too."

"I can imagine," Maritza said. She sighed. "When Sean and I first got married, it was rough. I was still looking out for me. Still trying to grab everything for myself, like I was afraid I would wake up one day and everything would be gone. But he was patient with me, and when I would ask him why, he would say because love is patient. I would give him a hard time sometimes, but he would always be kind to me, because love is kind. I thought I loved Sean, but he helped me understand what real love is. Real love comes from God, girl. It's all that good stuff in first Corinthians thirteen. Love is patient, kind; it doesn't envy; it doesn't boast. It's not proud. It doesn't dishonor others, it's not self-seeking, not easily angered, it keeps no record of wrongs."

Sydney closed her eyes as she thought of what Maritza said. Pride, dishonor, self-seeking, anger. It sounded like a complete description of what her life had been over the past few months.

"It doesn't enjoy evil," Maritza continued, "but rejoices in truth. It always protects, trusts, hopes, and perseveres. That's the kind of love that won't fail. If all you're doing doesn't match up to that, then it's not love. I thought I loved my husband, but I really didn't. In fact, I really didn't love anybody. I couldn't. Not until I understood this. Not until I understood who God was and how he loved me."

This was the other reason why she had let Maritza in so fast. Because there was something she had that Sydney wanted. She had somehow managed to make a real relationship with God seem attainable for Sydney in a way she had never seen it before. Sydney opened her eyes and wiped the runaway tears that had slid down her cheeks.

"I hurt him," Sydney said quietly. "Really, really badly."

"And yet, he still was selfless enough to do all this for you," Maritza said, waving her hand around the room. "Sounds like someone who is still committed to loving you. Why don't you try and love him back?"

"He won't let me," Sydney said. "And I don't deserve him, anyway."

"Sounds like pride and lack of trust."

"I trust him," Sydney said.

Maritza smiled and shouldered her purse. "Dub's not the one you need to be trusting right now."

Sydney paused for a moment before straightening up.

"So what are you saying?" Sydney asked, turning to face Maritza, who was halfway to the door. "I should just leave Dub alone?"

"I'm saying you should work on your vertical relationship with God before you start working on your horizontal relationships," Maritza said. "And since you're catering Sean's birthday party at the end of the month, you probably shouldn't give up that oven quite yet."

"Maritza!" Sydney whined. "You just told me to stay away from Dub. Now you're inviting me to a party where you know he'll be?"

"Uh-uh," Maritza said, wagging her finger. "I am not inviting you to attend. I don't need that kind of drama up in my husband's birthday bash. I am inviting you to cater. You know how Sean loves that key lime cheesecake from Decadent. He would eat it every day if I didn't stop him. I think he's been in withdrawal since the store closed."

Sydney laughed. Maritza was right. The reason they had become such good friends was because Maritza had been in the store almost every week getting the cheesecake for her husband.

"OK, fine," Sydney said with a smile as they headed toward the door. "I'll make the birthday cake and the cheesecake for Sean's birthday. Do you want slices or tarts?"

"Slices, please," Maritza said, slipping on her sunglasses as she stepped outside. "We're thinking it will be around two hundred people, but I'll call you with the final numbers for the order next week."

"OK," Sydney said, switching off the lights before pulling the door to the shop of her dreams closed.

"And speaking of calls"—Maritza unlocked the car with the key remote—"don't you have a call to make?"

Sydney sighed. "Oh, yeah."

She dug out her cell phone and pressed the redial button. The line answered after two rings.

"Hey, it's me, Maritza," she said. "I need to cancel my appointment."

Chapter 34

Sydney lay in bed and watched the numbers on her bedside clock turn from 4:29 a.m. to 4:30. She had woken up almost half an hour earlier and hadn't been able to get back to sleep. She had planned to get up a little earlier today—it was the day of Sean's party and she had to make thirteen cheesecakes as well as several platters of mini empanadas to serve as hors d'oeuvres. Maritza had come over when Sydney had been experimenting with a new recipe for the empanadas and, after "sampling" half of Sydney's batch, had decided that she wanted them for the party, too. Sydney was glad for the work, but she had had to call in Lissandra and Mario to make sure the whole thing was done in time for the five p.m. start of the event.

She wasn't worried, though. All the ingredients were sitting in the huge kitchen at 572 College Street and she had worked big orders like this with Lissandra and Mario before, so they knew what they were doing. Besides, she had done a test run in the oven and found it worked even better than she thought it would. But despite all of that, her mind didn't feel at ease.

By the time the numbers turned to 4:35, she realized she wasn't going to get any more sleep. She got out of bed, pulled a robe around her, and padded down the stairs to the kitchen. She put on the kettle, took out a mug and the box of berry tea, then went into the living room to wait for the kettle to hiss. As she sank into the couch, she saw the open book on the coffee table. Sydney knew it would be there. It had been there every morning for the past two weeks. And just like every morning before, she took it up to look at the portion that had been marked off the night before.

JJ's Bible was old. It was actually Leroy's father's Bible, which she had found in a box in the basement while they were clearing out the house after Leroy died. Sydney had always assumed that the highlighted sections were from their grandfather. But it suddenly occurred to her that they could be from her sister, because highlighters hadn't been around that long.

This morning the marker was at first Corinthians thirteen. Sydney read over the verses, which talked about love. She got stuck on the last two verses:

Love is patient, love is kind. It does not envy, it does not boast, it is not proud. It does not dishonor others, it is not self-seeking, it is not easily angered, it keeps no record of wrongs. Love does not delight in evil but rejoices with the truth. It always protects, always trusts, always hopes, always perseveres.

She closed her eyes and leaned her head back. Everything she had done, she had done out of love for her family. Or at least that was what she had convinced herself. But none of what she had done matched what the text said love was.

Love does not delight in evil but rejoices with the truth.

What truth? The last few months of her life were saturated with lies. Lies to her family. Lies to her boyfriend. Lies to herself.

She sighed again, closed the Bible, and placed it back onto the table.

"See something you don't like?"

Sydney looked up to find JJ standing at the bottom of the stairs.

"How come you're up so early?" Sydney asked, ignoring her sister's question.

JJ smiled and closed the space between them, sinking into the couch beside Sydney.

"I'm always up this early," JJ said. "I just let you have the living room while I stay in the kitchen."

Sydney raised an eyebrow. "So you knew that I was down here snooping in your Bible every morning?"

JJ chuckled. "You can't snoop in a Bible, Syd. It's not a diary. But yes, I've known. Why do you think I always leave it open the night before?"

Sydney smirked. "I should have guessed. Saint Judith. Always seeking the lost."

"Yeah, whatever," JJ said, putting her feet up on the coffee table. "So what part of first Corinthians did you have a problem with this morning?"

"The part where it says love is letting people take advantage of you."

"Ahh, chapter thirteen. The love chapter," she said knowingly.

"Yes, that part," Sydney said. "It's great in theory, but it's not very practical. What if I had let fly everything Sheree had done to us? I only did what I did out of love for my family."

"Of course," JJ said. "You betrayed your boyfriend, lied to your family, and almost got Sheree and yourself killed for love. That makes sense."

"Come on, JJ," Sydney said, turning to look at her sister. "You can't think this could have turned out any differently."

"I don't know," JJ said with a sigh. "Sometimes I think that if we had given Sheree a chance . . ."

Sydney's eyes widened as her sister trailed off.

"Given her a chance to what?"

JJ bit her lip. "Maybe if we had given her a chance to be our sister. If we had shown her genuine love, treated her like family, maybe she wouldn't have run off with the money."

Sydney raised an eyebrow. "Are you serious? Essie said she's already pulled this stunt twice. You think some TLC could have kept her from her plan this time?"

"I don't know, Syd," JJ said with a touch of frustration. "I've just been thinking about it, and you said Hayden said Sheree never had a family. She never had a father in her life, she barely saw her brother, and her mother is a bit of a nut job. She never had anyone show her real love, Syd. Maybe if we had done that with her, things could have been different."

Sydney didn't say anything, but she turned the words over in her mind. She wanted to believe that Sheree was just evil to the core. Her actions should have been proof enough of that. But if people were going to judge others based on what they saw of them, then Hayden had just as few reasons to forgive Sydney as she did to forgive Sheree.

"You know, when we found her, she said I was just like her," Sydney said, breaking the silence.

JJ turned to look at her.

"She said I pretended that I wanted the money for Dean, but really I wanted it for me," Sydney continued. "Sometimes I think she's right. Maybe I *am* like her."

"Or maybe she's like you," JJ said quietly. "Like all of us. We all think the reasons for what we do are justified. If we were in Sheree's head, as scary a place as it may be, we would probably have done exactly what she did. She was just looking out for herself."

JJ let out a sigh and leaned her head back against the couch.

"You know what I figured out, Syd?" she said after a moment. "It all comes down to love. We're all doing things out of misguided love. You killed yourself at Decadent out of love for Dad. You schemed to catch Sheree to prove to Dean that you love him, despite everything that happened. Hayden lied to you to prove to Sheree that he loves her. And Sheree stole so she could feel good enough about herself to love herself.

"Everyone in this world is just looking for real love. And when we get something that looks like it might be real, we scheme and lie and cheat to keep it, not realizing that if you have to do those things, it can't be love. Real love grows when you give it freely. The problem is, giving it away is hard. Loving people, with the patience and kindness and humility that real love from God requires, is really hard. Because in many cases you might end up getting hurt."

"You can only get hurt so many times in life, JJ,"

Sydney said. "When you've been hurt too much, you forget how to love."

"That's too bad. 'Cause the poison is the cure," JJ said. "Love is what is going to heal us from all that hurt. Sheree may be a mess, but I believe that loving her could have changed things. Just like it's changing you."

Sydney turned to look at her sister.

"Hayden loves you, Syd," JJ said. "If he didn't, he would have taken back the shop a long time ago and had you arrested for everything you did. You need to figure out how to love, Syd."

The exact same words Maritza had said to her a little over a week earlier.

"What if I can't?" Sydney could barely speak the words.

The kettle began to whistle in the kitchen, and JJ got up.

"You can't," she said as she headed to the kitchen. "Not without God."

Love does not delight in evil but rejoices with the truth.

Sydney closed her eyes. "God, I don't know how to do this. But if you want me to, show me how."

The soundless words floated up to the ceiling and, Sydney hoped, much higher than the roof on the house. Now she would have to wait and see what happened.

"Hey Mario, can you grab the last set of empanadas off the top oven?" Sydney asked as she carefully sliced the final cheesecake.

"Got it, boss," Mario said as he placed the long tray on the cooling rack. "I'm gonna start packing the cooled ones as soon as I finish this."

"Sydney, are we plating these beforehand?" Lissandra asked as she began removing the previously sliced cheesecakes from the refrigerator.

"No." Sydney gently removed the cake divider. "Maritza's kitchen is ridiculous. We can do it there. It will be easier and less risky."

"All right, then," Lissandra said. "In that case, we need to bounce. We've got to claim some space before the other caterers get in the mix."

Less than an hour later, Lissandra and Sydney were in the van, with Mario following in his car behind them. Out of the corner of her eye, Sydney saw Lissandra give her a once-over.

"That's what you're wearing?" Lissandra asked as they paused at a stoplight.

Sydney glanced down at her black slacks and matching wrap top.

"Yes," Sydney frowned. "What's wrong with what I have on?"

Lissandra shrugged. "Nothing."

Sydney narrowed her eyes at her sister.

"What?" Lissandra asked.

"What's wrong with what I have on?"

"Nothing," Lissandra insisted. "But if I was going to see the man I was in love with, for the first time in almost a month, I would bump it up a notch, you know what I'm saying? Put on some lipstick, show some cleavage."

Sydney rolled her eyes. "I am not going to see Hayden. I am going to deliver an order to my friend's party. I'm going to go in, set out the appetizers, sit in the van until the main course is down, then set out the dessert. After that I'm going to collect my check and go home."

"And you don't think you might run into Mr. Man during that time?" Sarcasm dripped from Lissandra's voice.

"Doesn't matter." Sydney eased down on the gas as the light changed to green. "I'm the help. I'm there to work, not to talk to Hayden. And since I know he definitely isn't interested in talking to me, I don't think either of us will have a problem."

And she had almost convinced herself that her little speech was true, until she almost dropped the last tray of appetizers when she caught sight of Hayden coming through the front doors. Only Lissandra's quick hand kept the empanadas from sliding off the tray onto the white tablecloths of the appetizer table.

"No problem, right?" Lissandra whispered.

Sydney lowered the tray onto the table with more attention than before and used a serving fork to quickly rearrange them evenly before dashing back into the kitchen.

She could hear Lissandra's footsteps behind her, but she couldn't stop. Pulling the cap from off her head, she pushed through the back door into the dusky evening, sucking in huge gulps of the night air. Her heart was beating so fast, she couldn't hear anything else above its echo.

Deep breath in. And out. In. And out.

She felt the blood stop rushing to her head, and only then did she realize her sister was talking to her.

". . . Syd, are you OK?" Lissandra asked, a touch of concern in her voice. "Girl, I thought you were about to pass out in there."

Sydney took a few more deep breaths. "I'm fine."

"You didn't look fine," Lissandra said with a shake of her head. "Who knew you would see him that soon. This thing hasn't even really started yet. And with Samantha? Man, does a brother move fast. . . ."

Sydney began to walk away from Lissandra. She knew her sister was not really the consoling type, and Sydney wasn't in a place where she could deal with her bluntness right then. Seeing Hayden had been bad enough. Seeing the Dolly Parton wannabe with him had been like a punch in the gut.

But she didn't have time to deal with this now. She needed to focus. Work came first. Maritza was depending on her, and she couldn't afford to have a mini-meltdown. Just two more hours, and a quick stop on the way home at Banjara, and she would be fine. She could do this.

She pep-talked herself all the way back to the kitchen, where she found Mario and Lissandra hanging around at the back doors.

"Have they finished setting out the buffet for the main course in the dining hall?" Sydney asked before they could say anything.

She saw the look exchanged between them but didn't acknowledge it.

"Uh . . . not yet," said Mario.

"OK, as soon as they've moved all the food out of the kitchen, we're going to start plating," Sydney said. "I'm going to see if we can have the same wait staff set out the dessert so it doesn't look like a hundred different people are handling the catering."

And also so she wouldn't have to go back out there again.

"OK, whatever you say, boss," Mario said.

Sydney looked across at Lissandra and she nodded her assent.

"OK, then," Sydney said. "Let's clear out a space so we can get started."

The evening went by fast. Sydney rarely enjoyed working with another catering team, but her team got along so well with the Fachellis team that Sydney, Lissandra, and Mario ended up pitching in to help them throughout the evening. By the time Sydney watched the last dessert tray walk out in the kitchen entryway, she had almost forgotten about Hayden. Almost.

"OK, guys, once we pack our stuff into the van, we should be able to go." Sydney wiped her hands on a dishcloth and looked around. "Grace from Fachellis said she would take care of the rest."

Lissandra cleared her throat. "What about our money?"

Sydney shrugged. "I'll handle it tomorrow. Right now I'm so exhausted, I just want to . . ."

The sound of voices and muffled commotion cut Sydney off.

". . . where is she?"

". . . ., this is not the place. Don't do this—"

"I just want to talk to her. . . ."

Sydney knew who it was before they even rounded the corner into the kitchen. She would recognize his voice anywhere. But before she could be any kind of prepared, Sydney was standing face to face with the one man she thought she would never be able to face again.

"I'm sorry, Syd. I tried to stop him," Maritza said. But Sydney didn't even hear her friend. All she could focus on was the look on Hayden's face.

His coffee-colored eyes had turned almost black as he glared at her. "It didn't take you long, did it," he said.

Sydney opened and closed her mouth several times before she was able to reply. "What?"

"To recover," he responded. "You lose a store, run your car off a bridge, and ruin a lot of people's lives, but here you are, back on your feet like nothing happened."

"Like nothing happened?" Sydney blinked at him, incredulous. "That's what you think? That everything is back to normal?"

"Why wouldn't I think that?" he shot back angrily. "You're already back in business. One thing fails, you just try something else, right?"

"You should know," Sydney shot back. "Looks like you got right back on the horse, judging from your company for the evening."

"Uh, we're just going to step outside." Lissandra pulled Mario with her toward the back door, even though no one seemed to notice. Maritza followed suit and exited the room.

"Don't turn this on me, Sydney," Hayden said, moving in and towering over her. Sydney stepped back and reclaimed some of the control he used his height to steal.

"It *is* on you." Sydney jabbed a finger at him. "You're the one who came storming in here, accusing me. And of what? Doing my job?"

"This is not about your job. It's about you. The way that you come into people's lives, mess it up, and just walk away as if nothing happened."

"So what am I supposed to do, Hayden?" Sydney threw her hands in the air. "I apologized over and over. I tried to call you and make things right. I tried to work this out, but you . . . you won't even talk to me. So what the hell am I supposed to do?"

"You're supposed to care. That's what happens when two people love each other. They care when things fall apart. They don't just go back to life as usual."

"I *do* care!" Sydney shouted. She could feel the tears running down her face, but she couldn't stop them even if she wanted to. "If I didn't care, I wouldn't think about you every day. I wouldn't stay up all night wondering how I could make this right. I wouldn't torture myself trying to figure out what to do with that property on College Street that I could never keep. I care, Hayden. More than you know. But I can't just lie in my bed all day. I have to keep moving. If I don't . . . if I don't, I'll lose my mind."

Sydney gripped the counter edge as her sobs pulled at her insides, pulling her toward the floor. She felt her knees buckle, but before she could sink to the floor, firm hands held her up and pulled her close. She buried her face against Hayden as he wrapped long arms around her.

"I'm sorry," she croaked into his shirt. "I'm sorry, I'm sorry, I'm sorry."

She felt him pull off her hat and tilt her head toward him, kissing her wet, closed eyes before resting his lips on her forehead.

"I know," he whispered against her hair. "I know."

"Then why won't you talk to me?" she sobbed. "Why can't we fix this? I don't want to lose you, Hayden. I love you."

She felt his grip on her tighten and she slipped her arms around his waist.

"I know." His voice was thick with emotion. "You know I love you, but . . ."

She felt him pulling away, physically and emotionally, but she held on tighter.

"It's not enough, Syd." His voice cracked with a pain that she felt all the way down to her bones. "It's not enough."

He began untangling himself from her, but she continued to resist.

"Hayden, please." She sobbed even as he gently removed her arms from around him. She knew she was embarrassing herself. She knew she was begging. But she didn't care.

"Dub, don't do this."

"I have to, Syd." His voice trembled. "I can't do this . . . not after everything . . ."

"Hayden?"

The female voice at the entrance of the kitchen severed the last bit of physical connection between Sydney and Hayden as they turned away from each other.

"What's going on?" The woman stepped farther into the kitchen and Sydney saw that it was the one woman in the world who provoked her gag reflex. Samantha looked back and forth between a teary-faced Sydney and a dishevelled Hayden.

"Oh. It's you," Samantha said, an annoyed expression on her face as she glared at Sydney.

Responding to Samantha would have been a waste of energy, and so Sydney began glancing around the kitchen for a napkin to wipe her face instead.

Hayden sighed. "Samantha, could you please wait for me at the table."

"Wait for you at the table?" Samantha echoed.

"Yes," Hayden ground out. "I just need a minute with Sydney. . . ."

"Why do you need a minute with Sydney?" she snapped. "You're here with me."

Sydney tried, but her patience was officially at zero.

"Samantha?" Sydney glared at Hayden. "Really, Hayden?"

Hayden shot her a look, but it did nothing to pacify Sydney.

"Of all the people you could come here with, you picked her?" Sydney asked.

"Excuse me?" Samantha tilted her head to the side and glared at Sydney. "What's that supposed to mean?"

"Nothing." Sydney backed toward the door, her eyes fixed on Hayden's. "Nothing at all."

Hayden shook his head at Sydney. "Don't go there, Sydney. You know what you're thinking isn't true."

"How do you know what *she's* thinking?" Samantha asked, her voice going up an octave. "Is there something going on I should know about, Hayden?"

"OK, I think this show is over," Maritza said, coming back into the kitchen. "Dub, why don't you take Samantha back to the main hall area? And please calm her down. No one ruins my man's birthday."

Maritza glared at Dub for emphasis. "No one."

She turned. "And Sydney . . ."

"Don't worry," Sydney said, heading toward the back exit. "I'm already gone."

She opened the door and Lissandra and Mario almost fell on top of each other getting out of the way.

"I'm going to go bring the van around," Sydney said, taking off her apron. "The two of you pack everything in and then you can take off for the night. I'll take everything back to the store."

Without waiting for their response, Sydney walked around the side of the house to get the van from where it was parked. Though she had not been able to avoid running into Hayden, like she had planned, the evening had not been a total waste. She had earned enough money to carry her over for the next two weeks. But more important, she had gotten the answer about her relationship with Hayden that she had been waiting for since that day at the shop with Maritza. They were over. Fully and completely over.

Chapter 35

It was already after ten by the time Sydney got back to the store. There wasn't much to put away, but she took her time transporting everything from the back of the van to the kitchen. Then she accessed a streaming jazz station on her iPhone and set to work washing up everything in the huge sink in the kitchen. Never mind the dishwasher staring at her. Sometimes all it took was some warm, soapy water to wash away the chaos of the day.

As she carefully cleaned the trays and cutlery, she began to remember Maritza's words about love the last time they had been at the store together. Love was patient, kind, humble, unselfish. What did it mean to be all those things? Could anyone be all of those things, anyway? Even Dub had told her that love wasn't enough. Who could possibly love like that?

I can.

Even though Sydney heard the words in her heart, she knew they weren't coming from her.

I loved you like that.

Sydney's hands stilled in the water. It wasn't possible. No one could love her like that. Not after everything that she had done. She had lied, stolen, and betrayed, and made other people lie, steal, and betray. When she thought of how she had involved Lissandra, her sisters, her sisters' family in everything she had done, it made her sick. She ran a woman's car off a bridge and almost killed her. And worse, the part that no one knew, not even her sisters, was that there was a moment when she had hoped Sheree was dead. It was brief, and she regretted the thought after, but for a moment she had wished Sheree was dead. How could someone love her, knowing all of that? How could God love her, knowing all of that?

I still do. I still love you.

Sydney didn't believe it. She pulled the stopper out of the sink and let out the soapy water, which had gone cold, and watched as it ran down the drain. Hayden was right. Love wasn't enough.

She rinsed everything off with more speed than she had washed them, then set them to dry. When she was finally satisfied that the kitchen was clean, she opened the refrigerator and took out the extra cheesecake she had left there earlier. She pulled up a stool to the island counter and cut herself a healthy slice. She almost never tasted the pastry she made. It was an old habit she had inherited from her dad. Instead, she let someone else taste it. Mario had been the happy guinea pig that morning and had certified that the cakes had been perfection, and as Sydney took her first bite, she had to agree that they were pretty good. But she didn't enjoy it. In fact, the interruption of her ringing cell phone was a welcome excuse for her to push it aside.

"This is Sydney."

"Hey, girl, how you holding up?" Maritza asked from the other end of the line.

"I don't know." Sydney used the fork to mash the remaining portion of the slice into mush. "I'll let you know when I start feeling things again."

"That bad, huh?"

"Shouldn't you be giving your husband the other part of his birthday celebration?" Sydney said, changing the subject.

"Yeah," Maritza said. "But he's in the shower, so I thought I would give you a quick call, make sure you weren't doing anything too crazy."

Maritza paused. "Where are you, anyway?"

"At the store," Sydney said. "I just finished cleaning up."

"Syd. It's 11:30."

"Is it?" Sydney looked around for a clock but found none. "Didn't even realize I had been here this long."

"Are you alone?" Maritza asked, concerned. "Do you want me to call someone for you?"

"No, I'm fine," Sydney said, putting some energy into her voice for the sake of her friend. Silence fell on the line between them and Sydney could tell that Maritza didn't know what to say.

"Look, Syd, I don't know what the full deal is with you and Hayden, but based on what I overheard, it sounded pretty serious. If you want to talk about it, I'm here. . . ."

"Remember when you told me all those things about love the other day?" Sydney asked.

"Yeah."

Sydney paused. "Do you think anyone could love like that? Like, really like that."

"Yeah, I think so."

Sydney bit her lip. "What if you did something really terrible? What if you hurt someone else, really badly? Could you still be loved? Could God still love someone like that?"

"Of course he could, Syd. He does. He loves all of us like that. Regardless of what we've done."

"But I don't deserve it," Sydney said quietly, tears brimming in her eyes again. "I've done nothing to deserve it."

"Honey, it's not about what you've done. We can't do anything to earn God's love. He loves us because he chooses to love us. He knows everything about us, everything we've said, everything we've done, even everything we've thought of doing. He knows us better than anyone else does, and he loves us nonetheless."

"I've done some really bad stuff, Maritza," Sydney said, sniffling. "And I'm not just talking about with Hayden. Just over my life until now, I've been so selfish, with my friends, with my family, with the people I claimed to love. . . ."

"It doesn't matter."

"It has to," Sydney insisted. "That's just how life works."

"But it's not how God works, Syd," Maritza said patiently. "You can't earn your way into his affections. There's nothing you can do to make him love you more, because he already loves you with everything he has, and nothing can change that. Romans 5:8 says God showed his love for us in that, while we were still sinners, Christ died for us. You know what that means, Syd? While we were still trifling, before we even knew that we were wrong, God already loved us, and gave up his only son to die to prove it, and to give us a chance at being saved with him. He loved you before you even realized that you didn't deserve his love. And he still loves you now, hon."

"I don't feel it, Mar," Sydney said as she wiped tears from her cheeks. "I don't feel any of it."

"It's not about feelings, girl," Maritza said. "Half the problems we have in life are 'cause we walk around letting feelings guide us. What I've been trying to show you from the start is that real love is not about feelings. There are times it will feel good, times it will feel terrible, and times it won't feel like nothing at all. But love means choosing to be there through all of that. God chose to be with us through all of our mess, even when being with us wasn't doing anything for him.

"And he's still with you, girl. He gave you a great family that has been with you no matter what you've been through. They're not perfect, but they're there for you, and that's one layer of his love for you. He gave you this amazing gift with food, and all these opportunities, so that even though you lost your business, your account balance still isn't at zero. And he gave you life, girl. You ran your car off a bridge—and I'm kinda mad you didn't tell me about that—but the fact that you're still here for me to be mad at means that God kept you. You may not be able to feel his love right now, but you've got to be able to see it in all that."

Sydney nodded. "You're right. I never thought of that."

"Of course I'm right," Maritza said. Sydney heard her sigh. "Look, Sean just got out of the shower and I gotta go, but think about this: the only way you're gonna be able to understand God's love fully is when you get to know him. Stop worrying about your own problems for a second and just get to know him. Maybe this is why he is letting all this chaos into your life. He just wants to slow you down long enough so you can get to know him and see how much he loves you. Promise me you'll think about doing that."

"I will."

"OK, girl," Maritza said. "You do that. Talk to you soon. Deuces."

Sydney put the phone down on the counter and let the silence surround her as she thought about what Maritza said. Get to know him. OK. That was something she could handle.

She glanced at her phone. Eleven forty. Time to go.

The remains of the slice of cake went into the garbage, just before she rinsed the plate, turned out the lights, and headed out the front doors. She was about to pull the door closed when she noticed JJ's jacket hanging behind it. Her sister must have forgotten it when she stopped by earlier. Sydney grabbed it off the hook, the movement shaking a piece of paper from the pocket. She picked up what turned out to be a flyer for Lost and Found, a bar a few blocks away.

Why would JJ, who had never tasted alcohol in her entire sanctified life, have a flyer for a bar in her pocket?

Sydney turned the creased paper over and noticed several dates on the back, the first of which happened to be today's date. She chewed on her lip a moment before stuffing the flyer into her own pocket and finally closing the front door. She glanced at her car parked in front of the store and headed away down the sidewalk. Going home would have to wait for a bit longer.

It was late, but a spattering of walking traffic still moved up and down the sidewalks of downtown Toronto. Sydney let the quiet sounds of the city wrap around her like a glove as she made the ten-minute walk to Lost and Found. The faint sound of jazz greeted her as she neared her destination. She pushed open the door to the dimly lit bar, and the previously muted sound of piano and bass filled her ears. It took her eyes a while to adjust to the low light, but her ears adjusted almost right away to the sound of a woman on stage covering Ella Fitzgerald's "Someone to Watch Over Me." The rest of the crowd seemed just as taken in, as the chatter was at a low din, and almost every seat in the narrow space seemed to be taken. Sydney did manage, however, to find an empty stool by the bar.

"What can I get you?"

Sydney looked up at the bartender, a scrawny young woman who really didn't look like she knew anything about jazz or alcohol, and considered, for a brief moment, breaking her no-drinking rule.

"Ginger ale, thanks," Sydney said finally.

"Coming right up," the girl said, fishing a glass from under the bar. "Nondrinker?"

Sydney nodded. "Almost all my life. Except for a slight detour during college."

The girl laughed. "I know what you mean. I barely drink myself."

Sydney raised an eyebrow. "A bartender who doesn't drink?"

"You would be surprised," the girl said, placing the glass in front of Sydney. "There are quite a few of us. In any case, I'm not really the bartender. We're just a bit short staffed tonight."

Sydney nodded and took a sip from her glass, glancing back at the woman on stage.

"She's pretty good, eh?" the girl continued.

"Yeah," Sydney said with a knowing smile. "Very good."

"Hey, do I know you?" the girl asked, squinting at Sydney.

"I don't think so."

It was the girl's turn to raise her eyebrow. "I swear, you look familiar."

Sydney bit back a smile. "I'm sure I do."

The woman looked like she was about to say more, but movement from the other end of the bar rescued Sydney from further conversation. She realized that it would be a while before the bartender would be back as the end of the singer's set had signaled drink refills for a lot of the patrons. Sydney took the break to make her way to the end of the bar near the stage, where the singer was getting a drink of her own.

"Nice dress," Sydney said. "Is that off the rack or did you make that one yourself?"

JJ's mouth fell open when she turned around and saw her sister.

"Sydney!"

"Yup, it's me," Sydney said, leaning against the bar next to JJ.

JJ sighed and took a sip from her drink. "So I guess you know now."

"Why you've been pretending to go to bed early every night and sneaking out of the house? Yes," Sydney said.

JJ's eyes widened. "You knew I was sneaking out?"

Sydney smirked. "Of course we knew. Lissandra thought you were seeing a married man."

JJ folded her arms. "And what did you think?"

"I thought it was a man, too. I just didn't think he was married. Saint Judith would never do that."

JJ rolled her eyes. "I'm no saint. You can already see that."

"Why, 'cause you're singing in a jazz club?" Sydney asked. "You're way too hard on yourself, JJ."

"It's a bar. No need to use euphemisms with me," JJ said. "Do you know what Mom would think if she knew I was doing this?"

If Sydney had a dollar for every time one of her siblings started a sentence with "Do you know what Mom would think," she could buy the house a round of drinks.

"Who cares what she thinks?" Sydney asked. "What's more important is what you think. If you think you're doing something wrong, then deal with that. But don't make your decisions based on what you think Jackie's gonna say."

JJ looked down and began stirring her glass of what Sydney assumed was tonic water.

"It's not that simple, Sydney," JJ said. "I'm not like you."

"And you should thank God for that." Sydney sighed. "He knows I'm a hot mess."

"How did it go tonight?" JJ looked up at her sister with concern.

"Bad," Sydney said. "Big-blowup-in-the-kitchen-with-the-new-jump-off-watching bad."

"No way! Hayden has a new girlfriend?"

"More like an old girlfriend come out of storage," Sydney said. "But it wasn't even about her. I know that's nothing serious. It was just a big mess, JJ. He's still really upset about everything that happened."

JJ grimaced. "Well, that is sort of to be expected."

"Yeah, I know." Sydney shook her head. "I don't want to talk about that anymore," she continued, waving off the topic. "I want to hear about this. How long have you been singing here?"

"Long." JJ smiled. "Almost a year."

Sydney's glass came down hard on the bar. "A year! We didn't even notice you were sneaking out until a couple months ago. You've been doing this for so long?"

"Yeah." JJ shrugged. "At first it was just occasionally. Then it became a regular once-a-week thing. Now it's about three times a week."

She laughed. "This is where I've been having all my secret meetings with your boyfriend."

Sydney's eyes widened. "What?"

JJ smiled.

"He told me he was thinking of finding a place where you could run the shop, in case things didn't work out with Dean," JJ said, stirring her drink. "He wanted feedback on a couple spaces and what he would need to make the place right. We couldn't very well talk at the house, so we met a couple times here. I had no idea he was going to buy a place for you outright. I was just as shocked as you were."

So JJ was having secret meetings with Hayden. If this had been any other woman, she might have been concerned. But she knew JJ would never even think of betraying her. She was still shocked, however.

"Wow." Sydney gave her sister a once-over. "You've been keeping all kinds of secrets, haven't you?"

She shrugged. "Everyone has a few."

Sydney nodded. "Don't worry. This one is safe with me. I won't tell anyone about you singing here."

"Not even Lissandra?"

Sydney rolled her eyes. "Especially not Lissandra. But didn't you think he would eventually slip up and say something to me?"

JJ tilted her head to the side. "Yeah, I guess. But you continuing Decadent was more important than me doing this. I just figured I would quit if it ever came out."

Sydney shook her head. "But I saw you on that stage, JJ. You loved it. Every moment of it. I know you love singing. And I know you won't do it at church anymore because of Josephine. But you would give up your chance to sing here, for me?"

JJ looked at Sydney as if she was crazy. "Of course I would. This is just a hobby for me, but that store is your career. You love it. And I love you, so why wouldn't I do that for you?"

Sydney felt her eyes brim with tears for the hundredth time that evening. Without thinking, she pulled her sister into a giant hug. Sometimes she forgot that there were people in her life who loved her. But now that she was looking, it felt like God was showing her how many there were.

"Are you crying?" JJ asked, when they finally let go of each other.

"No," Sydney said. She wiped the moistness from her face and they both laughed.

"Look, Syd, you may think I don't understand you, and it's true that I don't agree with some of the things you do, but that doesn't change the fact that I love you," JJ said. "I am always going to be here for you. Even though you're the older one, you can count on me. You don't have to deal with everything on your own. OK?"

Sydney nodded. "OK."

"All right," JJ said. She downed the rest of her drink

in one swig. "I gotta get back up there. Stay for the rest of my set?"

Sydney smiled. "Of course. I wouldn't miss it for the world."

JJ grinned and squeezed Sydney's hand before heading back on stage. Sydney watched JJ take her place at the microphone, and as she sang, Sydney said a quick prayer, thanking God for an amazing sister.

Chapter 36

"You ready?" Sydney asked Maritza as they stood outside the doors of the East York Athletic Clinic.

Maritza nodded. "Whenever you are."

"OK, let's do this," Sydney said, stepping off toward the entrance. "Door at the end of the hall. Right?"

"Right," Maritza said.

Sydney opened the door and let her friend step in ahead of her. Maritza headed straight for the receptionist while Sydney headed down the hallway to the offices.

"Excuse me, Miss, you can't go down there." The receptionist stood and began moving toward the hall after Sydney, but Maritza blocked her.

"Hey, girl, don't worry, she's with me," Maritza said. "I'm here for my two o'clock with Hayden Windsor."

"Yes, but she can't . . ."

"Don't worry, they're old friends," Maritza said, stepping in front of the woman and easing her back behind her desk. "She'll only be a minute. It's fine. Plus,

it gives me some time to show you what I broug.
you. . . ."

Maritza's voice faded into the background as Sydney moved deeper into the hallway. The door at the end
was half open, and as Sydney approached, a young
woman in a uniform stepped out.

"OK, the room is all ready and Mr. Windsor is already there," she said with a smile. "You can go right
ahead, Miss."

"Thank you," Sydney said, smiling at the woman before taking her advice. She stepped into the room and
closed the door behind her.

"Hey, Maritza, you're actually on time for . . ."

Sydney watched Hayden's jaw graze the floor when
he looked up and saw her. He swallowed so hard she
saw his Adam's apple bob.

"Sydney."

"Yes, it's me," Sydney said. Several different expressions passed over his face. He seemed to settle on res-
ignation.

"What are you doing here?" he asked.

"We need to talk. . . ."

He began to lift his hands. "Look, I don't want to get
into this now. . . ."

". . . about 572 College Street."

"Oh." He stopped. "OK."

He rubbed a hand over the back of his neck as if
thinking what to do next.

"Uh . . . have a seat, I guess."

Sydney sat down on one of the chairs against the
wall as Hayden sat down on the rotatable chair near his
desk.

"This is awkward," he mumbled, as he looked everywhere but at Sydney.

"It doesn't have to be," Sydney said calmly. She opened the folder she had brought in with her.

"First of all, I want to say thank you. The circumstances under which you gave me the deed for the property were not ideal, and I didn't get the chance to tell you how grateful I am for what you did."

He looked up, meeting her eyes for the first time since she had entered the room. The deep mocha latte pools sucked her in, and for a moment she forgot to breathe.

"No one has ever done anything like that for me before," she said sincerely. "And it's not just that you bought a place, but that you bought the place where I had my best memories with my father. Now that he's gone, all I have left are memories of him, and you giving me that place was like giving me back a little piece of him. So thank you. I will always love you for doing that for me."

"Sydney . . ."

She held up her hand to stop him.

"That being said, there is something we have to deal with. When you bought me that place, we were together. Now, our situation has changed, and therefore the terms of the ownership of the property have to change, too."

"I'm not taking it back." His eyes and his voice expressed his resolve. "I don't care what you say. I'm—"

Sydney held up her hand again to cut him off.

"We're not making any decisions about the ownership today," she said quickly. "But I am here to present you with some options."

"But I don't—"

"Option one," Sydney continued. "I relinquish all rights to the property and return sole ownership to you, for you to use however you want. You can keep it, or rent it, or sell it back to whomever you choose. I won't stand in your way, and I'll be glad to take care of any paperwork to make it happen."

Sydney reached over and placed the first sheet in her folder with the terms to option one on his desk.

Hayden folded his arms, his brows knotted. "Can I say something?"

"I'm not finished." She reclaimed her seat. "Option two, we can work out an agreement where you can sell your portion of the shop to me. Now, obviously, I don't have any money right now, but I think through catering contracts and sales at the store, we can work out a plan for payment."

"Any more?" he asked sarcastically.

"Yes," she said. "The last option, option three, is for you to remain co-owner of the shop. You would receive a share of income based on your percentage of ownership of the store. I would cover all costs, overhead, and upkeep, through income from my percentage."

"That's crazy. You can't run a business like that. You would never make anything—"

"Those are the options," Sydney said, placing the last two sheets on his desk and closing her now-empty folder. "I will give you a month to look over them and make your decision. If you need more time after that, let me know. In the meantime, I will cover utilities and all other overhead costs for the shop since I may use it from time to time for catering requests."

"The overheads are already being taken care of."

"I know," Sydney said. "And I called and spoke to someone at each of the companies and the bills will now be coming directly to me so I can deal with them."

Hayden threw his hands in the air. "This is crazy."

"Was everything clear in the options?" Sydney asked, ignoring his frustration.

"Yes," he said. "But can I say something?"

"No, not right now." Sydney got up. "I just came here to present you with the options. When you decide, you can e-mail me or sign the option you have selected and have it sent to me at the shop or to my home."

He scowled. "You definitely are the most stubborn woman I have ever met in my entire life."

Sydney moved toward the door but paused.

"One more thing." She turned to look at him.

Hayden sighed and clasped his hands together. "What?"

"I love you," she said simply. "And I'm probably going to love you for a very long time. You said love isn't enough, but I disagree. Real love, the love that's patient, that's kind, that doesn't envy or boast, that's not proud or selfish, that always protects and trusts and hopes and perseveres: That love is enough. And that's the love I've decided to have for you. That's the love that's going to wait for you until you're ready. Until you've forgiven me. Until God gives you the strength to love me, just like he gave me the ability to love you.

"So take your time, Dub. Whenever you're ready, I'll be here."

The look on his face told her he couldn't have spoken even if he wanted to. And so before she started telling him all her deepest darkest secrets, she slipped out of the office and closed the door behind her. Taking a deep breath, she led her shaky legs down the hallway to where Maritza was still sweet-talking the receptionist with Chanel samples.

"I'll be outside," she said, tapping Maritza on the shoulder as she passed by her on the way to the front door.

Once outside, she sucked in a deep gulp of air, hoping it would slow her rapidly beating heart. Where had that little speech come from? She definitely hadn't planned that part. But she knew it was the truth. She did love him like that. Somewhere between Sean's birthday party and the minute she walked into the clinic that day, she had realized it. And she wasn't going to let pride or anything else stand in the way of letting him know it.

"You did it?" Maritza slipped on her sunglasses as she remotely unlocked the car doors. "You told him about your plan for the store?"

"Yeah, I told him." Sydney opened the passenger side. She was about to say more when her phone rang. It was Jackie.

"Hello?"

Sydney felt her chest tighten as she heard sobs on the other end.

"What is it, Mom?" A feeling of weakness suddenly overtook her and she found herself leaning against the car for support.

"It's Dean."

Sydney's eyes began to burn. Please God, no.

"He opened his eyes."

"What?"

"He's awake. Sydney, your brother is awake."

Chapter 37

By the time she reached the two-week mark, she had decided that patience was entirely overrated.

"I'm calling him."

"No," JJ and Lissandra said at the same time, even as Lissandra moved Sydney's cell phone out of her reach.

They had been sitting in the kitchen at 572 College Street, eating the extra appetizers left over from an order Sydney had delivered the day before, when Sydney made the announcement.

"It's been two weeks," Sydney moaned, before stuffing a meat-filled wonton into her mouth.

"You gave him a month," JJ reminded, as she reached for a wonton from the quickly diminishing pile.

"I know, but I didn't think he would take the whole month," Sydney said grumpily. "How long does it take you to decide whether you want to keep, share, or sell a piece of property?"

"Apparently more than two weeks," Lissandra muttered.

The first couple of days hadn't been too bad. Dean waking up from his coma had completely consumed her and her family's minds. Every waking moment had been spent at the hospital with him. He was nowhere near fully recovered. His memory was foggy in some parts, he was easily fatigued, and the doctors said they needed a lot more observation before he could even think of being home. But seeing Dean sitting up, breathing and eating on his own, talking, had drawn Sydney closer to God in ways that she could never have imagined.

She could feel him in the room with Dean. He wasn't some deity out there. He was right there in the thick with her and her sisters and mother. And now more than ever before, something in her longed for him. She was still consumed with that longing for more. But her longing to move her life forward was also seeping in. And Hayden's lack of response was standing in the way of that.

"I'm just anxious about having to sit around with my business on hold," Sydney said, wiping her mouth with a napkin.

"I don't think it's just your business that you've put on hold," JJ said.

"What's that supposed to mean?"

"Syd." Lissandra rolled her eyes. "These are your sisters you're talking to. You can quit acting like your behind isn't thinking about Hayden twenty-four hours a day."

"Please." Sydney got up and headed to the fridge. "I am not."

"Yes, you are," JJ and Lissandra said together.

"Yesterday you called me Dub," Lissandra said.

"And last week when I asked you for Essies's work number, you gave me the number for the clinic," JJ said.

Sydney bit her lip. "I did?"

"Yes, you did," JJ said with a knowing smile. "Face it, Syd, you're still crazy in love with that man."

"Look, I just need to figure out what he wants to do with this shop, so I can figure out what to do next with this business," Sydney said. "I can't open up the front of the store, or make business cards, or try contacting my old clients, 'cause I'm not sure whether or not I'll have a space to work out of in the next week. So if Hayden's on my mind, that's the reason."

"OK, Syd," Lissandra said. "Whatever lies you need to tell yourself to get you to sleep."

Sydney was about to protest when they heard a knock on the front door.

All three women walked out into the main area, to find a dark, strapping, yuppie corporate type with a briefcase standing outside the glass doors.

"Who's that?" JJ asked.

"And can I have his number," Lissandra murmured.

"Maybe if we open the door, we might find out," Sydney said dryly as she pushed past her sisters to get to the front door.

"So sorry," Sydney apologized as she opened the door. "Can I help you?"

"Yes, I'm looking for a Ms. Sydney Isaacs," he said, his bright hazel eyes watching hers for signs of recognition.

"Why?" Lissandra asked, stepping closer to the door. "What you need her for?"

"I'm afraid that's a confidential matter I can only address with Ms. Isaacs. . . ."

"I'm Sydney."

"Oh." He glanced hesitantly at Lissandra and JJ, who were watching him with suspicion.

"It's OK," Sydney said, interpreting his unspoken questions. "These are my sisters. Whatever it is, you can say it in front of them."

"OK." The young Johnnie Cochran turned his attention back to Sydney before stretching out his hand to her. "I'm Kyle Jones, attorney for a Mr. Hayden Windsor. I'm here to discuss details relating to the ownership agreement for the property at 572 College Street."

Sydney and her sisters looked at each other. Guess he had decided.

"Come in." Sydney ushered Kyle to a table near the window. "Can I get you something to drink? Tea, coffee, juice?"

"Uh, some coffee would be great," he said with a smile as he took a seat.

Sydney nodded at Lissandra, who disappeared into the kitchen.

"So I guess Hayden made up his mind," Sydney said as she sat down across from Kyle.

"He has," Kyle said. "He wanted me to apologize for making you wait."

"It's no problem." Sydney waved away the apology. "I did give him a month."

"Yes, well, he knows that waiting for an answer may have kept you from proceeding with business matters as you might have." He offered a sympathetic smile. "He wanted to have this wrapped up as soon as he could so you both can move on with your respective lives."

Sydney turned to look at JJ, who had an uneasy look

on her face. Move on with their lives? That didn't sound entirely promising.

Lissandra returned with the coffee, two small containers with cream and sugar, and a slice of sponge cake from the kitchen.

"Oh, you didn't have to go through all of that," Kyle said, eyeing the cake eagerly.

"It's no trouble at all." Sydney watched Kyle's eyes close as he savored the first bite of cake. "I couldn't let you leave here without getting a piece of cake. You might be one of the last people to eat from this kitchen if we have to close down."

Kyle took a moment to swallow before opening his eyes. "I sure hope it doesn't come to that. But that would be your decision."

Reaching into his briefcase, he pulled out a slim, legal-size folder.

"Mr. Windsor has rejected your offers," he said.

"What?" JJ squeaked.

"All of them?" Sydney asked.

"Yes, all of them," Kyle said.

Kyle opened the folder and placed it in front of Sydney.

"Instead, he is proposing joint ownership of the property by both parties, with operating control held by you, Sydney Isaacs. Returns from sales will be applied first to operational expenses. From what remains, ten percent of profits will go to the church, fifteen percent into a fund for the business development, and the remainder split equally between both parties."

"Wait, he wants to give part of your money to the church?" Lissandra questioned. "He can't do that."

"It's tithe," JJ shot back. "And it's his property. He can do whatever he wants."

"I'm just saying," Lissandra huffed. "If I were you, Sydney . . ."

"But you're not," Sydney said gently, cutting her sister off. She turned back to Kyle. "Is that all?"

"Uh, yes," Kyle said, glancing at Lissandra warily. "You have fourteen days to decide."

Sydney closed her eyes and sat perfectly still.

A few moments passed and Kyle leaned forward to look at her, then looked over at her sisters helplessly.

Lissandra leaned forward. "Sydney? Syd—"

"Shhh!" JJ hushed her sister.

"But—"

"Just be quiet," JJ hissed in a stage whisper, as she sat watching her sister.

After what seemed like forever, Sydney opened her eyes and smiled.

"OK," she said. "I'll take it."

"B-but you have fourteen days," he stammered. "Don't you want to consult with someone? Talk to your accountant? Your lawyer?"

Sydney smiled. "I already talked to who I need to. Where do I sign?"

Chapter 38

By the time 9:30 p.m. rolled around, there were two things Sydney knew for sure. One, she made the best chocolate hazelnut brownies this side of Lake Ontario, and two, Hayden wasn't coming. The first she had determined by the number of people who had told her so, and by the complete consumption of her batch of three dozen just two hours into the party. The second had taken a lot longer to sink in.

Even as the crowd began to thin and Mario and Lissandra began to take the empty trays back to the kitchen, she had held out hope. She had checked the Raptors schedule, and there were no games for that night. But maybe he had training. Maybe the clinic had been booked up for the evening. She had filled her mind with excuse after excuse for him not showing up at Decadent's reopening. Even Jackie, who was more attached to Dean's bedside now that he was awake, had managed to show up for an hour.

"You did good, sweetheart," she had said as she pulled Sydney into an embrace. "I'm so proud of you."

"Thank you, Mom." Sydney had beamed. It really meant a lot to hear her mother say that.

"You're welcome," Jackie had said. "Now, pack up some of this food so I can bring it to Dean. You know that child eats like three grown men."

She had left not long after, and as the hours passed, so had most of the old clients, walk-in customers, friends, and family who had shown up to celebrate the business's new start. The one person missing was the one person who had made the whole thing possible.

"OK, Syd," Lissandra said with a sigh as she wiped down the counter. "We're all done here."

Sydney smiled as she watched her sister rinse the rag and hang it up before taking a scrutinizing look around the kitchen.

"I am so proud of you," Sydney said.

Lissandra looked up from her inspection to Sydney in surprise.

"You have really been there for me through this whole reopening thing," Sydney said. "All the late nights with the catering jobs, the long hours to prepare for today, even sticking it out before we knew what would happen."

"Sydney, please," Lissandra scoffed, looking away embarrassed. "What else was I supposed to do?"

"You could have gotten another job elsewhere." Sydney stepped toward her sister. "You have tons of experience, and skill. We both know there are places that would have scooped you up in a minute. But you stuck it out with your dear old sister."

Lissandra grimaced. "Oh God, are you going to start crying?"

"No." Sydney grinned. "But I am going to hug you."

Lissandra squealed as Sydney wrapped her arms tight around her sister, but she eventually hugged her back.

"OK, OK, enough," Lissandra said, easing Sydney away. "Geez."

Sydney laughed. "I love you, little sister."

"Love you back, big sister," Lissandra said with a smile.

Mario walked back into the kitchen as they stood there grinning at each other.

"OK, so are we ready to go or what?"

"Yeah." Lissandra grabbed her purse and turned out some of the kitchen lights. "You coming, Syd?"

"Yeah," Sydney said. She glanced behind her one more time, then followed Lissandra and Mario out the front door.

It was barely ten o'clock by the time Sydney got home to her empty house. She sighed, kicked off her shoes, and padded into the living room. With JJ out singing and Lissandra out with Mario, Sydney was getting used to spending her evenings alone. Sometimes there would be a catering job that would keep her out late or wear her out so much that she would go straight to bed. But most nights, it was just her and the Food Network.

She had just sunk into the couch and put her feet up on the coffee table when her cell phone rang.

"Syd, it's me. I totally forgot, but they're working on the lines on our block from midnight to five a.m. so the power's going to be out. You've got to go back and plug the refrigerator and freezer into the generator."

Sydney sat forward. "Me? Lissandra, you're the one who forgot to do it."

"And you're the owner of the store!"

"The owner who's already home," Sydney said grouchily. "You're still on the road; can't you just swing back and do it?"

"No," Lissandra said. "Would I be calling you if I could? Obviously, I don't have my keys."

"You better check that attitude," Sydney said. "Or I might just make your fat behind come here and get the keys yourself."

"Come on, Syd, please?" Lissandra had switched to her equally irritating whiny voice. "What about all that talk this evening about how much you love me and appreciate me. And you can't even drive twenty minutes over to the store for me?"

Sydney let out a growl and turned off the TV.

"Fine." She got up and headed to the door. "But you owe me for this."

"Yeah, yeah. Talk to you later."

Sydney slipped on the same shoes and jacket she had left by the door before heading out. She might as well. It wasn't as if she had anything better to do.

The drive over to Decadent took only fifteen minutes, thanks to the absence of traffic on the highway. There was no specialized store parking at this location, and so Sydney and the rest of her staff usually had to take their chances with the metered parking on the street. Thankfully, the spot right in front of the store was open.

She didn't bother turning on the main lights but went straight to the kitchen, where she plugged the refrigerator and the freezer into the generator and unplugged everything else from the wall sockets. They really needed to get a generator that was connected to their electrical system, instead of an emergency one that sat out back with a cord running inside. But they couldn't afford that kind of system yet. Maybe in a couple months. As a last precaution, she found the electrical power panel for the store and shut off the power at the main disconnect. Then, with all the lights out, she felt her way through the dark store to the entrance. One sore shin and bumped knee later, she found herself outside.

She had just pulled her keys out of the locked door when she saw him. The scattered leaves on the spindly branches of a tree near the edge of the sidewalk threw shadows over his face. But she didn't need the light to recognize him. She could pick him out of a crowd from one hundred feet away.

She stood frozen at the door, unable to speak, and afraid that if she did, he would vanish and prove to be nothing more than a figment of her overworked brain.

"Guess I'm too late," Hayden said after several moments had passed.

Sydney let out a cautious breath. "Depends what you came for."

He stuck his hands in his pockets. "I wish I knew. Maybe if I did, I wouldn't have spent the last twenty minutes circling the block."

Sydney tried to decipher some kind of meaning from his words, from his posture, from the way he looked at her but didn't. But she couldn't get anything.

"Why are you here, Hayden?"

"I don't know."

"Are you still mad at me?"

"I don't know."

She opened her hands. "What am I supposed to do with that, Hayden? What do you want me to say? Tell me what you want me to say. . . ."

"I don't know, Sydney." His frustration echoed hers.

"I've never been here before—in love with a girl I thought I knew, only to find out I'm wrong."

"You're not wrong," Sydney said, stepping forward. "It's still me. Just grown up and a little bruised from the journey."

She took a deep breath. "Besides, it's not just me. You're different, too."

He shook his head. "I'm the same person I used to be."

Sydney gave him a sad smile. "No, you're not. In so many ways you're not."

He looked confused and she shook her head in wonder. He couldn't see it even though it was so obvious to her.

"The Dub I knew was not as focused as you," she explained. "Not as caring. Not as forgiving. Not as connected where it counts. The Dub I knew never made me think about life outside of myself. About what real love is, and how it can't be real without God."

She dropped her gaze. "The Dub I knew could never have helped me see the things that needed to be changed in me. But you did."

He stepped out of the shadows, and in the glow of streetlight she could see everything clearly on his angular face. Everything he wondered. Everything he felt. Everything he couldn't say. She saw it in his eyes. And in that moment, she knew that in the weeks that had passed, she hadn't been the only one drowning in emotions.

"Dub." His name slipped from her lips with the breath she had been holding. "I can't lose you again." She searched his eyes as he stepped closer to her. "I think I kind of need you."

He was so close now that she had to tilt her head to meet his gaze. But as his hand touched her cheek, her eyes closed on reflex. She reveled in the feel of his firm hand against her smooth skin, his warm breath next to her ear.

"You never lost me." His words were like music to her ears. "I was always yours."

And then to prove it, he leaned down and touched her lips with his. It wasn't the most passionate kiss he had ever given her, but it was the most honest. And it took her breath away.

She closed her eyes and pressed her forehead against his as the cool night air swirled around them. He said he was always hers. She suspected that she had always been his—except she hadn't even known it.

"So what now?" Sydney asked, her eyes still closed.

His thumb stroked her cheek. "Now we start over. We do this the right way, get to know each other again. No secrets, no ulterior motives, no deception."

"I'm so sorry I lied to you," Sydney whispered. "So sorry I hurt you."

"I forgive you." He slipped his arms round her. "And I'm sorry for my part, too. We both could have handled things better."

She opened her eyes and stared up at him, amazed that the conversation they were having was even possible.

"So . . . we're starting over?"

He smiled slowly and a flutter of activity began in the pit of her stomach. "We're starting over."

She squealed as he suddenly lifted her into his arms and swung her around. Two guys passing by on the sidewalk snickered, but she didn't care. This was the new Dub. And she was so glad she had met him.

"So I guess I missed our party," he said when he finally set her down.

"Yes, you did," Sydney said, grinning up at him. "But I saved you something."

He shot her a curious look, but instead of answering, she grabbed his hand and pulled him toward the entrance. Once inside, she hit the switch by the door.

"Hey, what's up with the lights?" he asked, confused.

"No lights." Sydney squeezed his hand before placing it on her shoulder. "You're just going to have to trust me, Dub."

"OK, Nini," Hayden said, as he stepped closer and let her lead him toward the kitchen. "But remember, I'm a lot taller than you. So, no crawl spaces."

Sydney giggled but managed to lead him through an obstacle-free path to a stool at the kitchen island. She opened the refrigerator and a triangle of light flooded the large space.

"OK, Miss Isaacs. You want to tell me why you're using a generator to power the appliances in the kitchen?" he asked, an eyebrow raised. "Should I be worried?"

She threw a smile behind her from where she was rummaging in the fridge. "No and no."

Before he could conjure up more questions, she pulled a small square box from the back shelf of the refrigerator. Then, with the refrigerator door still open, she pulled three tea lights in vases from a cupboard below the island and placed them in the space between her and Hayden. She watched a smile curl his lips as she lit the candles before nudging the fridge door closed.

"This is yours," she said, sliding the box with his name in front of him.

His eyes sparkled in the glow of the candlelight. He gazed at her a moment before opening the box. The smile that he was already wearing spread even wider.

"Is this what I think it is?"

"Yes," she said with a laugh. "It's a red velvet cup-cake."

"It looks a bit larger than your average cupcake," he said, taking out the delicious-looking confection and discarding the box.

"It was specially made."

His eyes met hers and Sydney felt the symphony in her stomach start again.

"How did you know I would come?" he asked, still holding her gaze.

Sydney shrugged. "I didn't. But I love you. And love hopes all things."

She had spent a lot of her life hoping for all sorts of things. For approval from her dad, for success in her career, for more clients for her business, for less complication from her family. But she had never hoped for love. Not like the love she was beginning to experience with Hayden. Not like the love that God had been offering her all along.

He reached over and took her hand.

"I love you, too."

And as the beauty of his words filled her ears and her heart, she rested in the knowledge that now, for the first time, they both understood exactly what that meant.

Epilogue

Sydney entered the upscale restaurant and tried not to think too hard about why her sisters had decided to have lunch an hour away from Toronto in Orangeville.

"I'm here with the Isaacs party?" Sydney said to the hostess.

The woman smiled and led her through the restaurant to the back. When she pulled away the curtain to the private reserved section, she found Lissandra, JJ, Zelia, and her Aunt Essie waiting.

"I think you're the last of your party to arrive," the hostess said, leaving Sydney to enter. "Your waitress for the afternoon just started her shift. She should be here momentarily."

"Well, it's about time you got here," Lissandra said, taking a swig of something that looked suspiciously like red wine.

"Nice to see you, too, Sandi," Sydney said, taking the second-to-last seat at the table, after greeting her other sisters. "Next time you guys decide to have lunch out of town, maybe you could give me advance warning."

"Blame it on Essie," Zelia said. "This was all her idea."

Sydney's eyes narrowed as she considered her aunt. "What's going on, Essie?"

Her aunt smiled. "Just a little family reunion."

Just then the curtain swooped open and their waitress appeared.

"Welcome to One99! I'll be your waitress for the after—"

The rest of the words got lost as the menus slipped from the young woman's hands, falling to the floor. Her mouth fell open as she stared at the last five women in the world she wanted to see.

"Well, well," Lissandra said. "I guess now the whole family is here."

"Sure looks that way," said Zelia. With an outstretched leg, she slid the last remaining chair out from the table for Sheree, who stood frozen at the entrance to the private area.

Sydney sat forward—not sure she could believe what she was seeing

"Please, Sheree, have a seat," Essie said, her eyes fixed on the redheaded woman's. "I think we have a lot to talk about."

Sheree glanced around at all of them before sighing and sitting down, a resigned look on her face. As she sat, her waistless dress shifted to reveal her protruding stomach.

Lissandra swore and Sydney's mind spun back to three months earlier, before they knew Sheree was a liar.

"Yes, sisters," Sheree said with a wry smile as she rubbed her pregnant belly. "We certainly do."

Do family, faith—and fame—go together? In this capti-
vating new novel from award-winning author Tiffany L.
Warren, two brothers reach for the stars, but are they
prepared for a fall? . . .

Don't miss

The Favorite Son

On sale now, at your local bookstore!

Prologue

Camden was not going to forever hold his peace. His brother Blaine had committed the ultimate offense. But, there was a tiny window, a sliver of an opportunity to speak; to scream loud enough to reach heaven.

Camden rushed through the foyer of the church with his best friend Amber at his heels. "But Cam, Dawn said yes. She said yes! Maybe you should just walk away."

"I left her alone with him," Camden said as he turned the corner leading to his father's office.

"She made a choice," Amber protested. "Don't make this any harder for her."

These words stopped Camden in his tracks. "What about me? Did anyone think about how hard this would be for me?"

Amber threw her arms around Camden's neck and pulled him into an embrace. He felt his insides shudder. The hug almost made him lose it when he was doing such a good job trying to hold it all together.

He untangled himself from Amber's squeeze. "I have to do this."

"Then, let me go with you," Amber said.

Camden continued toward his father's office, where Pastor Wilson married couples who couldn't afford to have a real wedding, or those whose lust had left them in an undesirable predicament. Neither Camden nor Blaine were supposed to get married in the office. The two sons of the famed and illustrious Pastor B. C. Wilson of Dallas, Texas, were practically royalty—princes of the church. Their nuptials were destined to be star studded affairs with hundreds of guests in attendance.

Ironically, Blaine was the one who bought into that hype. Camden resisted all of the perks of their father's position, including the girls, and cougars who stuffed panties and hotel room keys into his pocket at church conferences. He refused to make a mockery of everything holy.

Finally in front of Pastor Wilson's office door, Camden reached for the doorknob. Amber covered his hand with hers.

"You sure, Cam?"

Camden's nostrils flared a bit. He wished he'd told Amber to wait for him in the foyer. "I'm sure."

Camden threw the door open and felt his resolve and determination evaporate at the sight of Dawn and Blaine. The couple stood before Pastor Wilson, gazing into each other's eyes. His mother, Lady Wilson, stood next to Pastor Wilson, looking on quietly. Dawn held onto Blaine's right hand for dear life.

Camden couldn't stop staring at Dawn's midsection, which held the evidence of Blaine and Dawn's lust. There was no bulge in her stomach. Not yet, but Camden knew the baby was there.

Dawn's mouth opened slightly when she saw Camden. Then, she looked away. Blaine didn't move a muscle.

"They're just about to recite their vows, Camden," Pastor Wilson said. There was no emotion in his tone. No joy for the son getting married. No sympathy for the other.

"I'm sorry, Cam," Dawn whispered.

"Do you love him?" Camden asked.

Dawn pursed her lips together tightly. Camden knew that face. She made that face when she was holding back a flood of tears.

"Of course she loves him," Pastor Wilson said. "They're getting married and having my first grandchild."

Camden waved his father's reply away with his hand. "Do. You. Love. Him?"

After a long and pregnant pause, Dawn nodded. "It doesn't matter, Camden. I do."

There was no conviction in her voice. To Camden, it sounded like she was still trying to convince herself that this marriage was necessary. It wasn't.

"Son, just go," Camden's mother said.

Camden was at a loss. Learning about the pregnancy and their shotgun wedding had thrown him off balance, as had the sight of Dawn looking incredibly pitiful. Amber lightly tugged on his jacket.

He looked down at Amber. At six foot four inches, he towered over her, but in that moment, he was the one who felt small.

Amber mouthed the words, "Let's go."

Camden nodded, and allowed Amber to pull him toward the door.

"Congratulations," Amber said. "Even though you cheated me out of my chance to be a maid of honor."

Dawn gave Amber a tiny smile. "But you're the baby's godmother. You can throw a baby shower."

"That will have to do, I guess," Amber said.

Pastor Wilson sighed loudly. "Are we ready to continue?"

"What about you, Camden?" Blaine asked, breaking his silence. "You gonna be the baby's godfather?"

Camden was almost out of the office when Blaine asked his question. He paused for a moment, thought of an answer to that question, but decided that he wouldn't say it in the walls of the church.

Camden stormed out of the office and out of the church. Amber couldn't match his long strides, but she ran behind him anyway, struggling to catch her breath.

In the church parking lot, Amber caught up to Camden as he got into his car. He glared at her through the window before rolling it down.

"You knew, that it was Blaine from the start. Why didn't you tell me?"

"I couldn't. I honestly hoped that somehow you two would end up together anyway, in spite of Blaine and your father's plans. Pastor Wilson told them they had to get married, or the group would be ruined, and so would the church," Amber said.

"All my father cares about now is the group! Isn't that funny? He never even wanted us to sing, and now the group means more than everything. It means more than me."

A single tear coursed down Amber's face. "You know that's not true, Cam. Pastor Wilson loves you."

Camden started the car. "Goodbye, Amber. I am never

coming back here. The next time I set foot in this church will be someone's funeral, I swear on everything."

"So you're gonna leave the group? We need you."

Camden looked at his father's church and couldn't see himself walking through the doors again. On the other side of those doors the only girl he'd ever loved was marrying his brother.

"You don't need me. As long as you've got Blaine, you'll be fine. He's the face of the group. I just play the keyboard."

"But you're the heart. You brought us together. So G.I.F.T.E.D. is your group."

Camden sighed and gave Amber a weak smile. He would miss her, and Akil, but he couldn't look at Dawn or Blaine without wanting to punch a hole in the wall. Or at his twin brother's face.

"I've got to go. Call me, okay?"

Camden sped out of the parking lot with no intentions of ever coming back to Graceway Worship Center. And no matter what anyone said, he wasn't running. Camden knew his presence would make things hard for Dawn, so he would give them miles and miles of space.

Camden was closer to Dawn than anyone. He knew what she wasn't saying—it was all over her face when she'd stared at him. Maybe she loved Blaine, and the child they'd conceived, but Dawn loved Camden still. But she hadn't spoken up. She'd held her peace.

And so would Camden.

Grab the Hottest Fiction
from
Dafina Books

Available Wherever Books Are Sold!

All available as e-books, too!

Visit our website at **www.kensingtonbooks.com**